Misplaced Magic

Editors: Rosie McCaffrey & Jennifer Bottum
Formatter: Susan Veach
Cover Design: Rena Violet
Page Art: Irina Beliakova, Jessica Dodge & Francesca Scillia

Published by Wizard Supply Co VT
Newbury, Vermont USA
ISBN:
Paperback 978-1-7376966-7-4
Hardcover 978-1-7376966-8-1
Ebook 978-1-7376966-9-8
Misplaced Magic Copyright 2023 by Jessica Dodge
All Rights Reserved

This book is a work of fiction. All the names, characters, businesses, events, and incidents in this book are either the product of the author's imagination or used in a fictitious manner. Any resemblance to actual persons, living or dead, or actual events is purely coincidental and a work of the author's imagination.

Dear Reader,

My love for folklore from around the world runs deep, yet Celtic lore holds a special place in my heart. It's a world where magic and myth intertwine, and I knew that I couldn't resist weaving these traditional tales into my book. This particular book is especially dear to me, and I hope that my passion for these tales shines brightly.

In the process of crafting this novel, I immersed myself in various sources, from books to online resources, and sought insights from the people of Wales, whose heritage and stories ignited my imagination and breathed life into the world I created.

While these stories pay homage to the rich tradition of Welsh folklore, they have been adapted to enhance the richness of this novel.

These adaptations, inspired by the magic of Welsh folklore, form the essence of this story that I hope will transport you to a world where the whispers of ancient tales come alive.

Happy Reading!

Jessica Dodge

To my cherished readers,
Your unwavering support and enthusiasm for my work have
fueled my creative journey and filled my heart with gratitude.
This book is a tribute to your loyalty and the connection we
share through the written word.

To my beloved family and friends,
Thank you for your love, encouragement, and understanding.
You've been my rock through the highs and lows of this
writing adventure. Your belief in me has been my
greatest source of strength.

To my fellow authors and mentors,
Your guidance, wisdom, and friendship have been invaluable
on this literary voyage. I'm privileged to have you as
companions on this path, and I'm endlessly grateful
for the lessons and inspiration you've shared.

With heartfelt appreciation,
~Jessica

TABLE OF CONTENTS

Prologue: Vermillion 15

Chapter One: Ionna: The Letter 21

Chapter Two: Ionna: Moral Ground 29

Chapter Three: Kate: Trip to Nana's 33

Chapter Four: Kate: The Magic Lamp 41

Chapter Five: Ionna: The Delayed Outcome 47

Chapter Six: Ionna: John Brightmore 53

Chapter Seven: Kate: Berry Picking 63

Chapter Eight: Ionna: Beddgelert 71

Chapter Nine: Kate: Death's Wake-Up Call 81

Chapter Ten: Kate: The Ride 89

Chapter Eleven: Ionna: Lost and Found 97

Chapter Twelve: Kate: The Cabin 109

Chapter Thirteen: Kate: Memories 115

Chapter Fourteen: Ionna: Flowers and Dust 121

Chapter Fifteen: Kate: Backflip 127

Chapter Sixteen: Ionna: The Stray 137

Chapter Seventeen: Kate: The Market 145

Chapter Eighteen: Ionna: John & Jasper 153

Chapter Nineteen: Kate: The Fortune Teller 163

Chapter Twenty: Ionna: Kebabs & Old Books 171

Chapter Twenty-One: Ionna: Pies and Palms 179

Chapter Twenty-Two: Ionna: Fortunes and Forges 187

Chapter Twenty-Three: Kate: Lady of the Lake 197

Chapter Twenty-Four: Kate: Brangwen 207

Chapter Twenty-Five: Kate: Predator 217

Chapter Twenty-Six: Kate: The Truth 225

Chapter Twenty-Seven: Ionna: Oceans Apart 235

Chapter Twenty-Eight: Ionna:
The Red Book of Hergest 243

Chapter Twenty-Nine: Ionna: The Dinner 251

Chapter Thirty: (2014-1951): Kate: Ginger Biscuits 261

Chapter Thirty-One: (1951): Kate - Neala 267

Chapter Thirty-Two: (1951): Kate - The Trip Back Home 275

Chapter Thirty-Three: (1951): Kate: Death Rewind 285

Chapter Thirty-Four: Ionna: The Journal 297

Chapter Thirty-Five: Ionna : A Break in Reality 307

Chapter Thirty-Six: Kate: A Picture Worth a Thousand Words 315

Chapter Thirty-Seven: Ionna: Sweet Finding 321

Chapter Thirty-Eight: Darkness Follows 333

Chapter Thirty-Nine: Tea Leaves 343

Chapter Forty: The Trip 351

Chapter Forty-One: The Missing Piece 357

Chapter Forty-Two: The Lie 363

Chapter Forty-Three: On the Other Side 369

Chapter Forty-Four: The Story of Nyneve 377

Chapter Forty-Five: Dark Charms 387

Chapter Forty-Six: The Grasp of Darkness 395

Chapter Forty-Seven: Fernbeg 401

Chapter Forty-Eight: Gelert 411

Chapter Forty-Nine: Strange Connection 425

Chapter Fifty: The First 437

Chapter Fifty-One: The Song of Copper 441

Chapter Fifty-Two: Water's End 449

Chapter Fifty-Three: The Raging Storm 457

Chapter Fifty-Four: Read Between the Lines 465

Chapter Fifty-Five: Obsidian Sky 475

Chapter Fifty-Six: The Toll of Magic 481

Chapter Fifty-Seven: Up in Smoke 491

Chapter Fifty-Eight: Shadow in the Mist 499

Chapter Fifty-Nine: Malachite 507

Chapter Sixty: The Darkness 519

Chapter Sixty-One: Obsidian Pools 529

Chapter Sixty-Two: The Pull of Love 539

Chapter Sixty-Three: A New Story 547

Epilogue 551

Prologue
VERMILLION

It was a brisk May morning when Betty Shortbridge went out to the garden after finishing her morning tea to do a bit of weeding. The sun was just making its way over the treetops, casting its golden rays down upon the slate roof of her stone farmhouse. The birds sang as Betty set her gardening stool down on the dewy grass. With an old woven garden basket to her left, she got ready to start pulling up the stray weeds that had been encroaching on her delphiniums.

Slowly she pulled on her floral gardening gloves. Her hands didn't work as well as they used to, and the process took some effort. They had begun to swell with arthritis in her early seventies, and now that she was nearly eighty, they were twisted and stiff. However, she refused to let that stop her from doing what she loved best.

She was known for having the best-kept garden in Beddgelert, and she was determined to keep that reputation. Her flower beds were always meticulously weeded, and now that it was spring, the hyacinths and primroses were hardy and robust. Lately, however, one particular patch had been giving her a hard time—growing unnatural amounts of weeds that seemed hellbent on choking out her delphiniums. Betty prided herself on knowing almost everything there was to know about plants and gardening, but she couldn't figure out what kind of weed had taken over this section of the garden. The burgundy vine was unlike anything she had ever seen, and its large black thorns made it especially challenging to remove. So, Betty made it a habit to weed that area every morning before the vine became too large to uproot.

As she plucked and pulled the weeds and placed them in her basket, the sun snuck behind a cloud, leaving the world dim. Betty bent forward, closer to the ground where the dark vine had sprouted overnight once again. She grabbed a large handful and pulled. The earth around it moved slightly but the roots did not give way. She tried again with no luck. Her hands didn't have the strength they used to. Instead, she took a trowel from her basket and plunged it into the earth. As the shovel cut into the soil, it struck something, echoing back a muttered sound of metal hitting metal. She began to dig, filling the air with the earthy aroma of damp soil. Soon, she'd carved out a hole the size of a football. There, at the bottom, she spotted a bit of metal, dulled by the dark soil around it.

Betty sat on the grass, slowly removing the soil to reveal the brass head of a bird. The bird was fastened to a brass base with five leaf-shaped compartments, each with smaller birds upon them.

These smaller birds were handles of a sort, meant to pull open the leaf-shaped containers. *How curious*, she thought. Slowly, she got to her feet and made her way back into the cottage.

In the kitchen, she went over to her sink to remove the rest of the dirt and have a better look at the treasure she had found. As the water rinsed away the dirt, the species of bird became apparent: a peacock with five smaller versions of itself on each compartment. The container itself was designed to look like a flower, with petals surrounding the center.

Betty scrubbed until the dirt had been removed from each crack and crevice, leaving the brass shining once again. Once she had dried the strange ornament off, she sat down at the kitchen table to inspect it.

"Well, aren't you a curious little thing?" she said as she tried to open one of the leaf-shaped compartments with no luck.

On closer inspection, she discovered that the peacock in the center was a lock of sorts, holding all five lids shut. She used what little strength she had in her hands to try turning the bird. It would not budge.

"Must be rusted shut, Jasper," she said, addressing her cat, who sat close by looking with suspicion at this new, strange, shiny object. "Looks like it's been in the ground for quite some time."

Betty went over to the refrigerator and pulled out a stick of butter, breaking off a piece and warming it in her fingers as she walked back to the table. She rubbed the butter on the base of the peacock and tried to turn it once again. This time it did budge—just enough for her to lose her grip and slash the palm of her hand on one of the sharp tail feathers.

"Oh, good God!" she cried out, grasping her cut hand with her other. The cut ran deep, and the blood flowed freely down her fingertips, speckling the top of the brass container. She hurried toward the bathroom, leaving a trail of blood on the pine boards as she went.

The sun cascaded through the window and onto the brass container sitting on the old oak table, the fresh blood tarnishing its new shiny finish. As the blood ran down and dripped off its edges, the tiny peacock began to move, slowly spinning clockwise on its own. Once it reached its threaded end, it fell to the table with a thud, unlocking the five leaf-shaped compartments. One by one, the five leaf-shaped compartments opened.

A wind blew into the room, emptying the containers of the spices that lay within them. Then, from the hole where the peacock had been, a thin wisp of black smoke seeped. It coiled and swirled, mirroring the menacing growth of the mysterious weed in her garden. In mere moments, an ominous cloud of ebony had materialized, shrouding Betty's kitchen in a cloak of unearthly darkness.

Chapter One
Ionna
THE LETTER

The letter came registered mail on a late Thursday afternoon at the end of May. Ionna had returned home early after a dreadful day at work. Her main lead on a story had bailed, and her editor was breathing down her neck to finish some fluff piece on a dog trainer who had landed a spot on *America's Got Talent*. She was just about to pour herself a hefty glass of cabernet when the doorbell rang. She hadn't expected anyone and was surprised to see the mailman standing there with a letter in his hands.

"Sorry for bringing this by so late in the afternoon, it's been crazy," he said apologetically as he handed her a small electronic device to sign.

"No, it's fine," she said with a sympathetic nod. She knew

exactly how shitty a hectic day could turn out.

When she returned to the kitchen with the letter, she poured out the cabernet and sat down at the table, putting her feet up on the opposite chair. She took two rather large sips of the wine and rolled her shoulders, attempting to release the stress that had built up throughout the day. Her boss, Jenna, being the biggest literal cause of pain in her neck. She harbored a deep-seated animosity toward Ionna that dated back to the time when they had both just started working at the *Gazette*.

In the shadow of a triple homicide linked to the governor's son, a former classmate of Ionna's, their boss assigned her the story instead of Jenna. The hope was that her existing connection with the family would coax them into opening up—a strategy that proved successful. The family's willingness to confide in her resulted in the paper's biggest story in years, giving Ionna her first big break and leaving Jenna the unknown rookie.

Ionna cherished her role as a journalist, content with her position as a staff reporter for the *Gazette*. In contrast, Jenna had always sought to climb the corporate hierarchy. She relentlessly pursued her goals and ultimately attained them, becoming Ionna's superior. Jenna seized every opportunity to remind Ionna of her new position, savoring the chance to hold her authority over her.

Jenna thought that Ionna was too independent and didn't work well with others. Even if that was partly true, it was more that she didn't work well with her. She was the lone wolf of the newsroom, always taking off on leads without approval, which irritated Jenna to no end.

Ionna took another sip to wash down the day's stress before inspecting the curious piece of mail. The cream-colored envelope had a return address from Wales, United Kingdom, scrolled across the top in black inky letters. Wales? She didn't know many people outside *Maine* let alone from another country altogether. Baffled, she wedged her nail under the fold of the envelope and ripped it open. Inside was a formal-looking letterhead from Brightmore Law Firm.

At the sight of it, her heart raced. Was she personally being sued over a story she had written? There was that one about the tourist couple arrested for indecent exposure behind the Lobster House. They had been from somewhere in England.

But upon further inspection, she saw that it had come from an estate lawyer. This calmed her racing heart and piqued her interest. She unfolded the letter, smoothed it out, and began to read.

Dear Ms. Bellmore,

I regret to inform you of the passing of your grandmother, Betty Shortbridge. Our law firm holds her final will and testament. These documents name you as the sole heir and beneficiary of her estate and holdings. We will need you to come to our offices to sign the proper paperwork and claim what she has left you. We understand that you are abroad and that it may take you some time to make the appropriate arrangements; therefore, we have set up the closing 12 days from the date of sending, on June 12th at 9 a.m. Please contact us with any questions you may have. You can reach us via email, phone, and fax.

Sincerely,

John Brightmore

She wanted nothing more than to confront them about this, but she'd never be able to have that conversation. Five winters ago, her parents had died in an accident on the Casco Bay Bridge, and in that moment her world upended. For a long time, nothing felt right or good. She'd buried her grief in her work and hadn't resurfaced until this past year. Any knowledge of this long-lost grandmother had died along with them.

Suddenly, she was angry. Just when she was finally starting to recover from the loss, this letter appeared out of nowhere, making her question everything, making her wonder things she'd never get the answers to. It was a devastating blow. How could they have kept such a significant secret from her? And why?

It had to be a mistake.

She picked a pen up off the table and began clicking it, a nervous habit she'd developed in the newsroom, as she read the letter for a second and then a third time.

"What the hell?!" she said to herself, putting the letter down again. She sat there, a mix of emotions running around inside her. Confusion burned alongside anger, then faded into curiosity with a hint of excitement at the prospect of an inheritance. Guilt for feeling this way at her apparent grandmother's demise quickly followed.

She walked back over to the counter and retrieved her laptop from her travel bag. Back at the table, she Googled "Brightmore Law Firm." She wasn't going to dive any deeper into this rabbit hole until she was certain the letter wasn't a scam.

Within seconds, the law firm's website popped up on the screen, followed beneath by various news pages detailing high-profile estate cases the firm had been involved in. Intrigued, she clicked on their webpage and scrolled down to explore the services they offered. She found that it was quite a large firm based in London and appeared to be genuine. Continuing her search, Ionna opened another page and entered "Betty Shortbridge, Wales" in the search bar. Numerous results appeared, ranging from the webpage for a baker in southern Wales to the Instagram of a dog groomer in Aberaeron. However, one particular result stood out from the rest: "Betty Shortbridge wins the 2018 Golden Garden Award." Ionna's mother had often teased her for having a "black thumb" compared to her grandmother's innate ability to cultivate any plant.

She clicked on the webpage and scrolled, skimming the article, when she came across a picture at the bottom. An older woman with snow-white hair standing in a large flower garden. She recognized her in an instant. The woman on the computer screen was an older version of the one in the photograph that had graced her parents' mantelpiece for years.

Without a second thought, she sprang from her chair and made a beeline for the corner cupboard in her living room, her heart pounding. She fished out an old shoe box and returned to the table, removing the top and sifting through the photographs until she finally found the small framed picture of her grandmother. She went back to her laptop and held the picture to the screen.

"Holy shit," she said as she compared the photos. That solidified it; there was no doubt about it—Betty was her grandmother.

Ionna's heart sank as she realized that her honest and kindhearted parents had been lying to her all these years. Why, though? Were they running from someone or something, or perhaps even from Betty? That would explain why she hadn't reached out after their deaths, instead leaving her to grieve on her own. She downed the remaining contents of her wineglass and promptly refilled it, then picked up the phone and dialed a number without even glancing at the keypad. The phone rang only twice before someone on the other end of the line answered.

"Hello," said the soft voice.

"Meg, you're not going to believe this!" Ionna blurted out, her words sounding more forceful than she had anticipated as the wine kicked in. If anyone was going to help sort this mess out in her head, it would be Meg. She was her best friend and knew everything about Ionna, including the things she wished she could keep from her. Like how she had shut down after her parents' deaths. Meg had tried to get her "out there" after a few lonely years, but she didn't feel ready. Being alone, she didn't have to worry about anyone else but herself—it just seemed easier that way.

"Don't tell me, you hooked up with the copy editor at work?"

"God, no! I'm not quite that desperate. I got a letter from an estate lawyer in England today. I inherited my grandmother's estate in Wales. Yup, you heard me—grandmother."

"I didn't think you had any family left," Meg stated, seeming confused.

"Well, I guess I did but no one decided to tell me. Instead, I had to find out from some law firm in London. Can you believe that shit?"

"Ionna, are you sure this isn't a scam? You hear about this kinda thing all the time."

"No, I looked up the law firm, and everything seems legit. It came registered mail and everything. It didn't ask for any bank account information or anything shady like that. Catch is, I need to be in London on June twelfth for the reading of the will. I don't know if I should go. I really want to get the river waste story out there. I don't have time to be flying halfway around the world. A week away kinda throws a wrench in the works if I can't get it done before the will reading."

"Oni, that's some heavy stuff. Are you sure you're okay?" Meg said sympathetically.

"Yeah, I have no idea what to even think. Why the hell would my parents have lied to me about it? How could they have kept my grandmother from me?"

"Maybe it was some sort of family feud thing," Meg suggested.

"Well, whatever it was I plan to find out," Ionna said with a forced sense of optimism that was grinding its way through the anger.

"Just think, though—maybe you're gonna inherit a huge fortune and you can fly me over there and we can live out our days as crazy old eccentric ladies in a manor house."

They both laughed.

"We'll see," Ionna said, still chuckling. Meg always looked on the brighter side of most situations; that's why she was her best friend since they were twelve. Ionna had always been the pragmatic one, viewing her experiences in life as puzzles to be solved. Meg balanced her out with her exuberant, spontaneous personality, forcing Ionna to relax and enjoy the moment while they were together. She was the sun to her moon.

"I'm gonna be in Tampa until the twentieth, and you'll be over there by then, so make sure you keep me updated. I am so curious to see what this mysterious grandmother has left you. Oh, and be safe; no getting into cars with shady lawyers."

"Haha, I'll do my best. I'll catch up with you once I'm there and find out what's going on. Talk to you soon, bye," Ionna said, hanging up the phone and going back to examining the letter for the fourth and final time. There was nothing more to be done tonight. She drank the last sips of her wine and then lay down on the couch and picked up *The Way of the Peaceful Warrior*, a novel she had been reading to try and calm her mind. Two pages in, her eyelids felt heavy and before she knew it, she had fallen asleep, slumped over onto the armrest, book resting open on her chest like a bird in flight.

Chapter Two

Ionna

MORAL GROUND

The sound of the book hitting the floor jolted Ionna from a sound sleep. She slowly sat up and gripped the back of her neck with both hands. It was sore and aching from the unnatural position she had fallen asleep in on the couch.

She picked the book up off the floor, setting it back on the coffee table before looking into the kitchen to see what time it was. The clock on the stove read 5:55 a.m. It was going to be a double pot of coffee kind of morning if she was going to be awake enough for the staff meeting at seven.

After she was suitably caffeinated, she jumped in the shower, threw on a pair of black slacks with a white blouse, and pulled her hair up into a messy bun. There was no time for makeup, so she quickly brushed on a bit of mascara and dabbed on some lip gloss. She gathered up her laptop and phone and threw them into an old, worn leather courier bag. With a fresh cup of coffee in hand, she raced out the door to her car.

The trip to work took her thirty minutes, which was just enough time for her to begin to stew over the events of yesterday. She had been working on a story for over a week about the sewage that was leaking into the Kennebec River from an old industrial building. The owner of the building was an out-of-town real estate flipper who had no interest in fixing the problem. Not only had he refused to give her a comment when she'd called to question him, but he had placed a complaint with the paper. This, in turn, got her kicked off the story, leaving it in the hands of her rival in the newsroom, Bailey Edwards. She was still fuming about it. It wasn't normal to be taken off a story for a complaint—people complained all the time. But she knew that Jenna had been gunning to push her out ever since becoming chief editor, and this was all the ammunition she needed.

Ionna made her way from the parking lot to the gray industrial building that housed the newsroom. Walking through the double doors, the deafening sound of a newspaper anticipating the next big story assailed her ears. As people rushed from one cubicle to the next, Jenna angrily paced the loft office above the newsroom.

"Ionna, thank God you're here. Jenna's in a mood and needs to see you in her office right away," said Tom, a lanky young man who was the paper's note runner. He was perfect for the job—his thin frame and hyper personality made it easy for him to zip around the office handing out copies and notes.

"Okay, thanks for the heads-up, Tom," Ionna said. She walked past him and over to her desk, dropping her bag and jacket off before heading up to Jenna's office.

Jenna's heels struck the floor in sharp taps as she paced the length of the room, phone to her ear. Ionna knocked on the glass doors and waited until she gestured her in, a look of utter annoyance across her face.

"Have a seat," she said as she cupped her hand over the receiver to block her voice.

Ionna apprehensively sat down in one of the deep burgundy chairs in front of Jenna's desk and crossed her arms, already feeling defensive.

"Okay, thanks, Sam. I'll be in touch after the meeting. Talk to you soon," Jenna said, ending the phone call and setting her sights on Ionna. "Do you know who that was?" she asked in a pissed-off tone. "That was Sam Walsh, the paper's lawyer. We're being sued, thanks to you."

"What? Who?" Ionna asked, even though she knew exactly who.

"Oh, don't give me that. You know. You should've just left it alone, Ionna. I told you to drop it. I took you off that story a week ago. Now they have you on camera snooping around the building that has a clear 'No Trespassing' sign out front. You broke several laws, and you're lucky they came here instead of just throwing your ass in jail," Jenna snarled.

"I'm a reporter. I don't let things go, I figure them out. That's what good reporters do. Plus, that guy's a complete asshole. He's ruining the water. People need to know what's going on, especially when it affects their local ecosystem. I seem to be the only one around here who's been able to get to the bottom of it all, or, hell, even *cares. Even the EPA is downplaying it*, and you're telling me to drop it?"

"Well, that asshole is also the mayor's godson."

"So what? That doesn't mean he's not liable for the damage he's causing to the environment."

"Ionna, just stop. You might be right, but there's no saving this piece. The only way out of this shit storm is to trash the article," Jenna said, running her fingers through her jet-black hair.

"You're seriously going to block this over politics? Did you even read the code of ethics before you became a journalist?" Ionna spat.

"Listen, it's done. The article is dead. You're lucky I've put up with your rogue bullshit this long."

Ionna stood, looking Jenna straight in the eyes. "*My* bullshit?"

Jenna set her jaw, refusing to respond, but Ionna could see she'd struck a nerve. She turned and headed for the door.

"You can either kill the story or kill your career here at the Gazette. Either way, it's not running in this paper. Your choice."

Five minutes later, Ionna had filled a box with her belongings and walked out of the newsroom, one hand raised over her head, middle finger pointed to the sky.

Chapter Three
Kate
TRIP TO NANA'S

The sun was out in full force, and it was hotter than any June Kate could remember. The bus ride from London to Beddgelert had been long and uncomfortable—five hours of motorways followed by winding country roads in the baking heat—and Kate felt sure she would have lost the will to live if she hadn't brought along Stephen King's newest book, *The Outsider* to keep her occupied.

She was full of anticipation for the next few months stretched out before her. After finishing secondary school, she'd decided to spend the summer at her grandmother's house in north Wales. Her grandfather had passed away in the winter, and she hated the thought of her grandmother being alone up there. Plus, there was the added bonus that it completely pissed off her mother. If it were up to her, she would be home all summer preparing for uni. Yet another reason to flee to the countryside since she didn't have a clue what she wanted to do with her life, let alone if she even wanted to attend uni. The time away could help her figure things out.

In a matter of weeks, Kate would be eighteen. Technically an adult and free to make her own decisions. Unfortunately for Kate, she had flown through her A levels with flying colors, and now her mother expected her to attend university. Kate had, up to this point, declined to reply to any of her university acceptances and the clock was ticking. Instead, she spent most of her time reading, rather than deciding her life's direction.

Her mother had attempted to involve Kate's father in the decision, but it proved to be a challenge since he spent most of his time vacationing with his girlfriends rather than being a responsible parent. As a result, she had given up on seeking his input and informed Kate that she expected her to have concrete plans for the autumn by the time she returned home or she would need to find a job along with her own place.

Kate could have spent the summer hanging out with her best friend Stevie, lazing around on their phones, and pissing away their time at the local café. That was all fine and good for Stevie, who had known from the time she was six that she wanted to be a meteorologist. She'd even gotten early acceptance into Greenwich University's engineering program, so she had nothing to do but wait. Kate, however, was like a ship lost at sea, not knowing what direction to go in. The only thing she truly enjoyed doing was reading books and keeping to herself, two things that didn't leave her many career options.

As the bus continued through the lush green landscape of the Welsh countryside, she looked out the tinted windows. Rolling hills lay as the backdrop to her reflection in the glass. Her hair had grown quite long in the past year and now flowed in crimson waves down to the center of her back. Her face caught the light, accentuating the freckles that graced her cheeks and the bridge of her nose. She had never been a pretty girl growing up, but in the past year, she had "come into herself," as her mother liked to say. It was too bad that it had taken all of her teenage years to do so. She was less than popular with the boys and spent one too many Friday nights inside reading rather than being part of the social scene. But that seemed to be the way her life went, always a step behind everyone else.

As they rolled into the small village, the bus driver announced their arrival. The town sat snug in a valley between the mountains, its stone storefronts and homes proving that time didn't change much this far up north. She figured the only thing that had altered there in the past hundred or so years was the people themselves. She liked the idea of a place that remained stable and predictable, as opposed to London, which was in a constant state of flux.

When she stepped off the bus, the smell of cut grass mixed with freshly baked bread wafted down the street from the local bakery to greet her. A more pleasant mix of smells than what she was used to in the city. The sun had moved behind thick cloud cover, and the temperature began to cool down as she waited in line to get her luggage. After grabbing her bag from under the bus, she walked into the car park and looked for her grandmother's Volkswagen, wondering if she would still be driving the ugly old thing. It only took a moment to spot it—still old, still bright pea-green.

As she walked over, she could see her grandmother's white hair poking up just above the steering wheel. She was a short, thin woman but she was fierce.

Kate bent to look in the driver's side window and gave her

grandmother a wave. "Nana! Hi!"

"Oh my. Look at you, all grown up. Come give your nana a hug," said her grandmother, slowly getting out of the car to envelop her.

It was almost six years since they had seen each other. While Kate had grown from an awkward kid into a young woman, gaining four inches in the process, her grandmother looked just the same as she remembered. Her bright blue eyes were still just as clear, and her smile lit up a small place in Kate's heart in a way no one else's could.

Since Kate was a small child, she had spent her summers in Wales with her grandparents. But the summer she turned twelve, something changed between her grandparents and her mother. All she knew was they had some kind of feud, and after that their only contact was through phone calls at Christmas and yearly birthday cards sent to Kate. Even though Kate had tried over the years, her mother refused to visit or let her stay there during the summer. But she was old enough now to travel without her mother's permission.

"Let's get going before the traffic gets bad. Toss your bag in the boot," her grandmother said, kicking Kate out of her own head and back into the moment.

She looked at the empty road that split the town in two; only three cars had passed by in the few minutes they had been standing there. She laughed a little to herself as she put her bag into the boot. *Nana would never make it in the city*, she thought.

The car ride to her grandmother's house was short compared to the trip on the bus, and they spent most of it chit-chatting about her plans after the summer. It was a question everyone asked her and one she didn't know how to answer. She had no idea what she wanted to do with her life; it was a complete mystery to her. Her mother had tried to push her into journalism after her A levels predictions had come back, saying she had always been a good writer, so why not give it a go? There was no way that was happening; just the thought of interviewing people made her stomach turn, she was way too much of an introvert for that kind of thing. All she wanted to do was escape from all the pressure and spend the summer relaxing. She would figure it out in her own time.

When they arrived at her grandmother's quaint little cottage, the sun was back out and lighting up the flowers in the fields behind the house like an ocean of pinks and yellows. She had forgotten how beautiful it was here. It may have been out in the middle of nowhere, but nowhere was breathtaking with its vast fields that broke away into slate-blue mountains beyond.

"Grab your bag, cariad. Get a move on. It's almost six, and I need to get in to watch the news," her grandmother said, trying to act as if no time had passed between them. But Kate could feel the space that had grown. Six years was a long time, and her grandmother would need to get to know the adult Kate now.

As Kate grabbed her bag out of the boot, she caught a glimpse of something from the corner of her eye. Some kind of animal darting from the edge of the woods into the tall wheat grass and wildflowers. She waited another moment, peering out into the open field. The head of a fox with one white ear popped up. Kate watched it leap into the air before diving back down into the wheat. He repeated this several times, then ran back into the woods with a mouse in his jaws. Stopping at the edge of the forest, he turned and looked at her; his eyes transfixed on hers for a long minute before he whirled around and disappeared into the thicket.

Kate had seen foxes in the city, of course, and often. But there they were skinny, scraggly, and ate mostly what leftovers they could find in people's bins during the night. To witness one hunting in the wild during the day felt a little magical, like a good omen for her stay here. She watched for several minutes, hoping the fox would come back. When it didn't, she turned and lugged her bags into the house.

The house was infused with the scent of cedar and woodsmoke, along with her grandmother's rosy-scented perfume, smells that instantly brought back memories from her childhood. Flashes of memories flooded her mind: moments spent with her grandmother in the small kitchen making jam, or with her grandfather taking walks as he smoked his pipe and told her stories. It was all a bit hazy though, coming to her in broken pieces, she guessed that was just another symptom of all the time that had passed.

Everything still looked just as it had the last time she was here. She could hear her grandmother in the kitchen, already beginning to cook dinner. An old box-style television blared from the living room, spouting off the daily weather report.

"We are looking at a fair bit of rain over the next few days," the weatherman said.

That figures, Kate thought, *it rains mostly all summer here.* She peered into the kitchen where her grandmother was slicing up carrots.

She glanced at Kate over her shoulder. "Go put your bag in the guest room and wash up. Dinner will be ready shortly."

She did as she was told, making her way to the stairs. She was glad to be back in her grandparents' house after so many years. It still seemed more like home than her own house in London. Yet, in the absence of her grandfather, the atmosphere felt altered, reflecting a more somber rendition of its former joyfulness. The thought of her nana enduring this empty house since her grandfather's death filled her with nauseating guilt. She should have insisted that her mother come to visit her after his passing. However, the summer carried the promise of redemption, a chance to restore lost moments and breathe life and happiness back into the house.

Chapter Four
Kate

THE MAGIC LAMP

Kate made her way upstairs to the tiny bedroom on the left. The wallpaper in her room was an overly cheerful relic of the sixties—bright orange and pink flowers and vibrant greenery against a periwinkle background. The windows were trimmed with pink lace curtains that matched the flowers on the paper. It was a far cry from her mother's world of sleek neutrals and minimalism back home. Well, at least the bed was a double, and from what she remembered, quite comfy. She sat down on the pink gingham bedspread and looked around.

As with the downstairs, it was like time had stood still in this room. Nothing had changed. She'd loved the room as a child, thinking it was the kind a fairy princess would have. Now, though, the bright colors and crazy patterns made her vaguely nauseous.

But she would manage. She only needed to sleep in here, and thankfully that was done in the dark.

She unpacked her bag and pulled out a small stack of tank tops and T-shirts, a few pairs of sweatpants, jeans, and an oversized sweatshirt, along with socks and underwear, and added them to the dresser before heading back down to the kitchen. When she came out of her room, she glanced across the way into her grandmother's. On the nightstand sat a framed picture of her grandfather. A twinge of sadness moved through her at the sight. He had been such a light-hearted person, always telling silly jokes and stories to amuse her. She felt sorry for her grandmother, who was living out here all alone in the country, her only daughter refusing to visit her. Whatever had happened between the two of them left her mother so bitter she hadn't even shown up for her father's funeral. This, in turn, had prevented Kate from attending it as well, adding to a lengthy list of resentments she held against her mother.

As Kate descended the stairs, she thought how lonely her grandmother must be without her husband around and not even her family to lean on for support.

"Kate, dear, can you grab me that bowl on the top shelf there?" her grandmother asked her as she entered the kitchen. She pointed to a large ceramic bowl resting on the top shelf of the old wooden cupboard. Kate looked up; it was the mixing bowl they'd always used to make biscuits when she was younger.

She took it down from the top shelf and handed it to her. Her grandmother took it over to the table and began filling it with a tossed salad.

"All these veggies came from Bryndu Farm just up the road. Do you remember Ben Dwyer and his son, Owen? You used to play with Owen when you were a wee one."

"Yeah, I guess. Aren't they the people with the mean ducks?"

"Geese, but yes," her grandmother said with a chuckle. "You must remember Owen, you two were inseparable in the summers. You used to get up to all kinds of mischief together." Her grandmother's tone was light but she seemed to be watching for Kate's reaction.

"Yeah, I remember Owen, I just don't remember much of what we did together. It's been a while, Nana," Kate said, her memories of her childhood friend and their adventures just as broken and hazy as all the other recollections of her time spent in Wales.

"You're right," her grandmother said quickly. "Now, help me set the table."

Kate went about setting the table as her grandmother pulled roast potatoes and carrots out of the oven, along with some hot rolls. Kate couldn't remember the last time she had eaten a home-cooked meal. Her mother was not what you would call a good cook, and most nights, it was takeout or cereal for dinner. She never quite understood how the apple had fallen so far from the tree. Her grandmother was a fabulous cook and a loving person—almost the polar opposite of her own mother.

"Looks delicious, Nana," Kate said, filling a plate and grabbing two rolls off the tray, then sitting down at the small kitchen table.

"Good Lord, is your mother not feeding you?" Nana said, looking at the heaping pile of food on Kate's plate.

"Not like this," Kate said through a mouthful of mashed-up roast potatoes.

"It's been a while since I've cooked for anyone. I forgot how much I missed it—and you. You've grown up so much since you were here last. I feel like I've missed out on so much," her grandmother said, with a sadness in her voice that made Kate's heart ache for her.

"I know, Nana, I missed you too. I don't know what happened between you guys and Mum but she didn't have the right to keep me away from you like she did."

"Your mother did what she thought was right for you at the time. You can't hold it against her, she was just trying to be a good mother," Nana said matter-of-factly, but Kate could still see the sorrow in her eyes.

Kate wanted to know the truth, but she didn't want to push her about it on her first day there. It was a difficult subject, and a lot of pain had taken root in the intervening years. There was time to talk about it. The whole summer stretched out before her. For now, she settled for the companionable silence that fell between them as they enjoyed the best meal Kate could remember having in years.

After dinner, Kate washed the dishes while her grandmother watched TV in the small living room off to the side of the kitchen. As Kate let the bubbly water cascade over the dinner plates in the sink, something caught her eye. The lowering rays of sunlight made their way through the window and illuminated a small table lamp sitting next to her grandmother. At the sight of the lamp's golden base, a memory began slipping into her thoughts.

It was a year after her parents' divorce, and her mother had dropped her off to stay with her grandparents while she vacationed in Italy with her new boyfriend. She was only seven years old at the time and had developed a fear of the dark that summer. Maybe it was the strange darkness of the countryside compared to the constant lights of the city, or maybe it was being away from both her parents so soon after their split. Whatever it was, the fear grew to the point that she ended up sleeping with her grandparents the first night she was there. The next day, her grandfather went into town and returned with a surprise for her. It was a special lamp for her room. He told her it was magical, and all she needed to do was touch it, and the light would come on, no switch required. Kate had never seen anything like it, and she was in awe of the magic she believed it possessed. That night, she was actually excited to go to sleep so that she could try it out.

As soon as dinner was over and her grandmother had succeeded in forcing them to watch *Britain's Got Talent*, she rushed upstairs, eager to use her new magic lamp.

As her grandfather tucked her in, he said, "Remember, if you get scared, all you need to do is give the magic lamp a tap, and it will light up your room. Why don't you give it a try?"

She reached over and touched the lamp. The light flicked on, bathing the room in a warm, safe glow. She touched it again and it shut off.

"Yes, just like that," her grandfather said, giving her a smile and a nod of his head.

Kate lay back, looking over at the lamp. Just knowing it was there lifted her anxiety. Her grandfather pulled the blanket up and tucked her in, giving her a kiss on the forehead before leaving the room.

The summer days in Wales were long and light, and her grandparents were tucked into their beds across the hall by the time it grew dim outside. Darkness began to spread its way across her room. She lay there in her bed, testing out the lamp, turning it on and off by touching it in different places. But as the darkness outside grew, the newfound joy of the lamp faded. The flowers on the wallpaper were transformed by the shadowy darkness into monstrous faces leering down at her from every angle.

She turned the light on.

Nothing. Just flowers and ferns.

She shut it off again and lay back in bed, wide awake. In the still silence of the dark, fear began to spread in her mind. She tried to keep her eyes shut tight but could feel faces leering down at her. Her heartbeat grew louder, echoing in her ears, then her chest tightened, and she felt the room begin to spin. Trying to calm herself, she turned the light back on one last time.

The lamp's soft glow lit up an unfamiliar room. Instead of monstrously floral wallpaper, there were stark wooden walls. A half loft hung over part of the room and under it was a table with two chairs. The only other piece of furniture was an old rocking chair that sat next to a stone fireplace toward the back of the room.

A dream, she must be in a dream.

Hand trembling, Kate reached for the lamp but grasped only empty air. Fear raced through her, and she shut her eyes as tightly as possible. The flowery pattern of the wallpaper was still emblazoned on her eyelids, and she focused on it as she gritted her teeth.

When she finally dared to open her eyes again, she was back in the guest room in her own bed, staring at the warm yellow glow of the magic lamp.

Chapter Five

Ionna

THE DELAYED OUTCOME

It was six days since she'd left the paper, and Ionna had spent the majority of it knee-deep in research. Just because the *Valley Gazette* wasn't going to publish her story on the sewage waste in the river didn't mean their rival, the *Bath Post*, wouldn't. After hours of further research, she had a solid story and emailed it to their chief editor, Mark Davis, as a final F-U to Jenna. Ionna knew the story was big, and if the *Gazette* hadn't been in the pocket of Mayor Dolton, then they would have run it in a heartbeat. Ever since Jenna became the chief editor, she had been pulling favors for town officials and trashing stories that should have been major headlines. Ionna assumed that in return Jenna was getting some cushy kickbacks and favors for holding the tongue of the paper for them. Her moral compass did not point due north. The *Post* was about to have a field day.

After sending the story to Mark, Ionna leaned back in her chair and stared at the laptop screen, clicking the pen in her hand. Now that she no longer had a story or job to occupy her mind, she had no idea what to do next. She gave the house a quick scan. The kitchen table, which had been serving as her impromptu workspace, had become a total disaster area, so she set about cleaning it up. She gathered the papers strewn across the table and stacked them neatly. As she did, the letter from the estate lawyer slipped from the pile and fell to the ground.

"Shit," she said, scooping it up and looking down at the letter for the first time in days. She had let herself get swept up in the sewage story as a distraction from this whole newfound grandmother idea. There had been a dizzying array of questions swirling around in her head that she had been trying to avoid, and she'd done such a good job of it that she'd completely spaced on calling the lawyer.

She thought for a moment. It was now the ninth, and she had until the twelfth to get to London and attend the reading of the will. When she'd first received the letter, the idea of just jumping on a plane across the Atlantic to claim an inheritance from a grandmother she'd thought dead for years seemed insane. But now that she'd sent off her story to the *Post* and her career at the *Gazette* was pretty much tanked, maybe it wasn't so crazy. She didn't have anything else lined up, and if she wanted to know why her parents had lied to her all these years, she would need to do some digging. What better place to start than her mysterious grandmother's place? At the very least, this could make for an interesting story to pitch somewhere and tide her over.

She picked up her cell phone and dialed the number on the

letterhead. The phone only rang twice before a woman with a thick British accent answered.

"Brightmore Law. How may I help you?" she asked.

"Hi, my name is Ionna Bellmore. I received a letter in the mail about my grandmother's will. I wanted to call and confirm the date and time for the will reading."

It was quiet on the other end; she could hear the tapping of fingers on a keyboard before the woman spoke again.

"Yes, I see you have an appointment with Mr. Brightmore scheduled for the twelfth of June at nine a.m. It looks like he's allotted an hour for the reading to get your grandmother's holdings transferred into your name," she told Ionna.

"Okay, great. Thanks," Ionna said before ending the call.

Next, she scrolled through travel websites. As she looked at the price of the tickets, she wished she'd decided about going sooner. Being so last minute, they were all quite expensive. Fortunately, she had always been careful with money, and after selling her parents' house, she had a sizable chunk in her savings account. She couldn't bring herself to spend any of it and had decided to keep it set aside for her retirement. However, discovering her true lineage seemed like a fitting way to use a small portion of it.

This was typical of her, though, putting decisions off until the very last minute. Here she was, three days from the point she needed to be in London, and just now getting around to organizing how the heck she was going to get there. If she could prioritize her life as well as she could her work, then things might be easier for her.

For the past five years, she had deliberately avoided almost all social situations. In the aftermath of her parents' deaths, she had thrown herself into work, using it as a coping mechanism to distract herself from the pain. In hindsight, she had probably become a little too consumed by it, to the point where it had taken over her life. She hadn't had a boyfriend in six years, and even that was little more than a brief fling. The only person she spoke to outside of work was Meg, but now that she'd begun a long-distance relationship with a guy in Florida, Ionna knew their friendship might not be the priority it once had been. It made her realize that her social life was practically non-existent.

Meg always said that writing other people's stories was keeping her from creating her own. And maybe she was right. Perhaps this was her wake-up call, a chance to stop avoiding life and start living it.

After searching for over an hour, she finally found a direct flight to London on Celtic Airways for a little over a thousand dollars. Although expensive, she was beginning to see this trip as a much-needed vacation. After the will reading, she planned to find a hotel, spend a few days in the city, and then travel around the country a bit. After all, there was no job or man waiting for her back home.

She shut her laptop and proceeded to sort out what she needed to pack. In the subdued glow of her bedroom, she carefully retrieved clothes from her dresser, laying them out on her bed. Her gaze shifted to the framed picture of her parents resting on the dresser's surface, and she removed it from its perch.

As she looked upon her parents' smiling faces, they didn't seem the same as they once had. They appeared different, as if a veil of secrecy had been draped over what she had thought to be their true selves. But now she could see there was something beneath the mask of normalcy they had always worn, and it unsettled her. Slowly, she returned the picture to its spot, placing it face down.

The weight of all the questions weighed on her as she finished packing. The trip could be her last chance to discover the truth. She couldn't help but think the answers to her questions lay amidst the Welsh countryside, hidden within the shadowed depths of her grandmother's house.

Chapter Six
Ionna
JOHN BRIGHTMORE

The next three days of last-minute preparations for her trip were a blur, and it seemed like in the blink of an eye, Ionna was waking up on the plane to the sound of the pilot announcing their descent into Gatwick Airport. She propped herself up, wiped the sleep from her eyes, and looked out the window. As the large gray landscape of the city grew closer, nervousness set in.

"Shit," she muttered to herself as the plane landed.

People began to disembark, and Ionna found herself swept up in a line of people pushing her forward through the gate and into the airport.

Once she had broken free of the crowd, she made her way to the baggage claim and then over to security. Both lines were rather long, and it had taken her some time to go through them; by the time she was cleared, it was almost seven a.m. Two hours until the reading of the will. She quickly made her way through the large glass doors that led to the taxi terminal. The place was dangerous, with taxis zipping in and out at all angles. It took four tries before she was able to flag a cab that wasn't already reserved.

"Alright, love, where ya going today?" the cabbie asked in his thick British accent as Ionna stuffed her luggage into the back seat and jumped in. He was an overweight older gentleman with dark brown hair, thick-framed glasses, and a kind smile.

"I need to go to 145 St. James Street, please," Ionna said as she adjusted herself into the seat and shut the door.

The cabbie tilted his head in acknowledgment and set off. After driving close to two hours, Ionna's eyes were drawn to the towering structure of the London Eye off in the distance, the first sign of the bustling metropolis that awaited her. She'd never been to London before, and only now did she remember how much she had burned to visit when she was younger. Somehow, the wanderlust had dwindled as she'd gotten older and life had gotten in the way.

As they passed through the diverse neighborhoods of Croydon and Bromley, Ionna couldn't help but feel a sense of awe at the towering structures that dominated the cityscape. The buildings stood over them like giants looming down from the thick, smoggy sky. The majestic Tower Bridge, its two imposing towers standing tall above the Thames, was a sight to behold. And then there was the Shard, a shimmering skyscraper that seemed to scrape the clouds themselves.

Colorful signs for shops and pubs broke up the ocean of grays rolling past the window.

The city was alive with the hustle and bustle of the working hours, transforming the streets into a chaotic tangle of cars and pedestrians. It took over two hours to get to her destination with all the traffic, getting her to the law office with only a few minutes to spare. Ionna was relieved; all the stopping and going on top of her nerves had turned her stomach.

The cabbie pulled as close as he could to a group of cars parked in front of the large stone building with a plaque that read 145 St. James.

"Here we are," he said in a cheerful tone, announcing their arrival.

Ionna hopped out of the cab and grabbed her bags, handing the cabbie his fee along with a nice tip.

"Thanks. Have a good day now," he said with a smile before pulling away.

"You as well," Ionna said, but her voice was drowned out by the sounds of the city that buzzed around her.

Brightmore Law Firm was housed in a tall stone building that appeared to be quite old, with hints of art nouveau in its architecture. She walked up the four steps that led to its enormous dark oak doors. To the right was a plaque engraved with the names of the businesses in the building along with the floor numbers. She hit button three and waited. A woman's voice came out from the intercom to the side of her.

"Hello, how may I help you?"

"Hello. My name is Ionna Bellmore. I'm here for the reading of Betty Shortbridge's will."

"Yes, Ms. Bellmore, we've been expecting you. Just come straight up," the voice said as the door buzzed and unlocked, letting her in.

As she stepped into the lobby, the smell of fresh flowers greeted her. Two ostentatious bouquets sat on a pair of oak tables on either side of the golden elevator doors. Gold-green floral wallpaper accentuated the dark mahogany trimmings, and the floor appeared to be freshly polished as she walked to the elevator, bags trailing behind her. As she waited for the doors to open, classical music filled the air, piped in from somewhere unseen. It was all so fancy and impressive, but somehow it reminded her of a Quentin Tarantino film. She half expected the elevator doors to burst open and two men to come rolling out onto the floor in a violent brawl. But instead, when the doors opened, she was greeted by an old man in a fine-looking gray suit.

"What floor, miss?" he asked politely.

"Floor three, please. Thank you," she answered back as she stepped in with her bags in tow.

As the doors closed, the classical music followed them into the elevator. She was full of nervous anticipation, but she put on her game face, determined not to let her feelings show as she prepared to enter the office. She watched the tiny circles light up until number three flashed, and the doors opened. She gave the older gentleman a smile and stepped out into an even more impressive room than the first. It was carpeted in rich burgundy, and a large mahogany desk sat front and center with two stained glass lights dropping down to create an ambient glow. Two well-dressed women sat behind the desk in front of computers, typing away. Ionna walked up to the friendlier looking of the two.

"Hello, I'm Ionna Bellmore."

"Yes, Ms. Bellmore. They're about to start. Let me show you to the room," the woman said in a kind voice.

They walked down a long hallway littered with doors. Ionna counted four before they stopped.

"Here you are. They should be starting shortly," the woman said, opening the door and gesturing for Ionna to go in.

The room looked like any corporate conference room, with a long oak table surrounded by chairs and a large flat-screen TV at the front for presentations. Two men in sharp suits sat toward the end of the table, and as she entered, they both rose to their feet.

"Hello, you must be Ms. Bellmore," the taller of the two men said, walking over to shake her hand. "Nice to meet you. I'm John Brightmore, and this is David Loft."

Mr. Loft, who stayed near his chair, greeted her with a brief "Hello" before sitting back down and rifling through some papers in front of him.

"Hello, nice to meet you," Ionna said, setting her bags aside.

"Why don't you have a seat, Ms. Bellmore," Mr. Brightmore suggested as he gestured toward one of the chairs. "I am so sorry for your loss. I grew up next door to Betty. She was a wonderful woman."

An awkward feeling came over Ionna, leaving her at a loss for words. This man knew her grandmother better than she did. Anger at her father resurfaced at that point, and she struggled to suppress it, swallowing hard in an attempt to push the feeling down.

She sat in the chair directly across from Mr. Brightmore. A large Renaissance painting hung on the wall behind him, and he looked as if he could have crawled out of it with his dapper clothing and dashing haircut. He was in his late thirties or early forties and was quite handsome, which caught her off guard. She half expected him to be an older man in his later years. At that moment, she became acutely aware of herself and wondered how disheveled she looked from rushing off the flight. She looked down at her black leggings and simple gray shirt, questioning her outfit choice, and quickly ran her fingers through her wavy brown hair in an attempt to smooth it down.

"First of all, I want to thank you for making the trip over," Mr. Brightmore said. "Having you here makes it a lot easier for David and myself. International estate law can be tricky. I know you must be exhausted from traveling, so let's get right down to business, shall we?"

He pulled out a large stack of papers from a folder in front of him. Thumbing through them, he pulled out several with little red X's highlighted in yellow.

"I assume you knew that this was being passed down to you? You were listed as the sole beneficiary the day you were born," he said, sliding over one of the papers to Ionna.

She looked down to see her birthdate—September 19th, 1983—scrolled in elegant handwriting across the bottom of the page next to her grandmother's signature.

"I did not," she said, in a daze. She ran her fingers across the fading ink of her birthday, hoping that this would start to feel more real. "Honestly, I didn't even know I had a grandmother still alive. My parents never told me anything about her."

Mr. Brightmore looked at her first with alarm and then confusion. "Are you quite serious?"

"Yes, I had absolutely no idea."

"Well, that's a new one," Mr. Loft said to Mr. Brightmore in a tone that suggested they had come across more than one thing from this will that surprised them.

Mr. Brightmore looked very seriously at Ionna. "Your grandmother left you her entire estate and holdings, which include…" He paused as he pulled out another piece of paper and began to read from it. "Ty Bryn, her estate in Beddgelert and everything within it; her Vauxhall Astra; holdings of thirty-two thousand pounds; and her safety deposit box."

Ionna's eyes grew wide. How was this happening? She took

a deep breath, trying to steady herself before she spoke. "I don't even know what to say. I feel like this must be some sort of mistake."

"I assure you it's not," Mr. Brightmore said reassuringly.

Ionna's heart raced, and her mind spun as she tried to process everything she had just been told. How could her parents have kept this from her for so long? They had set her up to be completely blindsided by the truth. A mixture of anger and betrayal surged through her as she sat there staring blankly down the length of the long conference table. She struggled to maintain her composure, her emotions threatening to overwhelm her.

"Now, I have a few pieces of paper I need you to sign, Ms. Bellmore," Mr. Loft said, sliding a pen and three pieces of paper over to her. "If you would sign on the line next to the highlighted X and date each one, please. These are the legal documents that will process everything over into your name—the house, the car, the bank accounts."

Ionna picked up the pen and scrolled her signature in shaky handwriting across the documents. It felt so surreal. Her grandmother had known about Ionna her entire life, but Ionna had never even heard the woman's name until a few days ago. Something significant must have transpired between them that kept her grandmother from reaching out after the death of her parents. Instead, she had just passed on all her worldly possessions to Ionna, along with a million questions. It felt wrong to be taking it all.

As she prepared to return the documents, her eyes caught sight of a particular paper revealing the cause of death. She paused and read the words before her. Until that moment, she hadn't given much thought to the circumstances surrounding Betty's passing, simply assuming it was due to old age. But what if she had died after some horrible accident like her parents had? What if she had died alone when Ionna could have been there? The unsettling thought dissipated a little as her eyes fell on the words "natural causes." Ionna hoped that meant she had passed peacefully in her sleep.

After she handed the papers back to Mr. Loft, Mr. Brightmore stood up and walked toward the door.

"We have arranged to have a car take you to the farm. That is, if you're okay with going up there today. If you have plans in the city, we can reschedule it for another day."

"No, actually, I don't. I had just planned to find a place to stay here. Did you say farm?" Ionna asked.

"Yes, your grandmother's estate, Ty Bryn, is a lovely little farm on the outskirts of the village of Beddgelert. It's beautiful; I grew up only a few miles from it," Mr. Brightmore said, giving her his dashing smile and gesturing toward the door.

"Then you must have known my father, Adam?" Ionna said. He had mentioned knowing Betty before, but it wasn't until now that Ionna realized this might be an opportunity to gather some information.

"I understand he emigrated to America. But I'm afraid I don't remember much about him. Before my time, perhaps," Mr. Brightmore said.

Ionna gave a smile, even though she was disappointed that her question had fallen flat.

As she got ready to leave, he stopped at a side table where a cardboard box sat. He picked it up and handed it to Ionna.

"Here is your grandmother's safety deposit box along with the keys to the house, the car, and the barn."

Ionna looked into the box to see a long, slim metal container and a keychain fat with keys.

"I hope that you can find some answers," Mr. Brightmore said.

"Thank you for everything," Ionna replied with a forced smile.

"Here's my card. Why don't you phone me in a couple of days and let me know how you're getting on out there?" he said, handing her a business card. Ionna took it, noticing that his personal cell number was scribbled on the back side. "If you need anything in the meantime, please don't hesitate to get in touch. There should be a car outside ready to take you to Wales. I'll talk to you in a few days."

Ionna thanked him again and returned to the grand elevator doors, bags in tow and the cardboard box tucked under her arm. As she descended in the elevator, she gazed down at the metal box, wondering if the answers to her questions lay locked inside.

Chapter Seven
Kate
BERRY PICKING

Kate sat at the kitchen table reading a local news article about a tourist couple that had gone missing while hiking in Snowdonia National Park. It had been three days since they'd been seen, and the officials were beginning to lose hope due to the impending weather front that was moving in. Her grandmother came into the room carrying a large farmers' market basket, and Kate tipped the paper down to look at her. Her silver-white hair was pulled up into a bun, and she wore a pair of coveralls that were two sizes too big. Kate figured they must have been a pair that belonged to her grandfather.

"Get off that lazy bum of yours and help your dear old nana, would you?" she said in her perky little voice.

"Okay, what do ya need?" Kate asked.

"You and I are going to go over to the Dwyer farm to pick some raspberries. I thought we could make a pie for dessert tonight. What do you think?"

In the three days since she arrived at her grandmother's house, Kate's dreams of lazing around reading, free from the judging eyes of her mother, had not entirely panned out. It seemed her grandmother had planned out most of their week in advance with little outings and errands. Kate wasn't sure if she was merely being folded into her grandmother's usual routine or if maybe this was the busiest she'd been since her grandfather had passed. Kate didn't want to disappoint her, but she would have been just as happy with her nose in her book.

The prospect of raspberry pie, however, made this outing a little more appealing.

"Let me just grab my shoes," Kate said, closing her newspaper and getting up from the table.

Since the memory of the magic lamp had resurfaced the other night, she had been trying to remember more of her summers here. Gradually, pieces of her days spent with Owen, the Dwyer boy, were coming back. She remembered playing with him in their hayloft and chasing the old farm dog through the fields. Riding horses and having chess tournaments, which she always seemed to win. In her mind, he was small and scrawny, even more so than Kate. It was strange to have these memories of someone who was now more like a stranger. She wondered if he remembered her at all.

Kate slipped her trainers on and pulled her thick ginger ponytail through the back of an old baseball cap before following her grandmother out of the house. Even though the Dwyers' farm was only a short walk away, they took the Volkswagen. Her grandmother was getting older, and even a short walk tired her out these days. Another thing that had changed since the last time Kate was here.

When they arrived at the farm, Ben Dwyer was outside, shooing some chickens from one of the smaller gardens. It was the quintessential small Welsh vegetable farm with lush green fields full of veggies and small greenhouses scattered throughout the property. In the middle of everything sat a modest stone house with light blue shutters and window boxes overflowing with flowers. To the left of the house was a large barn; its two gigantic doors were propped open, showing off four horse stalls. The driveway split the well-groomed lawn in two and led to a small parking spot to the left of the barn. Once they parked the car, Ben came over and greeted them as they emerged.

"Flora, what a wonderful surprise. And who might this be?" Ben asked, looking over at Kate with an inviting smile.

"You remember Kate, my granddaughter? We came over to do a bit of berry picking if you don't mind," Nana said, giving Kate a little push toward the man.

"Of course not, you know you're welcome anytime," Ben said. "This can't be Kate? Look at you, you're all grown up. I think the last time I saw you, you were only twelve. But I guess that stands to reason, seeing how Owen's eighteen now."

"Hello," Kate said sheepishly, glancing up at him and then looking down again. Her shyness was evident in every nervous movement she made.

"They certainly grow up quickly," Flora said, smiling with pride at her granddaughter.

Kate stood there, uneasy, in the center of the adults' attention, nervously picking at a small hole in the pocket of her jeans.

"Speaking of Owen," Ben said as a small black sporty-looking car pulled down the driveway and parked next to the pea-green Volkswagen.

Kate looked over, but the dark tint on the windows left it impossible to see the driver. However, she didn't need to wait long as Owen quickly emerged from the vehicle. He was nothing like she remembered; in fact, he was almost the opposite. A tall, broad-shouldered man with sandy brown hair and a strong jawline had replaced the scrawny boy with glasses. Kate became suddenly aware of her appearance as Owen approached. The faded graphic tee she was wearing, a throwback from her adolescence, and the worn-out trainers made her look disheveled. In that moment, she wished she had spent a little more time picking out something nice to wear.

With his tight white shirt and torn jeans, he exuded the bad boy vibe. Clearly, he was no longer that nerdy kid who liked to read in the hayloft. Kate had to keep herself from staring as he walked over to greet them. Her summer at Nana's had just got a lot more interesting.

"Hi," he greeted the newcomers, nodding in their direction.

"Hello, Owen," Nana said.

"Owen, remember Flora's granddaughter Kate?" Ben asked. "You two used to play together when you were younger."

Owen looked over at Kate. She was self-consciously smoothing her shirt down and fixing her ponytail. An awkwardness sat heavy in the air between them.

"Hey," he said, with a half-wave of his hand.

Kate looked up and gave him a small smile and a wave before looking back down enough to hide her eyes with the brim of her hat.

"Sorry, but I gotta run, taking Churchill down to meet the farrier. Catch up with you later," he said as he flashed them a dashing smile and walked off into the barn.

Kate felt her heart jump up into her throat, and it seemed

like it had decided to take up residence there. *How had the nerdy boy next door turned into that,* she thought as she watched him walk away from under the brim of her hat.

"Well, we better go pick some of those berries. That pie isn't going to bake itself," Flora said.

Flora and Kate walked a small pebbly path that led around to a berry patch on the back side of the barn. The bushes were well-groomed and overflowing with vibrant berries that looked like fat jewels in the sun.

"Best raspberries in the whole of Wales, I would say," Flora said, popping one in her mouth and eating it. "If you pick enough, I'll make some jam. Nothing better than a bit of jam on toast for breakfast." She winked.

"Okay, but only if you let me have some on ice cream," Kate said with a smile. It was something her grandmother had made for her as a special treat when she was younger.

"Okay, fine. You twisted my toe," Flora joked back. It was a playful thing she used to say to make Kate laugh when she was a kid.

Despite Kate's smile, an overwhelming sadness brewed within her. Being here, her memories beginning to come back, she was realizing just how much she'd missed her grandparents. How much of their lives she had missed, and them hers. The pain of it caught her off guard.

The first year of separation was the hardest, but after that, the ache of their absence was gradually replaced by other things in Kate's life. The fog of her teenage years rolled in and she wanted to impress her peers and explore the city and test her mother's boundaries. All the time, the little cottage in rural Wales grew smaller and smaller in her mind.

It hadn't helped that the subject of her grandparents was all but forbidden, and her mother certainly never brought them up. She didn't know what had caused the rift, and she wasn't sure if she should ask. Besides, she assumed it was just her mother overreacting about something trivial like she tended to do, which annoyed her to no end. She was always trying to control things, especially Kate's life. Yet, here Kate was, three days gone, and not a single word from her mother.

She couldn't help but wonder whether the silence was deliberate. A tactic to sow the seeds of doubt in Kate's mind. This wasn't the first time in her life she'd wondered whether her mother found more pleasure in wielding power over her than in truly caring for her. It was a lingering suspicion that had contributed to Kate's indecision about her university plans. She realized that choosing her academic path was the one thing her mother didn't have control over. Even though she had gotten good grades and could have her pick of universities, her mother's influence took away the fun of making such an important decision.

Carefully, Kate thumbed her way around the thorns of the raspberry bushes, taking her time in selecting the ripest berries, lost in thought about her mother. She glanced over her shoulder at Flora, who was hunched over, depositing a large handful of berries into her basket, and wondered what thoughts she might be lost in. She knew her grandmother wouldn't want her to see the small changes here and there that had taken root in the passing years—the slower way she moved, a certain tiredness around her eyes. There was a sadness to her, too, faint but always present. Kate wondered how much was due to her grandpa's passing and how much was due to the stress of being estranged from her daughter and granddaughter for so many years. She was putting on a brave face for Kate, trying to make the most of their time together—trying to make up for lost time.

Kate had filled almost a quarter of the basket with berries when she saw Owen shoot out of the barn and off into the rich green field on Churchill. As soon as she saw the colossal stallion, she recognized him. It was the same horse that Owen used to ride as a boy. He was unmistakable with his unusual coloring: gray front legs that broke away to a black body covered in spots of white and chestnut brown. If that wasn't an odd enough combination, his mane and tail were like golden wheat after the first frost of the season. He was just as spectacular as she remembered him. She watched as Owen rode Churchill through the tall wheat stocks and out into a clearing in the trees that led to the back pasture.

"He turned out to be quite a handsome young man," Flora said to Kate, snapping her out of the trance she had been in as she watched Owen ride off.

Her cheeks flushed with embarrassment as she realized her nana had caught her staring. "Well, he certainly isn't that scrawny kid I remember," Kate muttered as she went back to picking berries.

Once the basket was full, they made their way back around to the front side of the barn.

"I'm going to bring these back to the car and give my feet a rest. Can you go and give Ben this for me, dear." Flora handed her ten pounds and made her way slowly back to the car.

Kate walked back toward the front of the barn and found Ben in the stables, sweeping out the hay.

"Mr. Dwyer. My nana said to give this to you." She outstretched her berry-stained hand with the money in it.

"Call me Ben. Mr. Dwyer is my dad," he said with a chuckle. "Tell Flora she knows our deal. No need to pay if she makes me a jar of her famous jam." Ben winked.

Kate shoved the money into her pocket and thanked him.

She turned and headed back to the car, willing her feet to walk faster so she could leave the awkwardness behind her.

Just as she was about to open the door to the old Volkswagen, she heard Ben call out to her, and she turned around.

"Kate, why don't you come back on Thursday? Owen needs to take the mares out for a run and could use some help. I normally do it with him, but I have some crops to harvest for the big farmers' market on Friday. Think you still remember how to ride?"

Her heart jumped into her throat. She hadn't been on a horse in over five years. There was no way she was about to get on one in front of Owen and make a complete fool out of herself.

"Oh, I'm not sure. My riding skills are a bit rusty. I haven't been on a horse since I was twelve," she called back, hoping he would drop it and let her off the hook.

"Well, you know what they say; it's like riding a bike. He normally leaves around noon if you decide you're up to it."

"Okay, thanks, Mr. Dwyer. I mean Ben," she said, giving him a quick, awkward wave before slipping into the car.

"You should do it," her grandmother said as she shut the door. "It'll give you something to do other than sit around with your old nana."

"Maybe," Kate whispered as she gazed out the window toward the field where Owen had ridden off. Her heart raced with nerves at the mere thought of riding with him.

Thick, ominous clouds loomed over the peak of the mountain behind the farm, and she felt a sensation of dread settle over her as she watched the sky darken. A storm was about to sweep into Beddgelert, and with it, a darkness no one expected.

Chapter Eight
Ionna
BEDDGELERT

The car took the M1 out of London, then followed the M6 to the M54, a motorway that led through gray industrial cityscapes and into the lush green fields of the English countryside. The fields stretched out as far as Ionna could see, lying out like a jigsaw puzzle before her in a variety of greens and browns. The fields were studded every few miles with small towns full of quaint stone houses and shops. They had been driving for hours, and it seemed like they would never run out of green pastures filled with grazing sheep and cows. The deeper into the countryside they got, the more Ionna's excitement grew.

By the time they made it into Wales, her stomach was in knots of hunger. She had been in the car for five hours now and didn't have so much as a mint on her. Besides her hunger, there was something else that was causing her stomach to churn. She'd never planned on staying at her grandmother's house, but Mr. Brightmore had practically thrown her into going by having a car ready to take her there after their meeting. Her original intention was to book a hotel and visit the property before heading back to America.

As they pulled off the A5 and onto a small one-lane road, she figured they must be getting closer to their destination.

"Can we stop at a store so I can grab a few things before we get there?" she asked the driver.

"Of course, miss. Not a problem. I know just the place up ahead."

Within half an hour, the car slowed down, pulled in, and stopped at a local market. It was a lovely little place made of whitewashed brick with a large sign out front that read "Bowen Market" in rich red letters. The outside of the store was overflowing with planted flowers for sale, along with a few other garden supplies, giving it a charming farmstand-like appeal.

"Be back in just a minute," she said to the driver as she popped the handle and jumped out of the back seat.

"Take all the time you need," he called back.

Ionna smiled at the sweet smell of the flowers that greeted her at the entrance as she made her way into the little shop. The inside was even more charming, with wooden boxes housing a wide variety of vegetables on every open shelf and a butcher counter that looked straight out of the 1950s. It was different from the grocery stores she was used to. The ones back in Maine mostly sold premade meals and processed foods.

Her stomach growled at the sight of all the delicious food around her, and she grabbed a basket and began filling it. Now that her plans had changed, she figured she would need to get some food to stock up the house for the next few days at least.

The first things to enter the basket were a bag of apples, then three fresh peaches, a bag of potatoes, a bushel of carrots, two onions, a cut of beef from the deli, and a glorious-looking loaf of homemade bread. She then made her way into the back corner of the store where the dry goods were kept and grabbed a packet of pasta, a bag of rice, and a box of cereal. She had everything necessary to prepare a delicious meal when she arrived, but that didn't help her current hunger situation. Searching around, she found a small cooler with premade ham sandwiches in it and grabbed one for the road.

The clerk was a woman in her mid-forties with dark brown hair streaked with strands of silver. She was a petite woman, barely tall enough to see the top of the register. As she rang up the final items, she pushed herself up onto her tippy-toes and read the total to Ionna.

"Forty-three pounds, dear," she said with a broad smile as she began to pack the items up into bags.

"Can I ask you a question? How much further is Beddgelert from here?" Ionna asked, opening her purse.

"Oh, not far, it's the next town up the road. Are you here visiting relatives?"

"Not … exactly. My grandmother passed away recently, and I've inherited her farm."

"Oh, are you Betty's granddaughter?" the woman asked.

The question caught her by surprise. Was this woman aware that Betty had a granddaughter, or was she simply making an assumption?

"Yes, I am," Ionna answered hesitantly, the words feeling strange coming out of her mouth.

"Terrible tragedy. It really saddened the local community around here. She was well-liked by everyone. I'm so sorry," the woman said as she took the cash from Ionna and handed her the two bags filled with her groceries.

That was an odd thing to say, Ionna thought. From what she had read at the law firm, Betty had died of natural causes. A feeling of unease raced through her at the woman's comment.

"Yes, it was. Did you hear much about it?" Ionna asked.

"Not more than what was in the paper and, of course, the gossip around town. But you know how that goes. Everyone had their own idea of what might have happened."

"What paper was it in? I just arrived, so I'm not familiar with the local news outlets."

"*Caernarfon Herald* ran the story a few days after her death."

"Thank you," Ionna said, giving her a smile and walking to the door.

"Have a good day now," the woman called out as Ionna exited.

As they got back on the road, she took her cell phone out to query her grandmother's name alongside the *Caernarfon Herald*, in hopes of reading the article the clerk had talked about. It was time to let her journalist side take over and figure out what that woman meant when she'd said *It was a terrible tragedy.*

"Crap, no service," she said aloud.

"Oh, the mobile reception is spotty at best up this way. There are only a few places where you can get a bar or two," the driver replied.

"Great. Well, I guess that makes me officially cut off from the world then," she said, half joking as she unwrapped her sandwich and began eating it, giving in to the fact that her questions would not be answered now.

They drove for another fifteen minutes before they passed a

sign stating that they were entering the village of Beddgelert. It was a quiet little town nestled snug in a valley with large mountains rising up over it as if standing guard. The small road that led into the village was bordered by stone walls that guided them toward the village center. The road opened up into the town where most, if not all, the houses and shops were made of thick gray fieldstone. In the center of the village, the buildings merged together, creating long rows of conjoined shops with quaint little apartments above. There were a few small restaurants, a hardware store, a library, and a coffee shop. *Thank heaven for that*, Ionna thought as she looked at the "fresh roast" sign in the window.

The trip through town was short since there really wasn't much to it. As they drove on, the houses became ungrouped, and before she knew it, there were only a few stray homes here and there dusted throughout the countryside. Even though she was used to living in rural Maine, there was something different about the Welsh countryside—something ancient, almost magical.

As she looked out over the landscape that was a mix of fields and large mountains peppered with trees and stone walls, a sadness overtook her. A feeling of deep longing for this place, as if she had just come home.

"We're almost there," the driver announced, breaking her trance as they passed a small cottage.

They drove on until a beautiful farm came into view. It was a patchwork of vibrant green fields full of ripening crops. She hadn't expected it would be an actual running farm, with her grandmother's age and all. They drove closer, but as they came upon the driveway that snaked down to the barnyard, they drove right past it. Ionna looked out the back window, confused.

"That's the Dwyer farm," the driver explained.

"Oh, a neighboring farm?" she said, disappointed that it was not her newly acquired property. With her luck, the place she had just inherited would be some run-down shithole not worth a penny.

"Yes, your grandmother's farm is right up over this knoll here," the driver said.

As they crested the knoll, the farm came into view. There, sitting snugly at the very bottom of a giant mountain was a picturesque little farm. It was not a working farm like the Dwyers', more of a homestead with a small barn for a single horse and a quaint little garden tucked into its spacious yard. It was half the size of the one they had passed, but what it lacked in size, it made up for in its beauty. There were numerous flower beds scattered around the property, splashing color across its well-groomed lawns.

The house itself was made of gray fieldstone in a cape style with a blue slate roof. It had black shutters and a large wooden door that was stained green, the grain working its way through the aging paint, giving it a weathered look. The barn, unlike the house, was made of wood and had been stained a rich burgundy red. It stood out starkly against the bright green fields that surrounded it.

"It's beautiful," Ionna said.

"It is certainly that," the driver replied as he pulled up next to the house.

When the engine was turned off, Ionna opened the door and stepped out onto the sturdy, solid earth that held her grandmother's home. That deep feeling of sadness returned, racing around inside her. She wished she had been able to get to know her grandmother, to come and visit her here in this beautiful place while she was still alive.

"Where would you like your things, miss?" the driver asked, interrupting her thoughts.

"Can you set them there on the porch, please?" She pointed to a small porch on the left side of the house.

He walked over with her bags and placed them on the old, worn wood boards. "Well, is there anything I can do for you before I go?"

"Can you wait just a minute to make sure the key works?"

She rooted around in her bag for the ring of keys from the box Mr. Brightmore had given her. Once she retrieved them, she walked up the three steps to the front door and spun the keys around on the hook, searching for one that looked to be a house key. It took two attempts before one slipped into the old iron keyhole under the doorknob. She turned it until there was a click and then a pop, and the knob became loose. The door let out a loud creak that echoed into the empty house, a sound of welcoming to those who entered.

"Looks like it works!" the driver yelled out to her from the car. "I'll be taking off now. If you need anything, give Mr. Brightmore a call. He's a very kind chap. It was nice meeting you, Ms. Bellmore. Good day to you."

"You as well," Ionna called out, giving him a wave from the doorway as he drove off.

She stood there for a long while, feeling a bit apprehensive about going into the house. However, the sky began darkening as thick rain clouds covered the sun. This drove her forward; she retrieved her things from the porch and entered the house.

It was dim inside as all the curtains had been drawn. She fumbled around looking for a light switch but couldn't seem to find one. She thought it odd. She set her bags down and stepped cautiously into the room to her left, a small dining and kitchen area. She walked over to the window and pulled the curtains wide, sending a plume of dust into the air and letting in the late afternoon light. Golden rays broke through the clouds momentarily and streamed in, illuminating a large silver urn sitting on the table.

"Holy shit," she said. Somehow, she hadn't been expecting that, yet she was the last living relative Betty had, and these things would fall to her.

Next to the urn was a dried-up bouquet of flowers in a vase, petals littering the table around where it sat. She thought she could still smell the sweet floral undertones lingering in the stale air of the closed-up old house. She wondered who had left them there.

How strange it all was. She was in another country, at her grandmother's house, who she had been told died before she was even born. Now she was actually dead and contained in an urn sitting on the table right in front of her. A shiver ran down her spine and made her tremble for a moment. She embraced herself, rubbing her forearms as if they were cold.

An eeriness set in as the sun was obscured by clouds again, and the room grew dim.

"I need to figure out where these damn lights are," she said to herself, wanting to break the silence with something, even if it was just her own voice.

She looked around the room. Nothing. Not only were there no light switches, but there were also no visible light fixtures. Come to think of it, she hadn't noticed anything that used electricity.

"Oh, you have got to be *kidding* me. No electricity. Great, just great!" she said, throwing her hands up in the air. "That would have been nice to know." Looked like there would be no kicking back and watching TV—or charging her cell phone, for that matter.

Now she was in panic mode. Despite her normally unshakeable composure, the eerie atmosphere of the remote, poorly lit house and the haunting presence of her grandmother's ashes left her with an overwhelming sense of discomfort. She looked frantically for a flashlight or a candle but had no luck. Then she noticed there was an oil lamp on a little side table by the window. She started pulling open kitchen drawers looking for matches and found some in the third drawer she pulled open, along with several lighters and a pack of cigarettes. She took the matches out and struck one. It cast the room in a warm but brief glow as it petered out. She repeated the process again and this time was able to light the oil lamp. Thankfully, she knew how to use one. The power went out often at her house in Maine, and she always kept several on hand in case of storms as they were much more reliable and longer lasting than flashlights.

Once the lamp was lit, she picked it up and began to explore the house. She moved slowly into the next room, holding the light out in front of her. She felt like she had just stepped back in time, into some Victorian novel about wind-swept moors and secrets kept in attics. The lamp cast shadows that danced like ghosts on the walls as she entered the sitting room, causing her heart to quicken.

It wasn't an overly large room, but it was bigger than the kitchen. The walls were split in two, with white shiplap on the bottom and an intricate wallpaper above that reminded her of those old-fashioned blue china plates. In the center of the room was a blue floral sofa with two impressive-looking armchairs facing it. A fireplace graced the back wall, where a large landscape painting of a lake in between two mountains hung over it. It was warm and inviting, a place to spend time reading or in deep contemplation, and it instantly set her at ease.

As she inspected the room, she noticed another oil lamp on one of the side tables. Next to it were two framed pictures. She walked over and looked down in disbelief. The first was a picture of her at her college graduation. The second was her father as a young man standing next to a sturdy workhorse beside the barn that sat out front.

The sight of him made her heart ache but also ignited the confusion and anger of the situation she now found herself in.

Feeling weary, with so many unanswered questions racing around in her head, she sat down on the couch and looked out the window at the rolling fields and a burning horizon. Even though she had spent most of the past five years alone, the loneliness she felt at that very moment threatened to overtake her. Her chest tightened. She stared out of the window for a long while as she sat thinking; gradually the trees in the yard turned to silhouettes against a lavender sky. Her eyelids felt heavy and gritty, and before she knew it, she had fallen asleep.

The oil lamp sat on the coffee table in front of her, still burning bright, until its key slowly began to turn on its own, and the flame was snuffed out, leaving the room in the growing darkness.

Chapter Nine
Kate
DEATH'S WAKE-UP CALL

It was 6:45 a.m. when Kate was woken from her peaceful slumber by a loud bang reverberating off the bedroom walls. Shaken, she sat up and did a rapid sweep of the room, finding nothing out of place. With her heart still racing, she climbed out of bed and walked over to the window, half expecting to see that a storm was raging outside.

The curtains threw a lacey shadow of the early morning light around the room until she pushed them open, allowing a flood of golden light to fill the space. She looked out at the mountains standing watch over the valley. The sky was clear—not a single cloud in sight. Somehow the peacefulness, the stillness, unsettled her. There was no storm, no sign of any loud construction work out on the road. What on earth had woken her up?

She was just about to close the curtains when she saw something out of the corner of her eye on the walk below. She forced open the old window and craned her neck to see. A blackbird lay lifeless on the cold gray pavement of the path, its neck broken.

"Oh God," Kate muttered as she looked down at the dead bird. *It must have flown into the window*, she thought. That explained the sound that had woken her, the sound of death.

After that, she knew there was no way she was going back to sleep, so she got dressed and headed downstairs. Her grandmother was awake and already enjoying her first cup of tea at the kitchen table.

"Well, good morning, aren't you up early today!" she said.

Kate poured herself a cup of the strong black tea her grandmother had made and slumped down onto a kitchen chair.

"Well, I had an early morning wake-up call," Kate told her, taking a sip of tea.

"Oh, I'm sorry, cariad. I didn't mean to wake you. Thought I would get a bit of cleaning in this morning. I always try and give the kitchen a deep clean once a week."

"Oh, no, not you, Nana. A bird flew into my window and broke its neck. The sound scared me right out of a dead sleep. I can't believe you didn't hear it. It freaked me out."

"Oh, that's too bad," her grandmother said, looking pensive. "That's the circle of life, I suppose. You know, your grandfather and I used to love bird watching."

"I didn't know that," Kate said. "Do you still bird watch? It must be hard here without Grandad." This was the first time they had really talked about her grandfather since she arrived. She had been scared to mention him for fear that it might upset her grandmother. She knew that it had to be hard living out here with no one to keep her company.

"No, I don't as much as I used to. I spend most of my time reading books from the library or doing needlepoint. I started something years ago but still haven't finished it. To be honest, I'm awful at needlepoint, but it helps pass the time," she said, a sad smile on her face.

Feeling the sadness thickening the space between them Kate said, "It's still out in the walkway. I'll go and clean it up after I finish this."

"Oh, thank you, sweetheart. That would be very helpful. I'll cook up some breakfast in the meantime. Did you decide about that ride today with Owen?"

"I completely forgot that was today. I can't believe I let Ben talk me into it. I haven't ridden a horse since I was twelve. What if I don't remember how?"

"Oh, you'll do fine. You used to be quite the natural when you were younger. I can't imagine much has changed."

Kate sat and drank her tea, her thoughts shifting from her grandmother's loneliness and the little bird's death to the idea that she would be spending the afternoon with Owen. What if she couldn't keep up? What if she fell off and hurt herself—or worse, made a complete fool out of herself in front of him? Somehow she had to get through this afternoon without making it completely obvious that she had zero skills around the opposite sex. Self-doubt plagued her as she finished her now cold cup of tea.

Deciding she would rather deal with the dead bird than spend any more time thinking about the day ahead with Owen, she put on her trainers, grabbed her jacket, and went outside. She went into the small shed off to the side of the house and grabbed a shovel. As she walked back around the corner to where the dead bird lay, she stopped in her tracks. There, standing on the gray walkway, was the crimson fox. It was the same one she had seen in the meadow the first day she arrived. She could tell because one ear sported a white tip while the other ended in a tuft of fur as black as the moonless sky.

She watched, holding her breath, as it gently picked up the bird with its teeth. They stood there in shared silence, gazing at one another. The fox's golden-brown eyes shone brilliantly in the early light. Something about the way its eyes held her there sent a chill down her spine. She glanced over her shoulder, checking whether there was something behind her that was holding its attention instead, but there was nothing. Just empty fields.

By the time she turned back around, the fox had sprinted off into the woods, still clutching the bird securely in its teeth.

"Kate, are you alright, cariad?" her grandmother asked when she came back into the house. "You look like you've seen a ghost."

"No, not a ghost. A fox," Kate said.

"Oh, I see you've met Patch. Nothing to be frightened of, he's harmless. Unless you're a mouse or a squirrel, that is," her grandmother said with a chuckle.

"He got to cleaning up the bird before I did."

"I bet it made a fine breakfast for him. Nothing in nature goes to waste," her grandmother said as she brought their empty mugs over to the sink and began to wash them. "Why don't you go and have a shower? I can drive you over to the Dwyer farm once you're ready."

"I don't need to be there for a while, so I think I'll walk. If that's okay with you, I mean?" Kate asked.

"Of course. It's not too far, and Ben can drive you back if you're tired after the ride."

"What will you get up to while I'm out, Nana?"

"Oh, I think I'll sit down and finish my book," her grandmother said with a smile.

Kate envied her. She wished she could also curl up and read all day instead of the uncomfortable situation she was about to enter with Owen.

She gathered her clothes and made her way into the cottage's only bathroom. It was chilly, and Kate shivered as she stripped down. She stepped into the ancient clawfoot tub, longing for the hot water to warm her. The pipes were old and slow to heat, testing her patience, which she had very little of at the moment.

The moment the water was hot, she quickly immersed herself under the showerhead. She was hoping it might help wash away some of her apprehension about the day ahead but instead, she stood there thinking about how she should act around Owen. Should she be her awkward, boring self or try and play it cool, like Stevie? God, why did she have to be so self-conscious? If she had even a quarter of Stevie's confidence, she'd be fine. She had only gone on a few dates that never amounted to anything more than a bit of kissing at the end and normally weren't followed up with even a phone call or text. She was an anomaly. All her friends, even Stevie, had at least two serious boyfriends by now, but she couldn't seem to get out of her own way long enough to even score a second date.

Soon the water began to turn cold, and she turned off the tap and got out. No endless hot showers here, like at home. She wiped the steam off the mirror above the sink and stared at her reflection as she combed her hair.

She hated her freckles. She wished her complexion could be rich and tan like her mother's, but instead, she had her father's hair and skin tone. She looked so much like him that she often wondered if that was why her mother disliked her. She was a constant reminder of him and everything he'd put her through.

Since she had the time, she took a little extra time on her appearance, adding a bit of makeup to her eyes and giving her lips a dab of gloss. She had chosen a pair of worn jeans and a white shirt. She was trying for the casual yet sexy look but had missed the mark, looking more like she was about to go help work the farm than spend an afternoon horseback riding with a hot guy.

"You're kidding yourself, girl," she told her reflection. "Owen is so out of your league."

With that thought, she grabbed her stuff and went back into her room, pushing any thoughts of romance to the back of her mind. It was just a daydream anyways; in no way did she think she had even a sliver of a chance with him. Anyway, she was here this summer to figure out her future, not get lost in some romance that would have to end in a matter of weeks.

When she arrived back in the kitchen, her grandmother had a full-spread breakfast laid out on the kitchen table to greet her.

"Nana, if you keep feeding me like this, I'm going to get fat," she said, piling her plate with eggs and sausage.

"You could use a bit of meat on those bones if you ask me. I swear I'm going to have a talk with your mother," her grandmother said. "If I ever see her again."

An uncomfortable silence filled the room, and Kate didn't know how to respond. The mere mention of her mother not talking to her seemed to be her grandmother's way of opening the door to the conversation Kate desperately wanted to have. But her mind was already too full with worries to deal with anything else. It wasn't the right time. Instead, Kate filled her mouth with food and just smiled as if it was a joke.

Food was one of the few things that calmed Kate down, so after seconds of the eggs, she helped her grandmother clean up, then grabbed her small bag from the bench by the door and slung it over her shoulder.

"Do you need anything before I go?" she asked.

"No, I'm fine. Now, you go and have a good time with Owen. I'm sure you two have a lot to catch up on," her grandmother said with a mischievous smile.

"Well, okay then. I'll see you later," she said, making her way to the front door.

With each step, the rhythmic crunch of gravel beneath her shoes echoed in her ears. The anticipation coursing through her veins grew stronger, like a symphony reaching its crescendo as the farm came into her view.

Chapter Ten
Kate
THE RIDE

The day was still beautiful, not a cloud in the sky as Kate made her way down the driveway and onto the gravelly dirt road that led to the farm. The hedgerows and trees were in full bloom, and her nose was greeted with a variety of scents. From the flowers in the fields to freshly cut grass, even the scent of manure made the air smell like summer. The only sounds that could be heard as she walked were her own footsteps and the chorus of blackbirds that flew overhead.

It only took her about fifteen minutes to reach the farm. When she stepped onto the long driveway that led down to the barn, she paused. She wasn't sure if she had it in her to make the final steps as her nerves made her breakfast flip-flop around inside her.

"Get your shit together," she told herself, a desperate attempt at a pep talk that didn't work. Just as she was about to turn and walk back to her grandmother's cottage, she heard her name carried on the wind.

"Kate. Down here."

She looked around and spotted Ben not far from where she stood, his head poking up from the berry bushes that were up near the roadway.

"Owen's in the barn getting everything ready for your ride. Go ahead down," he called out to her.

"Okay, thank you," Kate yelled back, now forced to head to the barn instead of retreating. She walked as slowly as possible, trying to give herself more time to calm her nerves. But there wasn't enough time. There wouldn't be enough time if she had walked from London.

When she arrived at the barn, the old wide doors sat open, and she could hear Owen inside moving around. Why was she so nervous? She and Owen had known each other since they were children. They had spent entire summers together. It wasn't like they were meeting for the first time, despite how it seemed to her at that moment.

She crept in through the big barn doors where Owen stood with his back to her. The light from overhead cascaded over him and for a second Kate thought he looked like some kind of god. The wiry boy from her memories had all but vanished. His once slender frame had blossomed into a muscular physique, with broad shoulders and forearms that rivaled the size of her calves.

She remained there silently, waiting for him to turn around, not wanting to startle him or frighten the horses by calling out his name. However, it had the opposite effect. The sight of her standing there surprised him, causing him to drop the tackle he was holding onto the barn floor.

"Bloody hell! You scared the crap out of me," he said, bending down and picking up the tackle.

"Sorry! I was going to call out your name but then I didn't want to startle you or the horses. Guess that didn't turn out so well," she said with an awkward laugh.

"No worries. I was just getting the mares ready for our ride," he said in a tone that was hard for her to read.

"I have to warn you, the last time I rode a horse, it was with you when we were twelve. I'm not sure I remember how to at this point," she said. She moved her foot nervously around bits of loose hay scattered over the barn floor.

"It's something you never forget, trust me. Do you remember Ginger?" Owen asked her as he walked over to a mare in the stall next to him and ran his hand down her velvety muzzle.

"Of course. We named her after your dad's ginger cookies. I can't believe she's still around," Kate said, walking over and holding her hand out for the horse to sniff.

"Yup, the one and only. She's getting old, though, so I don't ride her as much as I used to," Owen said, looking Kate in the eyes for the first time since she had arrived.

His attention caught her off guard, and she found herself lost in his sea-blue eyes for a brief moment before jerking back to reality and looking down at her feet.

"Let me bring her out and get her saddled up. Go put on those riding boots over there. They might be a bit big, but they should do for today," he said as he walked Ginger out of the barn and hitched her to a post.

As Kate put on the old, worn leather riding boots, Owen slipped the saddle on Ginger and made sure everything was secure. He came back into the barn and took out a dark black mare with a striking white patch on her hindquarters that looked almost like a crescent moon.

"This is Luna," Owen said. "She's one of the mares my dad's trying to sell. I've been working with her every week, trying to break her of a few bad habits."

He tightened her girth and moved her out of the barn and to a post next to Ginger. Kate watched him with the horses, how careful and expert his movements were, how gentle he was with them.

"If you're all set, I can help you up," he told her with a gesture of his arm.

Kate walked over to him, focusing on each footstep in an attempt to calm her nerves. When she arrived at Ginger's side, Owen's hands met her hips, and he lifted her up and into the saddle. Her pulse quickened at his touch, and her stomach cartwheeled around inside of her. She thought she had done a good job of hiding her emotions, but her cheeks betrayed her, turning several shades of pink before blooming as red as a ripe tomato.

It felt at once alien and familiar to be on a horse again. Ginger was tall, and Kate couldn't help admiring her younger self for daring to ride the mare. Once she felt like she'd found her balance, she gave Ginger a gentle nudge, and the horse began to walk. Kate immediately wobbled and slipped sideways, almost falling off.

"Woah there, you okay?" Owen said as he mounted Luna.

"I'm fine," Kate said. It was a lie. Her nerves were shot. What shreds of confidence she'd had were now completely gone. She wasn't even out of the barnyard and she'd already made a fool of herself. Maybe she should stop right now. Get off the horse, turn around, and go back to the safety of her grandmother's house.

"Ready?" Owen said, riding up beside her.

She tightened her hands around the reins. "Ready," she heard herself saying.

Owen led them out of the barnyard toward the field. Kate got the feeling he was coaxing his horse to go slow so that she'd have a better chance of keeping up without falling on her butt. But when they made it to the edge of the field, Luna sped up, and Ginger went into a trot, trying to keep up with her. Kate bounced around on top, swaying side to side as she tried to get her balance.

She knew she looked ridiculous. Luckily, Owen didn't notice because he was paying no attention to her at all. His father had probably forced him into this ride and he was just trying to get it over and done with. A sick feeling rose in her throat at the thought, and she watched him as he trotted ahead of her into the field.

He took off into a full gallop, blowing wheat shaft up into the air in his wake. This in turn caused Ginger to break into a canter. The change in speed caught Kate off guard, and she held onto the reins as tight as she could. She'd been having a hard time sitting straight on the horse's back, and the force of the sudden run jarred her so much that she lost her balance and fell off.

She landed hard on the ground, knocking the wind out of her. She lay there in the tall wheat as Ginger continued to gallop ahead to Luna and Owen, feeling as if her absolute worst nightmare had just come true. Why hadn't she just faked being sick or come up with some other excuse not to come here?

Racked with embarrassment, she sat up, her head just peeking over the stalks of wheat, as Owen came riding up to her with Ginger in tow.

"Oh, shit. Kate, you okay?" he asked, jumping down from the horse and helping her back to her feet.

"Yeah, I think so. My arm's a little sore," she told him as she rubbed her right elbow.

He took her hand away from it gently and looked at it. "Looks like you're going to have a good bruise there."

"Well, turns out getting back on a horse after all these years is *not* quite like riding a bike," she nervously joked as he helped her to her feet. His touch sent goosebumps up her arm.

"I thought you'd be fine. You used to be a better rider than me when we were kids. I should have paid better attention. I'm glad you're okay. My dad would've killed me if you broke your arm or something," he said with a bit of annoyance in his voice.

And there it was, confirmation that his father had forced him into this. Now she felt like a thorn in his side. He probably would have preferred to be riding alone right now. Her stomach knotted up again as the idea poked at her insecurities.

The pain of the whole situation must have been visible on her face because Owen's expression softened.

"Maybe you're just overthinking it. Let's try again, but this time, don't think about it, just let your instincts kick in, okay?" he said in a gentle tone.

Kate stood there, taking a moment to steady her breathing. Ginger dipped her snout to gently nudge Kate's side. Kate turned to look at the horse; her big dark eyes oddly calmed her. She ran her hand over the horse's velvety nose. *Okay, girl,* she thought. In that moment she gathered up the courage she needed and mounted her again.

Back in the saddle, she took Owen's advice and tried to clear her mind, willing her natural instincts to take over. As Ginger began to move at a trot, she felt the rhythmic sway of the horse's body and followed its lead. Rather than trying to remain rigid, she allowed her body to move with Ginger's, smoothly gliding along with the horse's gentle rocking motions.

After a couple of minutes, Kate squeezed her heels into Ginger's sides and felt her speed up, going from a canter to a full-on gallop, eating up the ground beneath. Without overthinking, she surrendered to the experience, feeling the exhilaration rush through her as they moved as one, racing through the field.

Owen and Luna rode behind them, trying to catch up. They soon fell in sync and rode off toward the woodland trail, not noticing the dark storm clouds that had formed over the mountain and were moving at a quickening rate toward the farm.

Chapter Eleven
Ionna
LOST AND FOUND

It was 6:45 in the morning when Ionna was pulled from a sound sleep. She had been having a pleasant dream when the soft rays of morning light broke through the living room windows, beckoning her back from the dream realm.

As her eyes adjusted to the light, she momentarily forgot where she was. As soon as her feet touched the old wooden floorboards, they let out a creaky moan that snapped her out of her confusion. It was then she remembered she was in Wales at her grandmother's house. The previous afternoon the jet lag had taken over, and she had passed out on the sofa.

She shifted her gaze to the photographs of her father and herself on the tiny side table. Her first thoughts of the day returned to the array of questions. Her father had obviously stayed in touch with Betty over the years but had still chosen to hide her existence from Ionna. *Why would he do that?* The once unwavering foundation of her family was now nothing more than a dilapidated pile of crumbling lies. She wanted answers but it was too confusing, too painful.

You're a reporter, Ionna, she told herself. *Approach this like any other story. Objective. Pragmatic.*

Once she shifted her thinking, the weight in her chest lifted a little, and the knot of anxiety eased. She was determined to search around the old farmhouse for the answers to her queries, but not before coffee and a bite to eat.

She walked over to where she'd left her belongings on the floor and retrieved the two bags of groceries as well as the box from the law firm, then brought them into the kitchen and placed them on the table.

She looked at her grandmother's ashes sitting there where she was contemplating having some breakfast. *Maybe not.* She picked up the urn and took it into the living room, placing it on the side table next to her father's picture. The last thing she needed was to knock the ashes over—and with her clumsy ass, it was very possible. Once it was moved and resting safely in the living room, she began unpacking her groceries.

"Shit!" she exclaimed as she opened the first bag. She had forgotten about the slab of beef from the deli; it lay lukewarm in the bag, sporting a new tone of light gray. "What a waste," she said as she slid it to the side and went about unpacking the rest of the items. It wasn't until everything was out on the table that she realized she hadn't picked up any coffee.

Double shit! She cursed herself. *How the hell am I going to get through the day without any coffee?* Maybe her grandmother had some tucked away somewhere. She rifled through the kitchen cupboards, but the only thing she found was tea—lots and lots of tea. She grabbed a box of English Breakfast from the cupboard beside the stove and set it on the counter.

"This will have to do, I guess."

She filled the kettle with water and lit the old gas stove with a match. The majority of the items in the house appeared to be powered by propane, including the appliances and lighting. *It must have been difficult for an elderly woman to keep up with it all*, she thought.

While she waited for the water to boil, she decided to go through the paperwork from the lawyer and open the safety deposit box. If she was lucky, it might hold answers to the mountain of questions that were piling up. The letter was mostly a bunch of legal jargon stating the legality of the will, but the last section had been handwritten in neat cursive explaining what Betty wanted to be done with her remains. "*I wish to have my ashes spread around my flower garden throughout the property and at the base of the mountain behind the house.*" Ionna's heart beat rapidly at the thought of carrying out this task. Didn't Betty have friends or other relatives who could have done this for her? How could she have been sure Ionna would even be able to make the trip? It felt wrong that she should be the one to carry out Betty's wishes. She hadn't even known her.

She pulled the heavy metal container out of the cardboard box and retrieved the ring of keys, trying each one in turn. The first key slipped halfway in and then stopped. She tried to wiggle it but it wouldn't budge, so she moved on to the next one. The second one didn't even fit in the hole. She went through every key on the ring, with no luck. It looked as if the contents of the box would remain a mystery until she could get hold of the lawyer.

Feeling defeated, she threw the keys back into the box and decided to go hunting for answers elsewhere in the house. She hadn't even been in any of the other rooms yet. To the left of the kitchen was a small, narrow hallway with two doors. The first door led to a sizable bathroom, decorated in cream and blue with a beautiful old cast iron tub and a built-in wardrobe-style closet recessed into the wall.

The next door led to what she assumed to be her grandmother's bedroom. On the queen-size bed was a handmade quilt, patched together from various fabrics in different colors. A wide braided rug in vivid greens and blues covered half the floor, and underneath it were the beautiful pine wood boards that flowed through the rest of the house. A large window sat in the center of the longest wall, overlooking the lush green fields and majestic mountains off in the distance.

There was one small dresser with a jar of face cream, an odd brass container, and a small jewelry box resting on top. Ionna walked over and opened up the jar. The scent of wild roses and honey poured out, and she imagined it was the way her grandmother had smelt. Setting it back down, she opened the jewelry box—it was not full, but rather the opposite. There were two small wedding bands, a thick silver bracelet with Celtic knotwork, and a necklace with a green stone pendant. It was all very simple yet elegant.

Next, she tugged open each of the four large dresser drawers, carefully sifting through neatly folded clothes in search of anything that might shed light on the mysteries surrounding her newfound grandmother. But, to her disappointment, she found nothing of significance. It felt odd going through her things, even though they'd been her grandmother's. Perhaps even *because* they'd been her grandmother's. They had never even met each other and here Ionna was rooting around in all her worldly possessions.

What if Betty had left everything to Ionna in the hopes she would come here and uncover the truth?

She closed the drawers and noticed a small closet off to the right behind the bedroom door. Slowly, she opened it and found a closet full of her grandmother's clothes. Wool coats, dresses, rain jackets, blouses—you name it, she had it. The floor inside the closet was scattered with a wide variety of shoes in different styles. Her grandmother had obviously been a well-dressed woman.

Three worn cardboard boxes sat on a shelf above the clothing. Ionna took them down one by one and examined them. The first was stuffed with hats, gloves, scarves, and belts. The second was smaller and held a few Christmas ornaments, while the third contained old documents and a few stray photos.

"Bingo," she said, thinking she may get some answers at last, or at least a lead. She placed the other boxes back on the shelf and headed out of the bedroom with the third tucked under her arm.

In the kitchen, she sat down at the table and started sifting through the contents of the box. It mostly contained old bank statements, phone bills, and shopping receipts. She thumbed through a small stack of photos, hoping to come across a familiar face or *anything* that could point her in the direction of the truth, but they were all just photos of flower gardens.

Frustrated, she pushed the box aside when she noticed a letter wedged under the inside fold of the box. Carefully, she pulled it out. The envelope was yellowed with age; the word "Mum" was scrolled on the front in dark blue ink.

Just as she was about to open it, the kettle let go of its steam, startling her with its loud whistle. She got up, shut off the stove, and poured the water over the tea bag in her mug. She sat back down with her tea, then peeled open the cracking paper of the old envelope.

The letter inside was fragile and degrading with age, and she gently unfolded it. She recognized the handwriting almost instantly; it was her father's. Her heart sank, and a sadness overtook her as she looked down at his neat handwriting. The last time she'd seen it was on a birthday card, a few months before the accident.

The letter read:

Dear Mum,

It's not wise for us to stay here any longer. I have a child to look after now. I'm sorry that you won't get to watch her grow. I know how much it would have meant to you, but we can't take the risk. I know you understand that we need to start a new life far away from here. Someday when Ionna is older, I will bring her to see you, but for now, I think it's best if we stay away.

I love you,
Adam

Ionna's heart caught in her throat as she finished reading. It sounded as though he had committed some sort of transgression that resulted in him having to assume a new identity. That was not like the man she'd known at all. The father she knew had been a mild-mannered rule follower who paid his taxes on time and volunteered every Sunday at church. Questions cascaded through her mind, bigger and more urgent than before. What the hell had her father been running from?

In that moment, she felt utterly lost, like she had in the weeks following her parents' deaths. More than anything, she wished she could sit down with her father and ask him why this was all happening. She had always been a daddy's girl, and throughout her life, she and her father had shared what she thought was an unbreakable bond. Yet the whole time he was hiding this huge part of himself from her. The more the questions grew, the more the image of him seemed to shift, casting shadows of uncertainty over the man she had always thought she understood so well.

She combed through the box one more time in case she had missed something, but there was nothing else. Defeated, she tossed the box to the floor. As she did, she knocked over her tea, spilling it across the table and onto the letter. It spread across the paper, washing her father's words away into an inky blue puddle.

"Crap!"

She picked up the letter and let the tea drip off it, but it was no use; the words had been stretched and warped into an inky cloud on the paper, permanently lost. She quickly ran over to her bag, grabbed a small notepad and pen, and began to write what she remembered down, trying to save what little was left. A sharp pang of sadness sounded deep in her gut as she watched her father's words melt away. It was just another part of him lost to her.

Just as she finished transcribing the last line, a phone rang somewhere in the house. She sprang to her feet and started searching for it.

There, in the small entryway, was an old powder-blue corded phone. Its corkscrew cord looked almost long enough to walk around the entire house with. She hesitated for a moment and then decided to pick it up.

"Hello?"

"Ms. Bellmore, it's John Brightmore. Glad to see that our driver successfully got you to the house," John's voice said on the other end. "I just wanted to see how you're doing. I felt awful after you left the office yesterday—forgot to tell you that your grandmother's ashes had been brought to the house the day before. I'm sure that was an unwelcome surprise."

"Yes, it was a bit of a shock, but I'm her only surviving relative, so it does fall on me to do that sort of thing, I guess."

"Yes, I suppose it does, but I still feel awful not giving you a proper heads-up," he said.

"That's fine, really. To be completely honest, I pretty much fell asleep as soon as I got here yesterday. Jet lag knocked me for a loop. I haven't even seen the whole house yet, not to mention the barn or the grounds."

"Well, you certainly inherited a beautiful estate. Your grandmother was well known in the area for her amazing flower gardens."

"I did see those when we pulled in yesterday. Definitely looks like she had a green thumb. I wanted to ask you something…" she said, winding the cord around her finger. "Do you know how old the house is and if it's been in our family long?"

"I believe it was built in 1756," Mr. Brightmore said, "although the barn is newer. That was built in 1952 by your great-grandfather. As far as I know, it's only been in your family since around then. Your great-grandfather purchased it in 1950, according to the deed."

"Oh, good to know," Ionna said, looking around at the house.

"I plan on coming up in a few days to visit my brother. He lives on a farm not far from you. If it's okay with you, I'll pop in on Saturday and see how you're doing."

"That would be wonderful. Not sure I can take being alone and without cell service that long." She laughed.

"Well, if you really get desperate for a few bars, hike out into the field toward the woods. There's a big cluster of rocks there—if you stand on the tallest one, you can get two bars."

"Thanks for the tip," she said with a chuckle.

"See you in a few days. If you need anything in the meantime, you can call my mobile from the house phone. If there's an emergency, my brother Ben lives a mile up the road from you."

"Thank you, Mr. Brightmore. I look forward to it."

"Of course. Oh, and call me John."

"Okay, John. Bye," she said, blushing a little as she hung up the phone.

She paused for a moment, looking back into the kitchen at the box on the table. *Crap,* she thought. She had completely forgotten to ask about the keys to the safety deposit box. She'd just have to wait until John came by in a few days.

As for the remainder of today, she'd carry on exploring the rest of the house. There was much more to see and with some luck, she'd come across something that would shed a bit of light on, well, everything. She decided to check out the room off to the right of the entryway. It was the only room that graced this side of the house with its gray weathered door shut tight.

Ionna turned the old brass doorknob, but it seemed to be locked. She gave it a slight jiggle and then tried again. It still wouldn't budge.

"Come on, open damn it," she said, twisting it a bit more. The thought of yet another thing locked away from her made her blood boil with frustration. She gritted her teeth as the doorknob continued to be jammed. "Come *on!*"

And with that, as if giving into her commands, an almost musical chiming sound reverberated out as the latch popped free and the door opened. The smell of leather and old books poured out into the hallway through the cracked door. She stood there, slightly surprised but triumphant, and then pushed the door open.

She couldn't see much at first and skirted the edge of the

room until she found the window and drew back the emerald-green velvet curtains. Light flooded in, illuminating the huge plume of dust that had just sprung free from the curtains and into the stagnant air. Ionna coughed and waved her hands to disperse it, then turned to look at the room.

In the center sat a large ornate oak desk with a Tiffany-style stained glass oil lamp on top, veiled in cobwebs. The desk was magnificent, with its intricate detail and craftsmanship. Each leg was delicately carved with a vine of leaves and berries that worked their way up and around the legs and onto its sides. Each line trimmed out the edges and the top with such precision that it looked more like a piece of art than a desk—something that should be sitting in a palace, not some farmhouse in Wales. She had never seen this level of detail or craftsmanship in a piece of furniture before, and she stood there admiring it for some time.

Behind the desk sat an old captain's chair, worn with age, and behind that, the wall formed one extended bookcase, filled from top to bottom with a variety of books. She walked over and tilted her head to read their spines. A large section of them looked quite old and rare—most of the titles she had never even heard of. A sizable portion of the bookshelf was full of historical books on wars and politics. Then there was a whole shelf dedicated to books about gardening and botany and another full of books on quilting and sewing, followed by a large number of romance novels with well-worn covers. She smiled at this; Betty obviously had a certain type of book she enjoyed.

It seemed that Betty had been a widower for many years, this room being the only remnant that a man had ever even lived in the house. It felt masculine, with tiny bits of Betty tucked in here and there as if she had taken it over at some point yet tried to preserve it. Maybe it had been her husband's or a room for her father since he'd been an avid reader. He had been Betty's only child, or at least from what she knew he was. At this point, she was questioning everything she had been told about her family since she was a child. There was no way to discern the truth from the lies at this point and no one to ask, leaving her in a state of uncertainty.

She pulled out the chair and sat down at the desk, placing her hands on its smooth wooden surface. As her hands connected with the wood, a rush of energy pulsed through her.

"What the hell was that?" she whispered to herself, her breath catching in her throat. Her palms tingled where they'd met the surface of the oak desk.

Then, almost out of nowhere, a memory appeared at the forefront of her mind. A memory that was not hers. A man reaching under the desk.

Following his movements, her fingers brushed over what felt like a button hidden in the grooves of the wood. She pressed it.

A small drawer shot out from the side of the desk. Ionna let out a small gasp, then gathered herself and peered inside. In the drawer was an envelope, yellowed with age. Across the front was a single word scrawled in black ink: Neala.

Chapter Twelve

Kate

THE CABIN

The wind rushed past Kate's ears, blocking out the sounds of the world around her as Ginger galloped across the field toward the woods. As they raced through the tall grass, bursts of pollen blew back in their wake, creating a golden hue in the air. Up ahead, a path emerged, cut into the edge of the dense forest between two large pine trees. She remembered the trail as soon as she came upon it, how it wound its way up the ridge of the mountain to a lookout spot that lay the valley out below. It was the only trail they were allowed to venture onto alone as children. One clear spot in her memory among so much that was still murky.

As Ginger's hooves made traction with the dark brown soil of the trail, they kicked up the scent of the rich, musty earth and pine needles from the forest floor. The familiar smell pulled at Kate's memories, and she tried to untangle them, but she still couldn't remember more than small flickers from her time spent in Wales. She reasoned that it was normal to lose bits and pieces of her childhood in order to create room for the ocean of new memories she would need to make in her adult years.

She broke away from her thoughts as Owen rode up next to her, Luna's strides falling in sync with Ginger's. His light brown hair was windblown, and he had a look of utter enjoyment in his eyes.

"See, all you needed to do was let go," he said.

"I guess so," she said, smiling.

She glanced behind her, back through the trees, and saw the darkening sky. She was about to say maybe they should turn around when Owen spoke, interrupting her train of thought.

"So, what are your plans? You going to uni?" Owen asked.

"I don't know yet. That's why I came here for the summer. Clear my mind and try and figure it all out, you know. What about you?"

"Nah, my dad needs me here right now. Maybe someday, though."

Kate smiled and gave him a nod. She understood—she had it better than some, having the choice to go to uni. There were lots of people like Owen whose futures had been set for them without much of their say in the matter.

"Well, if you did go, what would you study?" Kate asked.

"Sounds childish but I always wanted to be a train driver. Don't really need to go to uni for that but it seems like a fun gig."

"Cool."

Silence fell between them, punctuated by the soft rhythmic sounds of the horses' hooves falling in step, the occasional far-off call of a bird.

"Kate," Owen said suddenly, "can I ask you a question?"

She glanced over at him, but his eyes were averted. Nerves squirmed inside her.

"Uh, sure, of course," she said.

He hesitated for a moment and then said, "Why did you never come back here?" When he looked at her now, there was a sadness in his eyes.

"Oh. Um. My mum had a falling out with my grandparents. I only saw them a handful of times after that summer. Not sure what happened, to be honest," she said. She ducked and weaved around low branches and fallen trees as Ginger continued up the steep slope.

"Your gran missed you," Owen said, lifting a branch up and scooting under it.

It was at that point she realized that Owen probably knew her grandmother better than she did now. There was an ease and familiarity between their families that Kate felt on the outside of.

"I missed her too. My mum can be a selfish bitch," Kate told him with a raise of her eyebrows and a slight shake of her head.

"I know all about that," Owen murmured.

Even though Kate's memories of her summers in Wales were patchy, she did remember the summer that Owen's mum left. He had stayed in the hayloft most of that summer reading the Harry Potter books. By then, her own dad had already left. She knew what it was like to have a parent abandon you. There wasn't anything anyone could do or say to make it better, so she had decided to just be present and read beside him.

As the horses continued on up the ridge, the darkening

clouds followed them, covering the once vibrant sun, dimming the world around them. Kate slowed down; the dense woods had darkened dramatically in the fading light. She thought about the missing hikers she'd read about in the newspaper. In a setting like this, she could understand how easy it would be to go off trail and become lost. Her gut churned at the image of the couple wandering around out here in the mountains somewhere. She looked at Owen, who was looking up at the storm clouds. Worry crossed his face as a low, guttural rumble rolled across the sky. Kate could feel it reverberating in the ground beneath them.

"We better get to the cabin," Owen said. "There isn't time for us to get back to the barn. Keep going."

Another low rumble of thunder echoed off the mountain ahead of them. Both horses perked up their ears.

"It's okay, girl," Kate said, edging Ginger onward just as the first drops of rain began to fall.

After a few minutes, she spotted the cabin up ahead. It seemed to appear from nowhere, stepping out of the gloom and thick evergreens. A tiny stone chimney poked up from the weathered logs, and Kate instantly felt like she'd stepped back in time. It was somewhat familiar, another hazy memory covered in the thick cobwebs of her mind.

As they drew closer, a sharp crack of thunder rang out, scaring the horses into a frantic race to the cabin. Kate held on with all her strength as Ginger galloped up the final stretch of the path. The rain made her grip slippery, and she swayed off to the side more than once but managed to keep her movements fluid with Ginger's.

"Woah, woah, girl," Kate said as they reached the cabin.

Cautiously, she dismounted and guided Ginger under a small extended roof that hung off the back of the cabin—once a place to keep wood dry, she assumed. Owen came to a halt in front of the cabin and jumped off Luna, then quickly tucked her next to Ginger. The rain was coming down in buckets, and they could see the storm working its way up the ridgeline from the cabin's vantage point.

"Let's get inside," Owen said, skirting the edge of the cabin. Kate followed, managing to stay somewhat dry under its eaves.

"That came on so fast. I saw the clouds when we were down at the trailhead but they still looked pretty far off," Kate said as she wrung her hair out.

"The storm wasn't supposed to come in until tonight. I wouldn't have taken us up the ridge trail if I knew it was going to rain. It's too dangerous," Owen said. He lifted a loose board on the side of the cabin, pulled out a small brass key, and unlocked the thick wooden door.

The space was darkly lit. The smell of pine, mildew, and lingering wood smoke greeted them, and beneath the pummel of rain, Kate could hear a small critter scuttling across the floor. There was just one small window, and the only things visible were murky silhouettes of unknown objects scattered throughout the room.

"Hold on," Owen said as he walked blindly into the dark room. The hiss and pop of a match echoed out, and a small flame brought light into the room before quickly fading out. "Crap," Kate heard him mutter.

As she stepped cautiously into the room, her eyes gradually adjusted to the dim light. Beyond where Owen stood was a fireplace, which she walked over to in search of a candle or other light source. The light streaming in through the little window illuminated a carving on the mantel, and she moved closer to get a better look.

"There we go," Owen said, lighting the lamp and flooding the room with a soft, warm glow.

Kate's heart raced as she looked over at Owen standing there in the glow of the lamp. All she could think of was those steamy romance novels where the man and woman got caught up in a storm and ended up alone in a cabin with nothing more than their own body heat to keep them warm. Her cheeks flushed at the thought, and she tried her best to calm her mind from going down that rabbit hole and turned back to the fireplace.

The light brought the carving into focus, and Kate's fingertips traced the outlines of two initials—K and O—etched into the dark wood grain of the log. Turning her gaze back to Owen, she was about to speak when her attention was drawn to the rest of the room. Any thoughts of romance quickly vanished, replaced with a chill that crept down her spine.

The space consisted of a single room with a small loft covering half the interior. A rustic ladder made of what looked to be two small trees with branches wedged in to create its rungs sat to the far right of the room. Other than the small table with two chairs, an old wooden rocking chair near the fireplace was the only piece of furniture in the whole cabin. Kate choked down the anxiety building in her throat. It was the room she'd seen in her memory about the magic lamp the night she arrived at her grandmother's house. The very same room.

Chapter Thirteen
Kate
MEMORIES

Owen walked over to the old mantelpiece where Kate stood, looking down at the carving.

"Do you remember when we did that?" he asked.

She stared at the choppy O and K, weathered with grime and the passing of years, but nothing sprang to her mind.

"To be honest, no. I don't remember a whole lot from my time here when I was a kid. Just bits and pieces mostly," she said, running her fingers through her damp hair.

"We snuck up here on my twelfth birthday after I got my pocketknife," he told her, as she retraced their initials with her fingertips. "It was your idea, you wanted to leave our mark on this place."

Kate tried to remember. It was obviously a fond memory of his by the way the tone of his voice had changed while telling her. But as hard as she tried, nothing came to her. It appeared as though certain parts of her mind had been erased, leaving blank spaces in her memories.

"I'm sorry. I really don't remember. Even this place is kinda foggy to me," she told him, walking back over to the table and sitting down.

The light from the lantern cast a soft glow across one side of his face, leaving the other in darkness.

"It's been a long time since you've been here," he said after a moment. "I'm sure it'll come back to you."

He came back to the table, and they sat there in silence listening to the rain.

It was loud and insistent against the metal roof of the cabin. Kate wanted to break the silence between them but she didn't know what to say. It was then that she noticed he had a look on his face like something was wrong. A feeling of unease went through her.

"What is it?" she finally asked him, not being able to take another minute of the worried look that creased his brow.

"You don't remember anything about that summer we turned twelve? Like, nothing?" he asked, confusion filling his words.

"Well, some things. Like our horse rides and the time my grandfather took us to the river to look for rocks." She deliberately omitted the memory of the magic lamp somehow transporting her here in the dead of night. It had to have been just a dream, her mind flipping things around on her, mixing up memories with childhood fantasies. "I mean it wasn't a super eventful summer," she said. "Why?"

Now he was looking at her with pity in his eyes, causing her to feel even more confused. What was he getting at? She knew her memories were foggy, but he was acting like she had amnesia or something.

"Okay," he said slowly. "I'm not sure where to begin."

Lightning flashed through the small window, momentarily bathing the room in light, and then a low rumble of thunder trembled through the pine boards beneath their feet.

"Kate, do you remember where Ginger came from?"

She picked nervously at a splinter sticking out of the side of the table. "Not really. I thought she was just one of the farm horses."

"No, you found her when you went on one of your special trips," he told her.

"Trips? Like, coming here from London?" she asked, growing more confused by the moment. She didn't like the tone of his voice. It reminded her of how people spoke in TV shows when they staged an intervention for someone on the edge, or to tell someone a loved one had died.

"No. You're unique, Kate. You can do things that most people could only dream of," Owen said.

"What are you talking about?" she asked in a harsher tone than she had meant to. Was he just messing with her? Playing some sort of joke to make her think she had lost her mind or something?

"That was the summer we turned twelve. It was all so amazing—until it wasn't. You really don't remember any of it?" he asked. He was looking at her so intensely. A wave of embarrassment washed over her for not being able to pull the memories from the recesses of her mind.

"No," she said, wishing she could remember *anything*, even the tiniest detail, so she didn't seem like such a complete fool.

"I've heard that people who go through traumatic events sometimes repress whole sections of their memories," Owen said, breaking her train of thought. "Maybe you blocked it out."

Kate sat there, distressed, as she watched the lightning dance across the room in intermittent bursts. Owen was starting to scare her with all the repressed memory talk. She knew her childhood memories were sparse, but she thought that was just what happened when you got older—your mind packed away older memories to make space for new ones.

"What happened the summer we turned twelve, Owen?" she asked as a sinking sensation came over her. However, she was unsure if she really wanted to know.

Owen reached his hand out to stop her incessant picking at the edge of the table. "A lot happened," he said gently. "It all started here, in this cabin."

Owen's hand held hers, and she became instantly calmer. She looked up at him and saw a younger version of him looking back at her, smiling. That skinny, awkward boy was one thing she did remember, and that was how she was seeing him now.

"Listen, I'll do my best to help fill in the gaps," he said, pulling his hand back and breaking her vision of him. "But it's gonna take time. I don't think it's a good idea to just hit you with everything all at once. Maybe I can help you find the memories you lost."

It was sweet the way he was trying to help her, but she was worried about what he might stir up. Whatever her mind was hiding from her couldn't be good.

He stood and went to the window to inspect the storm that was now raging overhead. The rain was beating down on the cabin's tin roof so hard that he needed to raise his voice to be heard.

"It was a week before you had to go back home the first summer you stayed with your grandparents. You came over all upset one afternoon," Owen said, turning back and facing Kate. "At first I thought it was because you were going to be leaving early, but you dragged me to your grandparents' place and showed me a lamp that your granda had bought you. You told me that it was magic, that it took you to a secret cabin and you wanted me to see."

Her heart sank at the mention of the lamp. So she had told him about it. Was it possible that what she remembered was true? No. It couldn't be. It had to have been just an imaginary game she'd been playing with him or something.

"I had a memory of the magic lamp the day I got here," She said before he was able to go on.

From the window, Owen looked at her over his shoulder and gave her a reassuring smile. "See, I'm sure you'll start to remember things," he said.

The storm was beginning to pass. Patches of blue sky peeked out from underneath the blanket of thick clouds.

"We should probably get the horses back to the barn," Owen said. "My dad'll be worried about us. I can tell you more later, if you want me to. And maybe in the meantime, things will start coming back."

"Thanks," she said uncertainly.

Without glancing back at the room, she went to the old wooden door and opened it, stepping back out onto the damp earth. Owen followed. She was glad he had stopped his tale. She needed time to process the overwhelming mix of emotions swirling inside her. All she'd wanted was to spend the day impressing Owen, not discovering that she was more broken than she had ever realized.

They walked the horses out from the overhang, their hooves creating horseshoe-shaped puddles as they sank into the wet ground. Owen helped her up onto Ginger, and then they started back down the mountain path, treacherous now with slick mud. Kate's heart pounded in her chest, echoing her emotional turmoil. She felt consumed by worry and uncertainty.

As they made their way through the misty landscape, Kate couldn't help but glance back over her shoulder at the cabin, its shape barely visible through the foggy haze. A strange sense of foreboding settled upon her, like a cold arm around her shoulder. She knew, deep down, the cabin held secrets that were just waiting to be unraveled.

Chapter Fourteen
Ionna
FLOWERS AND DUST

Ionna gingerly took the letter from its resting place and inspected it. She could tell it was old; the ink had faded back into the fragile fibers of the paper. When she turned it over, she found that it had already been opened. The sound of old paper crackling echoed off the walls as she peered inside. She'd expected a letter, but no. There, resting snugly within its fold, was a lock of chestnut brown hair tied with a thin navy-blue velvet ribbon.

Gently, she plucked it out and examined it. Who was Neala? And why was her hair hidden away in the desk? Just when she thought she might find answers, more questions were the only thing that awaited her.

Perplexed, she started to slip it back into the fold of the envelope when she had an overwhelming urge to smell it. The faint smell of cinnamon and cloves clung to it, along with the unmistakable, delicate scent of a very young child. It must have been a lock of hair from a baby, but whose child was it?

Suddenly, a memory played across her mind. An older man with a beard and dark slicked-back hair was holding a crying infant and pacing the floor. A fire blazed in the hearth and cast dancing shadows around the room, the man bobbing in and out of them as he paced. He was rubbing the baby's back and singing to her in a foreign language Ionna didn't recognize. Russian, perhaps? Yet she knew the song. It was a lullaby her father had sung to her when she was little.

As quick as the vision had come, it dissipated, leaving Ionna standing in the study, staring at the tiny piece of hair in her hands. She was now even more bewildered than before. She dropped the hair back into the envelope, placed it in the hidden drawer, and shut it. That couldn't possibly have been her own memory. But if it wasn't hers, what the hell was it?

"Oh my God, I'm losing my mind. Freaking jet lag," she said, shaking her head as if to free it from the unwanted thoughts floating around inside.

All of the morning's events had given her an uneasy feeling that sent her mind spinning in a hundred different directions. She needed to get out of the house and get some fresh air.

She walked out of the study and shut the door slowly, glancing in one last time at the desk before she closed the room off to the rest of the house. Just before the door latched, she swore she saw a faint glow coming from the seam where the hidden drawer lay in the desk.

"The lack of caffeine is driving me mad," she said to herself as she rooted through her bag in search of something light to wear outside.

At the bottom, she found a thin knit gray sweater. She then pulled on her shoes before heading out into the dewy late morning air. It was just breaking ten o'clock, and the sun had made its way well above the treetops beyond the front yard, bathing everything in warm golden light. Its summer heat already beginning to burn off the dew-sodden world. The air smelled of blossoming flowers and freshly cut grass, a fragrance she was accustomed to from living in rural Maine. But there was something different in the way the air smelled here—familiar in a way she couldn't quite place.

She decided to walk the grounds in a big loop, starting to the left of the front yard. The grass was wet, soaking her shoes through almost instantly. She inspected a large group of flower beds that spread out from the corners of the house and worked their way up and over to the entrance to the driveway. Two large oak trees flanked the gravel path down to the house, like giant guardians standing watch over all who came onto the land.

Surrounding the property was a large field, its long wheatgrass dancing in the light breeze. Off in the distance, she could see two people horseback riding toward the forest's edge, kicking up a thick cloud of golden pollen in their wake. *Must be the people from the farm next door*, she thought.

She continued on past the barn and toward the backyard. The lawn was much bigger back behind the house, and there was another large oak with a small bed of flowers planted at its base. A picnic table sat in its shade, creating a picturesque place to eat lunch in the late afternoon. She could almost envision her grandmother sitting there in its shade on a sunny day, drinking tea and reading a book.

Ionna moved around the house, finding more and more flower beds as she went. She was not a gardener and hadn't a clue what half the flowers were. Even if she had, there were so many different varieties she would have needed a notebook to keep track of them all. However, she noticed one familiar flower—a cluster of yellow poppies growing near a small bench. It was the one flower her father had insisted on planting in their front flower bed, explaining it reminded him of his mother. Now it made sense to her, and she felt a flood of sadness wash over her, a longing for the family she thought she knew so well. As she stood there, fixated on the poppies, lost in her own thoughts, a feeling of loneliness gradually replaced the sadness.

She began walking again, only to find more flower beds tucked against the field. Betty had been known in the area for her impressive gardening skills, and Ionna could see why. She thought about how much work caring for all the flowers would be, not something that seemed even the slightest bit enjoyable. A pang of guilt moved through her at the thought that she might not be able to keep them as well-groomed and beautiful as her grandmother had.

As she rounded the front of the house again, she noticed a place in one of the flower beds that looked disturbed. Coming closer, she saw a small pile of dirt next to a football-sized hole in the ground. At first, she figured it had been made by some sort of animal—until she noticed a small trowel lying next to it.

A dark, black, thorny vine emerged from the hole, entwining itself among the flowers and crawling up the corner of the house. It seemed her grandmother had attempted to rid the flower garden of this invasive weed, digging out its roots, but with little success. She picked up the trowel, gently moved the mound of soil back into the hole, and tamped it down firmly with her heel, attempting to restore the spot's beauty. It was probably what her grandmother would have done if she were still alive.

On her way to the barn, the sky dimmed as a bank of clouds rolled in, shrouding the sun like a thick blanket. Ionna gazed upward, realizing that what had initially appeared to be a pleasant day was now about to be a rainy one. She slid open the worn barn doors and made her way inside.

The inside of the barn was well kept. Its floor was clear of debris, and its beams looked strong and unwavering. There was a small hayloft to the back and two horse stalls off to the right. She guessed there hadn't been any animals living in the barn in a long while since there was only a faint smell of manure lingering in the air. A small grouping of tools hung off the wall to her right in a neat, tidy row. Mostly gardening utensils with a few older saws and tree pruning gear.

To the left was what appeared to be some kind of storage room, its door fastened shut. Ionna went to the door and turned the glass knob. The latch made a popping noise, and she slowly pushed it open.

Inside were hundreds of dried bundles of plants. Some were flowers, some leaves, and others looked like roots. They hung from every inch of each wall and some even from the ceiling. There was a long counter that stretched the length of the back wall. On it lay an old pair of garden scissors, a stone mortar and pestle, and jars full of powdered herbs.

It looked as though her grandmother hadn't been growing all the flowers in her garden just for their beauty. She must have been drying them for tea or tinctures. Ionna recognized a few of the plants hanging from the ceiling, such as mint, rosemary, and chamomile, but beyond that, she was lost.

She walked through the maze of hanging plants and picked

up a jar filled with tiny seeds. She turned it around, looking for a label, but it was void of one. She took another from the counter next to it. This one, too, lacked a label. She had just unscrewed the lid to give the odd powder a sniff when a thunderclap rang out, startling her and causing the jar to slip from her grip. She reached for it as it fell silently to the floor, only missing it by an inch.

When the old glass hit the floor, it shattered into a million tiny pieces and sent a plume of powder up into the air. Ionna frantically waved her hands in front of her face, trying hard not to inhale the powder. However, her efforts were in vain; she felt it tickle her throat and enter her lungs, sending her into a fit of coughing. Trying to catch her breath, she bent down, retching.

Another loud crack of thunder rang out, and the room began to come in and out of focus. Then, before she could brace herself for the fall, she passed out, the weight of her body hitting the floor with full force, shaking the weathered boards. She lay there unconscious, face down in a pile of powder and glass.

Chapter Fifteen
Kate
BACKFLIP

The slow, treacherous trip back to the barn was marked by dense silence between them as Kate tried to piece together what Owen had told her. The rain had washed away sections of the trail, leaving large swathes of deep mud and loose earth on the steep path. They took their time descending the mountain, afraid the horses might slip and be injured if they moved too fast. The storm had ravaged the landscape, laying the tall wheat fields virtually flat to the ground in spots. The air was still damp and smelled like fresh rain and mossy earth.

When they arrived back at the stable, they cleaned up the horses and returned them to their stalls, giving them extra hay to make up for the ordeal they had just been through. While sitting on a little wooden milking stool, Kate took off her drenched riding boots and replaced them with her dry sneakers.

"I gotta get going. Nana's probably worried," Kate said, standing up. She needed more time to process the fact that she was missing an important chunk of her memory from her summers here and was eager to break away.

Just as she was approaching the barn door, Ben came in, winded.

"Oh, thank God you're both okay. I was just about to go looking for you. That was one hell of a storm. Came on sooner than they predicted," he said in long-winded breaths. He must have run from wherever he was on the property when he heard them return.

"We made it to the cabin just before it hit. Got a little wet, but we're fine," Owen reassured him as he wrung out his wet shirt.

"I was just heading out," Kate said, then turned to Owen. "Thanks for the ride. I forgot how much I enjoyed it."

He gave her a knowing smile.

"Oh, let me take you home," Ben offered.

"Thanks, but I think I'll walk. It's beautiful out now, and it's really not that far," Kate said, picking up her bag and slinging it over her shoulder.

"Okay, if you're sure," Ben replied. He and Owen walked her out and onto the driveway.

"I'm sure," she said with a smile as her sneakers hit the muddy driveway. The sun's warmth was already burning away the rain, leaving a low, lingering layer of fog over everything around her.

She waved farewell and began walking up the long driveway to the road that would lead her back to her grandmother's house. She was nearly halfway up the driveway when she heard footsteps quickly approaching from behind. When she looked back, she saw Owen running to catch up with her.

"Kate, wait!" he huffed.

She stopped when he reached her.

"Hey, I know what I told you must have shaken you up. Are you okay? You didn't say much on the ride back," he said. The bad-boy facade fell away, and he looked at her with the eyes of the boy she remembered.

"I don't know. My memories are all messed up. I'm just trying to figure it out." She looked past him and out toward the mountain where the cabin lay hidden in its thick forest.

"Yeah, I get that," Owen said.

"I'll be okay. I just need some time. Repressed memories stay that way for a reason." she said, her eyes still fixed on the mountain.

"Like I said, I'll help fill in what I can. Maybe we can go on another ride tomorrow?" he suggested, finally getting her attention, her eyes falling back on him.

"I can't. I'm going to the farmers' market with Nana tomorrow," Kate told him, trying to hold back the small spark of excitement she felt but also trying not to read too much into his offer.

"Oh, no problem. Another time. See ya later," he said, giving her his dashing smile before turning and walking back down to the farm.

Kate's heart started to pound in her chest as she watched him walk back, his smile awakening something deep within her.

"I'll give you a call Saturday!" she yelled out.

"Sounds good!" he yelled back, waving goodbye to her just as he faded from view.

Kate was happy she had made the decision to walk back. This offered her some vital alone time to reflect on the day's events. She couldn't understand why her mind had blocked out so many memories from her time at her grandparents' house. It wasn't like they were completely gone; she had memories of small things, like picking berries at the farm and playing in the fields with Owen. But when she tried to think of her summers spent there as a whole it was like a blank canvas. *God, what happened to me here?* she thought as she nervously kicked at muddy rocks on the dirt road while she walked.

All she could think about was the documentaries she had seen about people who had witnessed murders or other horrific acts as children and how they literally could not remember whole sections of their childhood. Weren't the doctors in those documentaries always explaining it like it was a built-in coping mechanism of the brain? A way for the child to move forward with their life? Then Owen's words echoed back at her: *"It was all so amazing—until it wasn't."*

She tried to focus on the road up ahead where the light was breaking through the trees. She listened to the birds calling to one another off in the distance in an attempt to calm her nerves and stop her mind from spiraling into the depths of uncertainty.

It was getting later in the day, and the sun was low enough in the sky to where it rested on the tops of the trees, casting long, twisted shadows down the road. Everything was still damp from the storm and the afternoon sun reflected off it, creating a prism-like effect, making the world around her sparkle. But inside her mind was brewing like a storm with dark thoughts. The unease was settling into her bones as she drew closer to her grandmother's. She jogged the last hundred yards, feeling like she had to outrun something. However, she was running from her own thoughts and those she could not escape.

She rounded the driveway and burst through the front door.

"Good heavens!" her grandmother exclaimed.

There, sitting in the living room, were her nana and an old lady who looked to be the same age, both holding teacups with surprised looks on their faces.

"Sorry, Nana, I didn't mean to scare you."

"Beth, this is my granddaughter I was telling you about, Kate. Kate, this is one of my neighbors, Beth Hasting," her grandmother said.

"Hello, Kate. Very nice to meet you," Beth said with a smile.

"Hi, nice to meet you too," Kate said, winded from running.

"How did the ride go? Did you and Owen get caught out in that awful storm?" her grandmother asked.

"It was okay. We made it to a shelter before the storm got really bad. I'm gonna go get some dry clothes on," Kate said, smiling as she left and headed upstairs.

She couldn't push down the uneasiness she was still feeling. She peeled off her damp clothes and kicked them into a pile on her bedroom floor.

She pulled on an old faded U2 shirt and her favorite pair of sweatpants and laid down on the bed. She closed her eyes, trying to calm her nerves, but it didn't work. She sat up and looked at the overly cheerful wallpaper when all of a sudden a memory of her and Owen as kids formed in her mind. The wallpaper seemed to have sparked the memory, pulling it from its hiding place.

They had been in the same room, sitting side by side on the very bed she sat upon now. They must have been about seven or eight years old at the time. Owen was holding the magic lamp in his hands, and she was telling him what he needed to do as the sun was just starting to descend in the sky.

"Turn it on and off three times and close your eyes. If you do it right, the lamp will take you to a secret room," she said in the sweet, innocent voice of a child.

Owen sat there in his green tie-dye T-shirt turning the light on and off, but nothing happened. A look of disappointment passed over his face.

"No, like this," she said, taking hold of the lamp and turning it on and off three times.

At the last touch of the magic lamp, the bedroom with its cheerful wallpaper fell away, and they found themselves transported to a darkly lit room.

"Bloody hell!" Owen cried out as he looked around in amazement at the dim interior of the cabin.

There was just one small window and not much in the room other than an old wooden table and a rocking chair near a stone fireplace. There was a loft overhead with an old wooden ladder made from two small logs that sat to the right of the room. Owen stepped away from Kate to explore.

"Owen, no. Stop!" Kate called out, trying to get him to come back to where she stood. She was scared to move from the spot, afraid she might not be able to get them back home if she did.

Owen ignored Kate, walked over to the door, and cracked it open, letting sunlight cut into the dark room.

"No, Owen!" Kate cried out, but he didn't listen. He stepped out the door into the light.

It was at that point she had no choice but to leave the spot she held, but before doing so, she took off one of her shoes and left it behind as a placeholder. She still had no idea how the transporting magic of the lamp worked, and she was afraid she wouldn't be able to get them home if she wasn't standing on the exact spot they'd arrived, so the shoe seemed like the best option. She rushed to the door, the sudden contrast of daylight temporarily blinding her as her feet met the soil.

"Kate, over here!" Owen called out to her.

Once her eyes adjusted to the light, she noticed Owen standing in a small clearing near the forest's edge. She drew closer so she could see what he was looking at. There, in the break of the trees, was a view of the valley below where Owen's house and barn sat. But something was off. It didn't look quite right.

"I know where we are. This is Lookout Point, on the horse trail on the mountain behind the farm, but there's no cabin up here. And look, that's my house, but it looks different. What happened to the blue shutters?" Owen said, echoing her thoughts.

"Are you sure?" Kate asked, not knowing what to think.

"Only one way to find out," Owen said as he took off running down a small dirt path that led down the mountain.

"No, Owen. Don't!" But before she could finish, he was off. She followed after him, running clumsily with only one shoe on.

When Owen reached the end of the path and broke free into the field, he stopped to catch his breath, giving Kate time to catch up. Owen knew his family's land like the back of his hand, so he knew the quickest way to the barn.

"See? Something's not right," Owen said, pointing at the house. "It's missing my bedroom and the blue shutters."

Kate looked around Owen to see. The addition his parents had built when they took over the farm wasn't there, and neither was the tractor or any other farm equipment.

He turned to look at her. "What the heck, Kate?" he said, fear spreading through his eyes.

"We better go. You're supposed to be at my house. We're going to get in so much trouble if we get caught," Kate whispered. She didn't know what was going on, and she didn't care, she just wanted to get them back to the safety of her grandparents' house.

At that moment, the front door of the house opened, and an old man stepped out. An old man neither of them recognized.

Both Kate and Owen instinctively ducked down, but it was too late. The man's gaze homed in on them, and he scowled.

"Hey, you stealing my eggs? You better not let me catch you, you little thieves!" he bellowed.

"Run!" Kate yelled.

They turned tail and sprinted as fast as their legs would carry them back up the trail, all the while hearing the man's footsteps following quickly behind them. They burst through the cabin door, and Kate ran over to her shoe and stuck her foot back into it, then closed her eyes and thought of her grandparents' house.

She waited a moment, then opened her eyes, but nothing had happened—they were still in the cabin.

"What's wrong?" Owen demanded.

"I-I don't know," Kate said, "it's not working!"

"Try again!"

"I *am*!"

Pushing down the panic that was squirming inside her, she closed her eyes and tried once more. Still nothing.

"Come on, Kate, quick! He's going to be here any second," Owen said frantically, his voice high with urgency.

Kate closed her eyes again and thought of the lamp, picturing it in her mind, thinking about being back in her grandparents' guest room surrounded by the floral wallpaper. Still nothing. Outside the cabin, they could hear footsteps approaching.

"Kate, *now*!" Owen yelled, grabbing her hands and looking her in the eyes. "You can do it!"

Steadying herself, Kate closed her eyes one final time. This time something did happen. At first, it felt as if all the air had been pushed out of her lungs. Then the room began to shift and shake. Everything moving and melding into itself. She watched the walls warp into the floors, the sunlight spilling in through cracked seams in the wood. The world trembled.

Then it stopped and everything was still. There were no more footsteps, just the pounding of her own heart.

However, they were still in the cabin. Kate didn't understand. Something had *happened*, she'd felt it. Owen looked at her with wide eyes and quickly ran over to the one small window, standing on his tippy-toes to see out.

"Holy shit," he said.

She felt a new wave of panic swelling within her. "Owen, what is it? Is he out there?"

Owen didn't say anything. Instead, he slowly walked to the door and cracked it open, peering out.

"I'm sorry," Kate said, her voice trembling, "I tried to get us home, but it didn't work."

"Kate, no, come see," Owen said and flung the door open.

Kate stepped outside into a very different-looking forest. This forest looked more like the one she knew, with a thick canopy of trees and a wide dirt path running right up to the cabin door.

"Holy crap, Kate! I think we time traveled, just like Doctor Who or the time turner in Harry Potter," Owen said as he raced over to the lookout point.

"You're nuts," she said, following him.

There in the break of the trees was Owen's farm, bird-egg blue shutters and all.

"*How?*" Kate asked.

"Your magic lamp!" Owen said, a huge grin spread across his face.

"Holy shit," Kate said. It was the kind of language her mother would never let her use, but the only thing that seemed appropriate in this moment.

"And we brought the cabin back with us too. This wasn't here before," Owen told her.

They stared at one another, unable to speak but with smiles slowly spreading across their faces. They had a magical lamp that could transport them back in time, and the possibilities for the summer ahead of them seemed limitless.

Chapter Sixteen
Ionna
THE STRAY

Day faded into night as Ionna lay motionless on the floor of the barn, surrounded by a halo of glass and fine powder. A soft purring sound pulled her from the toxic slumber that had enveloped her, and she slowly emerged back into the waking world. There was a dull, throbbing pain in her head, and as she opened her eyes, the room spun in and out of focus.

She sat up, being mindful not to stir the dust and glass, and gingerly touched her face. Her fingertips found sticky wet patches, and she realized she must have cut herself when she fell. She was lucky she hadn't gotten hurt worse; it would have been days before anyone found her. At that moment, the fear of being utterly alone in another country crept over her like a shadow.

She was still trying to get her bearings when she heard the soft purring sound again. She tilted her head back and looked up at the long counter above her. There, sitting directly above her, was a black and gray striped cat, its emerald-green eyes staring down. Ionna carefully got to her feet. Still feeling light-headed, she rested her hand on the counter next to the cat. It looked down at her hand and then leaned forward and gave it a tiny sniff before slinking around her arm, rubbing against it with its silky fur.

"Well, aren't you curious," she said to the cat as she reached out her hand to stroke it. The cat was more than willing to be pet. Ionna was surprised to feel he was nothing more than skin and bones, his thick coat giving the illusion of being plump and healthy. There was no collar or tags, from what she could see. She wondered if it was a barn cat of Betty's or maybe just a stray that had found its way inside for shelter.

After making sure she was steady on her feet, she glanced around the room one last time, still curious and a little unnerved now about the room's contents. She carefully skirted around the glass, deciding to deal with the cleanup when her head wasn't pounding, and made her way back into the main area of the barn. Now that the sun was almost set, it was quite dark and her feelings of unease doubled. She must have been out for hours. By now, the storm had passed, and the world outside was quiet once more.

She quickened her pace, wanting to be back in the safety of the house before the darkness completely overtook the land, the cat following closely behind her to the house. Ionna opened the door, letting the cat inside, and then shuffled in behind it, leaving the cool night air and the eerie feeling outside with the coming darkness.

She headed for the bathroom to search for some aspirin and to wash her face and arms, which were still covered in the fine powder from the broken jar. She grabbed a box of matches off the kitchen table and struck one, lighting the old oil lantern and pushing back the encroaching darkness that was now settling into the house.

When she entered the bathroom, the light of the lantern bounced off the mirror and cast a soft glow against the back wall, giving a warm and inviting feeling of times past. The cat padded softly behind her. She set the lantern on the sink's edge and stepped up to the mirror. The reflection that stared back was bruised and bloody, and there were three distinct cuts on her face. She found a washcloth in the cupboard and ran the water until it began to heat up, then gently dabbed at the dried blood and cuts with it. It was a painful process. By the time she was done, she sported a thin cut across her chin, a small gash under her right eye, and a cut on her temple shaped like a V. They stood out in stark contrast against her pale skin.

"Well, this is a great start to my vacation. I almost poison myself and now I look like something out of *The Walking Dead*," she muttered to herself, looking down at the cat who was now sitting next to her feet.

She opened the small medicine cabinet and rooted around for something to disinfect the wounds, finding a small glass bottle of alcohol and a bag of cotton balls. She poured the alcohol over a cotton ball and hesitated a moment before dabbing at the cuts. She knew it was going to burn like hell, and it did. She gripped the edge of the sink and gritted her teeth.

"Shiiiiit."

Once the sting subsided, she was able to assess that the wounds were more or less superficial and wouldn't need stitches. *Thank God.* She had no idea how she'd even begin to get medical treatment around here.

As she was putting the alcohol and cotton balls back in the cabinet, her stomach let out a loud groan.

"I guess it's time for some food, what do ya think?" she said to the cat as she threw the bloody washcloth into the sink, grabbed the lantern, and made her way back into the kitchen.

Setting the lantern on the table, she lit the two small oil lights on each side of the kitchen window. They illuminated the room, but the smell of the smoky oil made her empty stomach churn and reignited the throbbing in her head. She cracked the window, then began rooting around for pots and pans. She had searched through almost every cupboard before finding them in the small pantry. When she grabbed a small pan from one of the shelves, she noticed a bag of cat food next to a few dozen cans of mixed vegetables.

"Oh, you poor thing," she said to the cat, realizing it must have been Betty's pet after all. It had probably been surviving on mice in the barn—and not very successfully, judging by how thin he was.

She grabbed a small bowl from one of the cupboards and filled it with cat food. As soon as she placed it on the floor, the cat was nose-deep into it, munching away.

After watching the cat for a few minutes, she filled the pot with water and lit the old gas stove. There was a hiss from the match and then a pop as a blue flame sprang to life. She placed the pot on the stovetop and then went about cutting up onions and peppers. A relaxed quietness settled around her; the only sounds were the water beginning to gently bubble and the cat crunching its food.

After a while, though, she noticed that the cat had stopped eating and was looking at something behind her. She spun around and looked into the darkness of the living room, trying to discern if there was something amiss amongst the silhouettes of furniture.

Nothing.

The light from the oil lamp reflected off the silver urn resting on top of the side table, so it looked almost like it was glowing.

Just then, the cat let out a loud mew and streaked into the dark of the room, melting into the shadows. An icy chill pricked her skin, and the hairs on her arms rose.

"Scared of the dark at thirty-six. Really? Get a grip," she told herself, trying to shake off the eerie feeling that she was being watched. She was just overtired and probably still a little loopy from being out most of the day. She had hit her head quite hard; it was possible that she had a concussion and was experiencing a bit of delirium.

Determined to prove to herself that everything was fine, she grabbed the lantern off the table and followed after the cat.

She made it halfway into the living room when she heard the cat purring. She swung the lantern in the direction of the sound and found the cat balled up in an old rocking chair by the fireplace. It rocked back and forth on its own, creaking quietly.

The cat looked up at her with its wide green eyes and stopped purring just as the chair came to an abrupt halt.

Ionna stood there stunned, not knowing what to make of anything she had just witnessed. Then she heard a hissing noise coming from the kitchen.

"Crap!" she said, rushing into the room as the water boiled over and spilled onto the stovetop. She quickly turned off the burner and sat with a thud on one of the chairs, trying to catch her breath. Her lungs still felt heavy from whatever she had inhaled in the barn. Maybe the powder—whatever it was—had some kind of hallucinogenic effect? Was she just on some sort of bad trip?

In a final attempt to calm herself, she grabbed the oil lamp and decided to go make sure all the windows and doors were locked. It was the least she could do to help quell her anxiety.

She walked cautiously through the rooms, her nerves coiling tightly in her chest, painstakingly checking every window. Making sure they were tightly fastened, and then checking again. The study was the last stop on her inspection, and she had to suppress a shiver as she turned the doorknob.

This room had an entirely different vibe about it than the rest of the house, oozing with masculine energy. Without wasting a moment, she made her way to the windows, verifying each one was securely locked, and scooted back to the door. She exited the room and pulled the door shut behind her, but not before she looked back over her—shoulder into the darkness one last time. She felt as if she was running from her own shadow as she walked briskly back to the kitchen.

Her stomach was in knots. She couldn't bear the thought of a big meal now. Whatever was happening to her, low blood sugar wasn't going to help. She knew she had to eat something, so she opted for some of the cereal she'd bought instead.

Once she had filled herself with Cheerios, she grabbed the oil lamp and her bag off the floor where it had sat since she arrived and went back to her grandmother's room, the cat following her as she went. She shut the door tight behind her, still not completely rid of the uneasy feeling creeping around inside her.

She slipped off her clothing and threw on an old baggy pair of PJs, then climbed into bed, longing for the safety a pile of blankets always gave her. It felt strange to be here, sleeping in her grandmother's bed. She wondered what it would have been like to have slept here as a child. She had never gotten to experience being loved and doted upon by a grandparent. She only had movie references or tales from friends to go by, but she wanted to think that Betty would have been an attentive grandmother, warm and kind. Sadness overwhelmed her, and she took a deep breath, breathing in Betty's scent that still lingered on the sheets, and closed her eyes.

As she fell asleep, the cat curled up next to her, purring as it gazed at a figure standing in front of the closed bedroom door.

Chapter Seventeen

Kate

THE MARKET

It was early Friday morning when Kate's grandmother woke her with a gentle knock on the bedroom door.

"Wake up, sleeping beauty. Time to get ready for the farmer's market. I want to get there before all of Glen's fresh bread is gone, so get a move on," she called through the closed door.

Kate rolled over and eased her eyes open. The morning rays were just breaking the edge of the window frame and a thin, bright beam of light cut across the room, landing softly on her bed. She sat herself up, feeling sore from her and Owen's horse ride the day before. *God, I'm sore in places I didn't even know were possible*, she thought.

She picked up her phone and looked at the time—6:33

a.m. She had six missed calls, ten new text messages, and fourteen emails. Even though she was curious, she shut the phone off and tossed it back on the nightstand. While she was here, she wanted to disconnect from her phone and everything it represented—her life back home, its expectations. Her mother. And so far she had no desire to immerse herself in the vast ocean of pictures and videos on social media. It only led to comparing herself to others and feeling worse about her own life. She promised herself there and then not to use her phone while in Wales unless absolutely necessary.

Standing up, she took one step and almost fell flat on her face. Her legs were so sore she could barely stand. She sat herself on the cold wooden floor, spread her legs out to either side, and bent forward, reaching out toward the tips of her toes. She kept the pose until she felt the muscles in her legs begin to loosen and relax. With her head angled down, she noticed something on the underside of the bed frame. Tucked away from the light, it was hard to tell, but it looked as though something had been carved into the wood. She got onto her belly, scooting herself under the bed to get a closer look.

There, on the opposite side of the frame, was the name Neala. It was formed with hundreds of tiny lines, as though it had been etched into the wood with a paper clip. She didn't remember seeing it before, but then there were apparently a lot of things about her time here she didn't remember. It looked old. Maybe the bed had been secondhand and this Neala person had tagged it as her own when she was a child, leaving the scar for the next occupant to find, like a hidden message. Pulling herself back out from under the bed, Kate attempted to stand up again, this time with a bit less pain than before.

She walked over to her bag and pulled out a burgundy sweatshirt that had the word "France" written across its chest in fancy lettering, the A stylized as a silhouette of the Eiffel Tower. A Christmas gift from her dad. He always sent her something cheesy straight out of a tourist shop at the airport. Last year it had been one of those tiny snow globes with the tower in it, this year the sweatshirt. She hated it and wasn't quite sure why she had even brought it with her. But it was chilly at her grandmother's house this morning, and she slipped it on over her head, then pulled her red hair up into a low ponytail and headed downstairs.

Her grandmother was in the kitchen, as she was every morning, cooking up a feast for breakfast. She bopped her way around the kitchen, humming a catchy little tune. Kate smiled as she watched her dance around. She was a wonderful soul, so full of love and joy. The complete opposite of her own mother, who was serious to a fault. Never giving in to small joyful moments like her grandmother. She supposed her father played a role in the unhappy woman her mother had become. Feeling cheated out of the life she had so badly wanted and left disregarded alongside Kate when he left. Kate could understand that, but it had been years now and her mother seemed to be getting more bitter with age, letting the unhappiness consume her rather than moving on with her life. Kate became the focus of her mother's nitpicky, controlling behavior.

"You look really pretty today, Nana," Kate said to her as she whirled around in a floral dress, her white hair made up into a neatly tucked bun.

"Why thank you, Kate," she said, spinning around to greet her. "Is that a gift from your father?" She looked Kate up and down as if she was dressed for Halloween at Christmas.

"How can you tell?" Kate replied sarcastically.

Her grandmother laughed. "Are you sure you want to go to the farmers' market in that? You might boil, it's going to be quite hot today."

"You're joking, right? It's freezing upstairs."

Even as she said it, she realized it was noticeably warmer in the kitchen. It didn't take long before she was pulling off the sweatshirt.

"Are you feeling okay?" her grandmother asked, placing the back of her hand on Kate's forehead.

"I'm fine, Nana. It's just cooler upstairs, I guess."

"Well, that's odd. It's normally ten degrees hotter up there in the summer. Are you sure you feel okay? I don't want you going to the market if you're coming down with something. Maybe we should just stay home."

"No, I'm fine, really," Kate reassured her.

"Well, alright then, let's get some food in you and get going. I look forward to this market all year, so I'd like to get there early," her grandmother said as she flipped two fluffy pancakes onto a blue and white china plate in front of Kate.

They ate breakfast quickly, and Kate cleaned the dishes as her grandmother got her things together to leave. By 7:30, they were out the door and in the "bogey," Kate's nickname for her grandmother's car. It had been a joke between her and her grandfather because of its color and the fact that Nana always bragged about the fact that she had picked it. They used to get a good chuckle out of it.

Kate's heart hurt a little thinking about her grandfather. When he got sick, her mother had refused to visit, saying he was already gone as the cancer had spread to his brain, wiping it clean of any memories of the life he once had. Thankfully, he died peacefully one night in his sleep a short time later. She knew that her grandmother missed him terribly, but the man she had loved died months before his actual death, giving her time to grieve the loss of him while he was still present.

Kate looked over at her grandmother and held back the tears

that were forming in her eyes. How had she not come to visit her sooner? How had her mother not been here supporting her the months after his death? How had the rift between them been so big that her grandfather's death had not mended it? The more she thought about it, the more the disdain for her mother grew inside her.

"Oh, Kate, you're going to love this. There'll be vendors from all over Europe, and there are so many fun events. Storytellers, magicians, sheep herding, all sorts of things to see and do," her grandmother said, interrupting her thoughts.

"I can't wait, Nana," she said, forcing enthusiasm into her voice as she tried to choke down her emotions.

While they drove, the low, lingering fog of early morning began to lift, and the sky broke away to a vibrant blue. The trip to Llangernyw was almost an hour, and they spent most of the car ride talking about Kate's plans for the upcoming year. Whether or not she would be staying in London or going to France to stay with her father. It was something that Kate knew she needed to decide but was putting off. She didn't want to think about big life-changing decisions right now, she just wanted to spend the day hanging out with her nana at the market. All those things could wait for another day.

As they arrived in Llangernyw, the sun had fully burned off the foggy haze in the air and the temperature was reaching the twenties. She looked out over the sea of vendors occupying every inch of the large town green.

Her grandmother pulled in and parked the car in the front lot next to a disabled sign.

"Nana, you're not disabled!" Kate said, looking at her grandmother with a raised eyebrow.

"Being nearly eighty qualifies me, dear," she said, giving her a wide grin and a wink.

She popped the boot and pulled out an empty basket woven in greens, tans, and burgundy reeds with a wide mouth and an outstretched handle. Threading her arm through the basket, she shut the hatch and looked at herself in the reflection of the window, smoothed out her dress, and tucked a loose strand of hair back into her bun.

"Nana, is there someone here you're excited to see?" Kate teased her.

"Oh, you stop it," she answered back with a swat of her wrist and a cheeky smile across her face.

They walked through the fence opening into the large village green. The vendors were set up along all four sides, leaving an open center with tables for eating at and a small stage where performances were taking place. A set of twin girls were doing some sort of Welsh folk dance in front of a small crowd when they entered.

"Off to the right are all the food vendors, to the left handmade goods, to the front and back different artists doing demonstrations. Oh, look over there." Her grandmother pointed to a man sitting in front of a pottery wheel. He was in the middle of throwing what looked to be a sizable serving bowl. "That's Jason Grimm, the local potter. Every year he comes with his wheel. His wife sells their pots over there." She pointed to a tent to the left with a large vinyl sign that said "Blair Path Pottery." "Don't listen to a thing he says, though. He's a storyteller, that one. Was at the local grocery the other day telling people he saw a panther in his backyard," she said with a laugh of disbelief.

Amidst the bustling activity of people moving in and out of colorful tents, Kate took in the delightful aroma of freshly popped corn mingling with an array of spices filling the air around her. A lively band played folk music, trying their best to be heard over the cheerful chatter of the festivalgoers. The atmosphere was charged with excitement, so much so that she could feel the energy in the air around her.

"This is so cool, Nana," Kate said.

"See, I knew you'd love it," her grandmother said, patting her on the shoulder. "Now, I'm going to go over and get some of Glen's bread before it's all gone. You go have fun and explore. I'll be floating around if you need me." She handed Kate a small bit of money before walking off with a pep in her step.

So, Glen must be who she got all dressed up for, Kate thought as she began to wander around the green. She was about to go and get a toffee apple when she heard her name being called out from down the line of food vendors. When she spun around to look, she saw Owen waving at her from behind a booth that said "Bryndu Farm Organic Produce." Her heart skipped a beat at the sight of him, and she felt a deep, primal pull in her gut. But she pushed the feeling down, hoping to keep herself from blushing as she walked over.

"Hey, I thought your dad was vending today?" Kate said as she approached the stand. Trying to make small talk wasn't easy after yesterday and the mound of questions that had been piling up in her head ever since, but she did her best to keep it light.

"He was going to, but there was a problem at the farm, and I had to take his place," he answered, lifting a large wooden crate of potatoes onto the table.

"Oh, no. Are the horses okay?" Kate asked.

An older woman stepped up beside her and started looking at the array of colorful vegetables laid out in front of the tent. Owen gave the woman a smile and a nod as she turned and walked away without purchasing anything.

"Yeah, the horses are fine," Owen said. He added some fresh red radishes to a barrel that was half empty. "It's the berry crop. The entire lot rotted overnight. Never seen anything like it. Dad was super pissed. It's his best-seller at the market every year."

"That's weird. Does he have any idea what caused it?"

"Nope. Not a clue. There's a local botanist coming to the farm today to see if she can figure out what happened. Totally weird."

"Yeah. I hope they can figure it out. So, I take it you're stuck here the rest of the day then?" Kate asked. She picked up a bushel of carrots and looked them over, their bright orange almost matching the color of her hair.

"Yeah, but it's not so bad. At least I got stuck next to these guys," Owen said, pointing at the booth to his right. A rich aroma of spices seeped from the tent and wafted toward them. The sign on the top said "Patawa's Indian Food."

"So, you like Indian food?" she asked, giving him a knowing smile. She watched him wipe dirt from a bunch of carrots and put them in a basket.

"Yup, it's my favorite," he said.

She was about to tell him it was her favorite as well, happy to find something they had in common other than their past, when a small group of people came over to the stand. She stepped aside to let them browse. Owen looked over at her, and she gave him a smile and wave as if to say *see ya later*. He waved back, giving her a nod of acknowledgment, then went about helping the customers.

She was glad in a way that he got busy—the small talk felt strange after their last conversation and the market was not the place to bring any of that up. So she walked away from his tent and out into the crowd in the center of the market to explore.

Chapter Eighteen
Ionna
JOHN & JASPER

The next morning, Ionna awoke before the sun had graced the edge of the wheat fields, and the world still lay quiet in the stillness of early dawn.

She made her way into the bathroom and looked in the mirror to inspect the wounds on her face. She was bruised, but the redness of the cuts had slightly subsided. She decided to dab a bit more alcohol on the larger gash that hadn't begun to heal quite as nicely as the rest. As she blotted the cut she winced—it was still sore to the touch. She thought about how lucky she had been to walk away with just a few small cuts and a bruise or two. Things could have been much worse. The thought made her shiver, and she looked about the room, remembering how utterly alone she was out here in the Welsh countryside. She took a deep breath, surrendering to the thought, and washed her face before heading into the kitchen.

After brewing herself a large mug of tea, she picked up one of the lanterns and headed into the study to do a bit more snooping around. She sat at the large oak desk and ran her hands over the smooth surface, feeling where each grain of wood spun into the next. She marveled once more at its size and craftsmanship, admiring whoever had taken the time to create such a beautiful work of art, for that was precisely what it was: a functional work of art. She felt a deep connection to the desk, as if it was intended for her in some manner. But that was a ridiculous idea—it was an antique and had been around long before she was even born.

She gingerly pulled open each drawer, thumbing through piles of old papers in hopes of finding something that might explain why her father had taken her away to America. Most of the papers in the drawers were old bank statements and clippings from newspapers. Nothing of interest pertaining to her parentage. She sat back in the chair and clicked the pen in her hand incessantly.

There was so much more to the story, but all she had at the moment was the proverbial tip of the iceberg. Bits and pieces of her past no longer added up, and her whole identity was now in question. If she had been born here in Wales, then why did her birth certificate state she was born in Portland, Maine? Her parents must have had the documents forged. Something criminals or people on the run would do.

And why had her grandmother left her the estate with no explanation? She must have anticipated that Ionna would have questions. She thought again of the safety deposit box—perhaps a note was in there? Her head spun as threads of memories began to snap, knotting up into a jumbled mess of questions in her mind.

She looked down at the thin outline where the hidden drawer lay. Sliding her hand under the desk, she pushed the button that unlocked it and gently pulled it open. She plucked the envelope with the lock of hair from its resting place and turned it over in her hands. The name Neala written on the small degrading paper sent a wave of unease through her, and she dropped it back into the drawer. It wasn't abnormal for parents to save a lock of their child's hair as a baby, lots of people did it, but it left her feeling troubled every time she looked at it. Who was Neala? Then another thought formed in her mind; perhaps she had a sister she didn't know about. She swallowed hard and closed the drawer abruptly.

She began picking the loose papers up off the desk and depositing them back into the drawers when a newspaper clipping slipped from the stack and landed softly on the old wood floor between her feet. She reached down and picked it up, flipping it over as she did. There, on the opposite side of a Yardley soap ad, was an obituary for a woman named Elizabeth R. Rogowski. The photo at the top of the paper showed a smiling middle-aged woman with shoulder-length salt-and-pepper hair. She wore thick-framed glasses and looked to be in her late fifties or early sixties. Under the image, it read:

> Elizabeth (Rose) Rogowski
> 1917–1980
> Elizabeth died peacefully in her sleep on October 20, 1980,
> after a long battle with cancer. She is survived by
> her daughter, Betty Shortbridge,
> and grandson, Adam Shortbridge, of Beddgelert.
> She was predeceased by her husband, Artemas,
> and her infant daughter.

The rest of the obituary had been obscured by a large water stain, yet the woman's image captivated her—her eyes looked so familiar, maybe because they looked similar to her own. It made sense, she supposed, since this woman was her great-grandmother. She felt a deep sadness overtake her as she stared down at the picture. All this family she had never known. She folded the image over on itself, leaving the line "and grandson Adam Shortbridge of Beddgelert" exposed.

Ionna sat there staring down at her father's name, Adam Shortbridge. But that wasn't his name; his name was Adam Bellmore — or at least it had been to her. How had he lived such a lie for so many years without anyone finding out? Or was she just the only one that had been kept in the dark about it all? What had started out as sorrow melded into anger and disappointment once again.

There was a knock at the front door. Startled out of the downward spiral she had found herself in, she stood and went toward the window to see who was calling on her so early in the morning. When she looked out, the sun was halfway to its precipice in the sky. How long had she been in there rooting around? She looked down at her watch — 9:49 a.m.

"Nine forty-nine?" she whispered to herself. This tended to happen to her when she was deep-diving into a story; time just seemed to stand still while she was working, then, suddenly, it would catch up with her.

She peeked around the curtains to see who was on the front steps, trying her best to hide behind the edge of them. To her surprise, it was John Brightmore, the estate lawyer from London. He knocked again, and she quickly headed out of the study, shutting the door behind her and opening the front door just as he was turning to walk back to his car.

"John, what a nice surprise. I didn't think you would be here until later," she said, causing him to stop in his tracks and turn around.

"Sorry, did I wake you?" he asked. Then he caught sight of her face. "Oh my God, what happened? Are you okay?" He walked quickly over to inspect her injuries.

She was confused at first, then remembered the cuts on her face from the fall. She reached up, wincing at the pain when her fingers grazed the wounds. As she pulled her hand back down, she caught sight of her shirt and the small green frogs speckling it. At that moment her cheeks turned from pale pink to rose red. She had been so engrossed in her search that she had completely forgotten she was still in her PJs.

"Oh, I'm fine," she said with a nervous laugh. "Took a bit of a fall in the barn yesterday. Just a few scratches, that's all. I've been up for hours. As you can see, I just haven't made it out of my PJs yet," she said, waving a hand from her chest down toward her feet in an awkward acknowledgment.

"I'm sorry for coming so early. Why don't I come back later?" he said, in turn blushing and matching her embarrassment with his own.

"No, don't be silly. Come in," she said, swinging the door wide and gesturing for him to come in. She had no idea why she had just said that. It would have been a much more comfortable situation if he *had* just come back later. But she'd been isolated for too long and was happy for another person to talk to. Plus, she had questions for him that couldn't wait.

She led them into the kitchen and lit the stove to heat up the kettle.

"Give me just a minute," she said, walking out of the kitchen and down to her grandmother's room.

Shutting the door quietly, she quickly pulled off her PJs and threw on a worn pair of jeans, a fitted white shirt, and a knit button-down vest. She pulled her hair out of its messy ponytail and brushed it out, leaving the long brown waves flowing down her back. Next, she dabbed concealer over the cuts and bruises on her face. It stung as she blended it in but the result left her looking more like herself and less like a cage fighter who'd lost a match. Glancing at herself in the mirror, she was happy with the result. She made her way back into the kitchen where John was now making them both coffee from a press.

"Where did you find that?" she asked as she came in.

"Top shelf over the toaster, behind the food processor. It's where she always kept it," he said with a smile.

"Oh my God, that little bit of information would have been great to know two days ago—along with the fact there's no electricity here," she teased.

John looked at her, confused. "What are you talking about? There's power here," he said, walking over and flipping a switch hidden behind an apron on the wall to the right of the sink.

Ionna looked up at an old milk glass light fixture on the ceiling adorned with cobwebs. Its soft yellow glow lit up the room. She looked from the light to John and back again.

"You have *got* to be kidding me. I've been here for two days surviving like it was the eighteen hundreds and the whole time there was power?" She was completely dumbfounded. How had she not seen the lights? She had even looked for them the first night she arrived. Had it been some sort of weird displacement from the jet lag or all the emotional exhaustion and stress of the last few days? No, there was no way she would have been that out of it.

"Did you think I would send you here with no power and not say anything?" John asked with a raised eyebrow.

"I don't know," Ionna said, shrugging and trying to laugh it off.

He turned to the coffee and began pouring it into mugs. "What have you been doing for light?"

"Lanterns. I thought everything in the house was gas-powered. There were so many oil lamps everywhere." She stumbled over her words, feeling like a complete idiot for not checking more thoroughly. However, she had a suspicion that even if she had, she wouldn't have found anything. She glanced up again. How had she missed the lights on the ceiling? She *knew* they had not been there before.

There was something very strange about the house. She'd been brushing it aside as anxiety over being alone and isolated, but she was certain of it now. Something was just... off.

"Oh, those old oil lamps are common around here. The storms roll off the mountains and cut the power a lot, so most people have one in every room," he said.

He handed her a steaming cup of hot coffee along with a reassuring smile. She smiled back, but she couldn't help feeling like she was going a bit mad.

Just then, the cat came slinking in and walked over to John, twining itself around his legs.

"Jasper!" he said, surprised. "We thought he had run off. No one could find him after Betty died. Was he here in the house when you got here?"

"No, actually, he found me in the barn yesterday. I didn't know if he was Betty's pet or a barn cat, but then I saw the cat food in the cupboard."

John placed his coffee on the table, picked up Jasper and put him in his lap. "Well, you're not wrong on either count. Jasper was a kitten from our barn cat Madeline. Betty came over to buy veggies one afternoon and walked home with a cat instead. He must be fourteen at this point."

Ionna looked down at the cat, purring softly in John's lap. It made her think of the night before, purring in the darkness on the creaking rocking chair.

"I keep forgetting that you grew up around here," she said, changing the subject.

"Yep, just beyond that field is my family's farm." He pointed out toward the front living room window. "My brother still runs it."

"I think I might have seen your brother riding a horse the other day."

"That was probably Owen, my nephew. He's the horse rider in the family." He took a long sip of his coffee and then set the mug down with a decisive thud. "You up for an outing? There's a big farmer's market in Llangernyw today. It's a nice ride up there, and they have some great food vendors. What do you say?"

"Sure, but on one condition: you help fill in some blanks for me, if you can, about my grandmother. Deal?" she said, in the voice she often used while interviewing a lead on a story.

"Deal!" he said, picking up Jasper from his lap and placing him back on the floor. He stood and placed his mug in the sink. When he turned around, he stopped, catching sight of the urn sitting on the side table in the living room. He walked over to it.

"I haven't done anything with her remains yet. I just haven't been able to bring myself to do it. It feels kinda odd, not knowing her and all," Ionna said, nervously twirling a hair tie around her wrist.

"I understand. There's no rush. Just take your time and do it when it feels right," John said sympathetically.

"Oh! Hey, I wanted to ask you if you have a key for the safety deposit box? I wasn't able to get in. None of the keys on the ring worked."

"Really? I thought it would be on the ring. I'm sorry, I don't have another. Your best bet would be to look around here. She probably kept it in the house somewhere."

"I bet you're right. I'll have a look around later."

"Good idea, because I'm starving. Are you ready to go?" he asked.

"Just a minute, let me grab my bag," she said, going back into the kitchen and grabbing her sling purse off the back of the kitchen chair. She took one last glance up at the ceiling light and shot it a look as if it had played some sort of trick on her.

As she walked back out to meet John, she noticed the outlets and other light fixtures she hadn't seen before. As soon as she was back, she was going to find that key, open the safety deposit box, and figure out whatever strange secrets this house held within its walls.

Chapter Nineteen

Kate

THE FORTUNE TELLER

The crowd at the farmers' market swelled as the day went on. Kate's grandmother spent most of her time with Glen in the baker's tent while Kate wandered about looking at all the vendors and their goods, drinking in the atmosphere. She found herself drawn to a tent that sold a wide range of vintage goods—records, cassette tapes, posters, eclectic clothing, and a mix of odds and ends from every decade of the past century.

She'd already picked up a small zipper pouch with Iggy Pop on it, a David Bowie record, and an old The Cure world tour button when a striking necklace caught her eye. It hung off an old coat hook attached to a display on the back wall of the tent. Nestled in the center of a simple Celtic knot was an odd-looking green stone. She picked it up, letting the cool metal chain slip through her fingers. As soon as she touched it, a surge of calmness pulsed through her body, and for a second she thought she saw a flash of bright light radiate from the stone's center.

"It's a beauty, isn't it?" the woman vending the tent said, noticing how captivated Kate looked. "It's the Triquetra, the symbol of the Holy Trinity. I found that trinket at an estate sale in Beddgelert."

Kate blinked and looked up. "It's lovely," she said. "How much for it?" She turned the stone in her fingers, trying to recreate the glow she had just seen. But the light only reflected off of it, causing a rainbow to dance across the surface of the stone.

"For you, how about fifteen pounds?" the woman said.

Kate looked down at the items she had collected, not wanting to blow the whole forty pounds her nana gave her in the first tent she went into. She knew she needed to put something back, but the necklace was calling to her, and she couldn't leave without it. So, she took the record out from under her arm and set it back down on the stand next to the counter.

"Great, I'll take it, along with these as well," Kate said, handing the woman the pin and the Iggy Pop bag.

Once she'd paid for her newfound treasures, she moved next door to a glassware tent where she found a blown glass pipe that looked as if it was made of tie-dyed glass. She immediately thought of her friend Stevie back home, who was an aspiring pothead. She knew Stevie would be thrilled to have a proper pipe rather than the ones she fashioned out of apples or old soda cans when she'd steal weed from her brother to get high on the roof. She looked around to make sure her grandmother was nowhere in sight and hastily paid for the pipe. She quickly tucked it into the Iggy Pop bag, zipped it up, and stuck it into her back pocket. The last thing she needed was for her grandmother to see it; she would never hear the end of the "Drugs will ruin your life" talk.

Kate walked around, indulging in a bag of candy floss and thinking about Stevie. She was envious of her and the fact she knew what she wanted to do with her life when another tent caught her eye. It had a hand-painted sign that read "Palm Reading" in beautiful crimson letters outlined in gold, with a mandala spreading out in the shape of an open hand sitting in front of it. She stopped and laughed to herself. Maybe she should go in and see what her future held. That would save her angsting around for the rest of the summer.

"You, there," the woman sitting next to the tent called out to her. "Yes, you with the ginger hair. Come over here."

Kate did her best to act as if she hadn't heard her, but the woman was persistent.

She sat on an old wooden stool only a foot or so off the ground. Her long skirt draped down over her legs and pooled on the ground, covering her feet. She was an older woman, in her late sixties, Kate assumed. She had long white hair that flowed down her shoulders and onto her ample bosom. Two thick braids with sprigs of lavender tucked into them hung off to one side. She certainly looked the part of a fortune teller, but it was her eyes that pulled Kate in. They were like dark pools of infinite blackness, otherworldly.

"I'm sorry, I don't have any money for a reading," Kate lied.

"That's okay. You come in and sit with me," the woman said, parting a panel of the tent and pointing to an oversized floor pillow on the opposite side of a small table.

Kate looked around for her grandmother or Owen to come to her rescue but both were out of sight. She took a deep breath and then walked into the tent, apprehensive but intrigued at the same time.

The inside of the tent reflected the sign; it was decorated with a large mandala rug in rich reds, blues, and golds and small tables covered in burning candles. Strings of twinkle lights cascaded down from the tent's peak, giving off a soft, magical glow. A copper bowl with burning incense sat on a table in the back and filled the air with the thick aroma of sage, cedar, and cinnamon. Kate knew most fortune tellers had to be great at setting the mood for readings. It was part of the illusion. If people felt like they were in the presence of a mystic, their minds would do the rest.

"What is your name, my dear?" she asked Kate, breaking the enchantment she was under from the beauty of the tent's interior.

"Kate."

"Hello, Kate, I'm Karena. May I see your hand?" she asked, holding her own wrinkled hand palm upward over the table for Kate to rest hers in.

She was reluctant at first but reached forward and placed her hand on top of the woman's. As soon as their flesh touched, the old woman flinched, and her eyes went wide. She looked up at Kate as if seeing her for the first time and then looked back down at her palm. Kate fought hard not to roll her eyes at the woman's theatrics.

The fortune teller sat there examining her palm for a long while, tracing her finger up and down the lines etched into her skin. After what seemed like several minutes, she spoke.

"Palms are the road maps to our lives. Some people's journeys are short and they have small rural maps, while others are long with maps of the world laid out upon them. My dear, you have the map of the universe on yours," she said with a soft excitement in her voice. "You see here." She ran her finger along a line that wrapped from Kate's pointer finger down around to the base of her thumb. "This is your lifeline. See here where it has two splits?" she pointed to the top section of the line. "This is a point in your past that caused you much distress. You have another one of those breaks a little further down, which means you may be experiencing something similar to those events again very soon."

She looked up at Kate, gauging her reaction, and then back down, tracing out a new line.

"Your head line starts below your heart line, which can mean the absence of a parent in your life."

Not exactly a stab in the dark, Kate thought. *The rate of divorce is over fifty percent.*

"Your fate line runs quite deep. This is the sign of a person controlled by destiny. And here, at the end, it forks, meaning that you have two destinies, depending on the choices you make."

Uni here, or uni in France. Bingo.

The woman stared down at her palm for a long while before speaking again. She moved her aged hand over each crease in her palm with the tip of her pointer finger, a look of bewilderment on her face as she worked.

"This is very interesting," she said.

"What is?" Kate asked, annoyed at herself for being curious.

"You have two distinct marks on your palm. Do you see that cross on the thumb side of your life line? That is a Saint Andrew's cross. It means that you have saved or will save a life. And here, between your head and heart lines, are witch marks, showing that you have a special ability. Not everyone has these, and you have several that run the length between lines. You, my dear, are very special. In the thirty-seven years I've been reading palms, I have never seen one such as yours. You have marks that seem to be from another realm altogether," she said, letting go of Kate's hand and looking up at her. The woman's eyes were as black as obsidian, and when she looked at Kate, it was as if she was gazing directly into her soul.

"Thanks for the reading, but I'm definitely not that special," Kate told her as she stood up, feeling uncomfortable and wanting to leave.

The woman rose slowly to her feet, her old body taking time to straighten. Kate went to give her what little money she had left when the woman grabbed her outstretched hand and pulled her close so that they were only inches apart. She leaned toward her ear and whispered.

"There are things from your past that you must remember in order to protect yourself from the danger in the present. You must stay vigilant. You're an obstacle in its path. Stay on guard. Use your abilities to protect yourself."

Kate shook the old woman off and pushed past the hanging lanterns and silk, out the door of the tent, and into the fresh air. Without even looking back, she shoved her way into the crowd of people until she was at a safe distance from the tent, her heart racing.

She found herself in a group of people watching a marionette act on the center stage, trying to catch her breath and slow her racing heart. What the hell had that been all about? At first, it seemed like all fun and games, an old woman dressed as a fortune teller to make a little extra money at the market, but once she had looked into the woman's eyes, she knew that she was much more than that. How had she known Kate's memories weren't whole? How had she known to refer to Kate's "special ability," just as Owen did? It made her deeply uneasy.

She felt a hand grab her shoulder. Already on guard, she spun around abruptly, almost knocking her grandmother over.

"Jesus Christ! Nana. I'm so sorry. I thought…" She stopped.

"Katherine! What have I told you about using the Lord's name in vain," her grandmother scolded.

"I'm sorry. You just startled me."

"Well, I'm ready to head home, I'm a bit tired. Are you ready to go?" she said, handing Kate her basket that was now piled high with bread, cheese, vegetables, and a small box of pastries.

"Yes, perfect timing. I was just about to find you. I think I've had enough for one day," Kate said as they weaved through the crowd.

Before they broke free of the market's edge, Kate looked back over her shoulder toward the palm reader's tent. There, standing in the doorway of the tent, was the old woman, staring back at Kate with her piercing black eyes. A chill ran down the length of her spine, and the palm of her hand felt as if it was on fire. She looked down. The crossed lines the fortune teller had shown her looked as if they had been branded into her flesh in a burning red hue. Kate quickly turned away and ran directly into a woman who was just entering the market.

"Oh, God, I'm so sorry," Kate blurted.

The woman turned back and gave her a forgiving smile. "No worries," she said in an American accent and continued into the market with a tall, well-dressed man by her side.

There is something oddly familiar about that woman, Kate thought, but she couldn't quite put her finger on it. She watched the couple disappear into the crowd, their heads slowly fading away into the mass of people.

Chapter Twenty
Ionna
KEBABS & OLD BOOKS

They arrived at the bustling market a little after noon and went in through the makeshift entrance between two tents when a young ginger-haired girl spun around and ran directly into Ionna.

"Oh, God, I'm so sorry," the girl said with a frightened look on her face.

"No worries," Ionna replied, smiling.

She had the strangest feeling come over her upon seeing the girl. She could have sworn she knew her somehow, but that was impossible; she had never been to Wales before. *She must just have one of those faces,* Ionna thought as she and John made their way through the crowd. She looked over her shoulder to get another glimpse of the girl but she had been erased from view by the people moving in and out of the market.

"Over here!" John called out to her over the sea of voices. "You gotta try this." He walked over to a tent and handed the man behind the table some cash in return for two kebab-looking things. He handed Ionna one with a smile. "Best part of the market is the *food*!" John said with the wide eyes of a child who was just given a very large piece of candy. "These are Turkish chicken kebabs. One of my favorite treats, and this guy makes the best ones in Wales." He took a huge bite and gave the vendor a thumbs-up.

Ionna gave hers a sniff and eyed it apprehensively. She wasn't much of a fan of Turkish food, but she decided to give it a try. She took a small bite and then another. The spices danced around in her mouth as the bread and meat melted like butter. It was one of the most delicious things she had ever tasted.

"Oh my God, you weren't kidding. These are amazing," she told him, taking another bite, then wiping off the corners of her mouth.

"Told ya! Let's go find my brother. He's around here somewhere."

John led them around the square, starting from the right and working their way toward the back. It only took them about a minute to see the farm's stand when the crowd broke around the center stage as a band exited and the next one began setting up.

John walked over with Ionna in tow toward the tent. It seemed the market was going well as most of the bushels were half full if not altogether empty. There, behind an old wooden folding table, was a boy in his late teens, who looked like a younger version of John. He was pulling out another barrel of potatoes to replace the half-empty one sitting in front of the stand.

"Owen! What are you doing here? Where's your dad?" John asked.

"Uncle John, hey! I didn't think you were coming until later. Dad's back at the farm. There was an issue with the berry crop this morning, and he had to stay behind. So, I'm vending today. Feel free to jump in and help. It's crazy busy this year," Owen said, wiping sweat off his forehead.

"Ionna, this is my nephew, Owen. Owen, this is Betty's granddaughter, Ionna."

Owen reached a hand across the table to greet her. She moved her kebab to the other hand and shook his.

"Nice to meet you, Owen," she said with a kind smile.

"Same. I'm really sorry about your grandmother. She was a really nice old lady," Owen said, offering his condolences.

"Thank you." She felt a bit odd at this young boy consoling her for the death of someone he knew better than she did. She felt as if it should have been the other way around.

"I see my uncle has already made it to the kebab tent. No surprise there," Owen said, giving John a playful nudge.

"The first and most important stop. Well, I'd love to stay and help but it's my duty to show Ionna around. I'll catch up with you later tonight. Good luck with the rest of the day."

"He seems like a good kid," Ionna said as they strolled toward the next vendor.

"He is. By far the best thing my brother ever did," John said with a smile.

Ionna could see how much Owen meant to John, the way his eyes lit with a kind of pride when talking about him. It made her ache a little inside, wishing for something like that. At this point in her life, she was the only family she had left. There was no one else, no one to be proud of or share memories with. And now even her memories were distorted, warped by the lies she had been told. It was then that she decided to ask him the question that she had been holding back since he had picked her up.

"John, can I ask you a question?"

"Of course. Fire away."

"How did Betty die? In all the craziness of everything, I never even thought to ask."

John slowed his pace and looked at her as if to say, *Are you really asking me this now?* He took her hand and guided them over to a small picnic area set up with benches and tables under a row of oak trees near the back of the market.

"It's a bit of a mystery really," he said, sitting down on one of the benches. "A neighbor she played bridge with found her. She came by for their weekly game, but Betty didn't answer the door. She found Betty sitting at the kitchen table, dead in her chair."

"It sounds like she must have had a heart attack or a stroke or something," Ionna said, the relief audible in her voice. After what the woman at the grocery store had implied, she was relieved Betty hadn't died in some horrific accident, or worse.

"Stroke is what the autopsy said, but the weird thing was that there was a significant trail of blood from the kitchen to the bathroom. The bathroom sink was stained too, but there was only a tiny cut on her palm, from what the coroner's report stated. The police did a small investigation into it but found no evidence of foul play. The blood they found matched Betty's, so the case was closed."

"That doesn't seem all that strange to me," Ionna said. She had seen similar things as a reporter. Older people died like this often.

"Maybe it's not, but something just seemed off. The neighbor's statement on the report said, at first, she thought Betty was alive because when she entered the kitchen, she was sitting upright in one of the kitchen chairs, eyes open with a frightened look on her face as if she had startled her coming into the house unannounced. She told the police she believed someone else had been in the house with her because things were in disarray and Betty was a very meticulous woman—" He stopped himself abruptly and looked over at Ionna. "Jesus, I shouldn't be telling you all this. It's not what you need to hear right now. I'm sorry. It's just that Betty was like a grandmother to me and my brother and—" He stopped again, a flushed redness spreading across his cheeks. "Wow, I'm not doing very good here, am I? I'm sorry."

"Don't be. I want to know what happened—the whole story, not some PG version," she said, trying to calm him down as he was obviously upset.

"She was like a grandmother to you? Tell me about her. I'd really love to know what kind of person she was," she said, hoping this would help smooth things a bit more.

John looked over at her gratefully. "She was wonderful. Ben and I would go over in the summers and help weed her flower beds. She would pay us each five pounds, which to a kid was a lot of money. Then, when we were done, she would always have a plate of homemade biscuits ready for us. She was an amazing storyteller as well. Some afternoons when we got out of school, we would go over, and she would tell us tales in the backyard under the oak tree. She called it her story spot." He spoke with such fondness in his voice. "Ionna, I wish you'd had the chance to know her, truly."

"I do too," she said. At that moment, a couple came over and sat on the bench next to theirs. Lowering her voice slightly, she asked, "Did you know my father, Adam?"

"Not really," John said. "I only met him once or twice when I was really little. He was a lot older than me. Betty never spoke much about him. In fact, I didn't even know he had a daughter until Betty came in to have her will drawn up. She was a very private person when it came to her personal life."

Ionna was a bit disappointed he couldn't tell her much about her father, but more than that, her heart ached at the thought of what she had missed out on. She had never known the love of a grandparent. The more she thought about it, the deeper the anger grew toward her father for stripping her of it. From the way John spoke of her, she was a Norman Rockwell kind of grandmother, and she hated her father for taking that from her, no matter what his reasons. The anger burned in her, doubling her determination to find out why he had made the choices he did.

"Let's go find something sweet to eat after all this heavy talk," John suggested, seeing the weight of emotion in her eyes.

He stuck out his hand to help her up, something most men didn't do these days, she thought. She noted that it was the second time that day he'd taken her hand. She smiled at him, glad he was able to break her away from the reporter side of her that wanted to keep questioning him. She stood up, took his hand, and followed him back into the crowd.

They walked the perimeter of the market, peeking into tents to see what they were selling. One tent in particular caught Ionna's eye, marked by a sign painted with the words "Vintage Goods," and she walked over to it.

"Oh, I have to have a look around in here," she told John as she moved a flap of the tent aside to enter.

"Okay, while you're in there, I'm gonna go grab some fresh bread from the tent next door. I'll be right back."

Ionna was thrilled when she walked in to see a huge array of records, books, clothing, and odds and ends scattered over every inch of the inside of the tent. She knew she'd have to restrain herself—she currently had no income and very little luggage space. But it would be nice to find something small to take back to America with her as a memento. She ran her fingers across a row of vintage velvet dresses, leaving trace lines on the fabric as she went. An old, ornate-looking bookshelf filled with books caught her eye from the back corner. She found herself drawn to the books and began thumbing through them. The top row looked much older than all the others, most being from the turn of the century. She scanned titles but recognized none of them. The one that stood out was an antique book with an embossed cover depicting a mountain and trees on each side, with the word "Lore" etched in the center in gold. She pulled it out and carefully began leafing through its pages. It was full of folklore and legends from Wales, something that would make a perfect keepsake from her time spent here.

She decided it was something she couldn't leave without, so she returned to the front of the tent and gave it to the lady behind the makeshift counter.

"Will that be it, dear?" she asked Ionna as she tucked the book into a small paper bag.

"Yeah, that's it."

"Isn't that a beautiful book? Came from an estate sale in Beddgelert a few years back. Twenty pounds, please."

Ionna reached into her bag and pulled out the money, handing it over to the woman, who in turn handed her the bag with the book inside. "Thank you so much."

As Ionna turned to leave, the woman called out to her.

"Miss!"

Ionna turned around as the woman approached her, handing her another book.

"I believe this book goes with the one you just bought. Both books came from the same estate sale. They should stay together. You take it, free of charge," the woman said, slipping it into the bag before Ionna was even able to look at it.

"Thank you, that's very kind of you," she said.

"You're welcome. These books never sell anyway. Not sure why I keep lugging them around with me." She chuckled.

Ionna smiled, then turned to walk out of the tent once again and almost ran directly into John.

"Woah, easy there, don't run me over," he teased.

Ionna laughed as they walked out of the tent together. John was so easy to be around. He was funny, smart, and handsome to boot. If she wasn't careful, she might just find herself falling for a guy like him.

Chapter Twenty-One

Ionna

PIES AND PALMS

As the afternoon crowds started to thin out and the market began to wind down, Ionna and John meandered their way through the remaining stalls. A Pibgorn piper had taken to the small stage in the center of the square, and the sad cry of his pipes filled the air as they looked for a tent selling sweets. Some of the merchants were freshening up their stalls and putting out the last of their inventory in hopes of making a few last-minute sales before the market closed. As they walked around the rear of the square, John's attention was drawn to a little tent. It was relatively smaller in size compared to the others. In the center, behind a foldable table, sat an old woman who looked to be in her late seventies or early eighties. The table was strewn with jams and pies of several varieties.

"We have to grab one of Sandra's pies. She makes the best rhubarb and redcurrant. Literally tastes like heaven," John said, raising his voice to be heard over the music.

Ionna read the simple handwritten sign on the table as they got closer. "PIES 6 pounds, JAMS 4 pounds, ADVICE free." *What a strange little message*, she thought.

"Sandra is the local bishop's wife. Don't ask for any free advice or we'll be here all day," John said under his breath as if he had read her mind.

Ionna gave him a knowing nod and a comical smile as they walked to the table. The air in the tent was filled with the rich aroma of freshly baked sweets—a mix of nutmeg, ginger, and cinnamon. It reminded her of her favorite little coffee shop back home in Maine. This, in turn, caused a tinge of homesickness in her. *Funny how smells have the capacity to take you to a certain time and place; they could be the closest thing to time travel we have*, she mused.

"Hello, Sandra. What a lovely day for the market. Can I please get two of your famous rhubarb redcurrant pies?" John asked in an overly friendly manner.

"John. Hello, dear. I haven't seen you in ages. How's the big city treating you? And who is this lovely young woman by your side?" Sandra asked him, giving Ionna an appraising look.

"City life is different. You know what they say, you can take the boy out of the country but you can't take the country out of the boy," he joked. "This is Ionna. Betty Shortbridge's granddaughter. She'll be staying at the farm for a little while," he told the old woman as he took out his money and paid for the pies.

"I'm so sorry to hear of her passing," Sandra said, her voice full of sincerity.

"Thank you very much," Ionna said graciously.

Sandra reached her old, weathered hand over to John to take the money. "John, this is too much, dear," she said, handing him back the extra twenty pounds he had handed her.

"Sandra, these pies are worth double the price. Take whatever is left and donate it to the church for me, okay?" he told her. His gentle and friendly demeanor was so endearing. Seeing him like this, she thought how practicing law in a huge city so far away seemed an odd fit.

"You're too kind. This won't go unnoticed by God," Sandra said with a smile and placed the two pies in wide paper bags with handles. With some effort, she picked the bags up and passed them over the table to John, who took them easily into his hands.

"Thank you, Sandra. Have a great rest of your day."

They turned to walk back out into the dwindling crowd of people.

"You two lovebirds have a wonderful rest of *your* day," Sandra called out.

Ionna couldn't help but crack a smile at that. *We must look quite good together if people already think we are lovebirds*, she thought.

As they made it almost to the end of the sea of vendor tents, a sign resting against a white tent with red and gold trim caught her eye. "Palm Reading" it said in fancy red letters outlined in gold. John saw her looking and smiled.

"Want to get your fortune read?" he asked her teasingly.

"Why not!" Ionna answered. If she was lucky, maybe this fortune teller could shed some light on her past. She had never had her palm read or fortune told before, but hell, at this point she would try anything to get some answers.

They walked toward the tent, threading in and out of the people heading to the center stage area to see the band that had just begun to play. Some sort of bluegrass rock band that was pulling in a sizable crowd.

The entrance to the tent was bathed in strips of red silk that hung down to create a makeshift doorway. There was a strong smell of incense working its way into the market air, enticing passersby to come in and be enchanted.

John held the silks back for Ionna. At first, they didn't see anyone upon entering; the inside was covered head to toe with rich fabrics in golds and reds, oriental lanterns, candles, and throw pillows scattering the floor. It wasn't until John almost ran into the old woman that they saw her. She had been sitting on a stool low to the floor, and her long pooling skirt and shawl had all but camouflaged her.

"Oh, I'm so sorry, I didn't see you there," John apologized.

With great effort, the old woman rose to greet them.

"Pay no mind. Come, come. Sit down and let me have a look at you both," she said, gesturing toward a group of floor pillows.

Ionna sat first while John clumsily tried to position himself on a pillow much too small for a man his size.

Ionna couldn't help but stare at the old woman. She was stunning for her age, in her early seventies, she guessed. With her long, flowing white hair and her piercing black eyes, she certainly looked the part of a mystic.

"Let's start with you," she said, looking over at John.

"Oh no, I'm not getting my palm read. I'd rather not know my future," he said, nudging Ionna forward toward the small table that separated them from the woman.

"It's not all about the future, it can be about the past and the present as well," the old woman said.

"Well, if that's the case, I'd be grateful for some insight into my past," Ionna told the woman as she placed her palm on the table between them.

The woman gently picked up Ionna's hand and rested it on her own. She looked into it for a long while, traveling the lines that crisscrossed her palm. Ionna caught a look of bewilderment crossing the woman's face. A quiet pulse of worry went through her as she waited for the woman to speak.

"My dear, you have a very peculiar palm. See this here?" She traced her finger down a line running vertically to Ionna's thumb. "This is your life line. You have another line here next to it that mirrors the first. It's as if you have two lives, and both lines are abnormally long."

Ionna raised her eyebrows. *Two lives?*

"Did you lose your father at a young age?" the woman asked, her eyes still on Ionna's palm.

"I did lose my father, but not when I was young. It's been a little over five years since he passed," Ionna told her. *This woman already seems full of bullshit,* she thought. She guessed that she asked every other person who came in her tent that same question, and chances were that some of them had lost their father at a young age, either to death or divorce.

"Well, I can see a separation that changed the course of your life when you were young. You also have the mark of a healer. Here." She ran her pointer finger down to a mark in the shape of an X that sat in the center of her palm. "There are few people who have this mark, and the ones who do hold great power within. Your lines do not follow the common rules. However, I did see something very similar with another young woman here today. Very peculiar," the woman said.

That was probably another thing she told just about everyone whose palm she read, trying to pull on their intrigue. Everyone wanted someone to tell them they were special. It probably brought in good tips.

"Can you see anything about my past that might give me any insight into why my family moved away from here?" Ionna asked in a last-ditch attempt to gain something useful out of the reading.

"Well, I do see there was a drastic move when you were young. A possible tragic event that led to the uprooting of you and your family."

Ionna's stomach turned at the words. The uprooting of her and her family. Hadn't that been what happened to her as a child?

"Might this have something to do with being separated from your father?" the old woman continued.

"No, I was never separated from my father. He raised me with my mother until they passed a few years back in a car accident," Ionna answered with confusion.

"Well, that *is* very strange. You didn't happen to be adopted, did you?"

Ionna's heart sank. That was one thing she had not considered. No, it couldn't be—she had her father's eyes and her mother's hair. She looked like them. She couldn't have been adopted.

"No. I wasn't," she said, uncertainty sneaking into her voice. She wanted to ask the woman a hundred more questions but she didn't want to put her entire hand of cards out on the table for John to see.

"I'm sorry I couldn't be of more help," the old woman said, letting go of Ionna's hand. "As I said, your palm seems to break the rules."

"Thank you for trying," Ionna said as she stood up and fished through her bag for some money.

The woman stood as well, her body moving slower than it should for someone her age. "Would you like me to pull a tarot spread for you? It might shed some light on why your palm is giving us mixed messages. Free of charge, my dear."

Ionna looked at John, who raised his eyebrows in a manner that suggested she should go for it. So, she sat back down as the woman walked over to an old wooden table in the corner and grabbed a purple silk bag. Seated once more on her low stool, she first pulled a clear quartz crystal out of the bag and placed it on the table between them. Then she removed a very old deck of cards that looked stained and cracked with age. They appeared to be much older than the woman herself. As she shuffled them, fanning them out and doubling them over on each other, they made a crisp, sharp sound as they moved the air out in quick bursts.

She cut the deck in half and then placed it back on top of itself before she spoke.

"I want you to pick up this deck and pull three cards from it. Place them down in front of you, face up, as you pull," she instructed.

As soon as Ionna touched the cards, a shock of energy shot up her arm and into her body. She jumped, almost dropping the deck to the ground. *With all the silks and fabrics draped around the room, I must have conducted an electric shock*, Ionna thought.

"Are you okay?" John asked.

The old woman looked at her as if she knew exactly what had just happened.

"Yes, I'm fine. Just a chill," she reassured him.

Ionna began to pull the cards out one at a time, laying each one in front of her on the table. When all three cards had been placed down, the old woman looked at the spread and seemed unable to conceal the intense worry that was now etched onto her face. She peered up at Ionna, her dark eyes suddenly filled with what seemed to be dread, and Ionna knew whatever she was about to tell her wasn't going to be good.

Chapter Twenty-Two

Ionna

FORTUNES AND FORGES

The palm reader sat motionless, staring at the cards laid upon the table in front of Ionna. A thick silence filled the air inside the tent—even the crowd and band playing outside seemed to be drowned out by it. Like a layer of fog resting upon the land in the early hours of the morning before the world was awake. It made Ionna uneasy. She glanced over at John, who was looking at the palm reader in anticipation of her explanation of the cards.

"This echoes the reading of your palm in many ways," the old woman said, finally shattering the heavy silence. "Let's start here, this is your present." She pointed at the card in the center. "The Seven of Swords. This card suggests you are or will soon be in a situation where things are not clear, and you should use caution. There is conflict on the horizon, and you must stay vigilant because deception is likely to arise. For your past, you pulled The Magician, but it is in reverse. This is very interesting as it suggests you were not able to achieve your true potential because of the events that happened to you when you were young, leaving you without the true power you were meant to have." She bent forward, studying the cards with intensity, as if they were revealing secrets only she could see.

She spun the next card around. "As for your future, you pulled the Seven of Wands. This card tells us there is a battle approaching with an enemy. The Seven is encouraging you to stay strong and focused in order to overcome the fight. It seems that you have a great deal of turmoil about to happen in your life, and it will fulfill part of the destiny that was set upon you as a child."

A look of pity sat upon the old woman's face, creating deep creases between her eyes as she waited for Ionna's response.

Ionna sat there, trying to take it all in. Nothing made sense, and why should it? It was coming from a fortune teller at a market. She had become so desperate for answers that she had gotten tangled up in this illusion instead of sticking to solid facts. Wasn't this what these people did, play on others' fears and insecurities to make a few bucks? It wasn't like any of this was real—she might have gotten the same reading in the daily horoscopes in the paper.

She stood up once again and grabbed her bags off the floor.

"Thank you," she said, ushering herself toward the opening of the tent. John followed behind, flashing a smile and a wave to the woman as they exited. But before they could make it through the doorway of silks, she called out to Ionna.

"These might not have been the answers you seek at present, but they will help you in the near future. Trust in your instincts and follow them. They are rarely wrong. You have great power in you locked away. You must find the key …"

Her wispy voice was drowned out by the crowd's applause outside the tent as the band finished their set. Ionna gave the old woman a brief, polite smile as she and John left. Once they reached the fresh air outside, she let out a sigh of disappointment.

"Well, that was interesting," John said, leading them back through the crowd of people in the center of the market.

"Interesting but not helpful. Who was I kidding, trying to get answers from a fortune teller? Desperation's a bitch," she joked, trying to lighten her own mood. She wasn't going to try and deny that the whole thing left her with a bit of an uneasy feeling in her gut and a few new questions in her mind, like whether or not she had been secretly adopted. But there would be no answers to those questions now; those would have to wait for another time.

As if reading her mind once again, John interjected. "Well, maybe we can find some of those answers ourselves. I know a few people in town who might have known your father. Let me ask around. There's still one last tent I want to show you before we go."

She followed him to a tent they had passed on the way in. A thick crowd stood in a semi-circle around it, and the smell of wood smoke and hot metal filled the air around them, accompanied by a loud banging noise coming from the center of the circle. John pushed through the crowd, making a small space for Ionna to creep in behind him. He turned sideways to reveal a man hammering out a sword on an anvil. He wore work pants and a long-sleeved plaid shirt with a leather apron over the front. He struck the blade with a large metal hammer, his hands protected by a pair of thick leather gloves as he worked. She had seen this kind of thing in movies and on the Discovery Channel but never before in real life. It captivated her, seeing the warped piece of steel being flattened and shaped into a fierce-looking blade.

"Amazing, isn't it?" John asked, seeing the look of amusement in her eyes.

"Amazing!" she agreed, entranced by the shapeshifting of the steel into a blade.

They stayed and watched until the swordsmith finished, ending the demonstration by dipping the blade into a tall container of oil to cool the metal. The crowd applauded, hooting and laughing in wonder. The swordsmith held up a hand and bobbed his head in humble gratitude. Gradually, the crowd began to disperse, and John approached the man as he removed his gloves and apron. Ionna followed a little sheepishly behind. The man was tall, well-built with blond hair, and sported a thick five o'clock shadow that gave him a rugged look. As they drew closer, she could make out the color of his eyes; they emulated a late autumn day, with their rich chestnut tones trimmed with a tinted green rim. *He is quite handsome*, she thought.

"Alright, mate. Looking good out there. Your skills are getting better by the day, I see," John greeted him.

"John. Long time. How's it going, mate?" the man asked, shaking John's hand.

"I'm doing really good. This is my friend Ionna. Ionna, this is Zeke Evans."

Ionna leaned forward and shook Zeke's hand. "Nice to meet you, Zeke. That was a really impressive demonstration. It was like watching Excalibur being forged," she said, thinking she was being witty by throwing in a bit of King Arthur lore.

"Ha, thank you, but I'm not sure this sword is up to that caliber. Your accent, it's American. What's brought you here to Northern Wales?" he asked, giving her a charming smile that made her stomach flip. Not only was he handsome, but there was something primal about a man who could turn steel into a sword.

"I came for the reading of my grandmother's will," she said, wishing she had a less morose reason.

"I'm sorry to hear that," he said, his dashing smile fading with the turn of the conversation.

"Yes, her grandmother was Betty Shortbridge," John said.

"Oh, I didn't know her well, but she always waved to me when I passed by if she was weeding her flower beds," Zeke said.

"How do you two know each other?" Ionna asked, eager to change the subject. She was good at that, deflecting conversations back onto other people. It was a valuable skill to have as a reporter.

"Zeke and I are old friends from uni," John explained. "He moved up this way, and I stayed in the big city."

"It's true, I was not cut out for city life," Zeke joked. He dipped his hands in a bucket of water next to his forge and washed them off. "I much prefer the rural life. How long have you guys been at the market?"

"Most of the day. We're actually heading out now. I just wanted to stop over and say hi before we left. It was nice seeing you, mate. It's been too long. We should grab a beer while I'm in town."

"Yeah, that'd be great. Here, hit me up when you're free," Zeke said, handing him a business card. "My mobile is on the back. It was really nice meeting you, Ionna." He gave her a flirtatious smile.

"Same," she said, feeling a blush burn in her cheeks.

"Sounds good. Catch up with you later, mate," John said, turning toward the opening to the market, Ionna following behind.

The drive back was filled with lively chit-chat as John entertained her with tales of his childhood and a few about him and

Zeke's wild college days. As they grew closer to Beddgelert, the conversation changed from funny stories about Zeke saving John in a swimming pool after jumping off a balcony to John's love of the city.

"Don't get me wrong. I love coming back home to the country but I have a thirst for culture that this area just can't quench. You know what I mean?" he asked her.

"Yeah, I get that. But, I think I prefer the more chill pace of small-town life. I'll stick to getting my culture from books and the travel channel," she joked. It was true, though. She never did like the city much. She had gone to college in Portland, Maine, and hated every second of it, driving home every chance she got.

"Ha, well, I at least hope you indulge in a fine glass of wine while you watch the travel channel," he joked.

"Always." She laughed.

John was so easygoing and fun to be around; it was as if they had known each other for years, not days.

Before she knew it, they were pulling into the farm just as the sun was slowly dipping behind the mountain, painting the field and lawn with long shadows set against an amber hue that lingered upon everything the sun touched.

"Thank you, John. I had a great time today," Ionna told him as he put the car into park.

"You're more than welcome. It was fun," he said, looking at her.

His eyes made her want to melt as she stared into them. She waited a moment, hoping that he might lean in for a kiss.

"Do you want to come in?" she asked when the moment had passed. She knew it was a bit presumptuous, but they were both adults and they had great chemistry together. Her stomach did flip-flops as she waited for his reply.

"I would love to but I have to pick up my husband from the train station in an hour. I have just enough time to swing in and say hi to my brother before I go get him. But we'll see you tomorrow. Ryan and I will come by in the afternoon. Maybe with some information about your dad for you," he said, smiling.

"Okay, that sounds great. See you guys tomorrow then," she said, practically leaping out of the car and hoping beyond hell he hadn't seen the look of disappointment cross her face.

She was halfway to the house when he called out to her.

"Hey, your pie and books!" He jumped out of the car and ran them up to her.

"Thanks, John. I completely forgot about them."

"No problem. Have a great night, Ionna."

Ionna couldn't get into the house quickly enough. As soon as she opened the door, Jasper was there to greet her, making S curves around her legs as if to say hello. She rested against the door and slid down until her butt hit the floor. Jasper jumped up into her lap.

"You could have told me he was gay. Would have saved me a whole lot of flirting, which I am not very good at," she said to the cat.

Of course John was gay. He was perfect and handsome, had a good job, a sense of humor, and she was actually interested in him. This was typical of her; she almost always fell for someone who was unattainable. This was not the first time it had happened, and she knew it wouldn't be the last. She was just not good at the whole dating game, which was why she never played it.

"Trust your instincts, they're almost never wrong," she said, mimicking the fortune teller's words. "Ha! Well, that's one way to tell the woman was totally full of shit. My instincts are about as good as a broken compass."

She looked down at the cat as if he might offer some wisdom, but he just blinked his green eyes slowly at her.

"Well, I'm beat. I guess it's just you and me tonight, Jasper. How about we eat some junk food and do a bit of reading in bed?"

She placed him on the ground and stood up, picking up her bags from the market. She went into the kitchen and took the pie out of the bag, then went to the cupboard for a plate. But something stopped her.

A loud creaking sound echoed from inside the living room. It was the same sound the floorboards made when someone walked on them.

The hairs on the back of her neck rose. Her heart sped up in her chest like an indie racecar as she grabbed a knife out of the cutlery drawer. As quietly as she could, she walked toward the living room, knife held out in front of her as she peeked around the doorway and into the shadows. She ran her free hand along the wall, looking for a switch that had not been there the day before. Yet, as her hand swept the edge of the wall, she found one, and with a flick of her pointer finger, the room was set aglow.

No one was there. Everything seemed to be in its place. But there was an eerie feeling, as if someone had just been in there, their energy leaving its mark on the room. Heart still pounding, she searched for a viable explanation for the sound she heard. Maybe it was the wind outside, moaning as it passed.

After giving the room one more full inspection, knife still in hand, she found nothing. She turned off the lights, looking over her shoulder one last time, before heading back to the kitchen.

She walked back over to the pie and then thought *Fuck it*, she wasn't in the mood for pie anymore, so she grabbed the Cheerios box and a bottle of wine instead. She tucked the cereal under her arm, held the wine bottle in one hand and her bag of books from the market in the other, then made her way into the bedroom.

When she entered the room, she inspected it for light switches and an overhead light. Sure enough, there were both.

"What the hell is going on? I swear there were no lights in this place yesterday. I think I'm going bat-shit crazy here. God help me," she muttered to herself as she flicked the light on. She hoped it had just been the jet lag playing tricks on her mind, but another thought lingered. Perhaps the house was haunted. Her grandmother had *died* right in the kitchen, after all.

She set the bag of books on the bed and the bottle and cereal box on the nightstand, then stripped down to her T-shirt and underwear and climbed into bed. Jasper was already ahead of her, curled up on one of the pillows, purring away.

Ionna unscrewed the wine top and took a slug, looking at the cereal box and deciding the wine made a better dinner. Sitting cross-legged, she took out one of the books from the bag and flipped it open. The room became rich with the scent of old books. The smell sent a feeling of longing through her but for something she couldn't quite put her finger on.

The book's pages were yellowed with age on the outer edges but crisp white in their centers, giving them an ombre effect. The paper was frail, making her take her time as she turned them. She scrolled through the book until the title of one particular tale caught her eye. It was called "Lady of the Lake." She remembered this tale; it was one her father had told her many times as a child. King Arthur's stories were some of her father's favorites, which made so much more sense to her now. They must have been the tales he grew up with here, in this very house.

She began to read the story, but it was not the tale her father told her as a child. This was the tale of a goddess who came out of the lake's waters to marry a human man, only to leave him and their three sons when a spell placed upon her was broken.

The story was dark and left her with a sadness she couldn't quite explain. It lingered with her as she tried to distract herself with other tales from the book. Soon, the wine began to kick in, and on top of the busy day, she soon drifted off to sleep, the book falling to her side as she broke away into the dream realm.

Chapter Twenty-Three
Kate
LADY OF THE LAKE

By the time Kate and her grandmother arrived home and put away their things from the market, they were both tired and hungry. After some persuading, Kate convinced her grandmother to let her order pizza for dinner from one of the only local restaurants that had a delivery service. There was no need for one of her three-course meals when she was obviously exhausted from their day out. It was at times like this that her grandmother's age began to show, and it sent a feeling of worry through Kate, knowing her years were now numbered.

While they waited, they turned on the TV and relaxed side by side on the plaid sofa. Her grandmother flipped through the channels until she landed on a documentary on the History Channel about Welsh highland folklore.

"Oh, look at this. Your grandfather loved this stuff. Do you remember the story he used to tell you about Lady of the Lake?"

Kate thought for a moment. "Oh yeah, was that the one about the woman who came out of the lake and married a man from the village?"

"Yes! Your grandfather swore his ancestors were direct descendants of one of the lady's three sons. We have a book somewhere that shows the lineage all the way back to one of the sons of Einion, who would have been your far-off great-grandfather of sorts." She lifted herself from the sofa and went over to the bookshelf on the wall behind the TV.

Running her frail fingers across the spines of the old books, she was halfway along the fourth shelf when she stopped and tipped out the corner of a book. She slid it off into her hands, turning it around and dusting off its edges.

"Here it is. Your grandfather loved looking through this. It's a family history of sorts. He must have read it front to back more times than I could count. It always seemed like he was searching for something hidden in the pages. God only knows now if he ever found it," she said, nostalgia thick in her voice. Smiling down at the book, she ran her hand across its cover, then turned to Kate. "I know how much you love reading. You might find it interesting."

Kate was now sprawled out on the couch, head cocked at an odd angle to see the TV from her position. "Cool, I'll have a look at it tonight when I go to bed," she said as her grandmother handed her the book. It was highly unlikely she would even pick it up again, but she wanted to appease her grandmother. She had little to no interest in genealogy—that kind of stuff bored the crap out of her. Knowing her parents was more than enough family history for her. She much preferred getting lost in fiction—in fact, she was looking forward to finishing *The Outsider* later on, which was waiting for her on her nightstand.

The documentary cut to a commercial just as there was a knock on the door. Kate jumped to her feet to answer it.

"I got it," she told her grandmother, setting the book down on the coffee table and heading over to the front door.

The pizza had taken much longer to arrive than it should have, and she was starving. When she opened the door, a teenage boy around her age with greasy black hair and an aquiline nose greeted her with a large pizza box in hand. He looked annoyed.

"Hi, did you order a double cheese pizza with bacon and olives?" he asked in a voice much deeper than should have been possible coming out of a guy his size.

"Yup," Kate answered as she pulled out the leftover cash she had stuffed into her pants pocket from the market.

"No charge," he said, handing her the pizza box. "There was a freak accident up the road, so we didn't get you the pizza on time. If it's over twenty minutes, it's free," he said, pointing to a slogan on his shirt that said "Montebello's Pizzeria guarantees 20 minutes or it's free."

"Oh, cool. Well, here's a tip for the delivery at least," Kate said, handing him five pounds. "What kind of accident?" she asked curiously.

"Thanks," he said, pocketing the cash before going on. "Totally weird. It was MacClure sheep farm on the edge of town. The entire flock drowned themselves in the river." The boy paused, shuddering a little. "That river isn't even deep. For forty-plus sheep to drown in it seems nuts to me. They had to shut the road down while they dragged the bodies out." He looked at her with wide, questioning eyes, as though she might be able to conjure an explanation that made sense.

"Oh my God. That's so awful. And disturbing. How does

something like that even happen?" Kate said.

"Right? I don't know, maybe the town has a curse on it or something," he joked, but Kate could see the deep unease in his eyes.

"That's as good a guess as any," Kate said, unsure what else to say.

"Yeah. Well, anyway. Thanks for the tip. Enjoy your night," he said, turning and heading back to his car.

Kate shut the door and took the pizza to the kitchen, where she found her grandmother pulling two plates from the cupboard. Kate flipped the box open, and to her surprise, the pizza was still warm. A thin wisp of steam rose up and filled the room with the smell of cheese and Italian spices.

"Oh, that smells wonderful. It's been ages since I had pizza. I'm glad you suggested it, Kate," her grandmother said, reaching into the box and pulling out a slice, thick with cheese fringe dangling off the sides. She handed Kate a plate and went back into the living room, placing hers on one of the foldable TV trays that sat next to each recliner.

Kate grabbed herself two slices and followed her grandmother, setting her plate on the other tray closest to the sofa.

"Nana, did you hear what that guy said about the MacClure farm?"

"No, what about it?" she asked, dabbing a bit of grease off her chin.

"The whole flock drowned in the Colwyn. Like, more than forty sheep. Isn't that crazy?"

"*What?* How could that even be? He must have been mistaken."

"He wasn't," Kate said. "He said the road was closed so they could ... remove the bodies." She set down her pizza, her stomach turning at the thought of all those dead sheep floating in the river.

"Why would they do that?"

"I have no idea," her grandmother said, her face drawn with concern. "I've never heard of something like that happening. One or two sheep during a storm, yes, but to lose the whole herd … and that river's no more than a few feet deep! Poor Gareth, that farm was barely surviving as it was. I hope that boy was wrong."

They sat there, letting the television fill the empty space in the wake of their conversation. Both of their minds turned to the possibilities of what had scared the sheep so badly that they ran for the river. It was an unsettling thought. The documentary played out, but neither of them were really watching it.

When it was over, her grandmother got up from her recliner and put her dish in the sink.

"I'm going to head off to bed, dear. Goodnight," she said.

"Goodnight, Nana. Sweet dreams."

Kate watched her grandmother make her slow ascent up the old staircase. It had been a long day and now that her stomach was full, the tiredness was kicking in, and Kate was also ready to call it a night. She turned off the TV and the two side lamps in the living room and headed for the stairs.

Catching a glimpse of her grandfather's book out of the corner of her eye, she stopped. She had told her grandmother she would have a look at it, so she turned around and grabbed it. Even if she had no intention of reading it, at least it would look like she had if she brought it up to her room. She tucked it under her arm and headed up to bed.

When she opened her bedroom door, a chilly breeze blew past her and into the hallway, as if to escape down the stairs. She walked over to shut the window but saw it was already closed. It felt drafty in her room, but she couldn't find the cause of the cold. Where was the chill coming from? Instead of stripping down into her PJs, she opted for her Paris sweatshirt and jumped into bed, turned off her lamp, and pulled the covers up to her chin to warm up.

She lay there a long time, completely exhausted but unable to fall asleep. She tossed and turned, but the harder she tried to shut her mind off, the further sleep eluded her. Finally, she sat up and turned the lamp back on, reaching for her novel. Mid-reach, she changed her mind and grabbed her grandfather's book instead, thinking it would be so boring it might lull her to sleep.

She ran her hands over the smooth red leather surface and flipped open the cover. She was surprised to see it was a handwritten book with names, dates, and stories all scribed in it. The first part seemed to have been written hundreds of years ago. There were pages of names and birth and death dates. Marriages, children, towns, and stories. Some of the handwriting was faded out or altogether too hard to read due to penmanship, but for the most part, she was able to decipher it. Punctuating some of the margins were single words or names, some with question marks next to them and some with lines through them. The further into the book she got, the more modern and legible the writing became. She skimmed around the book, flipping page after page until she came across one with bold handwriting on the top that read "Lady of the Lake." She stopped. This was the story her grandfather had told her at bedtime when she was little. A pang of sadness passed through her at the thought. She sat upright and began to read.

The story had been penned in onyx-black ink with what Kate guessed was a quill, going by the small inky blots that pooled around some of the letters. It read:

> One day, a young man named Rhiwallon peered dreamily into the cool, clear waters of Llyn Y Fan Fach Lake and was astounded to see the shape of a beautiful

lady gently emerging from the water towards him. He'd never seen a woman so beautiful in his life and fell in love with her instantly. He didn't know whether she was a fairy or one of the ancient goddesses, but she was most certainly a magical creature. He was immediately captivated by her beauty.

She introduced herself as Nyneve and told him about the future she envisioned for him, promising that if he accepted her marriage proposal, he would become wealthy and respected. Rhiwallon was so charmed he would have done whatever she requested, even if it didn't come with the benefits of riches and status, so he gladly accepted. However, there were a few conditions in order for him to marry her. The first requirement was that he never, ever strike her. If he did so three times, she would be forced to return to the lake. The second was that he must keep her origins hidden and never divulge the magical foundation of their love and good fortune to anyone. These terms were easily accepted by him, and he took her hand, leading them back to his home.

Rhiwallon's sheep became larger after the wedding and produced many lambs that year. He became a wealthy man as his farm expanded, as did his wife's belly. They were happy for many years until, one day, on their way to a friend's wedding, the man smacked his wife playfully on her back with a pair of gloves. She turned to face him and told him he had struck her.

The second incident occurred at a village baptism when his wife began to sob while everyone else joyfully cooed over the baby. Rhiwallon patted his wife on the shoulder slightly harder than normal and inquired as to the cause of her tears. Nyneve, who had the gift of foresight, informed him that she could see that the unfortunate infant's life would be brief, which made her weep. She then warned him that he had just struck her for a second time and reminded him of their marriage conditions. He didn't understand, for his actions had not been in anger. He pleaded for forgiveness, promising never to strike again.

The third incident came at the burial of the child whose baptism they had attended. While everyone wept for the child, Nyneve burst out laughing. Dumbfounded, he patted her on the shoulder and inquired why she was laughing during such a tragic event. She told him that, with her second sight, she could see the child in another realm, free of pain and happy. She also informed him that he had struck her for the third and final time, and their marriage had come to an end.

As if under a spell, she turned and walked out of the church and back toward the lake from which she had come. Driven by a force beyond her control, she traveled their land, the animals following her to the lake. Rhiwallon and his three sons ran after her, sobbing and pleading with her to stay, but she didn't seem to hear them. She stepped into the cool waters of the lake, disappearing under its surface, followed by all of the animals. Rhiwallon mourned the loss of his wife and spent the rest of his days filled with sorrow and regret.

Their three sons often traveled to the lake in search of their mother, with little success, until one day, during a solar eclipse, she emerged from the water. She sat with them and taught them the techniques of healing and herbalism and assured them they would be renowned healers and that they would be known as the Physicians of Myddfai.

And so it was, the three sons became well known as the Physicians of Myddfai. Their ancient remedies have been preserved in the *Red Book of Hergest*.

Finishing the story, Kate glanced around her room. It was eerily silent, and the darkness outside had now fully encroached, the only light coming from the lamp on her nightstand. She wondered what had happened to the magic lamp. She felt like a child again, unable to sleep, afraid of what the shadows held.

So much for boring old stories, she thought. Now she was even more awake. She began studying the margins of the book where words were scribbled in cursive. They were a bit hard to decipher at first, especially in the low light, but as she brought the book closer, she could make out three names: Cadwgan, Gruffudd, and Einion. "Einion" was underlined, and underneath was the word "descendant."

Turning the page, she found a family tree spread out across both pages. At the top of the tree were the names Rhiwallon and Nyneve, Lady of the Lake. Below them were the names of their three sons, Cadwgan, Gruffudd, and Einion, and their wives. From there, the tree expanded with children, grandchildren, great-grandchildren, and so on.

As Kate followed the tree to its lower branches, she found her grandfather's name, her mother's, and then hers, all broken off from Einion's lineage. A chill ran up her fingertips and into her body as she traced her finger over their names. Was she descended from the actual lady of the lake? It was a bit unbelievable; more likely, the tale had been spun to hide the real reason the woman had gone missing. Then, perhaps, over time, it had become folklore.

Nevertheless, it seemed like whoever did the family genealogy had done a thorough job of it. She thought back to what the fortune teller had told her: *"You have marks that seem to be from another realm altogether."* The words raced through her mind as she stared down at the family tree, trying her best to find a logical explanation for everything. The magic lamp. The mysterious blankness of her memories around that last summer. The cabin in the woods …

It was no use. She could feel deep in her bones that what she was reading was all true.

Chapter Twenty-Four
Kate
BRANGWEN

Kate was coaxed from her sleep the following morning by the first rays of sunlight penetrating her eyelids. Somewhere in the distance, she could hear birds chirping as she rolled over and sat up, wiping sleep from her eyes.

Something felt wrong. As her hands dropped away from her eyes, they touched something cool and wet.

She looked down.

Instead of the soft, warm bedding of her grandmother's guest room, she found fresh, dewy grass.

Whipping her head up, she looked around. She was on a small patch of grass between two boulders. In front of her was a pristine lake tucked between two large mountains that loomed over it. A hot seam of panic rose in her. She couldn't see a house or anything she recognized in any direction.

Then, as if she had materialized from the water itself, a beautiful woman stood before her at the lake's edge.

"Go, my child. You are needed back in your own time. There are important things you must do to protect the ones you love," she said in a voice as sweet and soft as a summer's day.

In complete shock, Kate scrambled to her feet, and as she did, something dropped from her lap, landing squarely on her foot with some force.

Crying out in pain, she looked down. There, resting open against her bare foot, was her grandfather's book and a large red welt forming where it had landed. Kate quickly bent down to retrieve it.

As she straightened, she was once more standing in the center of her grandmother's guest bedroom.

"What the hell?" she said, looking down at the book in her hands.

It was open to one of the older pages where the handwriting was faded with age, yet one word stood out. In fact, it didn't just stand out, it jumped out. There, in the margin, was the word "Timewalker."

What in the hell had just happened? She must have been sleepwalking, and the book hitting her foot sent her crashing back to reality. It had to have been a dream; she had been reading her grandfather's book before she fell asleep. But it had felt so real—she could still smell the earthy scent of the wet ground where she had woken up. And the woman, had she been Nyneve?

It was then that she looked down at her feet. Not only was there a large red welt turning a dark shade of purple, but bits of mud and grass peeked out from between her toes.

Kate went over to the bed and sat down, leaving a trail of muddy footprints on the hardwood floor as she went. There on the yellowed page of the book was the tale of Einion's great-great-great-granddaughter. Her name was Brangwen, and she was from the village of Llanfair. The first part of the page told of her birth and lineage, but it was the second half that really sparked Kate's interest. There, scrolled in deep burgundy ink, it read:

In the ancient land of Caernarfon, there lived a couple named Seren and Deri. They were humble villagers, content with their simple lives. On the twenty-second day of the month of October in the year of Our Lord 1402, a remarkable event took place—the birth of their daughter, Brangwen.

The night of Brangwen's arrival was filled with enchantment. The full harvest moon, shining brightly in the sky, suddenly vanished, enveloped by a total lunar eclipse. With the disappearance of the moon, an unusual warmth swept through the air, as if the breath of summer itself had embraced the world. It was at this extraordinary moment that Brangwen came into existence, born into a world devoid of the moon's gentle glow. This in turn earned her the name Brangwen Awel, meaning "dark wind."

However, the villagers did not welcome Brangwen's arrival with open arms. They believed that her birth had brought a curse upon the land. Shortly after she was born, the barley crops were plagued by a mysterious white mold, leading the villagers to whisper of dark forces at play. Some even speculated that Brangwen was the daughter of darkness, conceived by her mother's unholy union with the Devil himself.

Unable to endure the torment and accusations any longer, Seren and Deri were forced to leave their village behind. In search of a place where the knowledge of Brangwen's birth had not reached, they journeyed north and settled in the small village of Bekelert. There, nestled between the mountains, was their new home, a place to build a fresh life and raise their beloved Brangwen.

As the years passed, Brangwen blossomed into a young woman of remarkable beauty. Her golden hair flowed like liquid sunshine, and her eyes sparkled a vivid blue, mirroring the sky itself. Yet, it was not just her physical appearance that set her apart. Brangwen possessed a heart brimming with kindness and generosity. She was known throughout the village for her selflessness, always giving more than was required, even if it meant sacrificing her own well-being.

Brangwen learned the ways of a healer by assisting her mother, Seren, who was a respected midwife in the village. One fateful day, they were called upon to aid a woman in labor. Sensing that something was amiss upon their arrival, they discovered that the woman was suffering from excessive bleeding.

Seren, wise in her knowledge of remedies, instructed Brangwen to fetch a tincture of hawthorn berry and nettle from their stores. Brangwen hurried to their home, her feet flying over the path, and retrieved the life-saving herbs. However, when she returned, she found the woman and her newborn child lifeless, lost to the world beyond.

Overwhelmed with guilt and unable to bear the sound of the grieving husband's sorrow, Brangwen stepped outside into the cool embrace of the autumn day. She rested her head in her hands, cursing they had not brought the tincture with them in the first place and wishing it were so. To her bewilderment, when she lifted her head, she found herself back in her croft. Seren stood before her, packing her birthing sack, as if the events of the day had yet to unfold. Confused, Brangwen questioned her mother. Seren told Brangwen to hurry, reminding her of the urgent need to attend the birth.

Brangwen, still bewildered but compelled to trust her mother's words, chased after Seren toward the home of the laboring woman. Brangwen called out to her mother, asking if she had brought the tincture of hawthorn berry and nettle. Seren halted in her tracks, turning to face Brangwen, and motioned for her to turn back and retrieve the herbs. Brangwen's legs carried her swiftly back to their dwelling, and she retrieved the tiny bottle of life-preserving potion. With urgency, she raced down the hill, back to the woman's home.

Upon her arrival, Brangwen was greeted by the cries of a woman in labor. She entered the room, surprised to see the woman, who was thought to have perished, lay alive and in labor. Seren beckoned for the tincture, and Brangwen handed it over without hesitation. Within the hour, the baby was born, and mother and child were safe. Seren, her curiosity piqued, questioned Brangwen about her seemingly prophetic knowledge of the dire need for the medicine. Brangwen, unable to explain her newfound ability, stood silent, her mind awash with unanswered questions.

Initially, Brangwen believed her ability to perceive future events was a mere premonition, occurring only when her emotions were heightened. However, with the passage of time and years of practice, she learned to control her extraordinary gift. She could now "time walk" whenever she desired. Brangwen's reputation as a healer grew far and wide, and she was revered for her vast knowledge of herbs and countless lives saved. Only a select few were aware of her ability to traverse time, for she understood the possible consequences of meddling with the course of fate.

Guided by her innate wisdom, Brangwen lived a long and fulfilled life, reaching the ripe age of eighty. Throughout her journey, she only utilized her time-walking abilities on a handful of occasions and always only in dire situations. She understood that her power was a rare and precious gift, passed down through the generations of her bloodline. Legend had it that The Lady of the Lake, a mystical being of ancient origins, bestowed the power of the Timewalker upon the most exceptional members of her son, Einion's lineage. Born on the darkest of nights, two hundred years apart, Brangwen was a vessel of this extraordinary legacy.

"Wow," Kate murmured.

A Timewalker.

Was that what she was? She sat there for a long moment, looking at the word scrolled on the aged paper. A feeling of excitement built in her as she realized this might explain the weird memories that had been floating around in her head since she arrived.

She jumped to her feet, threw on a new set of clothes, and rushed downstairs with the book tucked under her arm. She needed to show it to Owen. As she rounded the corner into the kitchen, she came upon her grandmother, already cooking up her morning feast.

"Good morning! Sleep well? I didn't expect you up for at least another hour or so. I'll put more bacon on."

"Morning, Nana. Do you know Owen's phone number?"

"Yes, it's on the list on the fridge. It's a little early for calling, though, don't you think?"

Kate looked up at the weird little cuckoo clock above the microwave, its jumpy arms showing the time to be 6:23 a.m. Now she would have to wait at least another two hours before she could even think about calling Owen, and this new information was burning a hole in her. She picked up the newspaper in hopes it would preoccupy her when the phone rang.

"Who in the dickens would be calling at this hour?" her grandmother spat as she began to flip the bacon. "Can you get that for me, Kate?"

Kate walked over and picked up the old turd-brown phone that looked straight out of the nineteen seventies.

"Hello?"

"Kate? Good morning, it's Ben Dwyer."

"Oh, hi, Ben. How are—"

"Did you and your grandmother buy anything from the church bake sale at the market yesterday?" he interrupted her, getting the words out in a rush.

"Uh, no, I don't think so. Nana said the woman's pies were overpriced and never have enough sugar. Why?"

"Oh thank God." She heard Ben breathe a sigh of relief. "It's the bishop's wife who makes them. She's old. Somehow or another, she put *yew* berries in the pies instead of redcurrants. A lot of people are sick in hospital."

~ 213 ~

"Oh, my God, that's awful," Kate said. From the corner of her eye, she saw her grandmother pause her cooking to glance over.

"I know. An accident, of course, but terrible. I'm just happy you didn't buy anything from her," Ben said, the worry slipping from his tone.

"Yeah, me too," Kate said, looking over at her grandmother as she flipped the bacon once again. She didn't want to think about what might have happened if they had.

"Well, sorry again to phone so early, but I just wanted to check."

"No, thank you, that was really thoughtful. Um, Ben … is Owen up yet?" Kate asked as she twirled the phone cord around her finger.

"He's out at the barn just now, Kate. I can have him phone you when he gets back in."

"That's okay. I'll just walk up to the farm after breakfast. Can you tell him I'll be there around eight?"

"Can do. Oh, I almost forgot. I wanted to invite you and your grandmother over for dinner tonight. My brother is back in town and wants to see everyone before he leaves. Can you pass the invitation on for me? We can be each other's messengers today, eh," he said with a little chuckle.

"Sure, I'll let her know. Thanks," Kate said, hanging up the phone. She sat back down at the table and reached for the cup of steaming tea her grandmother had poured her during her talk with Ben.

"So what was that all about?" her grandmother asked.

"Nana, you're not going to believe this. You know that old lady selling pies for the church?"

"Sandra Sealy, that old bat. What did she do, give the town food poisoning?" she said, rolling her eyes.

"Well, kinda, yeah. Apparently, she put yew berries in the pies instead of redcurrants. Ben said a lot of the people who ate them are in hospital. He was phoning us to make sure we hadn't bought anything from her yesterday. What happens if you eat them? Is it like regular food poisoning or worse?" Kate asked.

"Oh, that's awful," her grandmother said, all traces of sarcastic joking gone. "Yew berries are very poisonous. Just a few can be deadly, never mind a whole pie. I don't know how she took them for currants, they're twice the size. And why would she even be picking yew berries to begin with?"

"That's really weird," Kate said, a sick feeling washing over her at the thought that the woman could have made such a life-threatening mistake. Or had it been intentional? She didn't know which would be worse.

"She's much too old to be baking things for the market," her grandmother continued, setting a plate of toast on the table. "She should have stopped years ago."

"Oh, come on, Nana, you're her age and you're still cooking up a storm," Kate joked.

"Ahh! I'll have you know I *am* six years younger than her," she scoffed, smacking Kate lightly with a dish towel.

Kate laughed and then tossed a thin crust of toast at her, which her grandmother caught in mid-flight. At that moment, she was more than glad she had opted for a summer in the country with her, even if strange things kept happening. Chances were that if she were back home, she would just be sitting in front of the TV or mindlessly scrolling on her phone. Here, she felt more alive, like it was where she was truly meant to be.

"Oh, I forgot, Ben invited us over for dinner tonight. He said his brother's in town and wants to see everyone before he heads back."

"Oh, wonderful, a night off from cooking. I won't say no to that."

"I'll let him know we'll be there. I'm going to get cleaned up and head over. I think Owen and I are going to go out riding this morning up the ridge trail," she told her Nana as she finished the last bite of toast and got up from the table. The story from the book and the news about the pies were driving her forward to get to the farm as quickly as she could.

"But you only ate one piece of toast. Are you feeling okay? Normally, this whole pile of bacon would be in your belly before it even hit your plate," she joked as Kate pushed in her chair.

Kate grabbed three strips of bacon off the plate as she scooted past her.

"Who said you can't eat bacon in the shower?" she said, walking down the hallway to the bathroom, bacon waving in her hand like a flag.

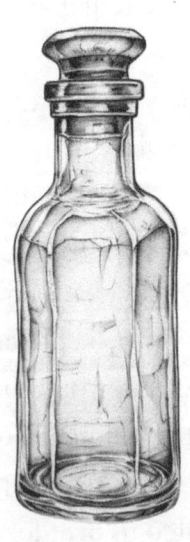

Chapter Twenty-Five
Kate
PREDATOR

Kate arrived at the farm shortly after eight that morning. As she walked down the long driveway, her thoughts kept returning to the story in the book she now clasped tightly in her hands. The experience of waking up in the middle of nowhere and the lingering impact of the mysterious woman's words had left her nerves on edge. As she walked, she traced her thumb along the edges of the book, trying to calm herself. Her mind was racing with everything she wanted to tell Owen, but the closer she got to the barn, the more she second-guessed whether or not she should say anything. Was he going to think she was completely mad?

When she crested the knoll, she spotted Owen standing outside the barn doors, looking up the driveway, as if he was perched there waiting for her to arrive. As soon as she came into view, he raised his arm above his head and waved hello, and her heart sank.

God, why did he have to be so attractive and charming? She was crushing on him hard, and now was not the time for butterflies. She had to keep her composure so they could decipher this book together and figure out what the hell it all meant.

Trying to shake off her nerves, she walked up to the barn and greeted him.

"Hey, you're up early. What's up?" he asked.

"I need to show you something. Something that's going to blow your mind."

"Okay, dish!" he said eagerly.

"Not here. Why don't we go for a ride? Are the horses up for it?" she asked, peeking into the barn at the horse stalls.

"Always," he answered, walking into the barn and pulling the tackle off the wall.

Kate sat down on the bench and pulled on the old riding boots, then grabbed an old backpack off one of the pegs above. Carefully, she tucked the book in, then pulled her arms through the straps while Owen got the horses ready and walked them out of the barn.

Ready in her boots and helmet, she walked over to Ginger and stroked her soft, velvety nose. There was something about her that calmed Kate into an almost meditative state. Just being in her proximity seemed to slow her heart. She stood there looking into the big dark eyes of her soul's companion, falling in sync with the horse's breathing. All the anxiety she was harboring from the morning's events dissipated as she stood there.

"Okay, all set. Let me just grab my helmet," Owen said, breaking Kate out of the trance she had fallen into. He grabbed an old sun-bleached helmet off the hook by Churchill's stall and clipped it on. "Here, let me help you up," he offered, picking Kate up and helping her onto Ginger's back.

Kate's heart was no longer beating slowly—Owen's touch set it to rapid fire, and she could feel her cheeks turning fifty shades of red. One of the downsides of being a ginger; there was zero hiding her emotions.

Once she was up and settled onto Ginger's back, she gave her one last stroke down the length of her neck and leaned down to whisper in her ear. "Let's give those guys a run for their money."

Owen mounted Churchill outside the barn doors, and they nudged the horses into a walk toward the field under the patchy morning sky. As soon as their hooves hit the soft cushion of the grassy field, Ginger and Kate took off in a full gallop toward the mountain.

"First to the trailhead eats grass," Kate yelled back. This time she felt at ease on the horse, riding her with confidence.

"Hey, that's not fair. You totally got a head start!" Owen yelled back, kicking his heels into Churchill's side, urging him to go faster.

Kate stayed ahead, but as they neared the trail, Owen was on her heels, and at the point where the woods split and the dark path sank into the dense woods, they were side by side.

"Well, I would say that was a tie," Owen said as he pulled on the reins to slow Churchill down as they drew closer to the trail opening.

"Ha! You wish. We were at least two beats ahead," Kate teased, giving him a victory smile before leading Ginger into the woods.

"Okay, so are you going to tell me what this is all about?" Owen asked.

The horses walked beside each other, rhythmic and steady.

"I found something last night. Something crazy. My nana pulled down a book that used to be my grandad's, full of family stories. At first, I wasn't even going to look at it—that genealogy crap bores the hell out of me. But then Nana said something about how my grandad had traced his family tree back to the actual lady of the lake. Do you know that folktale?" Kate asked. The image of the woman standing in the lake that morning flashed in her mind, sending an uneasy feeling through her.

"Of course. I used to have a book of old Welsh tales, and that was in it. It's just lore; she wasn't a real woman, you know?" Owen said.

"Yeah, well, that's what I thought too, but it turns out she *was* a real woman, and my granddad traced his bloodline back to her. My first thought was the story must have been, like, super exaggerated, a way to explain a wife leaving her husband kind of thing. But then I kept reading. That's when I came across this *other* story ..."

"You're kidding. There's no way your grandad was able to trace your family line back that far," Owen said in disbelief as he ducked under some low branches.

"He *did*. I brought the book with me to show you."

Kate slid one of the backpack straps off her shoulder and was about to swing it around into her lap when the hairs on the back of her neck rose, and an uneasy feeling came over her. She looked over at Owen—a worried look casting a shadow over his usually playful face.

The horses' ears perked up, and Churchill let out a loud snort.

"Something's not right," Owen said with worry in his voice. "The horses are sensing something. Let's pick up the pace a bit.

One of Murphy's hunting dogs might be up here in the woods or something."

He nudged Churchill to a quicker gait, and Kate followed suit with Ginger. The horses seemed as eager to be gone from this section of the forest as much as Kate and Owen were. They were moving quickly up the path when Kate realized the birds had stopped singing. It was then she caught sight of something large and fast streaking through the trees to her right. She whipped her head around. "Owen! Look!"

A sleek black animal was weaving quickly through the trees next to them. Her heart raced like a frightened rabbit, and she was overcome by the sensation of turning from predator to prey. Her hands gripped the reins tightly.

"Did you see that?" Kate asked, her voice high and thin with panic.

"We need to get to the cabin now!" Owen yelled. "Go!"

He kicked into Churchill's flanks as hard as he could, sending him into a full gallop up the trail. Kate did the same, keeping up with Owen and Churchill as they raced onward. She glanced to her left. The shadow raced in the woods next to them, keeping pace. Its long black body moved in and out of the thick undergrowth without slowing down. It was doing its best to gain on them, trying to cut them off at the next pass.

"Faster, Owen! It's almost on us!" Kate screeched, her voice strangled by fear as she pushed Ginger to the brink. The sound of the wind raced past her ears, and her quickening heartbeat was all that she could hear. Kate clung to the horse, the backpack slapping violently against her with each thud of Ginger's hooves.

Ginger began to slow, her age getting the better of her—Owen and Churchill were now strides ahead. From the corner of her eye, Kate saw the animal dart from the tree line. She turned and looked on in horror, her mind trying to take in what she was seeing: a black panther, only inches from striking Ginger's hindquarters, its claws glinting in the dappled light.

"Kate!" Owen cried out from somewhere ahead, seeing what was about to happen.

The panther lunged forward.

"No!" she screamed, as a surge of energy flashed through her body and her lungs tightened. She closed her eyes and braced herself for impact.

And then there was stillness.

The abrupt change of atmosphere was jarring, like a lightning strike on a cloudless day. She cautiously opened her eyes and found she was no longer flying up the trail on Ginger's back. Rather, she was slowly walking up the trail, the sun still beaming down, casting blotchy shadows on the forest floor. The world around her was calm, a harsh contrast to her rapidly beating heart. She was disoriented; her head was spinning from the sudden shift in events. *What just happened?*

It took her a minute to realize they were back at the start of the trail on the edge of the field. She looked over to see Owen riding next to her. He looked at her, eyes wide in amazement as he spun around to see the field behind them.

"Kate, did you just flip us back to before we rode up the trail?"

Kate just sat there on top of Ginger, looking up at the patchy sky, the sun breaking through the trees up ahead. "Did I?" she said to herself, confused and scared.

She looked back up the trail where they had just been moments before. She had no idea how she'd done it. It was as if her instincts had taken over, and the fear had caused her to jump time.

The lamp …

The cabin …

She realized then that every other time she had done this, it had been in response to some sort of fear. Even this morning by the lake, waking up in an unfamiliar place and then the appearance of the woman had frightened her, causing her to flip back to the safety of her bedroom at her grandparents' house.

"Was that a black panther?" she asked, looking back at Owen.

"Looked like one to me. I've heard stories about people spotting them in the mountains, but I always thought they were full of shit," he said. His eyes were wide. He looked just as shaken as she felt.

She sat silent for a moment, looking back up the path. "That's scary as hell. I guess that potter guy was right."

"Potter guy?" Owen asked.

"Nana was telling me the guy at the market who sold pottery was going on about seeing a panther in the woods behind his place. Guess he wasn't full of shit after all."

They fell quiet, both reflecting on how much worse things could have been if Kate hadn't flipped them when she did.

"How the hell did I just do that, Owen? I think I'm going completely mad."

Owen looked at her before speaking, as if he was trying to choose the right words for this very moment.

"Kate, I know this is hard for you, and you have tucked this part of yourself away for so long that you've all but forgotten it, but you're not crazy, you're incredible. You can do something most of us can only dream about. You have to embrace it and own it. You have to believe it. The lamp was never magic; it was you the whole time." He looked deep into her eyes as he spoke, and she felt his words resonate somewhere deep within her.

"Okay," she said, summoning her courage. "I think it's time you tell me what happened the summer I turned twelve. If I'm going to fully embrace this craziness, then I want to know what happened. I need to put these pieces of the puzzle back together so I can see it as a whole."

"Let's get back to the barn and talk," he said, nudging his heels into Churchill and turning him around. "I don't think the woods are a good idea anymore."

Kate followed as he led the horses back out into the field and headed toward the barn, leaving the dark predator behind but unknowingly walking into a new kind of danger.

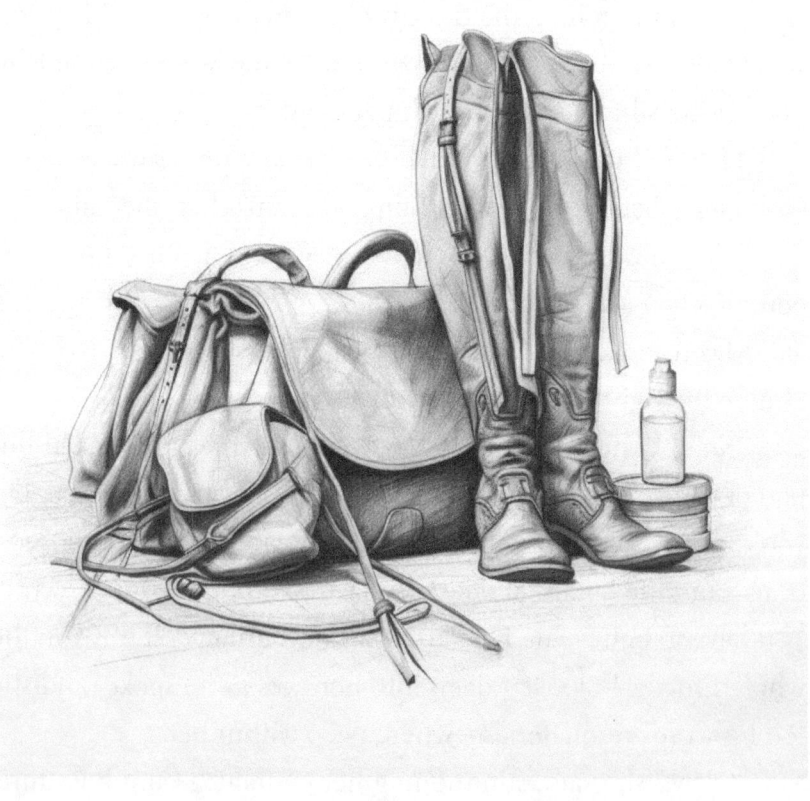

Chapter Twenty-Six
Kate
THE TRUTH

By the time they returned to the farm, the skies had darkened and it had begun to rain, churning up mud in the barnyard. A mix of relief and confusion flowed through Kate as they dismounted their horses and removed their riding equipment.

She picked up an old boar hair brush and began brushing out Ginger's wet coat.

"She's getting old," Owen said, patting Ginger's hindquarters.

"I know. I can see it in her eyes. The light in them seems a bit dimmer than it was just the other day," Kate said, stroking Ginger's head.

"You have a connection with her," Owen told her. "She usually isn't so relaxed, but for some reason, the moment she sees you, a calmness comes over her."

Kate looked at him and smiled as she grabbed some extra hay for Ginger and placed it in her stall. She was glad to know the horse felt the same around her, that they shared some kind of mutual comfort.

"So, want to go into the house and have some hot tea, and you can show me that book?" Owen suggested, hanging up the last of the tackle.

"Why don't we go up into the hayloft instead? I'm not sure this is something we can talk about in front of your dad and uncle."

Kate walked to the back of the barn where a ladder rested against the loft space above. She climbed up and clambered toward the window where hay was loaded in, then sat down on a bale in a pool of natural light, causing a cloud of dust and hay fibers to spring up around her. The loft smelled of fresh-cut hay and brought back a pang of nostalgia from her childhood.

Owen followed, grabbing a bale and placing it in front of Kate like a makeshift table. She unzipped the bag and pulled out the book.

"Okay, show me what your grandad found," Owen said, sitting down next to her.

Kate opened the book to the story of Brangwen and placed it on the bale in front of them. "Read this," she said, smoothing out the pages.

Owen leaned forward and began reading while Kate looked on. A few minutes passed as he took it all in, reading each line carefully. When he was finished, he looked up at Kate, his eyes wide with amazement.

"Holy shit, Kate. You're not the only one. It runs in your bloodline."

"I know. Even though I had all these, like, fractured memories of … time flipping"—she tested out the phrase—"I thought it was just me remembering wild stories we made up as kids. That was until I read this."

"I knew your memories would come back eventually," he said, looking at her.

Outside, the sun broke free of the clouds, and a stream of bright sunlight came in through the window, highlighting a sentence on the page. They both looked down at the words: *The Lady of the Lake vowed that every two hundred years, her power would be passed on to a descendant born during a total lunar eclipse.*

"Have you looked to see if there are any other stories that mention time travel?" Owen asked, picking the book up and turning its pages.

"No, as soon as I read that I went downstairs to phone you."

Owen flipped page after page while Kate looked on over his shoulder. He was skimming, looking for dates or any mention of a special ability, and then he stopped.

"Look at this," he said, pointing down at a passage scrolled in a dark rusty red handwriting different than the last. It read:

> Brynn, daughter of Glain and Arawn of Denbigh, was born on June 4, 1602, in the year of our Lord under a darkened moon. She was a wonderful baby with a delightful disposition. She demonstrated unnatural abilities as a child, such as the ability to move objects without touching them. In a time when anything beyond the normal abilities of man was seen as witchcraft, her parents tried desperately to hide her abilities. However, their efforts were for naught, and the poor child was accused and executed as a witch.

"Oh, my God. That's so sick, the poor thing," Kate said, aghast.

"This is crazy," Owen agreed, flipping the pages back to the first story and pointing down at the date. "Kate, look at the birthday—October twenty-second, 1402. That's two hundred years apart."

Owen flipped through the book again, looking for the next mention of a birthdate. Kate swiped at her eyes, not wanting to cry in front of him, but the story had struck her. Those were her ancestors. She couldn't bear to think of them being killed in such horrific circumstances. All because of a "gift." It didn't seem like much of a gift to her. More like a curse.

"Here we go again," Owen said, stopping on another page and pointing. "It says, 'On September eleventh, 1802, during a complete lunar eclipse, Alice Grant, daughter of Agatha and Edward Grant, was born. Alice was a pleasant child who demonstrated a great deal of potential in her academic pursuits. She developed into a stunning young lady who went on to play a significant role in the women's suffrage movement. She helped provide a path forward for ideas that were well beyond her time, earning her the nickname Future Thinker.'" Owen looked over at Kate, who was locked in a trance, staring down at the book. "I think we can guess why she had such forward-thinking ideas. And look, the dates match up again, exactly two hundred years apart," Owen said, setting the book back down in front of them on the bale of hay.

Kate bent forward and picked it up, running her hands over the right-hand corner of the page he had been reading. "Take a look at this; I first noticed it on the Brynn page and then again here. They all have the same mark in the upper right corner." She pointed to a small symbol near the top of the page. It was a Celtic knot with three points. Set within a circle, one point faced north, one east, and one west. "I know I've seen this symbol somewhere before," she said, trying to force herself to remember.

Owen took out his cell phone and jumped on the house's Wi-Fi, then began scrolling through some astronomy websites. "Okay, I know it's not much of a surprise now, but I'm sure you can guess what astrological event happened on June twenty-fourth, 2002, the night you were born."

Kate stopped reading and looked up at him. "How did you know my birthday?" she asked with an inquisitive smile. She certainly hadn't told him. Did he remember from all those years ago?

"I'm good with dates," he told her, his cheeks turning red.

In an attempt to skip over the awkward moment, Kate turned back to the book, landing on a page that made her heart still.

"Oh my God, Owen. Look at this." Her stomach grew sour as she digested the information laid out upon the page.

> Kate Jones was born on June 24, 2002, during a lunar eclipse, to Janice and Thomas Jones. She was an easy baby, an absolute gem, as all stories about these types of children note. Her abilities first manifested themselves when she was around seven years old here in Wales, and as far as I can tell, they only emerge while she is here. It began with small events such as shifting objects around the house. She wanted some sweets we had bought for her at the market but told her not until after dinner, placing them on the top cupboard out of reach. She threw an absolute tantrum on the floor of the kitchen, and before it was over, the sweets were sitting back on the table, as if they had just been taken out of the bag. Similar events took place over the next few summers she spent with us. By the time she was twelve, she was able to shift herself through

time. However, she had no control over her ability. Unfortunately, after discussing the events that happened during her time with us in the summer of 2014 with her mother, she refuses to allow her to return to spend time with us here in Wales. As a result, I am no longer able to track her progress for family records.

"Wow. So your grandad knew the whole time what was going on," Owen said, looking at Kate, who was now as pale as one of the sheets of paper in the book.

"He knew the entire time, and he was observing me like a lab rat. Was he just going to sit back and let me mess around with this until I lost myself in time — or worse?" She stood up and threw the book to the ground. "This is all so fucked up. I have no idea what to even think. This is why my mother never let me come back here. She must have thought my grandad was completely mad. Okay, I really need to know what happened now. You have to tell me, Owen," Kate pleaded as she bent down and picked the book back up, wiping straw and dirt from its cover.

"Are you sure you really want to talk about that now? After everything you just found out? Seems like a lot to take in," Owen said, concern in his voice.

Kate set the book down and went to the window overlooking the back field to the trail that led to the mountain. Sunlight fell upon the wet ground, making the wheat in the field sparkle like it was full of magic. Then as quickly as it came, the clouds covered the sun and muted the world outside the window. In Kate's mind, too, small flashes of memories moved in and out of the gloom. No memory was fully formed, just fragments, shattered into bits that made no sense to her. She turned back and looked at Owen.

"I want to know," she said firmly, letting him know with the strength in her voice that she was strong enough to withstand the mental load.

Owen walked over and rested his hand on her shoulder, brushing her long ginger locks aside. Kate's heart stopped. All the pain and confusion seemed to melt away at his touch.

"I'll tell you. But let's sit down. It's not an easy story to tell, and it's going to take some time for you to wrap your head around this," he told her.

Together they sat on a wide bale of hay, and Kate steeled herself for what was to come.

"It all happened about two weeks before the end of summer," Owen began. "We'd been trying to sneak some biscuits that my dad baked for the market when he caught us. I had the bright idea for you to use your ability to go back and grab a bag before he walked in and caught us. So, we went and hid in the living room behind the sofa. You closed your eyes and held my hands and then you vanished. For some reason, I didn't travel back with you that time. So, I sat behind the couch and waited for you to come back. But then you didn't. I don't know how long I waited. But I was panicking. Eventually, I went and told my dad that we were playing hide and seek and I couldn't find you. After an hour of looking, he called your grandparents. Your grandfather came and helped with the search." Owen stopped. A look of understanding came across his face before he went on. "He was so calm through the whole thing; I never could quite understand why. But it all makes sense now. He must have known what happened and knew it was only a matter of time before you flipped back."

Kate felt an ache in the pit of her stomach. It rose up, tightening in her chest. She was starting to second-guess this. Maybe she should stop Owen and pick it up another day. But before she could gather her voice, he continued.

"I convinced Dad to go up to the cabin to see if maybe you were there. But when we arrived, it was empty. I had this … *sinking* feeling you might never come back, and I felt like it was all my fault for putting the stupid biscuit idea in your head. By that night, everyone who lived on the road was out looking for you, convinced you had wandered off and got lost. Your nana, however, was in a complete panic, thinking you had been kidnapped. I prayed you hadn't got lost in time or been captured in some medieval century. Then, out of nowhere, you came riding up the road from Betty's house on a horse. Your face was dirty. You were crying. I'll never forget that. You looked like you'd seen a ghost."

Kate got up and went to the window again, looking out toward the mountain.

"It was Ginger, the horse I rode back on, wasn't it? We named her that because it was ginger cookies we had been after that day." She turned around, looking at Owen.

"Yes," he answered, waiting to see if she might remember anything else. When nothing came, he continued. "Your grandad took you home right away before anyone could ask where you'd been. I didn't hear from you or see you for four days after that. Finally, my dad let me walk over to your grandparents' house. When I got there, you were outside, sitting in the field, watching a fox cub playing in the flowers. You told me to be quiet and I sat next to you and we watched him until he ran off. Then you told me where you were. What had happened."

A memory started to emerge in Kate's mind. She could see them in the field. It had been a sunny day, and the wildflowers were in full bloom, towering over their heads as they sat deep in the field's grassy border. Owen's awkward twelve-year-old face stared back at hers, full of worry as he asked her what happened.

A sharp pain lanced in her head, and the memory faded into a pool of inky darkness.

"What did I tell you?" she asked.

"You told me that … you had tried to flip yourself back to right before my dad came in and caught us stealing the biscuits, but something went wrong. You ended up not only back in time but in a different place altogether. You thought you were gone for days, not hours, but you wouldn't tell me what happened. You kept saying you were afraid it had followed you back and that you hoped the baby was going to be okay. I don't know what exactly you meant by that. I don't know what happened to you when you were gone. But whatever it was, it scared you so badly that you refused to even come out of your room until that day."

"It was the fox," Kate said. "I saw it from my bedroom window in the field and went down to watch it. It was the one thing that drew me out."

"Do you remember anything else? Anything from when you disappeared?" Owen asked.

"No," she said. "Every time I try to remember, it's like a shade gets pulled down over my memories and blocks me from retrieving them. Whatever happened to me must have been bad. Bad enough that my mind doesn't want me to remember."

Chapter Twenty-Seven

Ionna

OCEANS APART

The stone house was chilly that morning as Ionna sipped her coffee at the kitchen table, trying to warm herself up. She wasn't quite sure if it was the chill in the house or a lingering feeling from the disturbing dream she'd had the night before, but she felt a sense of restlessness about her.

She had fallen asleep with a head full of questions and a stomach full of wine, creating the perfect cocktail for a night of disrupted sleep.

In the dream, she was beneath a canopy of trees that hung over a twisting trail that boarded a ridgeline. The leaves were at their fullest, and the trail was deeply shaded from the sun, which hung high in the sky, its rays beating down harshly on all that wasn't beneath the protection of the tree's outstretched arms. The dense undergrowth covered every inch of the forest floor, making the trail's rich brown soil stand out in stark contrast.

Ionna walked behind an older man up the winding path. There was a visible break in the trees up ahead, the sun illuminating the end of their journey. As they approached the opening, the salty smell of the sea greeted them, and gulls circled the cliff edge, their cries piercing and keen.

They stepped out into the brightness of the day and made their way to the top of the lookout point. She looked over at him. His soulful eyes stared back at hers, a kind smile creasing his aged face. She did not recognize him, yet her heart knew him well. She was overcome with a flood of emotions, rimming her eyes with tears.

The sun moved behind a cloud, muting the once vibrant horizon. They turned and faced the ocean together, looking out over its vastness, the rhythmic crash of the waves below locking them into a trance.

When the sun broke free of the clouds again, it was making its slow descent in the sky, painting it with hues of golds and pinks.

Still spellbound by the sea's call, they stood transfixed as the day slowly melted into night. She felt as if she could stay in that moment, standing there with this man forever, surrounded by a kind of peace she hadn't known before.

The light soon faded, and the moon echoed its silvery white reflection down into the sea when a violent scream broke them from their spell, the moon now covered in murky darkness. A shot of fear raced through her at the sound.

Looking at one another, they realized they were on opposite sides of a violent sea, no longer side by side but oceans apart. The feeling of fear and helplessness filled every ounce of her being.

The harsh realization they might never reach each other again struck her just like the sting of the sea had. Across the churning waters she saw the man begin to age rapidly. Before her eyes, he turned to nothing more than a pile of dust that was swept away by the harsh sea winds. She opened her mouth to let out a scream but nothing came forth other than a muted breath of air. A feeling of overwhelming loss and grief struck her like a bolt of lightning.

That was when she woke up.

After that, she'd tossed and turned all night, unable to shake the awful feeling the dream had invoked.

Even now, at the break of day, the smell of the sea lingered in her thoughts. She could still feel the darkness of the dream enveloping her like a cold fog. In an attempt to rid herself of the feeling, she reached for the book she had been reading the night before.

There were so many interesting tales tucked away in the pages. There was King Arthur lore about dragons and giants and chivalrous knights. There were legends of creatures lurking in the Welsh highlands, like the cyhyraeth, a banshee-like creature that screamed to foretell approaching death. She flipped past the story of the Afanc, a fearsome lake monster, not wanting to dive any deeper into dark tales, when she came across something that piqued her interest.

The story told of a very old yew tree in a churchyard, so old that it was said to be the oldest living thing in Wales, dating back over four thousand years. According to legend, a fairy spirit was said to reside in the tree and possessed extensive knowledge of both the material and ethereal planes. People traveled great distances to seek guidance from the spirit in all matters. She was rumored to speak only to those with the purest intentions and highest levels of integrity, and so the majority of people came away with their questions unanswered.

However, there was one night of the year when no one would risk venturing into the graveyard: All Hallows' Eve. Anyone who did ran the risk of hearing their name called out from within the tree, meaning they would not live to see another year of life.

On the opposite page was a hand-drawn image of a yew tree. Its base was wide with twisting roots like outstretched arms gripping the soil around it in all directions. It sat in the center of a churchyard, giving the impression that it was keeping watch over the gravestones that surrounded it. The caption under it read: *The yew tree in the Llangernyw churchyard.*

What a strange coincidence, Ionna thought as she set the book down. She'd purchased the book in Llangernyw, the same town where the tree stood.

The second book the woman had given her at the market still lay in the bag on the opposite chair. She leaned over and took it out. All the events of the previous day had prevented her from giving it any thought. She recognized it as soon as she took it out of the bag but couldn't place where she had seen it previously. It was a book called the *Red Book of Hergest,* and as she began to flip through its pages, the familiarity clicked: the study! Like any good journalist, she grabbed the book and went to investigate.

She turned the knob, popping the study's door just a crack. A burst of cool air from the unheated room broke free and filled the hallway, followed by the wonderful aroma of old books.

There was something different about this room. She had sensed it the first time she entered. It was just a plain old study, nothing particularly grand or interesting about it apart from the exquisitely carved desk, but she just knew there was something more lingering within its walls. She walked over to the wall of books and scanned the shelves, looking for the spine of the *Red Book of Hergest*. Walking the length of the wall, she ran her fingers across the spines, leaving lines in her wake, their true beauty peeking out from under the layers of dust. Then suddenly it felt as if her hand was being pulled toward a section of the bookcase, like a magnet to metal.

She reached up. There, at the tip of her fingers, was the book.

"I knew it," she murmured.

She pulled it down and held it next to its twin, immediately noticing a disparity. The book from the study was much thicker than the book from the farmers' market. Was it a later edition with supplementary chapters or something? But it wasn't just the thickness that was different. There was something about the book itself; it almost seemed to glow.

That's absurd, she thought, giving herself a shake. *It's just a book.*

The chill in the room began to creep its way through her robe, and she tucked the books under her arm and headed back to the kitchen for more coffee and a bit of pie for breakfast.

When she arrived in the kitchen, she poured herself another large cup and set it next to the pie on the table. She grabbed a fork and peeled back the cellophane from the pie. *Screw it!* She was just going to go for it and eat it right out of the tin. It wasn't as if she was trying to impress anyone after all; it was just her and the cat.

She broke through the flaky outer crust and was lifting a giant forkful up to her mouth when the phone rang. Startled, she dropped the fork into the pie tin, sending crumbs everywhere.

"Shit! Who the hell's calling at this hour?" she muttered as she got up and walked over to the corded phone. "Hello?"

"Ionna, please tell me you haven't eaten any of that pie?"

"John? Is that you?"

"Yes," he said, sounding frantic. "Now, please tell me that you haven't eaten any of that pie yet."

"I know you said it was good, but geez, a wake-up call to see if I liked it is a bit over the top, don't ya think?" she teased.

"Ionna, seriously, just answer the question," John said.

"No. I was just about to have it for breakfast before you called. It's literally sitting next to my coffee with a fork in it."

"Oh, thank God!" he said, relief filling his voice. "Don't eat any of it. Throw it away as soon as we get off the phone."

"Why?" she asked, eyeing the pie suspiciously. "Was it a bad batch?"

"You could say that. Remember the old woman selling them? I told you she was the bishop's wife? I have no idea how, but she put yew berries from the tree in their churchyard in the pies instead of redcurrants. No idea why she even picked them in the first place since they're deadly poisonous. The hospital has eight people in the critical care unit as we speak."

"Oh my God, that's awful." Ionna gasped as she walked over to the pie, the phone cord stretched to the max. She picked it up in one hand and threw it into the rubbish bin, fork and all. "Those poor people. Are they going to be alright?" she asked, walking back into the hallway, letting the cord retract back into its tight spiral. An eerie feeling crept over her. How weird was it that she'd *just* finished reading in the book about the yew tree before John called? The tree in the book had to be the same one the berries had come from.

"I don't think anyone knows just yet. At the moment the police are just trying to get in touch with anyone who went to the market yesterday. As of now, there are only fifteen out of twenty pies accounted for. Thank God Zeke called to tell me this morning. Ryan and I planned on having the pies at dinner tonight with Ben and Owen," John said, a noticeable strain in his voice.

And there it was again, the embarrassment for thinking she

had a shot with John, bursting forth at the mention of his husband's name. She pushed the feeling aside. John certainly wasn't making her feel weird about it, that was all between her own ears.

"God. I hope they can find the other five pies before it's too late. How scary," she said. She watched Jasper jump onto the table where Betty's urn sat, rubbing around it as if it were her leg.

"You're not kidding. Are you up for dinner tonight at the farm? I can introduce you to my brother and Ryan."

"Hmm, let me check my schedule. Well, it just so happens that I *am* free tonight," she joked.

"Great, we'll pick you up around six. Now, go throw that pie away," he told her.

"Already done. See you tonight," she said, then hung up the phone and stood there in the entryway for a moment. The whole morning had left her head spinning. *God, how weird my life has gotten in just a few short days.*

She looked into the living room again at Jasper. He was lying down next to the silver urn now, a deep purr echoing off the quiet walls. Ionna hadn't noticed just how quiet the house really was until that moment, and a feeling of utter loneliness settled into her bones. Was this all she now possessed of a family—a cat and the ashes of her grandmother, whom she didn't even know?

The dream drifted back into her mind, the sharp, serrated feeling of abandonment and loss that had woken her up. But she supposed that should be expected, as her dreams were just a manifestation of the events in her real life, and at the moment she felt oceans apart from the truth that her own family had been hiding from her for years.

Chapter Twenty-Eight
Ionna
THE RED BOOK OF HERGEST

Ionna made her way back into the kitchen, where she retrieved her cup of coffee and the books and headed into the living room. Jasper was still there, purring peacefully on the table next to the urn.

"Jasper, could you try and be a little less creepy?" she said as she walked by and sat in one of the deep blue armchairs. She set her coffee on the side table and laid both books in her lap, taking in the differences. The book from the study seemed to be an older print than the one from the market—the binding and material were slightly different. But that wasn't what made it stand out. There was something radiating from it, pulling her in.

She ran her hands over the cover, giving into the force that was compelling her to open it. As she gently flipped the book's cover open, a jolt of energy surged through her, awakening something that had lain dormant within her and propelling it to the surface.

Startled, she abruptly closed the book and tried to slow her racing heart.

"What the hell? Okay, I think maybe I've had too much coffee and not enough food." She tried to reassure herself as she sat with the books resting heavily in her lap. Jasper was now perched on the chair beside her, looking on with curiosity, as if waiting for something to happen.

Ionna looked down at the book again, desperately wanting to open it but fearful of what might happen if she did. Instead, she opened the copy from the market. The only sensation was the cool crispness of paper beneath her fingertips.

The book was filled with old Welsh stories and folklore, as well as a few herbal remedies scattered throughout. The title of the book sounded very familiar to her, and she knew she'd heard it somewhere before. Then it dawned on her. It had been in the story she read in the folklore book last night. The Lady of the Lake's children, known as the Physicians of Myddfai. Their ancient remedies had been preserved in the *Red Book of Hergest*. And here it was, that very book, written centuries before, sitting in her lap. It was, of course, just a copy, and it had been translated into English; however, the mere fact that it had withstood the test of time and was still in circulation intrigued her.

As she looked down at it, its twin below beckoned to her. Its pages calling out to be read. She closed the market copy and set it next to her cooling coffee on the side table. She sat with the other book in her lap for a long while, just staring down at its cover, desperately trying to understand the mystery within it without having to risk opening it again.

Finally, she gathered the courage and quickly tossed open the cover.

Nothing happened.

She looked down at the first page in surprise. It was not the same book; this one was full of handwritten pages, a journal of sorts, it seemed. *Well, that explains the reason for the difference in the size and spine.* It had been rebound as if someone was trying to hide its contents in plain sight as another book. But why?

Was this her grandmother's journal? A jolt of excitement raced through her at the prospect that this book might just bring her some answers. Not wanting to waste even a second more, she turned back to the beginning and began to read.

July 19th, 1948

The year anniversary of Abigail's death has come and gone, and not a day goes by that I don't second-guess my actions. I am not a religious man, but I pray that the binding will hold fast. I stayed on and looked after Fernbeg Cottage until Flora was able to sell her home and move to the cottage to take up her birthright. I know it is time for me to move on and try to live my life once more, yet I am directionless.

August 15th, 1948

I have met a lovely woman visiting from Wales named Elizabeth Perth. She is a widower who came to stay with family in Oban for the summer holiday. She has a charming young daughter named Betty, who is quite a little chatterbox. We have spent several weeks getting to know each other and now she is set to head back to Wales where she resides. I am not sure I can bear to see her go as I have grown quite fond of her and her daughter.

Ionna stopped reading. This wasn't her grandmother's journal; it was her great-grandfather's. Even though she was slightly disappointed, she was still curious about her family's story—especially since she hadn't even known this family existed two weeks ago.

The day passed quietly by as she got lost in reading about the courtship between her great-grandparents. She paused only for snacks and trips to the bathroom.

Through his journal entries, she learned that during the course of their summer romance, her great-grandmother Elizabeth had asked him to move back to Wales with her and Betty, which he did. Later on that year, just a few days before Betty turned ten, they got married and then bought the house where she was currently sitting.

Ionna had become enthralled by their love story. She read compulsively, as if pulled into another world by the words of her great-grandfather. She couldn't put it down, especially after finding out that Elizabeth had become pregnant.

She had just finished reading about when Artemas built the barn when she turned the page and felt that same jolt of energy surge through her.

She looked down at the words, where a faint glow emanated as if they were lit from below. She rubbed her eyes. Obviously, she had been reading too long. She stretched her arms up over her head and arched her back, only now realizing how stiff she was from sitting all day.

"Okay, boy, I think that's about enough reading for one day. Whatcha think?" she asked Jasper, who was curled up in a furball on the chair next to her.

Just as she was about to close the book, Jasper took one long leap from his chair to hers, landing on the book and forcing it to stay open. It was then that she looked down and caught sight of something that made her stop in her tracks.

There, on the aging white paper, was the name Neala scrawled in deep black ink. Jasper was blocking her from reading what was written around it. She shooed him off, making sure he didn't damage the pages as he fled.

The journal entry read:

> December 21st, 1949
>
> The sun was just beginning to set when Elizabeth's water broke. As little Betty and I rushed around the house, gathering everything we needed to bring to the hospital, our baby decided she didn't want to wait. She was coming and there was no time left, so I carried Elizabeth to our bed and within only a few minutes our beautiful baby girl came into the world just as the lunar eclipse broke in the sky. She glowed so brightly it was as if she could replace the moon itself, full of more magic than even I hold. We sat as a family together on the bed, all three of us looking down at this tiny miracle nestled snug on Elizabeth's breast. We decided on the name Neala, meaning "holder of light." It seems fitting that we would give her a Scottish name, for that is where our love began. I never knew my heart could be so full. I feel as if it might burst from the joy I feel at this moment.

Ionna stopped reading. She remembered seeing the obituary of her great-grandmother Elizabeth in the study. Hadn't it said that her husband and infant daughter passed before her? So, the hair she'd found in the desk had belonged to her great-aunt. *How sad*, she thought as she closed the journal, feeling a headache coming on from all the reading and overthinking. Even though the people she was reading about were long gone, it felt somehow intrusive to know that the child he had written with such joy and love about wouldn't survive past infancy.

She placed the book on top of the other on the side table and walked into the kitchen to look at the clock.

"Shit!" It was five thirty—she only had a half hour to get ready before John picked her up for dinner.

She went quickly into the bedroom and rifled through her bag, looking for something other than jeans and T-shirts. She couldn't quite remember what she had packed as she had been in such a rush. After spilling the entire contents of her bag out on the bed, she realized she had packed nothing other than jeans, T-shirts, and one navy blue blazer. Nothing that was even remotely presentable for a dinner with people she didn't know. She was about to think up some excuse to wiggle her way out of going when Jasper padded in and began pawing at Betty's closet door. She walked over to it, scooting Jasper out of the way as she opened it. It was a long shot, but maybe she could find something that didn't look straight out of the nineteen fifties and smell like mothballs.

Most of the dresses were much too uptight, with high collars and long sleeves, and others were way too floral for her taste. She was about to give up and call the whole thing off when a dark emerald-green dress with tiny white polka dots at the back of the closet caught her eye. She pushed past all the discarded options and retrieved it, carefully pulling it out into the light. It was mid-calf length with an empire waist, capped short sleeves, and an almost scandalous V-neck. She pulled off her shirt and kicked her pants to the floor, eager to see if the dress would fit. She slipped it over her arms and let it drop into place, then looked at herself in the mirror. It fit perfectly, hugging her in all the right places.

An odd feeling came over her at that moment as she gazed at her reflection in the mirror. A mixture of guilt and closeness to Betty. She wondered what occasions her grandmother had worn this dress to, what kind of evenings she'd had in it.

"This will do nicely. Thanks, buddy," she whispered to Jasper, who was snoozing away on the bed again.

She dug through the pile of shoes at the bottom of the closet until she found a cute pair of dark leather Mary Janes. She sat on the bed to try them on. *A tad big but they will do for the night.*

"Now, I need to tame this mane," she told Jasper as she stroked his back and went back to the mirror.

When she looked up, there was an old woman standing behind her, smiling at her reflection.

She let out a startled scream and spun around. No one was there. Except for her and Jasper, the bedroom was empty.

Heart pounding, she looked at the mirror again.

Nothing. Just her own reflection staring back at her, wide-eyed.

Okay, now she was truly going mad. But she was one hundred percent sure she'd seen someone standing behind her. Not a trick of the light. Could it have been her imagination going on overdrive after reading about her dead relatives all day? Or maybe … had she just seen Betty's ghost? A few days ago, she didn't believe in such things, but after all the weird, unexplained events that had happened to her since she arrived, she was beginning to believe anything was possible.

She turned from the mirror to face the room, and in a shaky voice, she said, "Um, hi. I'm Ionna, your granddaughter. I'm sorry I've been rooting around in your things. I hope you don't mind me borrowing your dress and shoes." As her words hung in the empty air, she shook her head and laughed nervously. "Okay, you're officially off the rails, talking not only to your dead grandmother's ghost but now yourself."

She shook off the uneasy feeling and went into the bathroom to do her hair. There was no time to be playing paranormal investigator at the moment. She lightly wet her hair in the sink and brushed it out, pulling half of it up and away from her heart-shaped face, then clipped it in the back so that her long dark waves flowed down over her shoulders. She grabbed her travel bag, pulled out some eyeliner and mascara, and trimmed her sea-green eyes. Lastly, she dabbed her lips with some gloss.

When she walked back into the bedroom, something was out of place. There, laid out on top of the dresser, was the pendant with the green stone that had been tucked away in the jewelry box. Ionna glanced around. The room was still, other than the purring coming from the bed where Jasper lay.

Well, I'm guessing Betty wants me to wear this...

Ionna walked over to the dresser and picked the necklace up, clasping it around her neck. As soon as her fingers linked the two chains together, a flood of energy rushed through her, the same kind of energy that had come from the book.

She pulled her hands back in front of her and looked at them, the shock still vibrating in her fingertips. Then, as though someone had just rested a hand on her shoulder, a sense of calm radiated through her. She looked at her reflection in the mirror, the necklace hanging softly between her breasts, and for a brief moment, she felt as if Betty were there, her spirit lingering in the air around her.

Chapter Twenty-Nine
Ionna
THE DINNER

It was ten minutes to six when John pulled in to pick up Ionna. Storm clouds had rolled back over the valley and the smell of rain hung in the air. John knocked on the door and Ionna came out with a bottle of wine in one hand and a small leather clutch in the other.

"Found her stash," she said, smiling and raising up the wine bottle.

John laughed. "That you did. You look amazing, Ionna," he said as he gestured toward the car. "Your chariot awaits."

Ionna chuckled and headed over to the car in the cool evening air. The whole yard was aloft with the smell of the flower beds, giving the moment an enchanting feel. However, John was not her prince, as much as she wished he were. He belonged to Ryan. She would just need to keep looking for hers.

She was surprised at how close their houses were when it only took about three minutes to get to the farm.

"I think I probably could have walked," she said as they pulled down the long driveway and into the barnyard.

"I'm sure you could have, but you would have gotten your pretty shoes all dirty," he joked. "I can't wait to introduce you to my brother and Ryan," John said as he turned the ignition off and opened the door.

Ionna hesitated for a moment, everything seeming to catch up with her all at once. All she could think about was how her once idyllic family had so quickly turned into the absolute opposite. The foundation that her whole life had been built upon was crumbling down around her.

Snap out of it, she told herself as John came around to open her door.

Taking a deep breath, she tried to quell her anxiety. She grabbed Betty's necklace and spun it in her fingers as she got out of the car, giving John the most convincing fake grin she could muster. A smile that quickly turned genuine as she took in the beauty of the farmyard with its lush gardens. The yard was well manicured, and the flower boxes were overflowing. *It truly is a picturesque Welsh farm*, she thought.

"Beautiful, isn't it?" John said, breaking her out of the moment.

"It truly is," she replied, giving him a nod and a smile.

"Well, we better get in there. Looks like Flora and Kate are already here, and that means the food must be close to done," he told her, walking to the door and holding it open for her.

She walked in, John at her heels, and immediately felt an

awkwardness come over her. After all, the only person she knew was John and that was just barely. He stepped in front of her and led her into a dining room with an exposed beam ceiling. Along one of the walls was a collection of picture frames featuring beautiful photographs of the farm as well as the family. The room housed a large, very old-looking farmhouse table where an elderly woman sat sipping a glass of wine.

"Ionna, this is Flora. She lives just down the road from here. She was part of your grandmother's bridge club. Flora, this is Ionna, Betty's granddaughter," John said, giving them a formal introduction.

Flora stood up, set her wineglass on the table, and walked over to Ionna.

"Oh, my dear, I am so sorry about your grandmother. She was a wonderful woman. You look so much like her." She took Ionna's hand and pulled her into a hug.

Ionna's emotions rose and it took all that she had not to burst into tears at the woman's embrace. "Thank you so much. Sadly, I never got a chance to know her," Ionna said as Flora stepped back. She found herself fidgeting with Betty's necklace once again, something about its presence comforted her.

"I know, dear, John told me. He said you had some questions about your family. I would be more than happy to help answer anything I can. Why don't you plan on coming over for some tea one of these days and we can talk?" Flora said.

"I'd love that. Thank you, Flora."

"Come over anytime," Flora said with a smile as she went back to the table and took up her wine again.

John looked at Ionna and smiled, knowing it was just what she needed to hear. "I'm going to take this and go find some wine-glasses and also my husband," he said, plucking the wine bottle from Ionna's hands and walking into a room off to the right of the table.

It was then that two teenagers came in from another doorway at the back of the dining room, chatting away. It was John's nephew, Owen, from the farmers' market, and a girl with long ginger hair whom she also recognized. She had been the girl she'd bumped into when entering the market.

"Ionna? Uncle John's friend, right?" Owen asked as he pulled a chair out and sat down. The ginger-haired girl perched on a chair next to Flora.

"Yes, hi again," Ionna said awkwardly as she took a seat across from them.

"Ionna, I see you've met Owen. And this here is my granddaughter, Kate," Flora said, gesturing over toward Kate who sat to the right of her at the table.

Kate raised her hand in a shy greeting. Ionna could tell by the look in her eyes that she had remembered her from their tiny collision at the market and looked a bit embarrassed over it.

"Yes, we met briefly at the market too," Ionna said with a smile.

John walked back in carrying four wineglasses, and following behind was a tall, well-dressed man with wire-rimmed glasses, holding an open bottle of wine. He looked slightly older than John, handsome with sleek streaks of gray through his sandy blond hair.

"Ionna, meet my husband, Ryan," John said, handing her a wineglass as Ryan poured the wine into it.

"So nice to finally meet you, Ionna. John has told me all about you," Ryan said cheerfully.

"Nice to meet you too, Ryan. Thank you," she said.

Ryan took up a seat next to Ionna, and John walked back out of the room.

"So, John told me that you're from Maine. I used to go there every year in the summer with my parents when I was a child. We used to stay in a small town called Wells where my uncle lived. Such a beautiful state. I haven't been back in ages," Ryan said, then took a leisurely sip of his wine.

"Oh yeah, Wells is a great little beach town. I've been there a ton. Good choice on your uncle's part," she said, giving Ryan a smile before diving into her wine. She was desperately hoping that it would be enough to cut the edge she was feeling.

A delicious smell of roasted vegetables and meat drifted in from the kitchen, making Ionna's stomach moan in hunger. She had been so wrapped up in reading all day that she hadn't eaten much and now she was feeling it.

"Owen, I could use an extra set of hands in here," a voice called out from the kitchen.

Owen and Kate both stood up and walked into the other room, returning a few moments later with plates and silverware. John returned carrying a long plate piled high with roast carrots adorned with sprigs of rosemary. A tall man followed him, carrying a large platter containing a steaming roast on a bed of fresh greens. He looked like John with his dark wavy hair and crystal blue eyes, but he was broader and more rugged looking, sporting a well-trimmed beard and a face that had been kissed by the sun. *Ben*, she thought as she sat there staring.

He walked over and placed the main dish in the center of the table.

"Ben, I want you to meet Ionna, Betty's granddaughter. Ionna, my brother Ben," John said, waving his hand between the two.

"Hi, nice to meet you," Ben said, turning around and walking back into the kitchen before she was even able to return the greeting.

"Oh, don't think anything of that. Not sure Ben remembers how to even talk to the opposite sex," Ryan joked.

"It's true," John echoed back.

Ionna looked across at the wall of pictures. There were pictures of John and Ben as children and many of little Owen with farm animals, but none of them featured a woman. Ben was obviously a single father and the nosey journalist inside her wondered what had happened to Owen's mother.

Ben returned with a large green salad in a beautiful wooden bowl. He set it down and then sat at the head of the table, John following suit and sitting beside Ryan.

"I want to raise a toast," John announced, standing back up with his wineglass raised. "I want to thank you all for coming tonight. It's not too often that I come home and get back to my roots. I want to thank Ionna for giving me the little push I needed to make the trip back, even if she didn't know she did it. Here's to old traditions and new beginnings." John said as he raised his glass into the air.

"To old traditions and new beginnings," everyone said in unison and then drank from their glasses.

"Okay, let's dig in. Ben made us a feast tonight."

The dinner was filled with conversation that Ionna happily listened to as she ate. She kept glancing over at Kate, who was quite the little wallflower. *We have that in common*, she thought.

"So, Ionna, what is that you do for a job back in the States?" Flora asked as she forked a carrot.

"I'm a journalist. I work, well, *worked* for a local paper in my hometown of Bath."

"Oh, does that mean you have plans to stay here and get a job with one of our local papers?" Flora asked.

The question made Ionna swallow hard. She had been avoiding thinking about work this past week and the direction of her life in general. She should have known this kind of thing might come up in conversation, but it had, for some reason, blindsided her.

"I'm not sure, to be honest. I haven't planned that far ahead quite yet," she said, hoping the answer would appease Flora for the time being.

Flora gave her a nod and a knowing smile and moved on. "Ben, did you figure out what happened to the berries?" she asked, changing the topic.

Ben sliced another hunk of meat off the roast and placed it on his plate, shaking his head. "No, they took samples, but I haven't heard any word back on them yet."

"Speaking of berries, I still can't believe Sandra mistook yew berries for currants. When I spoke with the chief inspector this afternoon, he told me she was acting very strange when they questioned her. Telling them she couldn't remember even making the pies. It's all so odd," John said as he finished off the last bit of onion cake on his plate.

"It's strange, especially because she came here to buy the currants for the pies," Ben said. "We talked a bit, and she seemed sharp as a tack. Telling me some stories about Grandad from years back. Then the next day my berry crop was completely rotten. It's all very bizarre."

"She is getting on in her years. It might be dementia kicking in. You know, people can be lucid one minute and doolally the next. I can't imagine she would have done such a thing on purpose," Flora said.

"Is there any word on how all the people who ate the pies are doing, Uncle John?" Owen asked.

"There were a few mild poisonings, those people have been released from the hospital and are back home. The others who ate more were not so lucky. There are two on life support and one passed away this morning," John told them, taking another sip of wine to wash down the dreadful words.

"Oh, how awful," Ionna said. Her stomach turned at the thought she had come so close to eating one of the pies herself.

"It is, and poor MacClure's sister is one of the people in intensive care. After what happened to his sheep in the river the poor man has had a rough go of it these past few days," John said.

"All the local farm owners had a meeting last night. We're trying to find a way to help him stay afloat while he builds back his herd," Ben said.

"Is that something that happens? Do sheep flee from predators in any means to escape, even if it sends them to their death?" Ionna asked Ben. She glanced over at Kate, who looked very uncomfortable. The heavy topic had obviously made her uneasy.

"You hear about things like this happening when they're cornered, and trying to cross a body of water as the only means of escape. You know, maybe in places where they have large wolf populations. But here, in rural Wales? What could have scared them so badly? I can't make sense of it, why they'd all choose to go to the river, almost like they were led there. And during a storm, too." Ben shook his head.

"Yeah, a lot of weird things have been going on around here in the last few weeks, don't you think?" Owen said. "The berry patch rotting overnight, the sheep, and now the pies. Not to mention Betty—" He stopped midway through his sentence, remembering Ionna was there.

The room fell silent. Everyone looked at him with wide eyes and then over at Ionna, as if she was a glass teetering on the edge of a table, about to fall and break.

"Kate and I might have spotted a panther on the trail today," Owen continued, trying to steer the subject away from his Betty comment. "I thought those stories of sightings were a load of crap, but I swear we saw one."

"I didn't know Wales had panthers," Ionna said, thankful that Owen had just given her a chance to make it known to all that she was not that easily broken.

"It doesn't, but some asshole brought a pair here a few years back and then released them into the wild. Now there've been multiple sightings of them in the mountains. And there aren't just two anymore. They've killed some livestock on a few different farms around the area. An officer on patrol caught sight of three on the outskirts of the McClure farm, not too far from here back last April," Ben said, then turned to his son with a stern expression. "You should have told me this earlier. You two stay off that trail until I call Creig and let him know there's been a sighting in the area again. You hear me?"

"Yes, Dad," Owen said, nodding. "Sorry."

"Well," John said, looking around the table at everyone's empty plates. "Anyone for dessert? Pie, perhaps?"

"No!" everyone said in unison followed by a bit of laughter.

John stood and began collecting the plates. Ionna got up to help, bringing the empty wineglasses into the kitchen. When she came back into the dining room, Ryan and Ben were chatting quietly with Flora while Owen and Kate helped clear off the last remnants of dinner from the table. There was a dark, somber mood from the conversation at dinner sitting heavy in the air.

Coming in from the kitchen, John almost bumped into her.

"Oops! Sorry."

"That's okay. John, I hate to interrupt your evening, but could you drive me home?" Ionna asked. The wine had gone to her head, and she was feeling tired and ready to get out of Betty's shoes.

"Of course," he said, wobbling a bit.

"Oh no, you don't. That wine gave you sea legs," Ryan told him, grabbing ahold of John and pulling him onto a chair. "Ben, could you give Ionna a lift home?" Ryan asked.

"No problem."

"Oh, thank you. It was really nice meeting you, Flora. I'm looking forward to our tea," Ionna said, outstretching her hand.

"Likewise, dear," Flora said, shaking it.

"You too, Kate," she said, reaching her hand forward and taking Kate's into her own.

"Yeah, nice to meet you," Kate said.

The moment their hands touched, the lights flashed, flickered, and went out. Ionna quickly snapped her hand back. As their hands parted, Kate went limp and then collapsed onto the floor, unconscious.

Chapter Thirty
(2014 -1951)
Kate

GINGER BISCUITS

The kitchen was filled with the sweet, spicy scent of ginger biscuits, which had wafted out the open kitchen window and into the barnyard where a twelve-year-old Kate and Owen sat talking. A light summer breeze guided the smell toward them.

"Dad's making ginger biscuits for the market. Let's go get some," Owen suggested, as he stood up and pulled Kate to her feet.

They went into the house and followed their noses into the kitchen where two large plates of biscuits were cooling on the long counter spanning one side of the kitchen. Ben was washing the last of the dishes as they tip-toed in and stood over them, looking down with wide eyes.

"Okay, you can have two each. The rest are going to the market with me tomorrow," Ben told them as he dried the last bowl and put it into the cupboard above where he stood.

Not having to be told twice, they grabbed their biscuits and went into the living room. Still hot from the oven, the insides of the cookies almost melted in their mouth.

No sooner had they sat down, however, than the biscuits were gone. Being adolescents with their never-ending hunger, two didn't come close to filling them up or stopping their craving.

"Those are super good," Kate said, licking crumbs off her fingers.

"I know. It's almost time for him to do barn chores. Let's wait here and when he goes out, we can sneak in and grab a few more," Owen whispered, looking toward the kitchen as they sat on the couch devising their plan.

He was right, within just a few minutes Ben was putting on his barn boots and heading out the door.

"Now!" Owen yelled as if he was commanding a squadron, rushing into the kitchen, Kate following quickly behind him.

Ben had covered the biscuits in plastic wrap and Owen was trying to carefully unwrap them in a way that would not be noticed when a loud voice rang out behind them.

"Owen! I said no more!" Ben had come back in. "Out of here, both of you!" he scolded, shooing them out of the kitchen.

Defeated, they returned to the living room.

"Well, that didn't go as planned," Kate joked.

"Not so much," Owen said, resting his head on the plaid sofa. Kate rested back against it next to him, disappointed at the prospect of no more biscuits when there was a whole tray of them just feet away.

But their rebellious pre-teen spirits weren't about to let the idea go.

"Kate, I have an idea," Owen said.

Instead of immediately explaining, he got up and pulled the sofa out from the wall, then beckoned Kate behind it. This was Owen's go-to hiding spot. They had many "couch meetings" as they called them back there. Kate grabbed a cushion and followed him.

"I think I know how we might be able to get a whole plate of those biscuits," Owen told her with a wide, mischievous grin on his dimly lit face.

"Oooh, how?" Kate asked, smiling back.

"What if you time flip us back to right after he bakes the first batch of biscuits and we grab them? Then flip back here and have a feast."

Kate thought about it for a long moment. She wasn't sure if she could even do it. She had never been able to fully control when or where she went when she flipped through time. It seemed a bit risky for a plate of biscuits, but she really didn't want to disappoint Owen, he was so excited.

"Ah, I don't know, Owen. I haven't been able to do that kinda thing before. I'm not sure I can," she told him.

"Kate, you need to just think about the point in time you want to go and where. Just concentrate really hard. You can do it," he insisted.

She bit her lip. "Okay. Fine. Let's try it."

She grabbed hold of his hands and closed her eyes, concentrating on the plate of biscuits in the kitchen and the image of Ben pulling the first batch out of the oven. She thought about the rich, spicy scent of the ginger, its fiery kick on her tongue, and the way the biscuits seemed to melt in her mouth. Then all of a sudden she felt energy rise up from her toes and into the tips of her fingers. Her body hummed with it, like she was a tuning fork that had just been struck. She felt the air being squeezed out of her lungs and the sensation of being thrust forward.

Then it stopped.

The first thing she realized was that she was no longer holding Owen's hands. When she opened her eyes to look for him, she was no longer crouched behind the plaid sofa in his living room.

She was in a barn, but it was not Owen's. She immediately closed her eyes and willed herself to flip back to the safety of their hiding spot, but as hard as she tried nothing happened.

Panic crept through her. Tears pricked her eyes as she looked around at the unfamiliar surroundings. There, toward the back stalls, was a small door with light seeping in around its edges. *A way out.* Once she was out, she might have a better idea where she was, and a better chance of getting back to Owen. She got up and raced over to the door.

Halfway there, she slipped on the loose hay that was scattered over the old barn floor. Her body hit the ground with such force it knocked her unconscious almost instantly.

She woke to the muffled yells of a man with a foreign accent. Slowly, she opened her eyes and looked around. She was lying on a sofa in a dimly lit living room, in a place she did not recognize. Her head was spinning and her stomach was queasy, like it had been turned upside down.

The last thing she remembered was flipping into an old barn. Now she was in a strange house.

Her heart raced as the man called out once again. This time

she could make out the words. Her vision was still coming in and out of focus but she could see the man was older, with the strands of silver in his dark hair.

"Elizabeth!" he yelled in the direction behind where Kate lay.

A woman in her forties with dark chestnut hair and a kind face came rushing in from another room upon hearing his call.

"Oh my. Who is this?" she asked, wiping her hands off on her apron.

"I don't know. I found her like this in the barn," the man replied, worry creasing deep lines into his forehead.

He moved aside so that the woman, who Kate assumed was his wife, could get a closer look. Kate stared back up at her with the eyes of a frightened rabbit.

"Is she alright?" she asked.

"I'm not sure."

The two of them stood there, looking down at Kate. Trying to avoid the stares of these strangers, she glanced around the room, taking in the details of her surroundings. Where was she? Or better yet, *when* was she? Everything around her looked odd, like something out of one of those old 1950s TV programs her grandfather used to watch.

From somewhere else in the house, the piercing cry of an infant broke the silence. The woman's face tightened slightly, and she took quick strides out of the room, leaving Kate alone with the man once more.

He stood there, looming over her, his big broad body casting a shadow across her face. Suddenly Kate felt like a cornered animal. She wanted to make a run for it. If she could just make it out of sight of the man, she could try and flip herself back again. Before she could talk herself out of it, she jumped to her feet and lunged toward the door but was only able to take a few steps before her legs gave out. The man stepped forward just in time and caught her mid-fall, then set her back on the couch.

"Woah, easy now. Looks like you're still not well enough to be running any marathons, child," he said to her in a gentle tone.

Kate rested herself back against the couch and took a deep breath, trying to steady herself as her head spun.

"I mean you no harm," the man said. "I found you unconscious in my barn. Do you know how you got there?"

She didn't answer. Instead, she just sat there not saying a word, her heart feeling as if it might beat out of her chest and run away without her. She had never found herself in the presence of other people when she had flipped time before, other than when she and Owen had ventured down the mountain to his house and they were chased away by the old man. She had no idea how to explain her appearance in his barn.

The man sat down in a chair across from her. He didn't press her for an answer, he just sat patiently waiting in shared silence with her. She could see genuine concern in his eyes. And something else that she recognized, something familiar that she couldn't quite place. Gradually, the acute sense of fear lessened. She dropped her shoulders, which she hadn't even realized had been raised, as if she was some cowering dog.

"What is your name?" the man asked gently, breaking the silence.

Kate hesitated for a moment before responding. "Kate," she said, her voice scratchy and dry. "My name is Kate."

Chapter Thirty-One
(1951)
KATE - NEALA

"It's nice to meet you, Kate. My name is Artemas," the man told her, extending his hand in greeting from where he sat.

Kate took his hand hesitantly and shook it. When their hands clasped together, she could feel an energy coming from him that she recognized. It was the same kind of buzzing that she felt before she flipped. This made her even more confused. She pulled her hand away and propped herself up a little more on the sofa to look around.

There was something very familiar about the house. She felt as if she had been here before but couldn't place where she was. It was furnished in 1950s style, just like her grandparents' home, but unlike theirs, nothing looked worn or dated from sitting around for decades. The bright oranges and pea greens stood out in their newness.

A boxy television in a wooden stand sat in the corner of the room, and on the coffee table right in front of her was a magazine with a picture of a young Queen Elizabeth. The date printed on the front read July 18th, 1951. *Well, that explains the weird choice of decor.* She had somehow flipped herself back in time sixty-three years. The realization sent a sharp pang of homesickness through her.

Trying to remain calm, she continued taking in her surroundings, noticing how big and cumbersome the electronics were here compared to her own time. Not only was the television as bulky as a small cabinet, but so was the radio. It was housed in a large wooden box with speakers built into its front and was studded with multiple knobs. She thought about the small MP3 player she had sitting on her nightstand at home as she looked at the ancient relic.

From somewhere toward the back of the house, the baby cried again.

"Is that your baby?" Kate asked.

"Yes. My daughter. She is very ill. Her mother is tending to her now," Artemas told her with a sadness in his eyes that aged him ten years in a single moment.

Kate felt sorry for him. She recognized his tone when he said she was very ill. It was the same tone her mother had used when she told her that her beloved cat, Boots, had died, a kind of hopeless sorrow.

"I'm sorry," Kate told him with genuine sorrow in her voice.

"It's okay. We are going to do everything we can to help her get better. But right now, I need to figure out how to get you home."

"Artemas! Come quick," the woman's voice called out from the back of the house.

He stood and rushed out of the room. Kate had a sinking feeling come over her. Something in the woman's voice sounded wrong. She got to her feet, slowly this time, and followed the sound of the baby's cries.

As Kate walked into the next room, a sense of recognition washed over her. The view outside the large window overlooked the familiar valley and mountains—the very same as her grandparents' and Owen's houses. It dawned on her; she had been in this house before, not in the past, but recently, in her own time, alongside Owen, delivering produce from the farm. It was Owen's neighbor Betty's house, just sixty years in the past.

As she walked down the small hallway, the baby's cries grew louder, accompanied by unsettling pauses in its breathing. Hesitating for a moment, she approached the room, unsure if she could bear witnessing the little one's struggle. Curiosity, however, got the best of her, and she peered inside.

The walls were covered in a light purple paper speckled with tiny violets. It was much too cheery of a place for the mood that had darkened it. A small crib sat by the window, and next to it, the woman was soothing the baby in an old wooden rocking chair. The baby was older than she had expected, closer to a toddler than a newborn. Her face was covered in a splotchy red rash, and her eyes were swollen and pink. However, that wasn't what grabbed Kate's attention. A dim halo of light surrounded the infant, a soft blue glow.

"She's getting worse. I think we need to call Dr. Morgan again," the woman said, her voice cracking with sadness as she handed the baby to Artemas.

Artemas rocked the baby in his arms and whispered to her. As he did, Kate witnessed a blue light emerge from his body and bond with the weak glow coming off the infant. Her crying stopped the moment the two lights fused into one. When Kate saw the strange sight, she let out a gasp, and the woman turned to see her standing in the doorway.

"Don't come in, we don't want you getting sick," she told her, lifting her hand in a halting gesture.

Artemas turned and smiled at her. "Kate, why don't you go with Elizabeth and get some tea? Once I get her back to sleep, I will come and take you home," he told her as he gently rocked the poor, sick baby.

Elizabeth ushered Kate out of the room and down the hallway into the kitchen.

"You sit here, and I'll get you some tea and biscuits," she told Kate in her kind voice. She was a pretty woman with dark hair and green eyes. There was a gentleness to the way she spoke, and Kate felt more at ease and less frightened than before.

She hoped that with a little food and some tea, she might have enough energy to flip herself back to Owen. Even if she couldn't flip back to his house, at least she was nearby. It was just a matter of finding her own time.

Just as the tea kettle let out its loud whistle, she heard the door open and shut, then the sound of someone running. She turned in her chair to see a girl her own age in an old-fashioned school uniform come dashing into the kitchen.

"Woah there, no running, please." Elizabeth scolded the girl in a way that only mothers could. "We have a guest. Betty, this is Kate. Kate, this is my daughter, Betty. I believe you are around the same age."

Kate sat there, looking at this girl in awe. It was Owen's neighbor Betty, whom Kate only knew as an old lady in her seventies back in her own time.

"Hi, Kate." she said with a friendly smile, then walked over and whispered, "Why is she dressed so weird?" in her mother's ear.

Elizabeth spoke to her in a low voice. "Don't be rude, Betty. Now, go wash up, and there'll be a plate of biscuits and tea when you get back. But be quiet; your father is trying to get Neala to sleep."

Betty ran off down the hallway and out of sight, and Kate turned back to Elizabeth, who was trying her best to keep a smile on her face. She poured Kate a cup of tea and another for Betty, then set them on the old, worn table. She fished through a cupboard, pulled down a tin full of biscuits, and piled a plate with them, setting it between the two mugs.

"Thank you," Kate said politely, giving her a smile of gratitude.

"Of course, dear. I need to go and make a telephone call. Betty should be out to join you in just a few minutes."

She walked around the corner, and Kate could hear her speaking softly into the phone, asking for Dr. Morgan. However, her eavesdropping quickly ended when Betty came bursting back into the room, a Polaroid camera in her hand. Before Kate could even blink, Betty had snapped a picture of her and plopped herself down in the chair opposite, shoving biscuits into her mouth with one hand and fanning the photograph in the air with the other to bring on the exposure more quickly.

"So, why are you here? Are you a war orphan or something?" Betty asked, spitting crumbs out as she talked.

Kate wasn't sure how to answer that question. She was going to need to get her story straight until she was able to recharge herself and get home.

"Um, no. I was visiting my cousin up the road and got a bit lost when my horse took off on me," Kate said, the lie flowing off her tongue.

"Where are you from? You sound funny," Betty said. She took another biscuit from the quickly diminishing pile on the plate and looked at the image forming on the thin piece of film.

"London," Kate replied.

Betty looked at her as if she had two heads and then said, "Okay," as if the answer satisfied her or at least pacified her for the time being.

In the hallway, Kate heard Elizabeth hang up the phone, followed a few moments later by her and Artemas talking in hushed tones. Kate could just make out that the doctor would be coming to check on the baby soon. After another minute, they came back into the kitchen.

"How are the tea and biscuits?" Elizabeth asked, putting on her forced smile again.

"Great, Mum, thanks," Betty said, getting up and walking into the living room with her camera. She'd left the small Polaroid image of Kate sitting on the table, crumbs littering its surface.

"Kate, why don't you come with me outside for a minute? You're not in trouble or anything. I just want to talk to you about how I can get you home," Artemas said, gesturing for her to get up and follow him.

They walked out into the dimming afternoon light. The sun was making its way down the mountains, which meant that nightfall was less than a few hours away, and she needed to get back. If she wasn't home by dark, her grandparents would be out of their minds with worry.

Artemas walked her over to a small bench in the center of a circle of plants. Around them, the garden overflowed with what looked like nothing more than weeds to Kate.

"This is my herb garden," he told her. "If you look at these plants, really look at them, what do you see?"

"Weeds," she said.

Artemas let out a chuckle, then said, "No, take another look. This time concentrate not only on the plants but the space around them as well."

She looked again, harder this time, like she had looked at Artemas when he held the baby, and then she saw it. There, around the plants, was a faint blue glow. Her eyes widened. She looked over at Artemas, who glowed even brighter than the plants.

"You can see it. I thought maybe you could," he said.

"What is it?" Kate asked, amazed and a bit frightened at the same time.

"Magic!" he told her, looking out to where the sun was starting to set. "You have the glow too, just like Neala. I could see it around you as you woke up. When are you from, Kate?"

With a slight hesitation, she answered him. "I'm from two thousand and fourteen," Kate said, as the word *magic* bounced around in her head.

Kate knew that flipping time was special, but she had never considered it to be magic. She had thought of it more like a thing of science, like how in *Dr. Who* space and time were forced together, creating a kind of portal she could step through and land somewhere else. The idea of it being a form of magic, like in the Harry Potter books, hadn't even occurred to her. Had she been using magic to flip through time all along and never known it?

She looked back over at Artemas with new eyes, taking in the glow surrounding him. Then she looked down at her own hands, and there, floating in the air around them like a protective shield, was a faint blue glow. The glow of magic.

Chapter Thirty-Two
(1951)
Kate

THE TRIP BACK HOME

Artemas sat quietly contemplating what Kate had just told him. He didn't appear surprised by what she said but rather deep in thought about it.

After a few long seconds of silence, he said, "Kate, do you know how you travel through time?"

Kate looked at him, at the blue aura pulsating around him. It appeared that once she had truly opened her eyes to magic, she couldn't unsee it.

"At first, it would just happen, and I'd flip back quickly. Then me and my friend Owen tried to figure out how to control it. But I was only able to move us a few times, and I think that was just luck. I've never flipped anywhere for this long. I'm scared I won't be able to flip myself back home. I tried, but it's as if my power is gone," Kate told him, her voice trembling.

"Don't you worry about that. Your power just needs to be recharged. I think maybe the hit to your head has temporarily mixed up your wiring, but I can see the magic getting stronger in you as we speak."

She looked around the yard with new eyes. Not only were the herbs in Artemas's garden glowing, but so were some of the trees on the farm as well. "How do you know so much about all of this?" she asked. "And how is it that we can see the magic?"

"Well, that is a very good question. I believe it is because we were born with something a bit extra. A tiny spark of magic passed down from our ancestors for us to carry and protect. We are the magic keepers. We hold the secrets of the universe in our genes. Your gift is the ability to travel through time; mine is to use the earth's elements to make things happen. We can both see the glow of magic because it's something inside of us that we recognize," Artemas told her, looking out into the field where the sun had made it past the ridgeline of the mountain, tracing its edges in gold.

"So, you're like a wizard?" Kate asked, doing her best to understand what he was telling her.

"Yes. Well, I used to be. Working with magic can be dangerous. It can bring unwanted evil into your life. When I was young, I spent most of my time traveling from place to place, never staying anywhere too long. When magic is performed, it lets off a beacon of sorts, and if you use it too much in one place, it can attract unwanted attention from those seeking its power. My magic's beacon had a darkness that followed it, and in order to keep my family safe, I had to give up that part of myself to have all of this." He waved his arm, as if drawing a circle around the farm and the house.

"Then why are you growing the magic herbs?" Kate questioned him.

"Well, the herbs planted around the house and in each of the window boxes are foxglove, sage, chamomile, and violets. These are all planted for protection. They keep my home safe from harmful spirits and unwanted visitors. The herbs here in my garden are a bit different—they are for cooking," he said with a laugh.

"I don't understand. Why are they glowing then?" she asked, confused.

"Well, that's because most of the herbs we cook with are also used in spell work. Like this." He picked a tall sprig with tiny green leaves that ran up the length of its shaft. "This is rosemary, one of the most powerful herbs. It's good for so many things, from love spells to protection charms, cleansing items used in spell work, and even healing. But I use it to make a delicious chicken and potato dish." He patted his stomach, smiling at her.

"Then why don't you use your herbs and magic to heal Neala?" she asked in a way that only a child could.

He stopped smiling and looked down at his hands. It was as if a dark cloud loomed over his face, casting it in shadow, the question catching him off guard.

"Because I swore I would never risk putting my beacon out into the world again. I can't jeopardize my family in that way. It's just too dangerous," he explained, his tone turning somber.

"Well, I think your baby is already in danger. Maybe you should make an exception."

Artemas didn't say anything in response, he just gave Kate a nod of his head and then stood up.

"Okay, Kate, let's take a walk back into the barn and see if we can work on getting you back home. If my wife or Betty come out, you must not say anything to them about magic. Neither of them knows that magic is real, so we are going to have to keep this just between us. Do you understand?" he asked.

Kate nodded, stood up, then followed Artemas to the barn where she had flipped into his timeline.

He pushed the large sliding door to the left, which opened with a loud squeak. Because the mountain had almost completely obscured the sun, he turned on a large tin light overhead. It didn't light up the entire barn, but it did illuminate the area where they were standing.

"Now, is there anything you can tell me that might explain how you ended up here?" he asked as he walked over to inspect the horse in the stall to the right.

"I don't know. I was with my friend Owen. We were just trying to flip back a few minutes to grab a plate of biscuits his father had just baked. I was holding his hands and then closed my eyes, trying to think about when and where I wanted to go. Then all of a sudden Owen's hands were gone, and I was here in your barn."

Now that it was dusk, she desperately hoped that he could figure out how to get her back before the sky turned completely dark.

"Hmm, okay. Have you ever been able to successfully move through time to where you wanted to go?"

"Yes, but only when I was scared. Anytime I've flipped somewhere I didn't mean to go, I would freak out and close my eyes and then think about being back at my grandparents' house. When I opened them, I would be there."

"Okay, now that's something. It seems that emotions play a role. Fear is a very strong emotion. Do you know what other emotion is even stronger than fear? Love!" he told her.

He walked back over and stood in front of her with a look of optimism in his eyes.

"Now, I want you to close your eyes and think really hard about someone or something you love very much."

Kate did as she was told and closed her eyes. She immediately thought of her mother, but love was not the first emotion that came to mind. Her father was up next, but that was as pointless as thinking about her mother. Then she remembered her grandparents. But as hard as she tried, the fear seemed to be a stronger emotion to her than love.

Artemas stood there observing her magical aura as she tried to invoke the feeling. However, her glow did not change. It stayed soft, ebbing and flowing like the tides.

"I don't think this is going to work," Kate told him, opening her eyes.

"You might just need more rest. Why don't we go in and have dinner with Elizabeth and Betty, and we can try again later?"

"No! I have to get back *now*. My grandparents are going to be completely freaking out," Kate insisted, looking out the sole window in the barn and seeing a darkened sky. A sinking feeling came over her. What if she was never able to get home? What if she was stuck here in 1951 with Artemas forever? The thought made her want to throw up.

Artemas looked at her. "Kate, don't worry. We'll figure this out together and get you home as soon as we can. You just need to build yourself back up so that you are strong enough. Traveling back six decades would exhaust anyone."

Kate closed her eyes again, squeezing them as tight as she could, and thought about being back home in her room at her grandparents' house, warm and safe. She felt an energy rising in her feet and moving up toward her chest, tightening her lungs. It sprang out into the tips of her fingers and the roots of her hair. She felt a shift and knew that she had moved in time. Yet the smell of the barn still lingered in her nose as she gently opened her eyes, hoping beyond all hope that she was back at Owen's farm.

There in front of her stood Artemas. A grin spread across his face, and his blue eyes were lit with wonder as he stared back at her.

"Crap. I thought I flipped," she said, her shoulders slumping in defeat.

"You did! You flipped a few minutes into the past," he told her, pointing up at the window where the sky was no longer black but a dusty pale blue. "And you took me with you. It was as if your magic grabbed hold of mine and dragged me along with it." Seeing the look of disappointment still on Kate's face, he said, "Well, it's a start. Magic is a fickle thing, and without proper nutrition and sleep, you could end up sending yourself somewhere other than home. So, let's go get a good meal in your belly and a full night's sleep, and by morning you should be able to flip back home with no problem."

They walked out of the barn and toward the house, where the windows glowed with soft yellow light. Artemas had a wild grin still sprawled across his face like a child just getting off a ride at a carnival.

"What will you tell your wife about me staying?" Kate asked.

"Don't you worry about that, I'll think of something," he reassured her.

Just then, a set of headlights cut through the dusk and came down the long, winding driveway. The sinking feeling returned to Kate as the car came to a stop, and an older man in a long jacket carrying a doctor's bag emerged from it. Artemas's grin quickly faded.

"Dr. Morgan. Thank you for coming back out to see Neala. Here, follow me," he said, guiding the doctor inside. Kate followed behind.

Upon entering the house, the smell of dinner filled the air, and Kate's stomach rumbled. From the back room she could hear the pitiful, weak cries of the baby. She sounded worse than she had just a few hours ago.

"Kate, why don't you go in and watch television with Betty in the living room," Elizabeth suggested, trying to make sure the girls were out of the way of the doctor. Kate did as she was told, but once Elizabeth was out of sight, she decided to walk into the hallway to listen in on what the doctor had to say.

The television blared with some black-and-white movie with cowboys and Indians. Betty sat only a foot away from it as if she was trying to block out the cries of her ailing sister. Kate felt bad for her. She was obviously trying to distract herself from the foreboding situation her family found itself in, but this kind of tension was hard to ignore, even with a TV blaring in your face. She knew that from trying to muffle out the sounds of her own parents' arguments when she was younger.

"We've done everything you advised but she's got so much worse. I've given her the medicine and fever reducer but nothing seems to be helping," she heard Elizabeth say in a voice woven with worry.

There was the sound of the doctor rooting around in his bag and then the weak cry of the baby again. It was silent for a few moments before the doctor spoke.

"I'm sorry," he said, his voice heavy and somber, as if saying those two words took all his effort. "The penicillin isn't working. The bacteria appear to be resistant to it. The measles weakened her immune system, and the pneumonia she developed has progressed more quickly as a result. At this stage, I don't think she's strong enough to fight it. I would normally tell you to bring her to the hospital, but to be very frank, she will be lucky to survive the night." The doctor paused for a moment. "She should be here at home with the people who love her."

"No!" Elizabeth cried out, then began sobbing heavily.

"I am so sorry. It took an unexpected turn. I wish there was more I could do," the doctor said, trying to console her.

"I told you we should've taken her to the hospital," she could hear Elizabeth say through muffled cries.

There was movement. Kate scooted herself back into the living room and sat on the couch. She could see Artemas walk the doctor to the front door through the small hallway that separated the living room and kitchen. The doctor rested his hand on Artemas's shoulder and hung his head in wordless sorrow.

Once the doctor left, Artemas came into the living room with two bowls of soup and round rolls for both her and Betty.

"Eat up, you two, bedtime in thirty minutes," he said, his eyes red and swollen from tears.

Betty looked up at him as he handed her the soup, a look of worry washing across her face. She turned back to the television, her eyes glued to the screen as if she were willing it to scoop her up and take her away from the sadness that surrounded her.

Kate sat there, the warm bowl of soup resting in her lap. Looking down into the bowl, she could see small flecks of magic mixed throughout it. That's when she stood up and walked into the kitchen, leaving her soup on the coffee table.

Artemas was standing at the sink, tears falling from his eyes and landing in the porcelain basin.

"You can save her. You need to save her," Kate said.

Her words startled him out of his sorrow. He turned around. "Kate…"

"You *can*. And I'll help. There must be a way my magic can

do something," Kate insisted.

"Kate, you are wise beyond your years, but I can't get you involved. It's too dangerous," he told her. He turned back to the sink and began washing a large cast iron pot, his eyes still filled with tears. "But you're right. I shouldn't have waited this long. My fear that I would lure evil to my home made me hesitate. I should have used my powers earlier. I didn't think the sickness would pull her under so fast." He paused, looking out the window above the sink in contemplation. "I will need to perform the spell as soon as possible. Elizabeth won't leave Neala's side, so I need to prepare everything now and then wait until she falls asleep. If you want to help me, make sure that Betty stays in her room tonight."

"What if I try and flip you back to before she got sick? Maybe you could prevent it from happening."

"No, Kate, that is too risky, and with the little time I have left to save her, I can't take that chance—for either of you. You just keep yourself and Betty safe in her room tonight, okay?" he told her, nodding his head as if he was asking her to nod along in compliance.

"Okay," Kate said, turning around and walking back to the living room. She sat down and picked up her bowl of soup that was now cool and tried to eat.

Though she'd only known these people for less than a day, she felt a deep sadness working its way to her core. In a way, they were family, connected by the magic flowing through their veins.

Chapter Thirty-Three
(1951)
Kate

DEATH REWIND

Kate had done as Artemas asked and kept an eye on Betty while she slept. However, eventually, her own eyelids grew heavy, and sleep took control. She was jolted awake by a wave of energy that shot through her like a bolt of lightning. She sat upright on the cot and looked toward the door. There was a blue glow seeping in through its cracks, and she could hear Artemas's hushed voice. Quickly and quietly, she got to her feet and slowly opened the door, doing her best not to wake Betty or disrupt whatever was going on outside the room. She tiptoed her way through the living room and stood in the shadow of the kitchen doorway.

Artemas held the baby in his arms above a cast iron pot resting on the kitchen table. Earthy-smelling smoke surrounded the baby as she lay silent in his arms. He guided the smoke up and around the infant, creating a circle around her, while in a low whisper, he chanted an incantation.

> "With this magic, break through the veil.
> From death to life now tip the scale.
> With darkness gone, the light will remain.
> Heal her from all sickness and pain.
> Pass her back through the veil.
> Where pain is lost, and health will prevail.
> By the power of three, so mote it be."

He spoke the words from the spell three times. Upon the final chant, a blue glow emanated from the pot and then became a bright white flash that left Kate blinded for a moment.

As her vision returned, she witnessed the baby begin to stir in Artemas's arms. It appeared that the spell had indeed worked, and her condition was improving. The light continued to pour out of the pot, glowing so brightly that it appeared to be a portal into another realm. Artemas set the baby down and began adding herbs to the pot, and as he did, the glow dimmed. Curious, Kate stepped forward, not looking where she was going and knocked over a small end table next to the doorway. Artemas spun around, and Kate stepped out from the shadow. Seeing that it was Kate and not his wife or Betty, he turned back around with a large bundle of herbs in his hands.

Then, from out of the dimming glow, a dark shadow appeared, slithering its way out into the room. Kate's stomach sank as she watched the shadow creature reach out and wrap a dark tendril around the baby's right arm.

"No!" Artemas cried out, throwing the bundle of herbs into the pot and stepping back.

The light went dim and then was snuffed out. The kitchen was plunged into darkness, all but the glow of one single candle. Its flickering flame danced around the walls and caught the shadowy figure as it moved around the baby.

"You are not welcome here! You must go!" Artemas commanded, his deep voice reverberating around the room. "Do you hear me? Go!"

There was the creak of a door and footsteps in the hallway. Then Elizabeth came running into the room.

"Artemas, what's going on? Is Neala…?" Her voice trailed off as she looked down to see a pink-cheeked, healthy-looking baby. "But how?" she asked, plucking the baby from the highchair and holding her tight to her chest.

"Herbs from the garden. I remembered an old remedy that my babtsya told me about when I was a child. I gathered the herbs from the garden and burned them so she could inhale the smoke. I think it worked. I think she's going to be okay," he said, taking Elizabeth and the baby in his arms.

Kate listened as the lies rolled off his tongue and into the air that was still filled with the aromatic smoke. Neala now glowed with a white light; it was no longer blue like Artemas's and hers. It was a white-hot light, like the kind she had witnessed coming from the pot's center. Like the light of the sun.

But Kate could still see a darkness following her, snaking its way around the light and hanging on its edge. She knew Artemas could see it too.

She slipped back to Betty's room, leaving Elizabeth and Artemas alone with the baby. She lay on the makeshift bed and felt a creeping sensation all around her. The air felt different; the gloomy foreboding that once filled the air with Neala's dying cries had turned to a dark, heavy energy that felt suffocating. Her mind was filled with unease, and it was a long time before sleep finally took her.

The sun was just beginning to rise when Kate woke the next day. Its bright, cheery rays broke through the window in Betty's room and left long streaks of golden light upon the floor. The sound of a happy babbling baby could be heard through the door, and the smell of bacon drifted in, drawing Kate out of the room with a groaning belly.

The sky was a clear blue, and the whole house was lit with the fresh rays of morning light pouring in through the east-facing windows.

In the kitchen, Elizabeth stood over the cookstove frying up a large pan of bacon, eggs, and mushrooms, humming a tune to herself. Little Neala sat in a wooden highchair pushed up next to the table, chattering away. Her color had fully returned, and no one would have ever guessed she had been on her deathbed the night before. She pushed around a bit of mushy egg on the tray with her fingers, blowing spit bubbles and babbling.

It should have been a happy scene, but the sight of the baby haloed in darkness left a pit in the bottom of Kate's stomach.

"Good morning," Kate said as she pulled up a chair next to the baby and sat down.

Elizabeth jumped. "Oh goodness me, Kate, I almost forgot you were here." She smiled. "Artemas went into town. He should be back in a few hours, and then he said he would drive you home. Are you hungry?" she asked, pulling a white plate with fine blue trim down from a cupboard.

"Yes, please," she answered, her stomach doing most of the talking now. "I'm happy to see that your baby is feeling better."

Elizabeth handed her a plate piled high with breakfast. "Thank you, Kate. I'm so relieved. She had us worried sick there for a moment. But it seems God answered our prayers and gave her the strength to overcome it."

"I'm really glad," Kate said, but she knew better. It wasn't God who saved Neala; it was Artemas.

Kate began eating and was joined by Betty, who had finally made her way out of bed, apparently in no hurry to get to school. Kate realized it must be Saturday, which meant she had been gone from her own time for over twenty-four hours. She stopped eating. She needed to get home, and as soon as Artemas was back, she was going to have to pull everything she had together to make sure it happened.

It was close to three in the afternoon when he finally arrived back at the house, a look of uncertainty plaguing his face as he walked in the door.

"Oh, love, perfect timing," Elizabeth said as she greeted him with the baby on her hip. "I need to drive Betty to her piano lesson. Can you take care of Neala? I don't think we should risk bringing her out just as she's starting to feel better."

Artemas slowly peeled off his thick canvas jacket and hung it on a pegboard next to the door. Then he plucked Neala out of her mother's arms and lifted her in the air over his head, bringing her down and kissing her nose. She squealed in delight, and the somber look he had walked in with faded.

"Of course. You take Betty, and I'll watch Neala. When you get back, I'll take Kate home," he told her, bringing Neala back down into his arms like a cradle.

Elizabeth hurried Betty, calling for her not to forget her sheet music and jacket as they scrambled around. Once they had pulled out of the driveway and the car could no longer be seen, Artemas's face grew pale and somber once again.

"Kate, I need you to do one thing for me before you go, and we only have a short amount of time to do it. Elizabeth and Betty will be back in a little less than two hours. I know you can see that Neala's light is different from ours now she's come back through the veil. She has pulled energy back from the other realm, and her magic is much stronger now than anything you or I will ever possess. I need to bind her so that she doesn't hurt herself or anyone else. No child should hold such powers freely," he told her. He handed Neala a small wooden rattle to play with, then looked back at Kate. "I know you saw the dark shadow emerge from the veil last night—"

"What was that anyway?" Kate asked, cutting him off.

"It was some sort of demon or dark spirit from another realm. The veil is the space that separates our world from the worlds beyond. It's the doorway between life and death. When I opened it to pull Neala back, the dark spirit slipped through with her. It has attached itself to Neala's soul." For a moment, Artemas looked as though he was going to be sick, then composed himself. "I need to cast another spell to send it back, and I'm going to need your help to do that."

"Yeah, of course. What do you need?" Kate asked, feeling as if she was being thrown into a world from one of her books. Magic, powers, evil forces—it was a lot to take in, and she was starting to think maybe she was just dreaming it all.

Artemas put Neala back in her highchair and then grabbed a pair of scissors. He snipped a small lock of hair from the back of her head and then pulled a piece of red thread from his pocket. He began wrapping the thread around the lock of hair and muttering something under his breath. When he finished, he plucked a dried violet off of a bundle that hung from the window and placed it on top of the hair, fusing it on with a bit of hot wax from a candle burning by the stove. He pressed his thumb hard into the wax, bonding the hair, string, and flower together as one.

"Okay, now I need you to watch Neala while I gather the herbs for the spell. Can you do that?" he asked, setting the hair down and taking a small basket and knife from the counter.

"Yes," she told him.

Kate kept Neala entertained with a game of peek-a-boo while Artemas gathered what he needed from the garden. When he returned, his basket was filled with sage, mugwort, basil, foxglove, and wild ferns. He pulled down the cast iron pot from a hook on one of the kitchen's exposed beams and set it on the table. Kate watched as he began layering the bottom of the pot with the herbs, making sure to leave an opening in the center. He took a large box of salt out of a cupboard and poured it in a circle on the floor around the table where Neala sat.

"Why did you do that?" Kate asked.

He stopped and looked up at her as if he had forgotten for a moment she was there. "Salt is used in spells for protection. A circle of salt around an object protects what lies inside it," he told her before going back to the task at hand.

Next, he pulled a small brick of charcoal out of the basket and placed it in the center of the pot, the herbs circling it like a wreath, then lit it.

"I send you back from where you came.

A portal back through wick and flame.

Break the chain, no tether be.

You must resend, so mote it be."

As he spoke, the flame doubled in size, and the center of

the pot burned with the white-hot light once again. Artemas was on his second chant of the spell when Kate noticed that Neala looked unwell. Her face was growing pale, and the red spots were appearing back on her neck and forehead. The darkness around her had turned into a whirling black mist, twisting and contorting violently as it was pulled from its host.

Fear bubbled up in Kate. She could now clearly make out a figure looming over the baby.

"Stop!" she cried out, breaking Artemas's enchantment.

He looked over at her, then at Neala, who was slumped in the highchair, tiny beads of sweat rolling off her face. The shadow of the demon retreated back into the safety of its hiding place within the child as the spell stopped.

"No!" he cried out, smoldering the fire in the pot. As soon as the fire and smoke were gone, Neala went back to being a pink-cheeked happy baby again. He picked her up and held her close to him.

"It's worse than I feared. I cannot kill or send the demon back. It has tethered itself to Neala's life force. I need to cut the tie that holds him to her, but he must stay in our realm or she will die." He paused, his eyes widening with the gravity of the situation. "I have to trap it. Contain it with something where he can do no harm," he muttered to himself.

He set Neala back down and then opened an old-looking leather-bound book that rested on the counter. He flipped wildly through its pages and then abruptly stopped, running his finger down its center as he read from it. Then he went feverishly through the house, gathering what items he needed and bringing them to the kitchen.

Kate watched as he took a thick hemp rope in one hand and a small tincture bottle in the other. He laid the rope on the table and then added drops of the pungent oil to it. Pulling it up, he wrapped it three times around on itself and then tied a knot with two equal ends. Walking over to the window above the sink, he grabbed a candle holder with a white candle in it. He placed it in the center of the table and then lit it with a match, muttering something under his breath as he went about his task. Holding the knotted end of the rope over the candle, he began to chant.

"Break the bond between two souls.

Let them find their separate roles.

Free them from the bond they share.

Break them free until they tear.

Separate, but in this world together,

Unbind them of their spiritual tether."

He spoke the spell three times, and on the third and final time, the candle had burned through the knot in the rope, splitting it into two pieces. Neala began crying, clearly distressed, as the spell took hold. As soon as the final thread burned, a dark plume of smoke seeped out of Neala and filled the room.

Kate shrank back in fear as the dark spirit spun wildly in the air, swooping down toward Neala in a desperate attempt to reenter its host. When it had no luck, it grew more violent, taking the shape of a man. A man made of soot and shadow.

The shadowy figure solidified, and with it came a voice as dark and deep as a moonless sky.

"You have no idea what you're doing, mortal," it said.

The sound of its voice pierced Kate's soul, and a fear unlike any she had ever known shook her to her core, leaving her frozen. Little Neala continued to cry, her glow almost nonexistent now that Artemas had bound her magic.

The shadow stepped toward Neala, arm outstretched.

"No!" Artemas bellowed.

Just inches from the baby's screaming face, the shadow recoiled as though it had touched fire. The circle of salt had stopped it, Kate realized. Artemas moved swiftly in front of Neala and pushed her highchair toward Kate without breaking the ring of salt.

Kate wanted to leap forward and grab the baby but fear held her tightly in its grip.

Artemas grabbed a bundle of herbs from the table and lit them on fire with the flick of his wrist. The smoke plumed out, and he blew it toward the figure, causing it to twist and move in an unearthly way.

"*Stay back!*" Artemas commanded, but his efforts seemed to only temporarily distract it.

The demon reformed, bigger and denser than before. A black tendril of smoke sprang from its body, and in one swoop, it cleared the table of its contents, cascading them over the floor. Everything except one thing—the blade.

Kate watched in horror as the demon stepped forward, wrapping its black, smoky fingers around the hilt of the knife, lifting it from the table. Artemas raised his arms to the sky and then brought them down in an X formation while yelling something out in a foreign language.

His actions were no match for the speed at which the demon had thrown the knife. Before Artemas's arms had even made their way to his sides, the knife struck him. He fell to the floor on his knees, the knife protruding from his side.

Kate's heart sank.

"Kate! Go! Take Neala. *Go now!*" Artemas yelled from the floor.

There was a look of defeat in his eyes as he slowly pulled the knife out, cupping his hand over the wound. A red river of blood flowed from his side, spreading down onto the old, porous wooden boards. He raised his hand to the sky, pulling what looked like magic from the air itself.

"*Kate!*" he yelled again. "Go."

Kate broke free from her fear, scooped the baby up into her arms and ran as fast as she could toward the front door. Neala screamed and cried into the air that was dense with magic as they fled. Her feet thudded on the floor, and her heart pounded in her ears. Not looking back, she ran out of the house, fear fueling each stride.

"Kate, can you hear me? Wake up, Kate. Come on, wake up," a faraway voice said.

Slowly, Kate opened her eyes. Above her, four faces stared back. Her vision was blurry, and it was a minute before she could make out who they were. Her nana, Owen, Ben, and John stood there with looks of worry and concern on their faces.

She locked eyes with Owen and said, "I remember." The words came out slurred and strained, but Owen heard them loud and clear by the look in his eyes. She sat herself up on the hardwood floor. "I'm okay," she said.

Owen took one of her arms, and Ben took the other, hoisting her up and onto one of the dining room chairs. Her nana came over to inspect her, placing the back of her hand against her forehead.

"She feels a bit feverish," she told Ben.

"I'm fine, really. I just stood up too fast. That's all." Kate tried to reassure them.

"You went down pretty hard. You sure you're okay?" Owen asked with genuine concern in his voice.

Kate looked over at Ionna, who was spinning the chain of her necklace mindlessly through her fingers with a puzzled look in her eyes. When their hands connected, had she, too, experienced the strange energy pulse? It appeared to have jarred loose a repressed memory from Kate's past, the one that her mind had been desperately attempting to hide.

"I think I better get her home. Ben, can you help me get her to the car?" Flora asked, guiding Kate to her feet.

"Owen, go grab Kate's jacket for her, would you?" Ben asked as he took up step next to Kate like she was some kind of invalid.

He walked her out of the dining room and into the entryway, but before she got any further, she turned back and looked at Ionna. She stood there next to the table, looking back at her, a wildness playing around in her eyes that Kate hadn't seen in them before now. She gave Kate a small smile and a wave goodnight as Ben urged her out the door, Owen following behind.

Kate's heart raced. The cool night air did nothing to subside the fear and adrenaline coursing through her. She tried her best to conceal the terror that was still playing out in her mind like something from a Stephen King novel.

Ben helped Kate into the car, and Owen stepped forward, handing her her jacket.

"Are you sure you're okay?" he asked. She could tell he knew she wasn't.

"Yeah, I just need some sleep. Why don't you come over tomorrow?" she told him.

He gave her a knowing look as his father shut the door, and Flora drove them off.

Chapter Thirty-Four
Ionna
THE JOURNAL

Ben and Owen walked back into the house after sending Kate and Flora on their way. John, Ryan, and Ionna were all standing in the entryway, chatting about the night's events.

"Why don't I take Ionna home for you, Dad? You still have all the dishes to do," Owen suggested as they walked in.

"See, this is how kids get themselves out of doing chores these days," Ben joked. He handed Owen a set of keys from a bowl that sat on an old milk can in the entryway. "It was nice meeting you, Ionna," he said, sticking out his hand for her to shake.

She took his hand and shook it firmly. "Thank you so much for the lovely dinner. It was delicious."

"Have a good night, Ionna," John said, pulling her into a tipsy hug. "I'll stop in and say goodbye before I head back to London."

She patted his back as she pulled away and smiled at him before walking out the door.

Stepping out into the crisp evening air, she followed Owen to his car. As she reached for the door handle, a chill caressed her shoulders, and the hairs on the back of her neck stood on end, as if someone was standing directly behind her. Turning swiftly, she expected someone to be there, but there was nothing, only an old gray cat slipping through the crack of the barn door. She paused for a moment, then got into the car.

"Thanks for taking me home," Ionna said as Owen pulled out of the driveway and onto the old dirt road.

"No problem," he said.

A long, awkward silence followed. Ionna had no idea how to talk to a teenage boy, and she wasn't feeling particularly sociable anyway.

"Can I ask you a question?" he asked, breaking the uncomfortable moment.

"Sure, what's up?"

"Tonight, right before Kate fainted, I saw this look in both your eyes like you had been shocked or something. What was that?"

"Oh. Um." The question surprised her. "To be completely honest with you, I have no idea. It was a strange surge of energy, like when you get a static electric shock. You know, like when you walk across a rug with socks on and then touch something metal, but stronger," Ionna told him. "It was probably just that. I don't know what else it could be."

"Well, it must have been one hell of a static shock to make Kate pass out. It's weird, don't you think?" he asked her as he pulled down the long, winding driveway toward Betty's house.

The moon was peeking its head up over the mountain's ridge line, giving just enough light to make out the silhouettes of the house and barn.

"Yeah, it's weird. I would be lying if I didn't say it shook me up a bit, but there's almost always an explanation," she told him, trying to convince him as much as herself.

"You're right. I'm sure there is a reasonable explanation," he said, sounding unconvinced.

He pulled up next to the barn and parked the car. It was an odd thing for him to say, and she wasn't sure how to respond.

"Well, here you go," he said, saving her from trying to think of something to say.

"Thank you for the ride. Night," she said, getting out of the car.

His headlights cut through the dark, and she followed the beam of light up to the front door. She waved a "thank you" as he turned around and drove back up the driveway, out of sight.

When she opened the door and flipped on the light switch, Jasper was there at her feet, awaiting her return. She slipped off her shoes and headed toward the kitchen when something caught her eye. There was a light coming from the living room.

Her blood ran cold.

She walked through the doorway, and there, next to one of the blue velvet chairs, was a lamp fully lit, its yellow glow illuminating her great-grandfather's journal. It sat there as if it was waiting for her return, calling out for her to come and read the rest of his tale.

Well, ghosts are better than intruders, she thought.

She set her bag down on the table next to Betty's urn and walked over to the book, giving into its pull. The possibility of finding some answers drew her in.

She grabbed a small knit blanket off the back of the sofa and threw it over her shoulders. It was quite cold in the house tonight, and she wished that she had a fire going to cut the chill, but the blanket would have to do.

Grabbing the book off the table, she sank down into one of the blue velvet chairs and opened it up, flipping to the page where she had left off. She paused, then squinted, holding the book at arm's length. Were the pages ... *glowing*? If she didn't know any better, she'd think there was a tiny light buried within the book somewhere. *One too many glasses of wine*, she thought as she flipped toward the back, but the glow seemed to get brighter. She turned to the last few pages to find there were no longer any journal entries but recipes. *Well, maybe not recipes*, she thought, skimming her eyes over them. Strange ingredients and instructions. Rituals. Spells.

No, how can that be? Spells, really? But that was exactly what they were. There was a page titled "Patch for a Broken Soul," another titled "Calling upon a Demon," and many more pages written to the brim with that kind of eerie content. Had her great-grandfather been involved with some sort of cult? The thought sent an uneasy feeling through her, and she swallowed hard. Something like that could explain why her father didn't want her to have any contact with his mother's side of the family.

She turned back to the part of the book where he had written his journal entries down and began looking for any mention of unnatural things. It didn't take her but a minute before she came upon a page that explained the spells in the book.

> June 20th, 1951
> It's been three years or more since I've practiced any magic. I swore an oath to myself when Elizabeth and I

married that I would not bring that kind of danger into our home. However, it has been a hard promise to keep. I have found myself looking through the spells in this book many times in the past week in search of something to help Neala out of her sickness. I know if I open the door to magic, even to cure her, it will also open a pathway for evil to find us. I must stay strong and believe that the doctor's cure for measles will work and that she will begin to get better.

June 25th, 1951

Neala grows weaker by the day, and it has taken everything I have not to step in and use the forces I know I possess to help her. I can no longer sit idly by and wait. It's time to do what needs to be done before it is too late. Her glow has grown weak and is almost nonexistent at this point, a telltale sign her spirit is shifting to the other realm. I must travel back to Fernbeg for the spell I need in one of Freya's grimoires. I don't have much time. Certain death holds her tightly in its grip now.

June 28th, 1951

Upon returning from Scotland, I was surprised by a visitor in my barn. A young red-haired girl named Kate, who I thought to be Freya reincarnate at first. However, she is not. Even though I have heard the stories of people who hold the power to bend time, I have never met one before until now. She was wounded upon her arrival and is unable to safely return to her own time in the future. It has taken all my efforts not to ask what the future holds, even though I am curious. I believe knowing too much can be a burden on the soul and could change fate's outcome. But just her presence gives me hope that the future has not been lost.

I convinced Elizabeth that she was visiting her cousins in Wales when they got into a fight, and she fled on one of their horses, got lost, and was bucked off on the mountain behind their house, leaving her stranded until she found her way to our barn. She thinks I have spoken with her parents and will be bringing Kate to meet them at the train station tomorrow.

The girl seems wise beyond her years and has reminded me that we have been gifted with powers to be used for the betterment of mankind, not to be hidden away. I think Kate was sent here to remind me of that from the Goddess herself. I plan to take the spell I found in Freya's grimoire and save my daughter. But I must do so after Elizabeth falls asleep. Even if I use magic to save our daughter, I do not want her to know about the powers I hold. I must remain my ordinary self to her and Betty.

There were no additional entries in the book; this was the final journal page. The remainder was comprised of strange spells and bizarre herbal remedies. Unnerved, Ionna stopped reading. Was her great-grandfather completely mad? How could a grown man believe in all this nonsense? He must have suffered from some kind of undiagnosed mental disorder. Either that or he had been some kind of devil worshipper. She wasn't totally closed-minded; there were lots of people who still performed pagan rituals and such. But time travel? *Come on*, she thought. His journal was starting to read more like some kind of fantasy novel than a diary.

Unsure if she wanted to keep reading, she set the book down in her lap. The house seemed to be getting colder, so much so that she could almost see her own breath now. She pulled the blanket tighter around her and shivered, looking over at the fireplace longingly. There was no firewood in the log box by the hearth, and she wasn't about to go out in the dark to root around for some in the yard. Not when there were panthers apparently stalking the land.

Without thinking, she grabbed Betty's chain that still hung around her neck and began spinning it through her fingers. A habit she had picked up, it seemed, since she had put it on earlier that night. Jasper came into the room and jumped up into the chair next to her, gazing fondly at the fireplace.

"I feel ya, boy. I wish there was a fire in there too. It's cold in here," she said, still spinning the chain through her fingers.

Then, out of nowhere, there was a flicker, a flash, and then a flame burst out, burning brightly in the fireplace. Ionna jumped to her feet, knocking the book to the floor.

"What the fuck!"

Ionna stared into the fire, the flames dancing in the reflection of her frightened eyes. *How did that just happen? There must be some sort of thermostat that kicked off a gas unit hidden in the fireplace*, she thought. She stepped forward to inspect it when she tripped on the book, temporally forgetting she had dropped it. She bent down to retrieve it, slipping her finger under its spine and picking it up, the two limp sides of the book hanging like a bird with broken wings. When she flipped it over, the words on the page immediately caught her eye.

> Fire from air.
> It takes two elements to create fire from air alone: garnet and gold.

The gold must be rubbed in a clockwise direction to generate friction. The garnet should be placed outside the circle, and the intention of fire should be expressed while visualizing the garnet as the spark and the circular movement of the gold as the air that breathes life into the flame.

Ionna's heart quickened. She pulled up the necklace and inspected it. Not only was the necklace gold but on the pendant above the green stone were two tiny red gems. She had been sitting there spinning the necklace around her neck, clockwise, and there outside the circle of the chain were not one but two garnets.

Had she just started the fire with a spell?

No, that was crazy. Her great-grandfather's journal was getting to her head.

She walked over to the fireplace and looked for the hidden gas nozzle where the fire had to be coming from, but there was nothing. It was as if the fire *was* burning on pure air alone. There wasn't even a small amount of ash or coal in the fireplace. It looked as if it had been swept clean and hadn't housed a fire for quite some time. Yet, there in the center of the old stone hearth was a fire burning brightly, and the room was already beginning to feel its warming effects.

Completely thrown by her findings, she sat back down and opened the book again, but this time with new eyes. If magic was indeed real ... then this journal held more secrets than just her family's. She was going to find out just what those were.

She had gotten through the entire book with tired eyes before she finally fell asleep sometime after midnight. As sleep overtook her, so did a dream.

It was a beautiful summer day; the sun was out in full effect, with not a cloud in the sky. Birdsong filled the air like a symphony, and the heady aroma of flowers danced with the soft breeze that blew through the Welsh countryside. The wheat was at its peak and ready to be harvested. Its tall stalks swayed in the wind, causing a wave that rippled through the field. Beyond, the mountain stood watch, guardian to all in its valley. There, in peaceful solitude at the base of the mountain, sat a mighty oak tree, its branches outstretched, providing shade to all who needed it.

Ionna walked toward the tree, across the field overflowing with wheat. At the base of the tree, sitting on a large rock, was the fortune teller from the market. She smiled and waved to Ionna, gesturing for her to come closer. She was saying something to her but the wind grew harsh and carried her words away.

All of a sudden, the beautiful day began to darken, and the chorus of birds fell silent. The fortune teller's happy expression turned fearful, and her gestures quickened, urging Ionna to come to her faster.

She tried to run, but her feet kept getting tangled in the thick wheat grass. The closer she got, the darker the sky became until both Ionna and the fortune teller were cloaked in total darkness. Ionna stopped, not being able to see, fear shooting through her.

It was then that she felt a cold breeze slither behind her and over her shoulders. She turned, and there in the darkness, a pair of piercing yellow eyes stared back at her.

Chapter Thirty-Five
Ionna
A BREAK IN REALITY

Ionna woke the following day, her neck stiff and the journal resting heavily in her lap, along with the nightmare resting heavily in her thoughts. *All this hocus pocus nonsense is messing with my head and causing nightmares,* she thought, as she picked the journal up and closed it.

Jasper was still sleeping soundly in the chair beside her when she got up and walked over to the fireplace. It lay empty; no flame graced its hearth, yet the room was warm as if a fire had burned through the night. She reached down and placed her hands on the smooth gray fieldstone. It was still warm to the touch, yet not even a single ash lay in its barren center. Even the faint smell of smoke still hovered in the air.

It wasn't a dream, then. She had started a fire purely from air and her own will.

She still couldn't wrap her mind around it. She rubbed her temples, trying to calm all the crazy thoughts that were spinning inside her head.

Ever since she stepped foot in Wales, her perception of reality had been flipped on its side. So many strange things had happened. The disappearing light switches, the poisoned pies, the sheep drowning in the river—even glimpses of what she believed to be Betty's ghost. Now her great-grandfather's journal of spells and the fire she couldn't explain rationally.

She'd read every spell, ritual, and remedy in the book the night before, and it still felt like something from a fantasy novel rather than real life. But she could sense its reality deep inside her, yearning to be acknowledged. As much as she tried to deny it, she knew deep down it was real. She feared that embracing the existence of magic might shatter her perception of reality, just as her trust in her family had been shattered after learning they had deceived her for years.

She looked down at the book still held tightly in her grip, the glow she had noticed the day before seeping from its edges. It was then that she felt a pull, some kind of force urging her to leave the room and enter the study. She let it guide her, and she found herself standing in front of the desk. She sat down in the old captain's chair and set the book down. As soon as it rested flat against the polished wood, a bright light shot out from one of the seams on the side of the desk. Ionna glided her hand down the thin crack to a small button hidden in a groove of its back leg. Another button, another hidden compartment. She was apprehensive at first, not knowing if she really wanted to keep going down this rabbit hole, but her journalist mind got the better of her, and she pushed it.

A small drawer popped out from the right side. How many secret drawers did this desk have? A thin piece of wood with a tiny knob sat snuggly over the compartment. She gently lifted it off, exposing a space no bigger than the page of a book. In its center was a Polaroid picture of a young ginger-haired girl.

Ionna lifted the picture up and inspected it closely. The image looked just like a younger version of Kate—it was uncanny. A date was printed in the corner of the picture: June 28th, 1951. There was no way it could be Kate. There was a good chance Kate's *mother* hadn't even been born then.

Then she remembered the last journal entry. She grabbed the book and flipped to the page dated June 28th, 1951. As she reread the entry, her eyes grew wide, and her heart began to race.

> June 28th, 1951
> Upon returning from Scotland, I was surprised by a visitor in my barn. A young red-haired girl named Kate.

She looked back at the photo, and an unsettling feeling began to brew in her stomach, sending waves of unease through her.

"No way!" she said, the rational thoughts moving aside, making space for the irrational ones that were forming in her mind at that moment.

No, this can't be. She tried her hardest to piece together a reasonable explanation. Maybe the Kate in the photograph was a namesake relative who shared a striking resemblance with the Kate Ionna had met at dinner last night. Maybe it was just some insane coincidence—the girl in the picture was probably in her early teens or younger, and didn't most pre-teen girls look sort of similar, with their baby-fat faces and shy smiles?

She looked again at the picture. Who was she kidding? The

girl in the photo could have been Kate's twin. She even shared a small freckle just above her right eye. Ionna had noticed it at the dinner as she had a similar freckle on the opposite side of her own face.

How was this even possible?

Okay, take it slowly, she told herself. *Somehow, and you don't need to know how just yet, it appears that the Kate you met at dinner last night visited your great-grandfather in the past.*

Is it nuts? Yes.

Is it highly improbable? Yes.

But it's also the clearest explanation you have for this photograph and the journal entries at the moment.

Ionna finally began wrapping her mind around the idea. And if all this craziness was true, then she needed to talk with Kate. She must have known what had happened to Artemas. She wanted—no, *needed* to know the rest of the story. The journalist instinct inside her would not be completely satisfied until the whole truth was revealed.

There were bits and pieces she could put together herself from what she had already learned in the past few days. Elizabeth's obituary stated that baby Neala died as an infant, so obviously the spells Artemas tried had not cured her. After that, the journal entries stopped. It was possible he was so grief-stricken he never wrote again, but what if something else happened? If Kate truly had traveled back to his time, then maybe she would be able to fill in what happened to Artemas.

There were so many questions and not nearly enough answers racing around in her head. She was never one to not get to the bottom of a story. It was one of the reasons she was such a good journalist. She just couldn't stop until she had pieced everything together and come up with the truth. Magic, time travel, demons—that was in a whole new league, and she had no idea how to go about questioning things that she herself wasn't sure she even believed in.

She closed the drawer and tucked the photo into the book, then carried it under her arm into the kitchen to make some coffee before opening any more cans of worms. She planned to call Flora and see if she was up for that cup of tea. Even if Flora couldn't shed any light on the mystery surrounding her father, then she could pull Kate aside and ask her about the events in the journal. Two birds, one stone.

It was going to be a long shot. A teenage girl wasn't going to spill her guts about anything to a total stranger, let alone about some crazy ability to bend space and time. But she needed answers before she went back to America, and her time was growing short. She had less than a week to get the answers she needed, so she'd better get a move on.

Chapter Thirty-Six

Kate

A PICTURE WORTH A THOUSAND WORDS

Kate did not sleep well that night; between the memory resurfacing and the nightmare she had after she eventually fell asleep, she appeared to be locked in an endless cycle of fear and anxiety. The memory was so horrifying and unbelievable that she could see why she had pushed it deep into her subconscious.

She sat there in bed, replaying the last thing she recalled from that time. She had grabbed the baby, turned around, and ran out of the house toward the barn. After that, her memory recoiled. How had she gotten back to her own time? And what had happened to the baby? That piece of the puzzle was still missing, and it seemed to be the most important part. She knew—or she hoped she knew—that her twelve-year-old self would not abandon a baby. But Owen had told her that when she reappeared back in her own time, she was alone.

It took her some time before she finally pulled herself out of bed and walked over to the dresser. She slipped off her PJs and pulled on a pair of jeans and an old Def Leppard shirt she'd found in a box of her mother's old clothes tucked away in the closet. When she bent down to put her socks on, she felt something poke her thigh. She jammed her hand into the front right pocket and felt something cold.

It was the necklace she'd purchased at the farmers' market. She'd totally forgotten about it. As she turned it in her fingers, its green surface reflected the early morning light. Two small red stones at the top caught her eye. She had forgotten how pretty it truly was.

Unclasping it, she slipped it around her neck, reconnecting it on the other side. When the clasp clicked into place and the cool metal touched her skin, a surge of energy shot through her, and for a brief moment she thought that she was about to flip time. But the sensation faded as quickly as it had come on. She tried to steady herself and then took a deep breath, happy that she hadn't sent herself spinning into another time again. *Weird*, she thought.

She tiptoed over to the door, trying her best not to alert her grandmother that she was awake. After last night, she'd want to keep a close eye on Kate the whole day, but she needed to see Owen. So she had to be a very stereotypical teenager and sneak out. Before she got to the door, she turned around and grabbed her mobile off the nightstand. She knew it was only a matter of time before her grandmother came up to check on her, so she wanted to have a way to call her once she was with Owen, just to reassure her she was fine. She slipped the phone in the back pocket of her jeans and headed to the door.

Walking downstairs as quietly as possible, she avoided the fourth stair to the bottom that creaked. She needed to make it over to her shoes and slip out the door before her grandmother saw her. She peeked around the corner and found her grandmother at the sink washing dishes and listening to the news on the radio. Kate waited until she turned to place a bowl in the cupboard before skirting past the kitchen and over to the entryway. She grabbed her trainers and opened the door slowly, her heart pounding in her chest as she said a silent prayer for the door not to creak as she opened it. Her prayers were answered, and she slipped out the door, closing it quietly behind her.

She hightailed it down the walkway in bare feet and then scooted behind a large bush out front to slip on her shoes. After her laces were tied, she took one last look over her shoulder at the house, half expecting her grandmother to be standing in the walkway with crossed arms. But the only thing she saw was a small blackbird hopping around on the patch of grass by the house, looking for a bit of breakfast. She let out a sigh of relief and turned toward the road in the direction of Owen's house.

It was a beautiful day. The sky was a robin's egg blue with only a few wispy clouds streaking its edges near the horizon. A light breeze blew in from the south, and with it came the smell of freshly baked bread from one of the neighboring houses. The smell made her stomach groan as she walked, her teenage hunger kicking in.

As she continued down the road, she caught sight of something out of the corner of her eye. Across the field at the base of the mountain was a lone oak tree. She had walked past this point many times but never paid the tree much attention. However, today, it caught her attention; it was the same tree from her dream the night before. Squinting in the late morning light, it looked as if someone was there standing under the tree. As if being pulled by an invisible cord, she couldn't help but walk toward it through the field of tall wheat stalks, cutting a thin path as she went. The grass tickled her wrists, and the crickets' song played softly throughout the field.

When she was almost upon the tree, she saw that the figure was a woman. Muted in the shade of the tree, her back was turned to Kate, and she was running her hands down the tree's rough surface. She seemed transfixed.

"Hello," Kate said, doing her best not to startle the woman.

But at the sound of Kate's voice, the woman jumped and turned quickly, alarm twisting her face. It was Ionna.

"Kate?" she said, a look of bewilderment replacing the alarm.

"Oh. Hi. What are you doing here?" Kate asked, a bit surprised to find that it was her standing under the tree.

"I was actually walking to your place to see how you were doing when I caught sight of this tree. I had the weirdest dream last night, and this tree was in it," she said, looking back at the tree with curious eyes.

"Really? Weird. I had a dream about this tree last night too. Well, it was more of a nightmare, I guess," Kate said.

Ionna's eyes widened. "This dream you had, it didn't happen to have the fortune teller from the farmers' market in it?"

Kate stood there stunned. *How? How does she know about the fortune teller in the dream? Is Ionna some sort of psychic herself?*

"Yeah, actually. How did you know that?" she asked, her tone turning suspicious.

"She was in my dream too. She was sitting under this tree calling to me, but—"

"The wind kept you from understanding what she was trying to tell you," Kate said, cutting her off and finishing her sentence.

They exchanged puzzled looks. What the hell was going on between the two of them? They obviously shared some strange connection, but why? They had never even met before the other day. What kind of connection could they possibly have?

"I don't get it. How could we have had the same dream?" Kate asked.

"I don't know. There seems to be a lot of unexplainable things going on around here," Ionna said, sitting down on the large rock at the base of the tree. "Kate, can I ask you a question? It's going to sound really strange but just hear me out, okay?"

"Yeah, I guess," Kate said reluctantly.

Ionna took a small breath, as if readying herself for what she was about to say. "I found a journal that belonged to my great-grandfather, Artemas. In it there was an entry about a girl with red hair named Kate." She paused, looking Kate straight in the eyes.

Kate's pulse raced.

"He mentioned that she had come from another time and that she helped him. I didn't think anything of it, other than he was raving mad—until I found this in his study." She pulled out a Polaroid from the pocket of her jacket and handed it to Kate.

Kate took the photo, staring down at the image of her young self, and any doubt she had about her time spent with Artemas vanished.

Chapter Thirty-Seven

Ionna

SWEET FINDING

Kate held the old Polaroid in her hands. It was like holding onto proof of the boogieman—it scared the hell out of her and thrilled her at the same time. She looked over at Ionna, who was regarding her with inquisitive eyes.

"Was this a relative of yours that you were named after?" Ionna asked her, breaking the awkward moment of silence that had fallen between them.

Kate just stood there looking down at the photo, not knowing what to say. How could she even begin to explain any of this? It was completely crazy; even she was having a hard time wrapping her own mind around it. She looked up at Ionna, and there was a silent acknowledgment between them. She could have lied to her and told her it was a relative, but Kate could see in her eyes she already knew that it was her in the photo.

"Did you visit the fortune teller when you were at the market?" Ionna asked, shifting the subject.

She could see how much the photograph had shaken Kate up and decided not to push the matter any further at the moment. If she allowed the fact that she suspected something to sink in, it would help Kate to open up when the time was right. It was a method she used when interviewing people for stories.

"Yeah, I did actually. She kinda pulled me in there. What about you? Did you get your palm read?" Kate asked, grateful that Ionna had not questioned her further on the photo.

"Yeah, John and I decided to pop in there when we were leaving. She couldn't really read my palm, though, so she read my tarot cards instead. She told me before I left that the only other time she had seen a palm like mine was when a girl walked in a little while before me. I think that must have been you."

"Yeah, she kinda freaked me out a little, telling me to be careful, that I needed to remember something from my past in order to protect myself," Kate told her. It was at that moment that she knew what the old woman had meant. She needed to remember her time with Artemas. The problem was that she couldn't remember everything, and it would be impossible to know for sure what danger was out there if she didn't have a complete memory of those last moments.

Ionna saw the strain in Kate's expression. There was more going on in her head than she was letting on, and she wasn't very good at hiding it.

"I have a ton of questions. There must be some sort of reason for this shared dream, we just have to piece it together." She tried to reassure her.

"You're right. We need answers, and the fortune teller might be the only one who can give us any. Do you have a car?" Kate asked, sliding the picture into the back pocket of her jeans and turning toward the road.

"Betty left me her car, but I'm not sure I'll be much good at driving it around here," Ionna said as she followed Kate down the narrow path out of the wheat field.

"That's okay. We can ask Owen to drive us. Let me text him," Kate said, pulling her phone from her back pocket, her long ginger hair swaying as she moved her phone around, looking for a spot where she could get enough bars to send a text. She stopped midstride and began typing.

"Do you even know where she lives?" Ionna asked.

Kate looked up from her phone. "No, but I'm sure it's not a mystery to the people who live around here. They probably think of her as the local loon." A moment later, Kate's phone vibrated. Owen had sent a text back. "He said he can meet us at your place in an hour or so after he finishes up some farm work for his dad."

"Okay, let's head that way then," Ionna said.

As they drew closer to the road, the sky darkened. The once light, wispy clouds were now thick cumulus clouds, turning the sky a dull gray. The sun had all but been completely blocked out by the time their shoes hit the gravelly road. They exchanged a glance, both thinking back to their shared dream. The clouds grew denser by the minute, and the midday sun was more like the setting light of a fall evening as they crested the knoll and passed the Dwyer farm onto the final stretch to Betty's.

Ionna noticed Kate look back at the farm in a way she remembered quite well from her own teenage years. Kate was crushing on Owen, and in a big way.

"How long have you two known each other?" she asked as

they made their way back up the road.

"Long time. Since we were seven or eight, maybe," Kate replied.

"Are you a couple?" She looked over at Kate as she kicked at the larger rocks on the road, her hands jammed into her front pockets. It made her look much younger than she was, and Ionna could see the innocence that she still held.

Kate's cheeks bloomed into a rosy hue before she had a chance to even answer, making it pretty apparent that she was smitten with him.

"God, no."

"Well, why not? You seem to both like each other by the looks of things," Ionna said.

"There is *no* way he would ever go out with someone like me," Kate said, sadness creasing her youthful face.

"What makes you think that? From my vantage point, I would say he's quite interested in you. He couldn't keep his eyes off you at dinner last night," she said with a conspiratorial smile.

Kate smiled in return, still blushing, but didn't say anything more as they continued to walk.

The sky grew darker still, and the birds' melodies had died down to only a few chirps here and there. The dark clouds loomed over the mountain, and a low rumble of thunder could be heard in the distance. There was a staleness to the air. It hung heavy around them, and the temperature had dropped significantly in just the past few minutes.

"Is the weather always this fickle in Wales?" Ionna asked as they made their way through the two oaks that flanked Betty's driveway.

"It's normally cloudy, but this week's weather has been abnormally weird," Kate told her, looking up at the sky.

As they drew closer, Kate's stomach began to turn. She feared that entering the house might cause the rest of the memory to resurface, and she wasn't sure she was ready to remember what had transpired that night. She hesitated at the front door, taking a step backward as Ionna swung it open. She peered in before stepping through the threshold, bracing herself for another flashback as she did.

"Come on in," Ionna said, waving her forward through the doorway.

Kate walked in slowly, surprised to see that the house had changed dramatically since the 1950s. She wasn't sure why it surprised her; it had been more than sixty years, after all. Maybe it was because her grandparents' place had stayed still in time, whereas Betty's house had been updated. It was now fashioned in a cozy country cottage style with hardwood floors and dark-painted walls with white trim. Other than the layout of the house itself, it looked almost nothing like she remembered it. This put her mind at ease a little, and she let the slack out of her shoulders as she followed Ionna in.

Ionna led her to the kitchen, but Kate hesitated again. The wall where the door used to be had been removed to create an open kitchen dining area. Despite the changes, a chill ran down her spine at the sight of the room. She could still feel the darkness there, like the room had been tainted by its very presence.

She sat down at the table, trying to steady her nerves. She scanned the kitchen, expecting something to happen, but everything was calm and still. The kitchen was stark compared to the slight chaos of a young family that she remembered. There were only a few items on the counter: a tea kettle, a set of canisters, salt and pepper shakers, and a funny-looking brass container with a bird on top of it, resting on the windowsill above the kitchen sink.

She reasoned that an elderly lady wouldn't require as much as an entire family.

It dawned on her then that everyone from her memories of this place was dead. She swallowed hard, thinking about the young Betty, so excited to show off her camera and take her picture. Now the only thing left of that time was the house itself.

"Okay, let me see what I have for lunch," Ionna said, the sound of her voice breaking into Kate's thoughts, making her jump. "How do you feel about grilled cheese sandwiches? I think that might be the only thing I have here to make unless you're down for a bowl of cereal," she joked.

She looked at Kate, who had turned pale, as if she had seen a ghost. Ionna glanced around quickly—at this point, it was quite possible. But the room was devoid of any ghostly apparitions, or anything else for that matter. There was something else going on with Kate, and she figured it had something to do with the fact she had been here before, a long time ago. It took everything she had not to ask her about it. Instead, she put her hands to work making their food.

As Ionna cooked, Kate sat at the small kitchen table and thumbed through the folklore book that sat next to a cold cup of coffee. She was happy for the distraction, as the tension in the room was palpable.

"Was this one of Betty's books?" she asked as she skimmed through the pages. She stopped when she reached "Lady of the Lake."

Ionna spun around, spatula in hand, and looked at what Kate had in her hands, letting out a sigh when she saw it was the folklore book and not Artemas's journal.

"No, actually. I got it from the vintage vendor at the market. Great little find, don't ya think?" she said, turning back around to flip one of the sandwiches in the old cast iron pan.

"Yeah, pretty cool. I got a few things from that vendor as well," Kate told her as she ran her fingers over the story of her ancestor.

She set the book of folklore to the side. There were two other books resting underneath. The one on top was a leather-bound book with the title *The Red Book of Hergest* embossed on the front in gold lettering. As she opened it, Ionna turned around.

"Order up!" she said, walking over to Kate with a slightly burnt grilled cheese sandwich on a plate.

Kate's hands fell away from the book as Ionna swooped in. "Oh. Thanks."

Ionna grabbed the books off the table and walked them into the sitting room, resting them next to the urn.

"Keep an eye on these, would ya," she told Jasper, who was sleeping on one of the blue velvet chairs. Back in the kitchen, she grabbed her plate and sat across from Kate at the small table. "So, do you come here every summer to stay with your grandmother?" she asked, trying to bring some normal conversation in to help Kate relax. There was obviously an elephant in the room, and at this point, Kate didn't seem remotely close to pointing it out.

"I used to. This is the first time I've been back in about six years. My granddad passed last winter, and I wanted to visit my nana before I start uni in the autumn," Kate told her, taking a bite of the sandwich and pulling a long string of cheese into her mouth.

"I'm sorry to hear about your grandfather," Ionna said.

"Thanks."

"I wish I'd gotten a chance to know my grandparents. I didn't even know I had a grandmother still alive until I got the letter from John a few weeks back. Both my parents are gone now, so there are lots of questions and no one to help answer them. That's why I wanted to talk to your grandmother. I thought maybe she might know what happened between my father and Betty," Ionna told her, disclosing more than she intended.

"I'm sorry too. Family can suck. Believe me, I have one as messed up as it gets," Kate said, taking another bite. "There must be something here in the house that can help answer some of it," Kate suggested.

"Yeah, you would think so, but so far, nada. The only thing I haven't looked at is her safety deposit box. She left it to me in the will but never gave the key to anyone. So, whatever secrets are in there will stay there until I find it or find someone to get it open."

Just then, Jasper came into the kitchen and jumped up onto the counter. He walked its length and then perched on the end near the sink. Three ceramic canisters sat there, stenciled with sixties-style gold and orange flowers, except for the places where the words "Flour," "Sugar," and "Tea" were printed. Jasper looked over at Ionna and then batted at the sugar container. With no more than two bats of his paw, the container fell to the ground. Broken ceramic shards and sugar covered the floor.

"Jasper! Bad kitty!" Ionna scolded, jumping up and going over to the mess.

"Do you have a broom?" Kate asked, taking the last bite of her sandwich and standing up.

"Um, yeah, I think it's over near the fridge. Can you grab it for me?"

Ionna bent down and began picking up pieces of the broken canister. Jasper looked down at her from the counter as she cleaned, a satisfied look in his eyes. She tossed the largest pieces into the rubbish bin and then grabbed the broom and dustpan from Kate. She had it almost all cleaned up when she noticed something shiny in the pile of sugar. There, hidden within it, was a silver key, the number 802 carved into its polished surface. Jasper jumped down and began rubbing himself around her legs in big S curves.

"You clever little kitty. Is this what I think it is?"

"I'm lost, what's going on?" Kate asked as she followed Ionna into the sitting room.

Ionna pulled a long metal box off a side table and sat in one of the overstuffed armchairs. Running her hands over its smooth, cold surface, she found an imprint of a number and spun it around to find 802 on its edge.

She took the key and inserted it into the lock, only turning it halfway when she heard the lock give way. The lid cracked open. She hesitated for a moment, but then excitement overtook her, and she flipped the box open.

Kate stood over her shoulder, looking down into the box as if it were a treasure chest, waiting to see gold jewelry and mounds of money. However, there in its center were just three things: a birth certificate, an envelope, and a picture. Ionna took out the birth certificate first. It was old and written in ink that was fading and hard to read.

> *Neala Rogowshi, born on December 21, 1949, at 8:00 p.m.*
> *Weight: 7 pounds 3 oz*
> *Length: 48.26 cm*
> *Mother: Elizabeth M Rogowshi*
> *Father: Artemas F Rogowshi*
> *Birthplace: Beddgelert, Wales*

It was her great-aunt's birth certificate. The edges looked as if they had been singed by fire, and a faint smell of old smoke lingered in the grains of the paper. The photograph had the same markers of fire on it. It showed a handsome man in his fifties and a beautiful woman holding a baby on her lap. Ionna stared down at the man. Something about him looked so familiar to her. His eyes. She was sure she had seen those eyes somewhere before. But she hadn't found any pictures in the house other than the ones of her and her father and the old, faded obituary from Elizabeth. Yet, she knew she had seen this man before.

Then it came to her like a wave crashing through her mind. The dream she had a few nights ago of a cliff edge near the ocean. He was the man in her dream. But how? She had never seen or met this man before. She didn't even know who he was.

Putting that aside for the moment, she took the envelope out of the box and opened it. In its fold was a letter addressed to her father.

Dear Adam,

After the fire in '94, I scavenged through the living room for any remnants that might have been untouched by the fire. Almost all of the photo albums were destroyed, but I was able to recover this photo that was saved by its metal frame and glass front. Neala's birth certificate was tucked away in a book that had halfway survived the flames. Everything else was a total loss. It pains me to know that this is the only image left of your grandparents. A tiny fragment of who they were to be passed down. I left it in here for safekeeping. I hope someday you will bring Ionna here and tell her the whole story. It's only right that she should know why you took her from here. Don't deprive her of the truth — sometimes it's the truth that saves us from ourselves. It pains me every day that I was not there to see her grow and guide you through parenthood as a good mother should. Just know that not a day went by that I didn't think of you two and love you.

Ionna sat back in the chair, the contents of the box laid out on its lid. She felt defeated. She'd finally been able to open the safety deposit box and inside were just more questions. What truth was her father depriving her of all these years? Why hadn't her grandmother reached out to Ionna personally after her parents' deaths? Was it possible she died not even knowing they had passed? She picked the picture up again. Her great-grandparents and little Neala stared back at her through sepia-toned eyes.

"Well, that wasn't what I thought would be in there," Kate said, startling Ionna out of her thoughts. She had forgotten Kate was there for a brief moment while the mounting questions about her past filled her every thought.

"Yeah, not what I was hoping for either. Just more questions with zero answers," she said, placing everything back in the box. For a split second, when she was putting the picture back in, she swore she saw a look of remembrance in Kate's eyes. Ionna felt as if this was her chance to bridge the gap between them and possibly have Kate open up to her. "Kate, how did you meet Betty?" she asked, hoping that it would be a good starter question to get Kate to loosen up a bit.

Kate looked up at her. She opened her mouth to answer when the sound of a car coming down the driveway distracted her. She walked to the window and peeled back the curtains.

"Owen's here," she said.

As Kate glanced out the window at Owen's car, her eyes held a secret, a glimmer of something Ionna couldn't quite decipher, leaving her with a burning question on her mind: What was Kate hiding about her connection to Betty and her family's mysterious past?

Part Two

Chapter Thirty-Eight
DARKNESS FOLLOWS

Kate pushed the curtains aside and looked down the long driveway. Owen's black car pulled past the two oaks at the entrance to the yard. He had arrived early, but in Kate's opinion, he was just in time because the tension in the room had been building since Ionna opened the box. Kate knew it was only a matter of time before she started asking questions about the picture tucked into the back pocket of her jeans, and she was still unsure of how she would go about answering her.

"We better get going," she told Ionna as she turned from the window.

"Great. Let me just grab a jacket, I'll meet you in the car."

Kate nodded as she walked to the front door and out into the heavy afternoon air. The sky was still thick with cloud cover, and there was a dampness to the air that foretold rain in the near future. The wind had picked up, blowing harshly from the north, and with it came an eeriness. Kate reached Owen's car and opened up the passenger door, slipping herself inside away from the sharp gale.

"Wow, the weather did a three-sixty today," she said as she shivered off the chill.

"Yeah, weird, right? But what's weirder is the shit that happened at dinner last night. What the hell was that, anyways? Spill it quick before she gets out here," Owen said, turning to Kate and waiting for her response.

"Okay, well, the quick version is I remembered what happened after I tried to get those biscuits. I flipped back to Betty's house in 1951 and saw some crazy shit go down between her dad and a pretty badass demon."

"Demon?" Owen repeated, alarm spreading across his face.

"Yeah. I know it sounds like an episode of *Buffy* or something, but I'm serious. And I'm still missing what happened at the end. How I got Ginger, and how I ended up back here. What happened there was bad, but whatever happened after must have been worse because it's still blocked out." Kate glanced up just as Ionna stepped out of the house and started toward the car. "Shit, she's coming. I'll tell you more later."

Ionna opened the back door behind Kate and got in, the wind blowing so fiercely now that it blew stray leaves in with her.

"Okay, so are you guys going to enlighten me on why we're going to see Karena Awbrey this afternoon?" Owen asked as he put the car in reverse and backed up.

"I think she might be able to help us. We both had a dream about her last night, the same dream. It must mean something," Ionna said. "Plus, if anyone's going to be able to shed some light on what's been going on around here, I'm thinking the local psychic might be a good place to start."

"Well, that's bloody weird. I've never heard of two people having the same dream. Are you *sure* it was the same?" Owen asked as he pulled onto the road and started driving toward town.

"Yeah, it was the same. The old fortune teller was trying to tell us something, but we couldn't understand her," Kate told him, turning the heat on. In the space of a few hours, the temperature outside had dropped significantly. It felt more like mid-autumn than mid-summer.

"Well, I guess it's worth a shot. I've heard she's pretty good. But what would be the connection between you two that would make you have the same dream?" Owen asked.

"I've been throwing that around in my head as well. I think Kate might have a better answer to that question than me," Ionna said, watching Kate's expression in the rearview mirror.

Her freckled cheeks blushed, and she closed her eyes, going silent for a moment. "I'm not sure what you mean?" Kate answered back, feigning innocence.

"The picture, Kate," Ionna said, but gently. "That image looks like a younger version of you at my great-grandparents' house. It's from 1951. I saw the expression on your face when you saw the image of my great-grandfather. You knew him, didn't you? But how?" She leaned forward, between the two front seats, trying to get a better look at Kate's face.

Kate was quiet for a long moment, gathering her thoughts on how to go about explaining this. She knew from the moment Ionna had handed her the photograph that this conversation was inevitable. But she didn't know whether she should tell her the entire truth or make something up that sounded more feasible.

Owen looked over at her with raised eyebrows, clearly wondering what he had missed. She hung her head and nodded softly.

"Yeah, you're right. It's me in that photo. It's a really hard thing to explain," Kate said, taking in a deep breath.

"You're a time traveler, I know," Ionna burst out before Kate even had a chance to go on.

She turned around in her seat to stare at Ionna. "How the hell did you know that?"

"Well, after I read Artemas's journal, then found the Polaroid picture, I kinda put two and two together. I'm a journalist, it's what I do." Ionna shrugged.

Kate turned around again, facing out the front of the car. "Well, you're right, that's probably why we're connected. You're his blood, and that bond drew us together. It must be why your touch brought on the repressed memory."

"Repressed memory? Is that what happened when you passed out at dinner? You had a flashback?"

"Yes, as soon as our hands met, I remembered the day I flipped back into Artemas's time. I figured because you were his blood, it triggered it," Kate said, pulling the picture out of her back pocket and staring down at her young self.

"That might have made sense if I was part of his bloodline but technically I'm not. Betty was his stepdaughter," Ionna said.

Well, there goes that theory, Kate thought. But then why had Ionna's touch caused her to have the flashback? Maybe it was just a coincidence, but then there was the dream. That was not something she could explain away. There had to be some sort of a connection there somewhere.

"Maybe it wasn't Ionna that caused the flashback. Maybe it was something *on* her," Owen suggested as he continued down the thin, winding road to Llangernyw.

The two women glanced at one another in the rearview mirror.

"What do you mean?" Kate asked.

"Like..." He sighed, trying to think of a way to explain. "Okay, you know in horror movies when someone touches something that belonged to a dead person, and it causes them to have flashes of the dead person's life? Like the object holds memories or something." He looked at Ionna in the mirror. "Did you have anything from the house with you last night?"

"Actually, yeah. I wore one of Betty's old dresses and her shoes. But again, Betty had no true blood connection to Artemas."

"Yeah, you're right. That wouldn't make much sense. I was thinking that if you had a watch or maybe a ring from the house, that it might have been Artemas's, not necessarily Betty's," Owen said, shrugging.

"I did have something else on, a necklace. I still have it on!" Ionna said, pulling the necklace out from under her shirt and letting it fall loose between her fingers as she showed it to Owen in the mirror.

Kate turned around to look, and her eyes grew wide. "Holy shit! No way?" She proceeded to pull her own necklace out of her shirt, showing it to both Owen and Ionna.

"They look identical. Where did you get that?" Ionna asked, leaning forward to inspect it between the seats.

"The vintage tent at the market. Remember I told you I got some things in there too? Well, this was one of those things."

"Okay, that's crazy. I figured it was a family heirloom or something, it looked so old. Definitely handmade and not something you find at a big chain store," Ionna said, looking down at her own necklace now and inspecting it closely. It made sense that it would be the necklace—after all, it was the thing she was

~ 337 ~

holding when she had started that fire from nothing more than air last night. Maybe the necklace itself was magical in some way. It wasn't a new concept that stones carried powers; people had believed that for centuries. *Maybe there is something to it,* Ionna thought.

"Almost there," Owen announced as they drove past a sign welcoming them to the town of Llangernyw.

The sky had grown so dark at this point it almost looked like twilight. Small drops of rain began to pepper the windshield, and the gusts of wind had become so intense that the trees bent and swayed in its grip. Owen had to swerve around a branch that had fallen into the road.

"What's up with this crazy weather?" he said. "It was supposed to be clear today. No rain until the day after tomorrow."

He turned the radio on and skipped through the stations, expecting to hear weather alerts being broadcast but every station was full of nothing but static.

"That's odd," he muttered, switching the radio off again.

Ahead in the distance, they could make out the spire of a church, a guiding post in the darkness of the storm around it.

"Look, there's the culprit of the poison pies right there," Owen announced, pointing at a churchyard with a large evergreen sitting in its center.

There was a huge split in the trunk near the base, bifurcating the tree, its two halves reaching in different directions. Its long, gnarly roots worked their way up from its large stump and crawled toward the gravestones. It looked like a two-headed monster.

Owen slowed as they passed it. "You know that's the oldest living thing in Wales?"

"I can believe it, that thing looks old as hell," Kate said, staring out the window at the tree. For a brief moment, she thought she saw the outline of a figure standing right where the trunk split. A creeping feeling worked its way down her neck, making the fine hairs stand on end.

Owen slammed on the brakes as a thick limb of an oak tree came crashing down on the road in front of them. The car skidded to the right, just missing it as they came to a halt.

"Holy shit," Owen said, putting the car in park and opening his door. He got out and inspected the limb. It had fallen off a giant old oak sitting back off the road. The rain began to come down harder, and the world around him began to blur. He made a visor with his hand and looked back at the car.

"I think if we all get on the smaller end, we might be able to move it just enough to get around," Owen yelled to the girls.

Ionna and Kate got out of the car and ran over to where Owen was standing. At that moment the sky let loose, and the rain came down in sheets. A crack of thunder sounded out, too close for comfort, as they hurried over to move the large limb. The rough bark dug into their hands as they tried to lift it. It took them three tries before they were able to maneuver it just enough for Owen's car to skirt by.

By the time they made it back to the car, they were completely drenched from head to toe. Kate turned the heat up and held her hands in front of the blowers. Not only was it pouring rain, but it had gotten even colder since they left the house.

"God, it's cold."

"This can't be right," Owen said, pointing at his temperature gauge in the car. "Five degrees? That's not possible."

The windows began to fog up from the rapid change in temperature. Owen turned the wipers to their fastest setting, trying to make the road more visible as he drove. The rain was coming down so hard that it was almost impossible to see even a few feet in front of the car.

"Maybe we should turn back, it's getting pretty bad out," Kate said as she strained to see the road.

"No, I've got it," Owen told her, his hands gripping the wheel tightly.

As he rounded a bend in the road, there was a sudden flash and then a blinding light that made him stamp on the brakes, coming to a dead stop in the middle of the road once again. They'd missed being struck by lightning by milliseconds. The road in front of the car now had a scorch mark in its center that resembled the rooting system of a tree. The singed tendrils stretched out in all directions around it. The interior of the car was permeated by the stench of charred road tar, seeping through the heating ducts from the smoldering pavement.

"Owen, we need to go back. Something's not right. I can feel it," Kate said.

"She's right, Owen. Something is trying very hard to keep us away from this woman. It's too dangerous," Ionna told him.

"We're closer to Karena's house than we are to home. It's just up the road a bit more. I think it's a safer bet to try and get there than travel back in this weather."

It was silent in the car as they moved slowly along the road, Kate and Ionna sharing the same single thought. The day's events were playing out just as their dream had, and something desperately didn't want them to make it to their destination.

The road grew narrow as they drew closer to where Karena lived. The temperature had dropped further, and the rain had become a wintery mix of sleet and snow. Thick, slippery slush accumulated on the road, and Owen's car whined with the effort to navigate it. The tires spun, and once or twice the backend slid sideways, almost taking the car off the road.

"Her house is right there," Owen said, shifting into a lower gear.

Ionna and Kate looked ahead. It was now beginning to snow. Large white flakes fell from the sky so heavily that the house became obscured, making it difficult to tell where they were on the road.

"Okay, now this is just bizarre," Owen said, slowing the car down to a crawl.

He looked around. In a matter of moments, a blizzard had set in, and they couldn't make hide nor hair of where they were.

"I can't go any further," Owen stated as he came to a complete stop. The snow was coming down so thick that it almost blocked out the light completely, making it too dangerous to drive any further.

A moment later, a dim yellow glow penetrated the white veil of snow that surrounded them. It flickered on and off as if to communicate to them where the house sat, guiding them forward.

Chapter Thirty-Nine
TEA LEAVES

The soft yellow glow cut through the snow like a beacon, combating the supernatural forces at play.

"Look," Owen said, pointing. "That's coming from her house."

"Don't try to drive, it's only fifty feet up the road. We can walk," Ionna said.

"Let's just hope she keeps the light on," Kate said.

They sat there working up the courage to venture out into the snow with nothing more than jeans and T-shirts on.

"Okay, let's do this. I think it might be a good idea if we all hold hands. That way no one wanders off to the side and gets lost in this whiteout," Owen said.

"Good idea, Owen," Ionna remarked as she unclipped her seatbelt and grabbed the door handle.

"Wait. We all need to get out at the same time. When you get out, put your hand on the car and use it as a guide to the front."

"Wow, you certainly know how to get around in a blizzard," Kate joked.

"I want to tell you it's just common sense, but I would be lying. You have video games to thank for this one," Owen joked back.

On a count of three, they opened the doors at the same time. The cold hit them with force, each snowflake stinging their skin like tiny pinpricks. Once they made it to the front of the car, they clasped hands and ventured out into the white nothingness in front of them. The small yellow flicker of light was the only guide they had. Even though the house sat no more than fifty feet ahead of them, the walk there felt like miles. There was a deafening silence to the world around them as the snow fell heavier still.

As the light grew closer, they slowed their steps, their bodies giving in to the frigid temperature. Snow clumped in their hair and clung to their already damp clothes, creating a bitter chill that seemed to penetrate their cores.

Kate's heart pounded in her chest as they made their way toward the light, yet her body was slowed by the cold, trembling with it. As Kate's hands began to shake, Ionna sensed the fear emanating from her and squeezed her icy fingers reassuringly. Her lungs burned with the bitterly cold air, and it felt as if her feet had frozen to the soles of her shoes in the short time they had been out in the storm. Ionna was used to harsh winters living in Maine but had never in all her years felt cold like this. This cold was unnatural.

It was Kate who ran her foot into what looked to be the steps leading to the house where the light still blinked. They slowly made their way up, one at a time, until they came to the door of the house. It was painted with snow but its plum color peeked out from around the edges. Ionna stepped up and gave it a firm knock. They could make out the sound of shuffling footsteps from within, and moments later, the door swung open, revealing the silhouette of an elderly woman bathed in the soft glow of the light behind her.

"Come, come! Get out of that nasty weather!" she called out to them, her aged voice guiding them forward.

All three stepped in from the harsh conditions and stood there in the entryway with snow falling off them in clumps as if they were snowmen on a summer's day.

"I've been expecting you. Come in and warm yourself by the fire," Karena said, leading them into a small living room. The house smelled of cedar, allspice, cinnamon, and ginger and was decorated with a mix of Celtic, Indian, and Middle Eastern vibes. "Now, sit yourselves down and warm up while I get us some tea," she said, shuffling out of the room.

They gathered by the fire, their backs facing its warmth. The room was toasty, like the fire had been going all day. But the chill of fear they all felt was slow to fade. Ionna thought there must have been a weather alert on the radio or TV warning people about the approaching storm, and they'd somehow missed it. She looked out of the window but could see nothing other than the white veil of snow.

"I feel like I'll never be warm again," Kate said, shivering. She stood as close to the fire as her body would allow.

"Well, then, this should do just the trick," Karena said, coming back into the room carrying a tea tray. Upon it sat four white cups arranged around the most beautiful teapot—a deep blood-red with golden mandalas linking together to form a border around it. The lid sported a golden leaf perched on its surface, creating the perfect handle for opening.

"You were prepared. This place is so nice and cozy. Was there a weather warning about the storm?" Ionna asked.

"No warning other than my own foresight," Karena said as she placed the tray on an old wooden trunk positioned in front of the sofa like a coffee table.

She bent slowly and picked up the teapot, then looked over at Ionna and muttered something under her breath before she poured. "This one is for you, my dear."

"Thank you." Ionna took her tea and went back to the fire.

Now it was Kate's turn to be stared at. Karena held her gaze for only a moment before she poured the second cup. Once she had filled it, she proceeded to fill the last two on the tray. She handed Kate hers and then the last to Owen.

"You said you were expecting us? How could that be?" Kate asked as she blew on the steaming cup. The smell of hibiscus, cinnamon, chamomile, and rose filled her nose, and just the smell warmed her.

"Fortune teller, remember?" Karena joked as she picked up her own cup. "I dreamt of you both. I could see a darkness following you, moving closer. I tried to warn you, but my message was not getting through. I knew that you would come to find me once you pieced things together," she told them, taking a sip of the hot tea.

"We dreamt of you as well. We had the same dream but couldn't understand what you were saying to us. We could see the warning in your eyes but your words were swept away with the wind," Ionna told her.

"What was the warning?" Kate asked, finally daring to sip at the hot tea.

"I had a vision," Karena said. "An evil has been unleashed, and for some reason, it seems to be coming for the both of you. I was hoping that maybe you understood why."

"How do you know this?" Owen asked her, stepping a little closer to the fire as he clutched the steaming cup of tea in his hands.

"I should have said more that day at the market, but it wasn't until the day after that I began to put things together. The pies were the first clue—and your palms. After thirty years of reading palms, I'd never seen a set that seemed to create a map as yours did. One led onto the story of the other. Apart, they didn't seem to make any sense but put them together and they create a whole."

"But why us? What's it after?" Ionna asked, spinning the chain around her neck with her free hand. Then it came to her. "Could it be after the necklaces?" she asked.

Karena stepped closer to Ionna, setting her teacup down on the mantel.

"Let me have a closer look at that," she said, stepping up to her and taking the amulet in her hands as it hung loose off Ionna's neck, inspecting it closely.

"We have a pair, Kate and I, but hers is silver," Ionna told her.

Kate pulled hers from the inside fold of her shirt and flashed it over at the old woman.

"They are protection amulets. Once you've clasped them, you must not take them off—to do so would break the charms that have been placed upon them. They look quite old, maybe sixteenth century," she said, touching the gem that sat in the middle of the Celtic knot. "The stone in its center is moldavite, one of the rarest stones on Earth. A piece of a meteorite. It's said to aid in bringing forth one's intuition and magical abilities."

"Well, that explains a lot," Kate said.

Karena turned the amulet over in her hand. "Whoever made these, made them for you," she said, pointing to a small engraving on the back. There, pressed into the gold, was Ionna's name.

Ionna looked down at the necklace. How had she missed that? Her name wound its way up and around the back edge of the setting.

Kate flipped hers over, and sure enough, "Katherine" was engraved into the silver.

"Wow. This day just keeps getting weirder by the minute," Owen said in a low tone.

"You're telling me," Kate said.

Owen went over to the couch and sat down, looking tense as he tried to take in the situation. Kate finished her tea and joined him.

"I don't understand. How could they have been made for us?" Ionna asked.

"A seer, I suppose. Someone who saw the future events and wanted to aid in your battle," Karena told her as she walked over and sat in one of the two plum-colored armchairs facing the sofa.

"Battle?" Ionna repeated with a look of confusion on her face.

Kate looked over at Owen, thinking about her grandfather's book of ancestors. It was possible one of them had made the necklaces in hopes of helping them.

Ionna took the last sip of her tea. It had done its job well in warming her insides and knocking the chill out. She went to place her cup in the tray when Karena stopped her.

"Let me see that," she said, holding her hand out.

Ionna placed the empty cup in her hands, unsure why the old woman wanted it.

Karena swirled the dregs around, then grabbed a cloth napkin off the table, turned the cup upside down over it, and spun the cup to the left. When she flipped it back upright, she looked into its empty center, inspecting it.

"Well, this is certainly not the reading I was hoping for," she said as she stared down into the cup.

"Reading?" Ionna questioned.

"Your tea leaves. It's called tasseomancy, a type of divination. It's been practiced for centuries. The particular way the tea leaves lie at the bottom of the cup reveals something about the drinker. Where they fall on the cup will tell me whether it's about the past, present, or future."

Ionna leaned forward and looked into the bottom of her cup. At first, all she could make out were clusters of tea leaves, but then Karena turned the cup so that the handle faced her. At the bottom, formed with wet tea leaves, was a skull staring back.

Chapter Forty

THE TRIP

Ionna took the teacup from the old woman and looked down into its center. The skull sat there staring up, almost taunting her. She had never subscribed to this witchy voodoo stuff, but after everything she had seen in the past few days, she was becoming a believer, and this made her anxious.

"You said you could tell when things would happen from the places the leaves fell? What does the center mean?"

"First of all, the skull doesn't necessarily mean death—it can indicate danger as well. The central placement tells of something in the near future that you need to be prepared for. If you look up near the rim, there is also a wavy line of leaves. That tells me what's to come is uncertain, that you will have a crossroads ahead of you," Karena explained. She leaned forward toward the tray with an outstretched arm. "Hand me your cup, Kate."

Kate walked it over to where she sat. She looked down into it with nervous eyes, expecting to see something similar to Ionna's, but it just looked like tea in the bottom of a cup to her. She handed it to Karena, who flipped the cup over onto the cloth as she had done before and then turned the cup in her hands, inspecting it from all angles before she spoke.

"Very interesting. I see three distinct symbols in your cup. Look here, see this shape?" She pointed down at a cluster of leaves stuck together.

"Not sure I see a shape. Looks more like a blob of tea," Kate said.

"No, no. It's a cloud, and it sits below the edge of the cup. This means there is danger approaching. And this here." She paused, sweeping her finger over to a line of leaves that split in the center and then reformed right below the cloud. "This space represents the present, and here is a line with a break in it. This tells me that you are missing something important. Without this missing thing, you will face danger soon."

Instinctively, Kate slid her right hand into her back pocket and touched the photograph. She knew what was missing but hadn't a clue how she was going to break it free of its hiding place in her mind.

"Then we have this here," Karena continued, pointing at a small line that looped up on one end. "This is a key. It's sitting in your near future as well. There's something you must unlock or master to help you."

She returned the cup to Kate and then looked at Owen, who was eagerly waiting his turn to see his future.

"Come, boy, bring me your cup. I can see you over there waiting with bated breath," she said, letting out a raspy laugh.

Owen stood and walked over, handing his cup to Karena. She flipped the cup over and peered into it as she had done with the others.

"Well, no surprise here. See these two spots?" She pointed at a straight line below the cup's rim. Underneath, the tea leaves had clustered in the shape of a small hand. "That line there shows us that you need to do a bit of careful planning in the present. And the shape there near the center, this hand, it means you will play an important role in helping these two in their battle."

Karena returned the cup to Owen. He took his seat next to Kate again, looking pensive. It was silent for a long moment as everyone's minds mulled over what they had just been told.

"You keep saying battle. What battle?" Ionna asked.

"It's not here yet, but it will be soon. These readings played out much like your palms," Karen told her. She propped herself up as if preparing for a lengthy conversation. "Your stories all connect to one another. If we look at them in order, we see Kate needing to find something, Owen helping with a plan, Kate learning to master something to help you from a future that is uncertain and lined with danger." She then looked at Kate. "First things first. Kate, do you know what it is you are missing?"

Kate sat there for a moment, not sure how to go about answering the question and not knowing if she could trust Karena with her secret. But if she wanted her help, she was going to need to tell her at least a little.

"Yes. It's not a thing as much as a memory. I can't remember something that happened to me when I was young, and I think it might have to do with the dark force you keep talking about," Kate told her in one long breath.

"Well, now, that's easy. Memories can be guided out from the dark with a simple tea," Karena said.

"What kind of tea?" Owen asked skeptically.

"The kind made of mushrooms!" Slowly, she stood and gathered the tea tray, taking it into the kitchen.

"There's no way I'm going on some psychedelic trip with magic mushroom tea," Kate said as soon as Karena left the room.

"Kate, you don't have to do anything you're not comfortable with," Ionna reassured her.

Kate stood and started to pace the room. Walking from one end to the other and then stopping in the center to stand by the fire.

"There must be other ways of doing this. I've never even smoked weed before, let alone tripped," she said, running her fingers nervously through her hair.

"It's not that bad, kinda fun, really. I used to do it all the time in secondary school with my mates," Owen said.

"Not helping, Owen," Ionna told him, standing up and walking over to Kate. "Listen, you don't have to do this. We can find a different way."

"We don't have time," Kate stressed. "You heard what she said—whatever that darkness is, it's getting closer to us. Just look at today. We almost died twice on the way here, not to mention all the horrible things happening to the community. I *need* to remember what happened," Kate said, talking herself into it.

They could hear Karena moving around in the kitchen, pots and pans banging together. The popping sound of a ball jar echoed off the walls. Soon after, a strong earthy scent wafted in and filled the room. There were hints of rosemary and jasmine in the air, along with a pungent odor they suspected came from the mushrooms.

When Karena came back in with the teapot, they had all gathered back on the sofa. She set the tray back down, then sat in her chair again.

"Kate, I want you to close your eyes and relax. Think about the last thing you remember from the broken memory," Karena told her.

Kate went to close her eyes, then stopped. "I don't know if I can do this. I've never done drugs before," she blurted out.

"Oh, my dear, no, these aren't *those* kinds of mushrooms," Karena said with a loud laugh. "This tea is made from rosemary, yarrow, mugwort, and reishi mushrooms. With a touch of chamomile to help you fall asleep. When you drink it, you'll doze off for a bit, and when you wake up, you should remember what you had forgotten."

"Oh," she said, as her cheeks reddened with embarrassment.

"You must pour yourself the tea. It won't work if you are not one hundred percent certain that you want to know what your mind has been hiding from you. So, take a minute to decide."

Kate closed her eyes. She pictured Artemas, wounded and fading away while trying to save Neala. That moment had changed her profoundly. What if what came next damaged her even more? She was already unsure of who she really was. Would this revelation make things worse and leave her utterly lost? But she needed to know. Otherwise, it would torment her forever. Plus, there were other people counting on her, not just herself.

She pushed away the doubts and sat quietly in her mind for a moment. Then she opened her eyes, took the teapot into her hands, and poured the pungent tea into the cup in front of her, still stained with her future.

"Now, I want you to close your eyes again and think back to that day," Karena instructed. "Find the place that is missing and stay thinking about that as you sip the tea. Once you have finished it, I want you to lie down and do your best to let the tea take you where you need to go inside your mind. Remember, if you fight this, it won't come."

Kate brought the cup to her lips and sipped. It was hot but manageable; however, the taste was something less than desirable. It tasted like musty earth and some sort of Mediterranean dish, not like any tea she had ever had before. It took all she had to finish the cup as it turned in her stomach. When she was finished, she rested back on the sofa and looked at Owen.

"Stay with me?" she asked him, already feeling a bit sleepy from the strong blend.

"I won't leave your side," he told her, taking her hand in his. He guided her body down on the sofa, resting her head on a pillow on his lap.

Gazing up, she recognized the look in his eyes. It was the way Stevie's boyfriend looked at Stevie and the way her grandfather used to look at her grandmother. By the time she realized what that look meant, her eyes were so heavy she could no longer keep them open. The last thing she remembered was the fluttering of her own heart as Owen looked down at her before she drifted off to sleep.

Chapter Forty-One

THE MISSING PIECE

"Kate, go! Take Neala. Take her as far away as you can. GO, NOW!" a voice screamed into the darkness of her mind.

Kate opened her eyes to see a baby in her arms. She looked up to where the voice was coming from. Artemas was holding his side, blood flowing through his fingers and down his leg, making a slick puddle on the floor. In his other hand, he grasped an oddly shaped brass container. It looked almost like a flower with tiny birds perched on top of it.

The demon twisted wildly above the container as it was sucked down into it like a whirlpool. It fought desperately to escape, its half-distorted body flaring about as it was pulled further into the brass flower, thinning the air as it went.

"Go!" Artemas cried out once again.

Kate looked down at Neala's tear-streaked face and then without hesitation ran for the door. The baby's cries split the dusky afternoon air as she sprinted toward the open barn doors.

Slipping into the barn with the baby on her hip, she ran to the horse stall. She tried to be as quiet as she could so as not to spook the horse inside. A large blanket was thrown up over an old saddle in the corner. She grabbed it and shook off the loose hay with her free arm before tying it up around the baby in a makeshift sling.

Opening up the stall, she walked the chestnut horse out into the center of the barn. She knew it was risky to mount a horse in the barn, especially with a baby in her arms, but she had no other choice. She kicked an old milk crate over and stepped onto it so she could reach the horse's back. It took several attempts before she was able to mount the large mare, her heart pounding in her chest at every second they remained in the barn. Fear raced inside her. Any second now the demon could break free of Artemas's efforts and come straight for Neala.

Finally, on the horse, she turned it toward the door when a darkness slipped in, filling the barn with the smell of rotten eggs. Kate watched in horror as it doubled in size and towered above them like a black wave about to crash down on the shore. The hair on her neck and arms rose, her animal instincts alerting her of the danger that was now only feet away. The baby began to cry again, her tears landing hot on Kate's chest, a burning reminder of the tiny life she needed to protect. She wrapped her arm tighter around Neala, pulling her even closer to her chest.

The darkness loomed over them, its wispy tendrils reaching out toward the horse.

"Give me the child, girl," a voice as dark as night called out, rumbling in the air like thunder.

The horse let out a loud whinny and reared up in fright, almost causing Kate to lose grip of Neala. She leaned forward, holding tight to its mane and digging her thighs into its sides. Swaying on the horse's back, she tried desperately not to fall as its feet collided with the barn floor once more.

At that moment, she closed her eyes. The only thought racing in her mind was saving Artemas's child. She felt her lungs tighten, pushing every last molecule of air from them. She gasped and her throat burned as she spun through the murky darkness of time, crashing on the other side as if she had been spit out of a whale.

When she opened her eyes, she was still in the barn, sitting on top of the horse with the baby wrapped tightly in the sling on her chest. She looked wildly around. The dark presence was gone. The air seemed lighter. She took a minute to steady herself. They had flipped through time, she was sure of that, but the adrenaline coursing through her veins still had her on high alert.

Through the crack in the barn door, she could see sunlight, a drastic difference from the stormy weather just moments before. Carefully, she maneuvered off the horse and went to the door to peek out, her heart still racing, not yet believing they were safe.

They were still at Artemas's house, but when?

The house looked the same, with the exception of large flower beds all around the yard and a fresh coat of paint on the front door. The car in the driveway was the real giveaway—it was the same style as the one in her dad's favorite TV show from the nineteen eighties, *The Cuckoo Waltz*. She had definitely flipped them to some point after 1951.

How would she explain all of this? What had Artemas told Elizabeth and Betty when they came home to find Artemas wounded and Neala missing? To say she was worried about how

Betty would react was an understatement.

She decided that she needed to try and flip Neala back, but she wasn't sure she could do that. She had never been able to pick a point in time and safely travel to it before. If she tried and failed, she might end up further back in the past. If she did that, she wasn't sure if Neala would even exist. She might end up losing her in time. No, she couldn't take that risk. Artemas had wanted Kate to protect her, to keep her safe, to take her as far away as possible. She had done that; she had gotten the baby away from the demon in her own time. Thirty years in the future was as far away as she had managed and she hoped that time counted as distance.

After weighing up her options, she decided that bringing Neala to Betty was the safest choice. She went back to the horse and grabbed a rope off one of the hooks, tying it to a post in the barn, then headed for the door. She slowly slid it to the side and walked out into the blinding light of midday. A warm breeze blew, picking up a myriad of scents from the flowers blooming in the yard. It was a harsh juxtaposition to the scene they had just escaped from, and it was jarring.

She looked down at Neala, who had cried herself to sleep, her rosy cheeks peeking out from the edge of the blanket. Kate walked up to the door of the house and knocked. As she waited for Betty to answer, her heart began to beat heavily in her chest again. Neala stirred in her arms. She cooed, looking up at Kate with wide green eyes, and then grabbed a handful of her red hair and gave it a hefty pull.

"Ouch! I see you're feeling better," Kate said, looking down at the baby.

The door creaked open and a guy in his twenties peered out at her. "Umm, can I help you?" he asked, looking at her and then down at the makeshift sling.

Kate was caught off guard; she hadn't thought anyone else lived there but Betty. "Hi, um, does Betty live here?" she asked him in a sheepish voice.

The man closed the door slightly and leaned back into the house. "Mum, there's some girl here to see you," he called out.

Kate heard footsteps and then the door pulled open. In the man's place was Betty—not young anymore, but not as old as Kate knew her. Her hair was streaked with gray and the lines around her eyes were just starting to deepen.

"Yes, how can I help you?" she asked, looking down at Kate from the doorstep.

Kate didn't say anything, she just stood there, looking up. Betty's expression changed from suspicious to perplexed as she tried to place who this girl with the baby was.

"And who is this?" she asked, peering down at the baby, as though hoping her question would prompt some response from Kate.

A moment passed. Kate hardly dared to breathe. She saw Betty's eyes widen in disbelief. Her hand came to her mouth, stifling a gasp.

"Neala?" she whispered. Her eyes darted up to Kate. "How is this possible? Oh God, am I having a stroke?" She took a step back, placing her hand over her heart, looking at them as if they were ghosts. "This isn't real. You can't be real," she said, stumbling over her own words as her face turned a pale shade of gray.

"This is really hard to explain," Kate said, untying the sling and pulling Neala out. She held her up to Betty and stepped forward.

Betty looked at her and then at Neala, a tear sliding down her cheek. She took Neala in her arms, bringing her up to her face and breathing in her scent.

"How? How is this possible? You ran away with Neala in 1951. You look the same age as the last time I saw you both."

Kate was unsure of how to answer. Betty was obviously in shock.

"Was this Artemas's doing?" Betty asked, breaking the tension in the air.

It was at that point Kate remembered that Artemas had never told Elizabeth or Betty about magic. They'd had no idea that magic was real but the way she asked the question made her wonder if that was still the case.

However, she wasn't willing to risk saying anything unless she was sure. She thought back to all the books she'd read, trying to come up with something that would sound feasible. *A Wrinkle in Time*, *The Time Machine*, or even the movie *Back to the Future* all seemed way too far-fetched to use. So, she just went with the first thing that came to her mind when she was being asked something she didn't want to answer.

"I don't know what happened. One minute we were in the house and the next we were here standing in your barn," Kate told her, doing her best to sound as shaken up as Betty looked. She figured that all of this was so mind-blowing that her explanation made as much sense as the rest of it did.

"Why don't you come in," Betty said, swinging the door wide.

The house still looked almost the same as it had when she left it, apart from the upgraded appliances and furniture. Betty led her into the living room where the man who answered the door and a young woman sat watching TV.

"Adam, this is Patricia. And this here, is baby…" She paused for a moment. "Ionna."

Chapter Forty-Two

THE LIE

Betty held baby Neala in her arms as she walked over to Adam. "Can you two watch Ionna while I talk to Patricia in the kitchen?" she asked, now holding the baby out for him to take. He smiled at the baby and took her in his arms, then began bouncing her on his knee. Kate looked at Betty, confused, but followed her into the kitchen.

"My name is Kate, not Patricia," she told her.

"I know that, but my son and his wife can't," Betty said in a hushed tone. She sat herself down at the table, the same table where Kate and she had first met. "They've heard the stories of you running off with Neala, and I can't risk them putting two and two together. Not that anyone would believe all this anyway. I wouldn't myself if you weren't standing here in front of me."

"I don't know what to do. I need to get Neala somewhere safe," Kate said, worry straining her voice.

"She'll be safe here," Betty said, looking toward the living room. "For years, my mother and I thought she had been kidnapped—or worse. We believed that someone was using you to get into homes in order to steal infants and hold them for ransom. But when no demands were made, we were at a loss for what really happened." Tears filled her eyes once again. "We thought Artemas was just in the wrong place at the wrong time when they came to get you both. Do you know what happened to him?" she asked Kate, catching her off guard.

It took her a moment to answer, but she decided to tell a version of the truth. "I don't. The last thing I remember was Artemas yelling for me to take Neala and get as far away as possible, that she wasn't safe here. So, I ran out of the house and into the barn. When I came out to see if it was safe, I was here. I swear."

"Why? What was it that he was trying to protect her from?" Betty asked, concern and fear playing across her face.

"I'm not sure. He told me a supernatural darkness was after her and that she needed to be taken far away from here," Kate said, withholding the full truth to spare Betty from the unsettling reality of a demon from another realm being present in their world.

"Supernatural darkness," Betty echoed, her tone absent of surprise or shock, revealing that she had harbored suspicions about such things for quite some time. She sat there quietly for a long moment, and Kate could see the pieces coming together in her mind.

"We came home that day and found his body in the herb garden," she said as she turned from Kate and looked out the window toward where his herb patch used to be.

Kate was stunned. She knew he had been injured but she

had hoped for his survival, even though deep down she knew the chances were slim. Sadness washed over her. Maybe she should have stayed and tried to help him; maybe she should have tried to flip them back to before everything had gone all wrong.

"I'm sorry. He was a really nice man," she said, the words finally finding her lips after a long pause. There was a lump in her throat, and her eyes swam with tears.

"He was," Betty said, tears welling in her eyes as well.

"What are you going to tell your son?" Kate asked.

"Don't you worry about that, I'll think of something," Betty told her.

As she watched Betty mull things over in her own mind, Kate started to think about her grandparents and how worried they must still be. She'd been gone for more than a day now. The whole town was probably out looking for her. She needed to leave and try to get back to her own time. But Betty would probably want her there to explain whatever it was she was cooking up in her head.

"You know, Adam and his wife have been trying to have a baby for years now with no luck," Betty said at last. There was something different in her voice now—perhaps hope. "They've had three miscarriages. The last time, the doctor advised them not to try again. They've been on the adoption list for a long time now with no luck. Neala will be the miracle they've been looking for," Betty told her.

This put Kate's mind at ease a bit more, knowing that Neala would be loved by her own family as if she were their very own child. "That sounds good," she said. "I think Artemas would've liked that."

"Yes, I think so too." Betty nodded. "Now, the question is what we do with you? Do you know how to get back to your own time?"

"I'm not really sure."

"I have no idea how to get you home either, but we'll figure something out," Betty reassured her.

Before Kate even had time to respond, Betty was walking out of the room. Kate got up and walked to the doorway, about to follow her into the living room, when she heard Betty talking to Adam.

"I'll explain more later, but you need to take the baby. She is the miracle you and Mary have been waiting for," she heard Betty say.

"Wait, I don't understand," Adam said, confused.

"You need to take Ionna and leave. It's not safe for her here."

"What do you mean not safe? Mum, I can't just take a baby and run away with her. We need to call the police or the social services or something. And what about the girl?" Adam insisted.

"You don't understand, Adam. We can't do that; you need to trust me," Betty said, a sharpness entering her voice.

"Mum, no. I'm calling," Adam said.

Then she heard him lift the phone off the receiver and begin punching in numbers.

Kate stepped back into the kitchen, panic rising in her. She couldn't let the authorities take her away—if she tried to flip from somewhere else, there was no telling where she might end up. It was possible there was something special about Beddgelert and it was the only place where she could flip time. After all, it never happened where she lived back home in London. If she ended up somewhere else she might be stuck there forever.

She could hear Adam's muffled voice coming in from the living room, still arguing with Betty. Fear raced through her, and she decided her only option was to flee. She stood up, and without a second thought, she ran.

She dashed through the dining room, past Adam and Betty, and out the front door.

"Kate, wait!" Betty yelled.

But Kate couldn't hear her. Her own heart was beating so loud that it echoed back in her ears, drowning out all the sounds around her. She burst through the barn doors and over to the horse, unhooking her from the post. She could hear footsteps approaching quickly as she threw herself up and then drove her heels into the horse's sides. It took off at a full gallop out the barn doors, nearly knocking over Adam. She rode up the driveway, and just as she passed beneath the two large oaks that flanked either side, she heard a car engine start.

Panic shot through her like a bolt of lightning, and when she got to the road, she instinctively closed her eyes, the fear working with her to ripple time. Then she felt it—her lungs clenched, and she began spinning, then it was as if time itself flipped her out on the other side.

When she opened her eyes, it was dark, and she was riding up by the Dwyer farm. She saw flashlights in the distance up ahead.

"Kate!" A man's voice she didn't recognize called out. "Kate!" Her name came again from another unknown caller. "Kate!" A chorus of her name was being called out by multiple voices. A search party. How long had she been gone? Days, weeks, hours? Tears filled her eyes. It didn't matter. What mattered was she had found her way back home to her own time.

Chapter Forty-Three

ON THE OTHER SIDE

Kate's body twitched as she lay there in Owen's lap. He looked down at her, worry spreading across his face.

"She'll be fine," Karena reassured him. "It won't be much longer now. The effects of the tea should be wearing off."

Ionna stood and started pacing the length of the room, anxiously awaiting Kate's arrival back from the dream realm. Her stomach turned, and she had a feeling building up inside her that she couldn't quite put her finger on. It had started the night of the dinner and seemed to be growing by the minute. It felt like something was racing around inside of her, trying to escape.

She walked over to the window and looked out. The storm clouds still hung heavy in the sky, snow falling softly as the sun had begun to set, rendering the world outside monochrome. It was hard for her to believe that less than a week ago the only worry she had was getting taken off the wastewater article. Now, she was chasing her own bizarre story that seemed to lead to nothing more than an ever-increasing number of questions.

"She's waking up," Owen yelled out, breaking Ionna from her thoughts.

She turned around to see Kate trying to sit herself up with the aid of Owen. Her eyes were still filled with sleep, and her head swayed as she tried to get her bearings.

"You okay?" Owen asked, concern filling each word.

Kate sat there for a moment before answering him, her blue eyes wide and wild looking. Karena got up from her chair and shuffled across to the tea tray. She grabbed the pot and then proceeded out of the room and back to the kitchen. Owen moved close to Kate on the sofa and put his arm around her to steady her swaying.

"I'm okay," she managed to say, her voice hoarse.

Just then, Karena came back in with the pot in her hands. The rich aroma of orange and cinnamon filled the air. She bent down and filled up the empty cup in front of Kate.

"Drink this. It will help with the dryness and wake you up a bit," she told her, handing Kate the cup. She looked at it skeptically. "Don't worry, it's just black tea with a bit of orange and cinnamon," she reassured her.

Kate sat there with the teacup in her hands and stared at Ionna. She was the missing piece. Baby Neala and her were one and the same. She had taken her from Artemas all those decades ago and brought her forward in time. Adam had kept good on his promise and raised her. How was she going to explain all of this? She knew that Ionna had questions about her parents but these were not the answers she would be expecting.

"Are you okay?" Ionna questioned her as she stared back, seeing the concerned look in her eyes.

Kate blew into her teacup and nodded, then took a tiny sip, testing out the heat on her lips. It was the same way she needed to approach things with Ionna, with tiny sips of information. She didn't want to overwhelm her.

"So, did you remember what you had blocked out?" Owen asked, breaking the tension and asking the question that was on everyone's mind.

"Yes. I saw what happened after I left Artemas's house," Kate said slowly.

"Artemas? Artemas Rogowski?" Karena asked, her eyes growing wide.

"Yes."

"How could you have known Artemas? He died in 1951," she said. And then a look came over her face as if she had pieced together her own mystery. "Are you the time traveler he told me about?"

Kate's eyes grew wide, and she looked over at Owen, who looked just as stunned as she felt.

"How do you know that? Your psychic thing?" Kate asked, setting down her tea and sitting up a bit straighter.

"No, Artemas came to me the day after you arrived in his barn. He was desperate to find a way to send back a dark entity he'd unleashed when he tried to save his daughter. I sent him to the churchyard to seek counsel with the spirit that lives within the great yew tree there. He returned here after, seeking a vermillion, which I gave him."

"He came here to visit you?" Kate asked.

"Yes, he was a dear friend. That was the last time I saw him," she told them, her sorrowful expression further creasing her wrinkled features.

Well, now that there were four of them who knew what she was capable of, there was no point in holding back. Knowing she wouldn't have to skirt around the time travel aspects of the story lightened Kate's mood a little.

"How did he die? There were all sorts of rumors going around about his death at the time and what happened to the baby. But none of them seemed right to me," Karena said as she rested herself back into one of the overstuffed armchairs.

"I'm not sure. He was fighting the demon off. It stabbed him, but he wasn't dead when I left. He told me to take the baby and go. He tried to stop it, but the darkness followed after me. It was trying to get the baby. I flipped us both out of the barn, and that was the last time I saw him," Kate said, glancing up at Ionna, who was still standing near the window.

"So what happened next? Where did you go after?" Owen asked, scooting up to the edge of the sofa and turning to look at her.

Kate rested herself back against the sofa before she began. "I flipped us forward to the eighties. We were still in the same place, just forward in time thirty years. When I knocked on the door, a man answered. At first, I was confused because I remembered you telling me that Betty had lived in the house her whole life, then I came to find out it was her son."

That caught Ionna's attention. She listened with more intensity as Kate went on.

"I had to lie to Betty and tell her I had no idea what had happened. I was in her kitchen in the 1950s one minute and in her barn in the 1980s the next. She was so stunned; I don't think she even knew what to think. She took the baby from me and handed it to her son and called her Ionna." Kate stopped and looked over at Ionna, whose face had turned pale. "She didn't know how to help me get back to my own time, and she panicked. Adam was insisting that she call the police or social services, and that's when I ran. I had no idea if I would be able to flip back if I wasn't in Beddgelert, so I went into the barn, got on the horse, and took off up the road. They were coming after me with the car when I flipped myself back to my own time."

It was a long time before anyone spoke. Ionna stood there in shock, looking down at her own hands and then up at Kate.

"Kate, am I baby Neala?" she asked, a wave of sickness threatening to take her over.

Kate stood up and walked over to her. She looked into her big green eyes, now realizing why they had always looked so familiar to her.

"You are, yes. Betty told me that Adam and his wife had tried to have children but they couldn't, that they would love and care for you as if you were their own. From what I can tell, they did," Kate said.

"It all makes sense now, all the lies and secrets," Ionna said under her breath.

Tears ran down her face, and the mounting feeling inside of her was about to spill forth. Then suddenly, a glow seemed to radiate out of her skin. It was faint at first and then burst out in a blinding light, sending her to the floor in an unconscious heap. The truth had unbound her magic, setting it free.

Gripping his side, Artemas raced out of the house, following the demon toward the barn. His strides were shortened by his wound, and he tripped over his own feet, landing hard on the ground. He lay there only feet away from the barn door where the demon had slipped inside in pursuit of Kate and Neala.

He was growing weaker by the second. He looked over at his herb garden, knowing he had the herbs he needed to save his own life, but there wasn't time to save both Neala and himself. There was only one choice in his eyes, and that was to save his only child. With all his might, he pulled himself back to his feet and stormed into the barn. A small ounce of relief washed over him when he saw that only the demon was inside. He prayed that Kate had been able to flip Neala far away from here.

Drawing on all of the magic left inside him, he continued the spell he had started in the house once again. As he began the incantation, the demon spun around and faced him.

"You're no match for me in your wounded state, mortal." His voice rang out like the wildest storm, rattling the floor beneath where Artemas stood, shaking the rafters of the barn. "Where I come from, I am a god with powers far beyond your comprehension. Your daughter is the key to the prison I have been bound to for centuries, and I will be damned if I am going to let you stop me."

"She is just a child," Artemas pleaded. "If you want powers, take mine."

"It is not power I seek." He laughed malevolently. "Thanks to your little magic trick, your child now possesses life energy from both realms. She is the only living descendant of Nyneve who possesses the ability to host a god from our realm. I hoped for a male descendant, but I have waited long enough. Once I have taken possession of her form and have rebuilt my strength, nothing will be able to stop me from taking over this realm."

"You won't get a chance," Artemas yelled, as he stuck his hand in his pocket and pulled out a powder that he blew into the air toward the demon. It was a mixture of herbs that held it captive for a brief moment, giving him just enough time to begin his spell once again. There was no way in hell he was about to lose this battle and subject Neala to a lifetime of servitude to this so-called god.

The demon gripped at the darkness in the shadows of the old dusty barn, but his efforts were futile as he was trapped within an invisible net. Artemas pulled the vermillion from his pocket. The brass container resembled a flower, and each of its chambers was shaped like a leaf with birds on top, each in turn filled with some form of aromatic herb or spice.

"From the veil and to my power,
Trapped until your final hour,
With the aid of earth, wind, fire, and sea,
I keep you, my prisoner, until I set you free.
Blood being the only key.
By the power of three
So mote it be."

When he spoke the final words, he removed a pin at the top of the container shaped like a bird. The darkness hovering over it began to spin violently, creating a vortex that was being sucked down into the tiny hole in the top of the container.

"This will not stop me. I will come for her, and when I do, I will take her over completely. Crushing her soul in my bare hands," the demon boomed in a voice that shook Artemas to his core, but he held fast.

Once the darkness was trapped inside, he slammed the bird back on top of the hole and screwed it shut. He washed the blood from his hands in the horse's water bucket and tied an old blanket around his waist, ensuring the blood wouldn't come in contact with the brass vermillion that now housed the demon. Then he picked it up and walked out of the barn.

The sun had broken free of the clouds and sat in harsh contrast with the situation as he grew weaker. He grabbed a small spade and began digging a hole in the flower bed amongst the rosemary and foxglove, two powerful protection herbs.

With each strike upon the earth, he felt his strength waning, yet he persisted, using the last remnants of his life force to dig the hole deep enough that no one would accidentally stumble upon what he buried there. Only when satisfied with the depth did he gently place the container inside and cover it with soil.

As he rose to his feet, he stumbled, attempting to steady himself, but the loss of blood was too great. He mustered just enough strength to move away from the hole, making sure his blood wouldn't seep into the ground and set free the demon he had fought relentlessly to confine. His body collapsed, his life energy nothing more than a tiny flame that was petering out.

As he lay there, with the warmth of the sun beating down upon him and the gentle summer breeze caressing his face, he took his final breath, and with it, he said, "Neala."

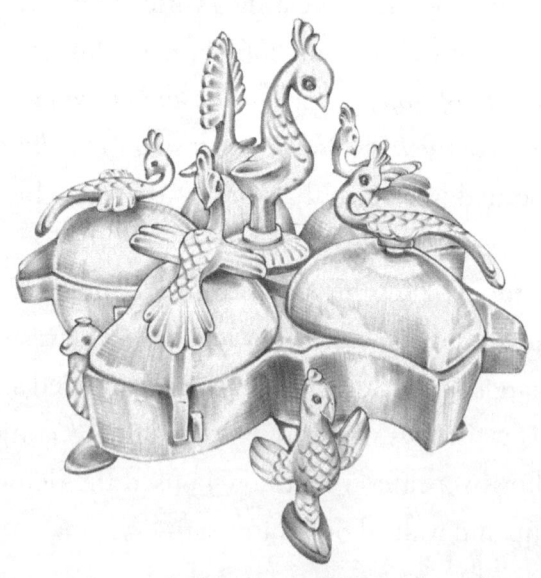

Chapter Forty-Four
THE STORY OF NYNEVE

Ionna jolted awake on the cold hardwood floor, her vision fading in and out. Kate, Owen, and Karena stood over her, looking down with concern. Slowly, she sat up and tried to get her bearings.

Something wasn't quite right; she couldn't tell if her eyes were playing tricks on her or if the blue glow that seemed to envelop both Kate and Karena was really there.

She rubbed at her eyes, but the glow was still present, floating around them like protective orbs. Owen, however, did not share this glow. He stood there staring down at her, the outline of his body crisp against the background of the room, his hand outstretched to her.

He was saying something, but she couldn't hear what it was—

there was a loud hum in her ears that was blocking everything else out. It seemed to coincide with the pulse of the glowing blue light that encircled the women. It was as if she was hearing the energy radiating from the light.

She closed her eyes and cupped her hands over her ears, trying desperately to calm her mind, which was becoming overstimulated. It didn't work. Even with her eyes closed and her ears blocked, she could still hear the deafening hum. She could feel it in her bones, in her teeth, gnawing at her, reverberating through her whole being. It grew so intense she thought she was about to explode. Just when she thought she couldn't take another second of it, she felt a hand on her shoulder, and everything died down to a dull hum. Ionna slowly took her hands off her ears and opened her eyes to see Kate kneeling down beside her. Somehow the connection they shared had calmed her overwhelmed senses.

"Ionna, are you okay?" Kate said, her voice penetrating the hum, pushing it into the background.

Ionna looked up into Kate's eyes and felt a sense of peace wash over her. It was then she felt the pull of reality calling her back, and she came fully out of the spell she had been under.

"I'm okay," she said as Owen pulled her to her feet, and Kate grabbed her by the arm, guiding her over to the sofa. She sank down into the cushions and looked at Kate. She still had the glow around her but it was softer now, almost invisible unless you were looking for it.

Kate noticed she was looking at her in an unusual way. She sat down in the armchair across from Ionna. "What is it?" she asked, though she suspected she already knew.

"I swear I can see a blue glow around you and Karena," Ionna said in a rush.

"Ionna, are you sure you're okay?" Owen asked gently. "You

hit your head pretty hard when you fell."

"She's fine," Karena reassured him. "That glow you can see around us is magic. Each person or thing that is magical has its own energy signature. It's like a fingerprint. Now that the binding spell your father placed on you has come undone and your powers have surfaced, you are able to see it."

"Binding spell? What do you mean, my powers?" Ionna asked as Karena poured a cup of tea for her and handed it over.

"My dear, your father had to bind your magic to keep you safe. The truth of your origins was what broke the final thread and released your magic. Artemas was one of the most powerful witches I have ever known. His magic runs through your veins."

"Me, magic? There's no way. I'm as ordinary as it gets," Ionna said, a small nervous laugh breaking through her words. The tea began to shake in her hands, and she set the cup down on the old trunk.

"It's true. I saw your father bind your magic when you were little," Kate said. "But it's not just his magic in you; it's also the power from the veil. When he pulled you back, your blue glow had turned white hot with the magic of the other world."

Ionna looked down at her hands. She could see it—there around the edges was a glow. It looked like Kate's and Karena's but instead of blue, it was a brilliant bright white.

"You not only brought back the power of the other world but the demon along with it," Karena told her. "That night after your father came to see me, I had a vision unlike any I had ever had. I didn't put it all together until recently. I believe Nyneve sent it to me so that one day I would pass it on to you, and I believe that today is that day. She revealed to me the true tale of her origins."

"Nyneve? The fictional character from the folktales?" Ionna asked.

"Yes, but she wasn't fictional. She was real and an ancestor of mine," Kate said.

"Is that so? How very interesting," Karena said, looking at Kate with new eyes. "The story came to me in a dream, guided by Nyneve herself. You see, Nyneve was destined to wed the deity Malachi, known for his chaos-inducing reputation. This arranged marriage aimed to forge peace between their families. However, Nyneve's mother foresaw the misery her daughter would endure if she married the evil Malachi.

"So, determined to shield Nyneve from this fate, her mother, an ancient sorceress, sent her to the human realm and erected a mystical barrier between the mortal and divine realms. This ensured that Malachi could only cross over in the company of Nyneve's bloodline from the realm of the gods. She also cast a protective spell upon Nyneve. It decreed that if a human man hit her three times, she would be transported away from the human realm for her safety," Karena said, her voice carrying a hint of otherworldliness. "When Malachi learned what Nyneve's mother had done, rage consumed him. A rage so great and terrible that he killed Nyneve's mother and father, unknowingly trapping himself in the realm of the gods. When he learned of her marriage to a mortal man, he was driven insane with vengeance; he vowed to break the barrier to kill all of her human descendants and wreak havoc on the human world."

Kate looked at Owen, who wore the same expression of fear on his face as she did. Karena continued to paint a vivid image of the horrifying story.

"When Nyneve surfaced in the human realm, it was in Lake Llyn Y Fan Fach. She found love and joy with a mortal man and bore him three sons. But her mother's spell, performed in haste, was fickle, and the day came when her husband's harmless actions triggered it, and she was torn away from her beloved family and cast out of the mortal realm. Nyneve sought solace within the watery realm of the lake. Mastering magic and healing, she became a guardian of ancient wisdom, guiding and protecting those who sought her counsel.

"In time, she discovered a way to briefly return to the mortal realm during an eclipse. Driven by her love for her sons and the desire to share her wisdom, she appeared before them on the water's edge and taught them magic and the techniques of a healer. She bestowed her powers on their bloodlines so that any descendant, born two hundred years apart amid a lunar eclipse, possessed powers from her domain. It was Malachi who attached to you, Ionna, finally freeing himself from the prison he had been trapped in, only to find himself trapped once again," Karena finished.

The room sat silent for a moment as the story sank in. Kate's and Owen's minds were spinning, filling in the blanks from the tales within Kate's grandfather's book with the one Karena had just told them.

"But why me and not Kate?" Ionna asked.

"Because you, my dear, hold magic from both realms. You were his key, being not only a descendant of Nyneve but also carrying the power and light force of his realm."

"So, how has he been surviving without her, then?" Owen asked.

"Outside the vermillion, Malachi can only survive a short time without a host. He must have been passing from one person to the next, living off the fear and chaos, but he will not be able to continue existing for much longer without his primary host, which is Ionna." Karena turned back to Ionna. "See, when your father pulled you back from death, your soul had already gone into the veil. When you returned, you not only brought back Malachi, but your soul came back with energy from the other realm. Making you the only host that he can stay in permanently as you carry magic within you from both realms. He will eventually die without you. He's desperate, and that's what makes him so dangerous," Karena said, pushing the teacup toward Ionna, urging her to drink.

"It's your soul he needs to stay in this realm. If you let your guard down or give him a way in, he will try and consume your soul to transform into a physical entity. This is something we can't let happen. So you must learn to practice your magic and safeguard your soul."

Ionna felt herself go pale. The gravity of the situation was sinking in, and the thought of being the host of this demon left her on the verge of being sick. She grabbed the tea and took a deep breath, trying her best to subside her anxiety. She looked down into the teacup. The dark amber liquid spun, and the loose leaves seemed to dance around in its wake. The more her mind turned over the day's events, the more the tea whirled around. Before she knew what was going on, the tea had spun up into a vortex and was hovering in the air above the cup. She gasped, breaking her downward-spiraling thoughts. The tea landed back, splashing its contents out over its sides and onto her lap.

"Crap," Ionna said, setting the teacup down and standing up to wipe off her pants.

"Well, I see your magic is alive and well," Karena said, handing her a cotton napkin with tiny violets embroidered on it. "Our emotions play a role in how we wield our magic. You must be careful until you have learned how your emotions control yours. Only small amounts of magic—we can't open the door for Malachi."

Ionna took the napkin and blotted the hot tea off her pants, letting Karena's words sink in as the tea had into the fabric of her jeans.

"How do I learn to do that?" she asked.

"The first thing you need to do is learn to focus your energy when your emotions rise," Karena said. She stood up and walked over to the old wooden mantel above the fireplace, pulling down a pewter candle holder with a tall white tier candle in its base. She brought it over and set it on the table. "Let's start with this. I want you to try and light the candle without touching it," she told Ionna.

"Ha, you're kidding, right? There's no way."

"Oh, but there is. Look at the candle's wick and picture it coming to life with fire. Use your emotions to generate your energy," Karena instructed.

Ionna sat there for a minute, her mind churning with all the new information she had been given in such a short amount of time. She had found out that her parents were not her parents, that her grandmother was actually her stepsister, that her real name was Neala, that she had some hell-bent demonic god from another realm on her ass, and that she now possessed magical powers. *Maybe there were magic mushrooms in that tea, after all,* she thought. She wished it was just that simple, but it wasn't.

She looked over at Kate and Owen, two innocent kids thrown into all this craziness. Anger began to build in her. It started in her chest and spread throughout her body, like wildfire in a forest. How had her seemingly boring life turned into this horrible nightmare? She almost wished she didn't know any of it. Ignorance would have been bliss. But that wasn't her; she needed the truth. She would never have been satisfied not knowing what had really happened.

She felt her cheeks burning as her anger grew and transformed into rage. It was at that moment that she looked at the candle, its thin white pyre sitting there untouched. The moment her thoughts turned to fire, a tiny plume of black smoke appeared in the air over the candle—and a moment later vanished. The second time she tried, sparks flew out of the tips of her fingers, but the candle remained unlit. It took two more attempts, one singeing the corner of one of Karena's chairs before she finally set fire to the candlewick.

She watched as it burst into a dancing flame, and small teardrops of wax gently melted down the sides.

"Oh my God! That was amazing," Owen burst out, breaking Ionna from the flame's hypnotizing trance. He looked at her with amazement in his eyes, then leaned forward to examine the candle.

"See, it only takes a bit of practice. I'm sure you'll catch on quickly. Just small bits at a time. Remember, too much magic and you'll open a gateway for Malachi," Karena warned.

"I hate to break this lesson up but now that Ionna's magic is unbound, isn't Malachi going to be even more eager to take her over?" Kate asked.

"You're right. We need to perform a protection ritual for each of you before you leave," Karena said. "And then there is the business of trapping Malachi and sending him back from where he came."

"We can't. Artemas tried when Ionna was little, and Malachi almost killed her and succeeded in killing him. And like you said, Artemas was one of the most powerful witches you knew. How can we even compete with that?" Kate said, her tone full of concern as she looked at Ionna.

"They must be linked still," Owen said, as a tense feeling

settled in the room. He glanced over his shoulder.

"I don't understand. Why hasn't it shown up until now?" Ionna asked, resting back against the sofa, her eyes still transfixed on the candle.

"I don't know, but somehow it escaped the trap your father had it in for the past thirty-six years," Karena said.

"Did you say that it would have to create fear and chaos to survive in another host for a short period of time?" Owen asked, resting his elbows on his knees.

Kate looked at Owen and then back at Karena. "Like making pies with yew berries?" she asked.

"Yes, just like that," Karena said.

"What about drowning a bunch of sheep? Or panthers stalking the riding trail on the mountain?" Owen asked.

"All great ways to spread fear and chaos I would say," Kate said. Karena nodded in agreement.

"Wait, when did this all start happening—before or after Betty's death?" Ionna asked, the gears turning in her head as she began to piece things together.

"After," Kate and Owen said in unison.

"It must have been Betty. She didn't know anything about magic, right? Well, when I first arrived, I found a spade in the garden next to a small hole with a black thorny vine coming out of it. It was out of place because the rest of her property was well kept. Like she had just been gardening and left everything in a hurry. I bet that Betty tried digging the roots of the thorn bush out and that's how she found the vermillion. And John said she had a cut on her hand when they found her," Ionna told them.

"Yes, I bet you're right. If the key to unlocking the spell on the vermillion was blood, a thorn bush would be a perfect way for Malachi to free himself. Clever," Kate said.

"So he was able to have some kind of influence on his surroundings, even though he was trapped in the vermillion?" Owen asked.

"Exactly," Karena said. "Think of it like something radioactive. Tainting the area around where it rests. The thorn bush was just a manifestation of the demon's evil, helping to free itself if it got the chance."

As Ionna's mind spun with newfound answers, relieving the burden of unanswered questions she had carried for days, an ominous realization dawned on her—the truth was far more terrifying than she could have ever imagined. She sat there grappling with the haunting uncertainty. Was knowing the truth a blessing or a curse, and what unforeseen consequences would it bring in the days to come?

Chapter Forty-Five

DARK CHARMS

Kate walked over to the window. Outside, the snow had stopped but the sky was still thick with clouds, and thunder rumbled somewhere in the distance. What scant light there had been was now fading. Kate had an uneasy feeling come over her at the thought of traveling back to Beddgelert in the dark. *What if the demon churns up another storm? It is scary enough driving in that kind of weather in the daytime*, she thought.

"I think it's time you headed back, before nightfall," Karena said, as if reading Kate's mind—*which is completely possible, seeing how she is a psychic*, Kate thought. "But before you go, we must figure out your next move and create protection charms for each of you," she told them, getting back up and walking over to an old box that sat on top of one of the side tables. From this, she pulled a black bag and poured its contents into her hand, closing her fingers over it in a tight fist. Then she sat back down and closed her eyes, tilting her head back.

Kate and Owen looked at each other with questioning glances as they watched the old woman fall into a trance-like state. She sat there silent for a long while with her head facing the heavens. Eventually, she lifted her head and opened her eyes, which were no longer black but a light gray, almost white. She blinked a few times as if to break herself from her vision, and her eyes turned back to pools of obsidian.

Ionna sat there on the edge of the sofa waiting to hear what Karena had seen. She felt desperate at this point for any information. Even though she had magic, she still felt like she was fighting a dragon with a toothpick. She was going to take any help she could get.

Karena's eyes pulled back into focus, and she propped herself up.

"The spell you need is in the fern library, but it will not work unless you find the guidance that you need. There is another that must assist you in your mission," she told them.

"Where is the fern library?" Kate asked, turning from the window and rejoining the group.

"I can't say. My vision is not always straightforward. There is always much that needs to be interpreted." She got up and went over to the small table again, slipping the mystery item back into the black velvet bag it had come from.

"Who is this other person?" Owen asked.

"It's a man. He will play an important part in the capture of the demon. You should not go forth with the spell unless he is present. Otherwise, it will not end well."

Owen looked over at Kate, and she saw him clench his jaw in concern.

Karena proceeded over to the doorway that led toward the kitchen. When she returned, she held a small tray with an array of bottles on it filled with different herbs. She set it down on the side table next to her chair and began pulling the corks off each bottle.

"Owen, come here. The first charm will be for you," she said. She pulled a small bag the size of her thumb from next to one of the bottles.

Owen walked over to her.

"Now, I need you to hold this as I fill it."

He nodded in compliance.

"The first and most vital thing for this charm is this small piece of black tourmaline," Karena said, holding up a small black stone that resembled a piece of coal. She picked up a bottle labeled "angelica root" and poured a tiny bit into the bag. Next, she added a touch of foxglove, basil, and mugwort. "Now, I need you to pull the strings tight and knot them three times around each other while saying, 'Shield my earthly body from harm and protect my soul with this charm.'"

Owen did as he was told and repeated the incantation three times.

Karena held out her hand, and he placed the charm bag into it. She took out a tincture bottle that said "Dragon's blood oil" on it and added three drops to it before slipping the bag onto a thin rope of leather, creating a necklace.

"Bend down," she said, and Owen did as he was told, bowing his head as if he was being knighted. She placed the charm around his neck and tied it securely.

Immediately, he felt a lightness come over him, as though some of his worries had been absorbed by the charm. He made his way back to the sofa, where he examined his new piece of hardware.

"Okay, Kate, you next," Karena said, repeating the same process as she had done with Owen. "Now listen very carefully." She leveled her gaze at Kate and paused. "This charm will protect you, but it will also keep you from flipping time. Be vigilant if you must take it off."

Kate nodded, taking heed of the warning.

Once Kate's charm was done, it was Ionna's turn. She stood and walked over but before she could make it the two short feet to where Karena sat, a bolt of lightning struck down in front of the window, blinding everyone inside the room and catching the mighty oak tree in front of Karena's house on fire. The tree's trunk bore the aftermath of lightning, leaving behind a twisting, fiery spiral, resembling a serpent constricting its prey.

"Oh my God," Ionna gasped.

The singed tree burned for only a few moments. The wet, heavy snow that sat upon it snuffed out the flames, leaving little more than a smoldering trail of ash on its bark. The fear of the demon's presence left everyone but Karena on edge.

"Someone is not happy about this charm I'm about to give you," Karena said. "But have no fear—he cannot penetrate the protection barriers I have on my home. You are safe," she reassured them all.

Apprehensively, Ionna stepped up to Karena and took the small bag from her as the others had done.

"You, my dear, need a charm of a different sort," she said as she picked up a bottle with "Moonwort" written on it. She put a small amount of the herb at the bottom of the bag before placing in the tourmaline. Then she added a sprig of mistletoe, angelica root, mullein, and St. John's wart to the small bag. The last thing she placed inside was a small, dried violet. Then she asked Ionna to close it.

"Now as you knot it, repeat these words three times: 'When dark forces are at play, with my magic, I keep them at bay. Protect my soul from evil's touch, may it never fall into its clutch.'"

As Ionna murmured the words, she could feel a mounting power with each repetition, and by the time she had finished, the bag was glowing with the white light that she held within her.

Owen looked out at the old oak that sat stoically in Karena's yard. The top branches were still smoldering from where the lightning had struck, and it sported a black singe mark that now looked like a dragon wrapping itself around the tree.

"Are you sure these protection charms will work?" he asked, pulling the small black pouch out of his shirt and running the smooth leather rope through his fingers.

"Yes, they'll work. Just make sure you keep them on you. If not around your neck, then in your pocket," Karena said. "Ionna and Kate have their other amulets as well for an extra layer of protection. You should all be just fine."

"How will we find the fern library and this man who's supposed to help us?" Kate asked, going over to stand by Owen.

"Things have a way of working themselves out. The universe will guide you to the answers," Karena said. It was a vague piece of advice only a fortune teller could come up with.

Knowing it was time to go, Ionna bent forward and blew the candle out, watching the magic she had created turn to nothing more than wispy tendrils of smoke. As she stood, she noticed something—the smoke began to twist and shift in an unnatural way. It spun up to form a point, then fell back and created a hilt.

Before she knew it, the smoke had created the perfect medieval-style sword. It hovered in the air for only a second before it vanished into nothing more than a thin strand of haze.

"Did you see that?" she asked with excitement, looking around at the others.

"I missed it. What happened?" Kate asked, stepping forward to inspect the candle.

"It was a sword, like Excalibur, there in the smoke," Ionna said, still looking at the candle as if it had more secrets to share.

"What does that mean?" Owen asked, taking a step closer to Kate and also looking at the candle, which was now just sitting there with its burnt wick.

"I'm not sure," Ionna said, looking over at Karena for guidance.

"It seems you are able to scry with smoke," she told her.

"Scry?" Ionna repeated.

"It's another form of divination that's been used for centuries. Those with the ability can see images in the workings of the smoke. These images are often things that will help or guide you."

Ionna looked back down at the candle one last time, willing it to give her a little more to go on. But the smoke was gone, and there was nothing left other than a sooty wick.

"What good is it if you can't understand the meaning behind the message?"

"It will come to you. It's something you already understand deep within, you just need to guide it to the surface," Karena told her as she walked them back to the entryway of her home. "I may not know what the future holds for you, but what I do know is that together you are strong enough to overcome the challenges set upon you. Now find your fern library and your other guide. You know where I am if you need me." With that, she opened the door.

"Thank you for all your help," Kate said, giving the old woman a big hug before walking out into the dewy evening air. Owen gave her a smile and a tilt of his head in gratitude as he followed behind Kate.

"Remember to practice your magic carefully, just small bits like lighting candles for now. Don't go trying spells that require large amounts of magic; that will only give Malachi a well to drink from. Do you understand?" she told Ionna.

"Yes," Ionna said.

Karena gave her a kind look. "You are your father's daughter, I can see it in your eyes. Which means you, my dear, are a very powerful witch. You need to be prepared and be on the lookout for Malachi. He will try to find a way in by whatever means possible, even coming after the people you love most." She pulled Ionna into an embrace.

"Thank you. I'm not sure what we would have done without your guidance," Ionna told her as she pulled away and walked out the door.

The three of them were surprised to see that the snow had all but melted, only leaving a few patches here and there. The temperature had warmed back up so it almost felt ... normal, yet a ghostly mist rose from the snowmelt, giving the landscape an eerie look.

They walked quickly to Owen's car, though it was parked only a short distance away. None of them felt safe out in the open. As they pulled away from the turning point in all of their lives, they looked back to see Karena standing in the little window, watching them drive away. A whispered *"Good luck"* entered each of their minds as they departed.

Chapter Forty-Six
THE GRASP OF DARKNESS

The car ride back was mostly filled with silence. Everyone was trapped inside their own minds, replaying the day's events. It wasn't until they reached Beddgelert that Owen broke the silence.

"Do you think that the sword might have something to do with the King Arthur legend?" he asked Ionna, who was staring out the back window, lost in thought.

"Not sure, why?" she asked.

"Well, you said it was a sword like Excalibur, and in the tale, Lady of the Lake gave that sword to Arthur. That can't be a coincidence. Maybe one of the legends might help us figure out where the fern library is or this other man who's supposed to help you," Owen said, the latter half of the sentence coming out a little bitterly.

It was at that moment that Kate realized what the expression was she had seen on his face when Karena had mentioned another man. It was a look of jealousy. He had been their knight in shining armor up until now, after all. It was highly unlikely that he wanted to share that role with someone else. And there was another consideration, too. It was his idea that had put all of this into motion five years ago, and she could see that he was harboring some guilt over it.

"Maybe. Let's look into it when we get back. There's a whole section on King Arthur in the study," Ionna said, pulling Kate out of her thoughts and back into the conversation.

Once they were back at Betty's house, they gathered in the study and began looking through the stack of books featuring the famous legends.

"Here," Ionna said, handing both Kate and Owen a piece of paper and a pen. "Now, make citations on anything that stands out; write down the page number and title. It will help in the end if we need to go back and cross-reference things," she told them, her newsroom skills coming out to play.

They nodded and set the paper and pen next to their books. For a while they all sat silently reading, no sounds but the shuffling of pages between them.

"Ionna, did you know that the mountain behind this house is said to have two sleeping dragons in it?" Owen asked her, turning a book around and showing her a drawing of two dragons sleeping, the earth falling around them to create the same mountain that sat behind Betty's house.

"No, but I *will* be more mindful when I take a walk next time," she joked.

"My dad used to tell me that if I was bad, it would wake the dragons, and the only thing dragons like more than a cow after sleeping for centuries is naughty little boys," Owen said with a chuckle.

"That's awful," Kate said, looking up from a book.

She was in her element. Reading was her favorite pastime, and she was good at it. She could speed read with the best of them and had made it through four stories in just the short time they had been there.

"I'm not seeing anything that sticks out, are you?" Ionna asked them as she closed one book and picked up another.

"Nothing," Kate said, setting down the book she had been reading and looking for something else.

"Owen, have you heard any update about the poison pie people in the hospital?" Ionna asked. She was skimming through a Welsh lore recipe book.

"Dad said that a few of them have been released but another one of the older chaps in critical care died late last night. That makes four dead from the pies. Can you believe that?"

"God, how terrible. What ever happened to Sandra? Did they end up arresting her?" Ionna asked.

"No, I guess she's in hospital too, in the psych ward. Completely lost it after finding out she had poisoned all those people," Owen said grimly.

Kate looked up from her book. "Oh my God, that's awful."

"You think that's bad—you know the little bed-and-breakfast just outside of town? It burned down last night from a lightning strike. Dad went over with some other local farmers to help clean up the damage. It's like the demon's unleashed a plague of bad luck on Beddgelert."

"Why didn't you tell us before now?" Kate asked, looking put out that Owen hadn't brought it up.

"Well, we were kinda busy today, you know?" he said, raising his eyebrows at Kate as if she had forgotten all that had happened in the past four hours.

Ionna's mind raced with all the awful things the town had been through in the past few days. Between the poisoning, the ruined crops, the sheep, and now the B and B, the community had taken quite a hit. She looked back down at the book in her hands. It was open to a page with a Welsh tale called "The Devil's Stone." It was said that the devil had thrown a stone from the top of a mountain in an attempt to hit a nearby church, but he missed, and the stone landed where it now stood in Llanharry.

The story sent shivers down her spine. It felt all too real. They had their own demon tossing stones at them, after all. She snapped the book shut, not wanting to read any more about devils causing chaos. She was scrutinizing the bookcase when she noticed a set of headlights pulling down the driveway toward the house. Stepping over to the window, she saw John's BMW pull up next to Owen's car.

"John's here," she announced, walking out of the study and over to the front door. By the time she had opened it, John was there, about to knock.

"Oh hey! Just wanted to drop in on my way back to London to say goodbye," he said.

"Come in," she told him, swinging the door wide.

"I can't, Ryan's in the car. It's just a quick stop."

Owen and Kate peeked around the door, books in hand.

"Owen, hey, bud. Glad I got a chance to see you before I head out," he said, stepping in and giving his nephew a bro hug.

"You guys going back tonight?" Owen asked as they pulled apart.

"Yeah, got to get back to the grind. We had a great last day though; took the horses out for a ride. It was a beautiful afternoon, wasn't it?"

Owen raised his eyebrows and looked over at Kate, who also looked surprised at the mention of the beautiful weather. Their experience had not been so pleasant.

John followed Owen's gaze over to Kate, who was standing next to him with a book in her hands.

"Wait, did you guys start a book club and not invite me?" he joked.

"No, we're looking for some of the legends of Excalibur," Owen said with a laugh.

"Oh really? If you want to know about Excalibur, you should ask my friend Zeke. He's an expert in all things swords," John said, taking out his wallet and handing a business card to Owen.

Owen took it from him and smiled. "Thanks, Uncle John."

Karena was right: the universe would help. It had guided John to them just at the right moment.

"Well, I better go. Ryan won't be happy if I leave him in the car too long by himself," John said, turning sideways and looking toward the car. Ryan rolled the window down and gave them a big wave.

Ionna smiled and waved back as John turned back toward the car. "Thanks again for everything, John," she called out after him.

He turned and smiled. "It was great getting to know you, Ionna. I hope you decide to stay."

She kept waving as they drove off, her mind getting stuck on the last thing John said. She hadn't thought about actually sticking around. This was supposed to be a quick trip over and back, a bit of a vacation of sorts, in its own morbid way. However, finding out that this was her birthplace, her original home, she wasn't quite sure she was ready to leave just yet.

Not to mention all that she would face in the coming days with the demon. There was no telling how much of Beddgelert would be left if they couldn't figure out a way to vanquish him.

She shut the door and turned around to see Owen standing there, holding out the business card like it was the holy grail.

"I think we found your guide," he said.

Chapter Forty-Seven

FERNBEG

The next morning came early for Ionna. She had spent most of the night lying awake, her mind racing with everything that had transpired that day. But it wasn't just her mind that kept her far from sleep; it was the energy she felt racing around inside her. Ever since her magic had come unbound, it was as if she had the power of an electrical storm rushing through her. Not that her mind was much better—her thoughts whirled in her head like a violent storm.

She spent a good part of the night longing for her old mundane life back and wondering what things might have been like if she hadn't boarded that plane and come to Wales. Maybe the *Bath Post* would have hired her and she'd be starting a new job, completely oblivious to the realm of magic and all its dangers.

But the not knowing would have haunted her. Not knowing why her parents hid her true origins. She wasn't sure she could ever go back to the life she once lived after all of this was over. But she also wasn't sure what future she would have if she stayed here in Wales. If she even survived, that was.

She climbed out of bed just as the sun peeked above the horizon, burning a thin gold line in its wake.

After making herself a cup of coffee, she went into the living room where Jasper was sleeping peacefully next to Betty's urn. She pushed one of the large blue velvet chairs around, positioning it to face the window. The sun seemed slow to rise this morning. She watched it paint everything it touched in shades of orange and gold. When it finally rose above its earthly bed, the sky was streaked with pink.

"Pink sky in morning, sailors take warning," she said to herself, as an uneasy feeling settled into her bones. *Even the most beautiful things can hide danger within*, she thought, looking out over the seemingly beautiful sky, knowing it foretold trouble.

As she sat looking out the window, the cup of coffee warming her hands, a thought formed in her mind, one that she had not considered before. What if she were to rid herself of the magic she held? Not bind it again but actually strip herself of it. If she no longer possessed the powers that Malachi sought, then maybe he'd leave her alone. She had lived for thirty-six years without magic, it wasn't like she was going to miss it—she didn't even know how to control it. But she knew it couldn't be that easy. A move like that would likely just enrage Malachi further, spurring him on to wreak more havoc on the people of Beddgelert. And at that point, she'd have no way of stopping him. She couldn't let that happen.

She thought back to what Karena had told her. She had to

practice focusing her emotions into her magic. She looked over at her father's journal sitting on the table next to Jasper. It was strange to think that Artemas was her real father. He'd lived so long ago that he could have been her great-grandfather. If she had never gotten sick as a child and Kate had never brought her forward in time, she would be an old woman now, spending her retirement knitting and watching her grandbabies grow up. Her family would never have been ripped apart. She would probably have lived in Beddgelert, happily, all her life. The thought was almost too much.

She got up and went to the table where the journal sat. When she approached, Jasper woke up and gave a leisurely stretch before jumping down and finding a new spot to nap. She picked up the journal and ran her hands over its cool leather surface.

As she held it, she could see the blue glow seeping from within and hear the distant song of energy that filled its pages. It somehow seemed so much more important now that she knew it had been her father's, a small piece of him still here for her to hold. She flipped it open and began looking at the spells. There had to be something in here that could help them get rid of this darkness. But she couldn't see anything that would be powerful enough. She flipped back to his journal entries. The words themselves thrummed with resonance now that she knew she was reading her origin story, not just some written account of a far-off grandparent.

As she sifted through the first entry again, she stopped. One of the lines caught her attention, glowing as if it was trying to tell her something.

"'I stayed on and looked after Fernbeg Cottage,'" she read aloud.

Fernbeg Cottage. Was this the "fern" in the fern library they were looking for? It was then that she remembered an entry she'd read before. She flipped through the book until she found it: *I must go back to Fernbeg to gather a spell needed.*

So, this was the place they needed to go. This Fernbeg Cottage held a spell book and within it a spell they needed to get rid of Malachi for good. Now, the question was how was she going to find this Fernbeg Cottage? It was in Scotland, she knew that much. Maybe with the help of the internet she could figure out just where in Scotland it was.

She walked into the bedroom, grabbed her phone out of her bag, and pulled on a pair of jeans, a sweater, and a pair of Betty's old mud boots, and headed for the door. John had told her that if she got desperate, the large rock in the field had two bars.

As soon as she made it halfway to the rock, an ominous feeling came over her—she was certain she was being watched. She spun around, scanning the field behind her. No one was there, yet she knew deep in her bones there was. Hidden in the folds of daylight was a darkness that followed her like a predator. Ionna waited a few moments, her heart loud in her chest. It seemed that Karena's charms were working. Whatever was out there was staying at a distance.

But its presence was palpable in the air, sitting on the nape of her neck. The feeling of being stalked.

"Fuck off," she said to the air, her middle finger raised above her head as she spun three hundred and sixty degrees, then stomped off toward the rock.

The bolder had to be as big as the double-decker buses she'd seen towering along the streets of London, and it took some effort to make her way to a spot where she could stand. Sure enough, just as John had promised, there were two bars. Just enough to bring up a Google page.

She typed "Fernbeg Cottage, Scotland" into the search bar and waited. It took a few minutes for the results to load. The second one down was a real estate listing for a cottage in Oban, Scotland. The title read "Fernbeg Cottage, a charming estate nestled in the Scottish Highlands."

"Bingo," she said, clicking on the link.

It seemed ages before the page loaded completely, and she was quickly disappointed to see there was no address—but there was a phone number to the estate company that had the listing. She took a screenshot and then slowly climbed down off the rock. There was no way she would be able to make a clear call with the crappy reception, so she decided to make her way back to the house and call from the good old corded landline.

The sun was above the tops of the trees by the time she made it back to the house, and the brilliant pink sky had faded to nothing more than a powder blue, giving a false feeling of calm to the world below.

In the house she picked up the landline and then pulled her cell out to look for the number. It rang for a while before someone picked up. She realized she had no idea what time it actually was; quickly glancing down at her phone, she was relieved to see that it was half past eight.

"Hello, Coney Estates, how may I help you?" a jolly older woman's voice rang out from the other end.

"Yes, hello. My name is Ionna Bellmore, and I saw an ad online for a cottage that I'm interested in," she said, the lie coming easily. She had gotten quite good at this sort of thing with her job, and she knew how to bend the truth to serve her needs.

"Of course, can you give me the estate number, please?"

Thank God I took a screenshot of the page, she thought as she read the number off to the woman.

"Oh dear, I'm so sorry, that cottage sold already."

"Oh. Do you happen to know who bought it? It belonged to a relative of mine, and I'd like to contact its current owner to see if I might be able to come over and have a look at it. Take some photos for genealogical stuff," she told the woman, more lies spilling from her silver tongue.

"Well, I'm really not supposed to give out that information…" the woman said.

She was going to be a tougher egg to crack than Ionna had first thought.

"Oh, I totally understand, but I truly am just trying to piece together some of my family's history. It would be a huge help to me."

"Well … I'm a bit of a family historian myself," she confessed.

She had her hook, line, and sinker now.

"Oh, so I'm sure you know how important photographs of places can be when putting together a historical record then."

"Oh, of course. Well, I'm really not supposed to be doing this, but…" She trailed off, and Ionna could hear papers being rifled through on the other end of the phone. "The woman who bought it is Helen Kent. Do you have a pen handy for the number?"

"Yes," Ionna said, her thumb hovering over the keypad of her cell phone.

"Okay, her number is 44-1631-571459. I hope that helps you."

"More than you know. Thank you," Ionna said before saying goodbye and hanging up.

She stood there looking down at the number. It was the next piece of the puzzle, and she was hoping that this Helen Kent was going to be as easy to persuade as the old woman on the phone had been.

She took a deep breath before she dialed. It rang, then rang some more, but no one answered, and no machine picked up for her to leave a message on. After a few more attempts, she hung up, resigning herself to the fact that she was going to have to wait. In the meantime, there was another phone call she needed to make.

She walked over to the kitchen table and picked up the small white business card with fiery red letters spelling out the name "Zeke Evans" and below that, "Swordsmith."

She turned it over and looked at his personal cell number scrolled in blue ink. His handwriting was neat, and the numbers stood perfectly straight, with no slant to them at all. Ionna had learned to read handwriting when she first started out at the *Gazette*. It was a great way of telling who someone was without too much snooping. Zeke seemed to be a pretty straightforward guy. His handwriting told her that he was well organized and disciplined and took pride in his work. He likely had a keen eye for detail and preferred structure in his life.

Of course, this was all speculation. What she knew for definite was he knew about swords, and he was disarmingly good-looking.

After a few minutes, she realized she was stalling. She wasn't quite sure how to approach this conversation, and the memory of how charming he'd been when she met him at the market made this even harder. But she pushed it all aside and picked up the phone, knowing there were too many lives hanging in the balance. She swallowed hard as she dialed, waiting with bated breath as it rang. And it did ring, for more than a minute. She was just about to hang up when she heard the raspy, tired voice break through on the other end.

"Hello?" he said. His voice was thick with sleep and confusion, probably wondering who the hell was calling him this early in the morning. *Must be a night owl*, she thought as she cleared her throat.

"Zeke?" she asked.

"Yeah, who is this?"

"Ionna Bellmore, John's friend. We met at the market the other day," she reminded him.

It was a while before he responded, and she heard things being moved around as if he was literally rolling out of bed. Well, she must not have made that big of an impression on him because it took him all of a minute to break the silence.

"Okay, yeah. Your American accent threw me there for a minute. Is John okay?" he asked, worry filling his words.

"Oh, he's fine. Headed back to the city last night," she told him, trying to figure out how to break into what she needed to ask him. *What was it I needed to ask him?* She froze. *Shit, I don't even know.* She didn't have the spell and had no idea what she even needed him for. She had been in such a rush to put everything in motion that she made the call prematurely. Now she was going to have to make something up off the cuff. "Um, John thought you might be able to help me. You see, I'm researching the Excalibur legend along with some of the other local folklore in the area for an article I'm putting together." *Lies, lies, and more lies*, she thought as she told them.

"Interesting. Yeah, sure, I'm happy to help. I'm free this afternoon. How about we meet in town around one?" he said. His tone had recovered from the sleepiness, and to her relief, he sounded genuine.

"Yes, that sounds great. Where should I meet you?" she asked.

"Let's meet at Gelert's grave. Don't worry, it's not a graveyard. It's just a monument to a long-dead dog of a king but also a fascinating piece of local lore," he said.

"Okay, I'll try and find my way to it."

"Great, see you at one, Ionna," he said, her name rolling off his tongue like silk.

"See you," she said in a girlish voice before hanging up. Internally, she cursed herself. Why did she have to be so awkward around men?

And *why* did lying come so naturally to her? Now she had to pretend she was writing an article about Welsh folklore. She told herself it would be better to ease into things with him like this than to straight up ask him to help her fight a demon. If she did that, he might think she was a total crazy and not give her the time of day. This way she would get to know him a bit better. She was good at reading people and even better at figuring out their weaknesses. With any luck, she would come up with a way to break into the conversation with him and find out just what role he was to play in saving her life.

Chapter Forty-Eight
GELERT

Ionna grabbed her cell from the table and sent a text to Kate, informing her about her plan to meet Zeke in town and her discovery of the fern library's location. Within moments, she received a reply: a smiley face, two thumbs-up, and a party blower emoji along with a short message letting her know that she and Owen had stumbled upon a lead of their own and were planning on doing some digging. Ionna smiled and tucked her phone into her pocket before picking up a box off the side table.

She dug through the box with the Brightmore law firm's insignia on it, scanning each item until she laid her hands on a set of car keys hidden at the bottom. She pulled them out and looked out the window at the old burgundy car sitting next to the barn.

"Okay, let's give this European driving thing a go," she said nervously to herself as she grabbed her bag and headed out the door.

A thick layer of dust covered the car like a shroud and she wondered if it would even start. It looked like it had been sitting there far longer than the month since Betty's death.

She unlocked and opened the door, sending a plume of dust into the air, and slipped inside. It smelled of mildew and pine air freshener but was neat and tidy, just as the house was. She put the key in the ignition and prayed that it would start. It turned over once with no success. She tried again, but nothing.

"Crap," she muttered, resting her head back against the headrest. "Come on, old girl."

She tried again, but the engine just skipped and petered out. "Really?"

She wasn't sure if the car wasn't starting because it hadn't been driven in a while or if it was Malachi trying to keep her from her mission. The thought fueled an idea and she tried to start the car once more, this time giving it a gentle nudge with her magic. She closed her eyes, searching deep within herself for the hum of magic. When her senses finally locked onto it, she grasped it firmly, coaxing forth a comforting warmth that blossomed within her chest. She channeled the energy into her arms, guiding it down to her hands, and then released it through the tips of her fingers, allowing it to flow seamlessly into the steering wheel.

It sputtered at first as she turned it over, then ignited and came to life with a low rumble. She smiled as the engine purred, not one hundred percent sure she had anything to do with getting it started, but she was glad it had.

"Now, let's just hope I can get the hang of driving on the wrong side of the road," she said as she shifted it into drive and headed for the town.

Her nerves were on edge as she drove, expecting Malachi to cause a sudden storm or something else destructive in an attempt to stop her. However, she made it to town with no incidents and parked near the spot Zeke had chosen for them to meet.

A large group of tourists were following a guide around the area. Ionna got out and looked around for Zeke but didn't see him. She weaved in and out of the people surrounding the large copper sculpture of what looked to be a wolfhound. It wasn't until she pushed past the crowd that she saw him. He was leaning on a stone wall looking off to his right at a small group of people.

The sun was still out in full force, not yet obscured by the clouds that loomed on the horizon. Its rays cast a glow upon him that made his hair look the color of dried wheat, and his eyes lightened, turning from a chestnut brown to a dark shade of melted gold, rimmed in the rich color of earth. His sharp jawline was peppered with a day's worth of stubble, giving him a rugged look that fit him quite well. And instead of the thick canvas pants and apron she had seen him in at the market, he wore a pair of faded jeans and a gray T-shirt with mountain peaks across the chest.

He was handsome, but there was something about him that drew her attention in a different way. She felt a pull toward him. She had noticed it when they first met at the market, but it had now grown into something more. *Something metaphysical?* she thought as she got closer to him, unable to pull her eyes from the upward curve of his mouth. He hadn't noticed her yet, as he was still watching the crowd off to his right.

Ionna stepped forward and caught his attention. When they locked eyes, she saw a glow emanating from him, as if her magic was sending her a signal. The glow seemed to reach from her body over to his, creating a bridge of light between them.

Zeke smiled and waved to Ionna as he made his way over to where she stood. As he moved toward her, the glow faded to a light mist, just as Kate's had done at Karena's.

"Hello, there," he said, his deep voice filling the space between them.

"Hey, thanks for meeting me," she said, a wide smile playing across her face as she shoved her hand inside her jeans pocket and twisted the cloth in her fingers, trying to steady her nerves.

"No problem. Not sure if you've seen this place yet but I thought it's a pretty good spot to start, being a big part of the local lore here," he said, waving his hand toward the large rock with the plaque resting next to the sculpture of the wolfhound.

"No, I haven't really made it into town much," she told him, thinking how very true it was. She had been so caught up in all this craziness since she arrived that she hadn't even gotten a chance to do any exploring. Maybe this was just what she needed, a day to clear her mind of all things supernatural and just be a tourist enjoying the beauty of the Welsh Highlands. But as they set off, she glanced over her shoulder, half expecting to see a shadowy figure watching her.

"Have you heard the Tale of Gelert?" he asked her, walking over and running his large hand across the surface of the stone that acted as a grave marker.

"No, I haven't. But it looks to be a popular tale," Ionna said, gesturing at the groups of people walking in and out of the small gated area.

"The town was actually named after the dog. Beddgelert means 'grave of Gelert.' I'll tell you the story as we walk into town," he said.

They walked a small footpath down near the river. The grassy riverbanks looked inviting and he found a place with three large rocks close to the water for them to sit on.

"The tale goes that Gelert was a loyal dog of Prince Llywelyn the Great. One day, Llywelyn returned from a hunting trip to find Gelert covered in blood and his infant son missing. Assuming he had attacked and killed his baby, Llywelyn killed Gelert in anger." He glanced over his shoulder back toward the monument. "Only moments later he discovered his son unharmed and a wolf dead in his home. He realized too late that Gelert had actually saved his son from the wolf's attack. He was so upset with what he had done that he promised no one would ever forget his dog's name. Thus, the monument and the town's name."

It was a tragic story and Ionna forced back tears that threatened to break free. She was never one for the story of animal deaths—*Old Yeller* and *Bambi* traumatized her as a child.

"I'm sorry, I sometimes forget what a sad tale it is. It's been told to me since I was a wee boy and the sadness has evolved into part of its lore, I guess," he said. He stood up, holding his hand out for her to take.

As she took it, she looked down. There, where their hands met, was a shimmery gold outline of magic unlike any she had seen before. It seemed to pulse with the beat of her own heart. She stared down in wonder for a moment and then a sinking sensation came over her. It felt as if they had just created some kind of magical beacon with their touch. And if they had, then Malachi wouldn't be far behind.

She knew what he meant; you could be dulled to certain emotions. Like her and loneliness, they were such close companions that she had all but forgotten what the emotion was.

"It's okay, I'm just a sucker for sad dog stories," she told him when she realized he was still holding her hand even though they had made it up to the path. She looked up into his chestnut eyes and he looked back down into hers. It was at that moment that she knew he was the missing piece, she could feel it deep within her. Her magic called out in a way that it hadn't before, as if to say she was close to the answers she needed.

He was the first to break the awkward stare, releasing her hand and looking away toward the path.

"Why don't we head into town for a coffee and a bite to eat? Carri Gwynant is truly a place not to be missed," he said with a smile.

She watched him walk ahead of her for a second before picking up her stride and catching up. She had seen something in his expression when their hands met—it was as if he could see the magic as well. But it wasn't a look of wonder or astonishment; it was a look of curiosity. Could Zeke see magic?

If he could, then he must have been able to see the glow that surrounded her when they met at the market.

She had thought it had been her own magic signaling to her at first but maybe it wasn't; maybe he held magic of his own. But it was the same color as hers, not blue like the other magic she had seen thus far. None of it was making any sense to her and she realized he had been talking while she was deep in thought.

"You ever been?" was the last thing she caught him saying.

"Sorry, what was that?" she asked, completely embarrassed.

"Oh, I was just wondering if John took you up the mountain trail behind your house. It's one of my favorite places to go this time of year," he told her. He had such an easy way about him that her embarrassment quickly faded.

"No, to be honest, I haven't gotten to do much of anything since I got here."

"I'm sorry, I'm going on about hiking when you've been dealing with the death of your grandmother. Forgive me."

"No, no, there's nothing to forgive. It's sad, but I didn't even know her. I had no idea she was even alive until I got the letter from John." She felt more than a bit weird referring to Betty as her grandmother now that she knew she was her stepsister. Something she was still trying to wrap her head around.

"Oh, I'm sorry to hear that. Family can be a rough thing sometimes. Believe me, I know," he said, giving her a nod as if he understood all too well the ways of a broken family.

She wanted to question him further on what he meant but she was reluctant to get to know him. It could complicate things and at this point, she had no idea how anything would turn out. She desperately wished she had met him under different circumstances, one where her life wasn't hanging in the balance.

Their walk into town continued with Zeke leading the way, engaging in casual conversations along the route. He introduced her to a cozy coffee shop, where they spent a good part of an hour sipping coffee and discussing local lore. The café was adorned with vintage Welsh decor and was a hub for the town's regulars, making it a perfect place to soak in the town's ambiance. As the day went on, Zeke guided her through the town, gradually acquainting her with various shops, local stories, and even a bit of town gossip. By day's end, she felt like she'd absorbed a treasure trove of knowledge about her new surroundings, thanks to Zeke's guidance and their enlightening conversations.

As the day faded, they walked back to a small lot where they parked their cars. The sun was low in the sky, sending the trees' shadows stretching out over the ground like long fingers reaching. Ionna was thinking how peaceful the afternoon had been when a feeling came over her—a feeling in the pit of her stomach, as if a storm was about to roll in, but there were no storm clouds in the sky. *A storm of another kind,* she thought as the chill set into her bones.

"Oh, I forgot to ask you what it was that you wanted to know about the Excalibur legend?" Zeke asked, pulling his keys from his pocket.

"Oh, yeah, I got so wrapped up in our other conversations I forgot to ask. I was just hoping that you might be able to tell me a little more about its origins."

"Well, a lot of people mistake the legend of Excalibur with the tale of the Sword and the Stone. But the real origin of Excalibur is much different." He told her, a boyish smile playing across his face. "It was said that Nyneve, an ancient goddess referred to as Lady of the Lake, came out of the waters to give King Arthur Excalibur. Because she was a goddess she enchanted the sword with special properties like super strength, indestructibility, a radiant light and some say even the power to heal. It was one of the reasons I got into swordsmithing. I was just really captivated by that idea as a kid. *But* I've never quite figured out how to add those kinds of qualities to my own swords," he joked.

Ionna smiled at him, but her mind was racing. Nyneve. Lady of the Lake. She was connected to the legend of Excalibur. Her magic was what created the sword. It was all tied together but what did it all mean in terms of furthering her own quest? Now she was even more eager to get back and fill Kate and Owen in on what she had found out today.

"Zeke, thank you so much for showing me around."

"I had a great time. Maybe I can show you a bit of the countryside one of these days. There is a great little restaurant near Caernarfon that has some beautiful hikes around it."

There was a flutter in her stomach. Was he asking her out on a date? She tried to suppress a smile but it was no use, it spread across her face and her cheeks blossomed rose red.

"Yeah, that sounds gr—"

Her last word fell silent as all the air was pushed from her lungs. She fell to her knees on the rough gravel of the parking lot, teetering on the edge of passing out when a voice broke into her mind. It was as deep and dark as the night itself, graveled and hoarse as if it hadn't spoken in centuries.

"Do you truly believe you possess the strength to vanquish me? Your feeble attempts amuse me, daughter of Nyneve," the dark voice said.

Ionna went rigid with fear, still gasping for breath. It wasn't the first time she had felt Malachi's presence, but it was the first time she'd felt his pull over her. He was inside her thoughts and had power over her body. It was as if he was twisting her insides, wringing them out like a wet rag. Every nerve in her body cried out and she felt as if the pain would consume her.

"Ionna!" Zeke called out. Dropping to her side, he grabbed ahold of her shoulders just as she was about to topple to the ground.

As soon as he touched her, everything went still, and as quickly as the air had left her lungs it came rushing back in bursts as she choked it in.

"Are you okay? What happened?" he asked, his voice filled with concern.

"I don't know," she said, still gasping. "It was like I got the wind kicked out of me," she told him as she pushed her feet out in front of her and sat on the ground.

"Bloody hell, I thought you were about to have a seizure or something."

"I'm fine now, really." She began to stand, but she was shaking.

Zeke grabbed her hands and helped her to her feet. "I don't think you should drive home. Why don't you let me take you?"

"No, no, it's okay. I don't want you going out of your way. I can drive, I just need a minute," she reassured him, turning toward Betty's car. She had got her bearings back by the time she fished the keys from her pocket but the fear of the moment still held her tight in its grip. She tried to steady her nerves but all she wanted to do was get the hell out of there.

Zeke watched her closely as she unlocked the car. "It's not out of my way—"

"Zeke, I'm fine," she said, looking over at him while he continued to watch her as if she was about to break in two.

"Fine, if you won't let me drive you, then I'm going to follow you back. It's on my way, anyways," he insisted.

"Okay," Ionna said, giving in.

On the drive back to the farm, her unease grew. *How did he do that? Malachi's powers must be getting stronger.* At first, the thought of his presence unnerved her, but now it had evolved into a fear that ran much deeper. Was that what it would be like if he gained access and possessed her? She had felt so weak and helpless, like a doll being tossed around from the inside.

She spent the entire trip back with her fists clenched around the wheel, waiting for something to happen. But when they made it back to Betty's unharmed, she relaxed a bit, relieved to be back on familiar ground.

"Thank you for following me back," she said to Zeke as she got out of the car, the unease of the events still tainting her words.

"Of course. Are you sure you're okay?" he asked.

"Yeah, I'm okay. Do you want to come in for some tea? Or

perhaps some wine after all that?" she asked before she even knew what she was doing. It was as if her magic wasn't about to let him go yet—it had plans and she was just its vessel.

A surprised look came over his face and he hesitated for a brief moment before responding.

"Um, sure," he said, smiling uncertainly as he shut the ignition off on his van.

Ionna gave him a forced smile, not happy that she was being played with like a puppet. She knew that Zeke was an important part of whatever they needed to do but this was just beyond awkward. They had just met. He must think she was some kind of loose American.

As she stood unlocking the front door, he stepped up behind her. She could feel the energy pouring off him as if his magic had risen up to meet hers.

The house was lit with dusty afternoon light, and she flipped on a few lamps as she made her way into the kitchen, Zeke following behind her. Jasper came running to greet them, slinking in S curves around their legs. Just entering the house set her at ease. Her fear began to dissipate.

"Zeke, meet Jasper, Betty's cat," she said as she rooted around the kitchen for wineglasses.

She was a bit embarrassed she didn't know where they were, seeing as she had been drinking straight from the bottle. She found them on the top shelf just slightly out of her grasp. Getting up on her tippy toes, she reached for them but came up an inch too short. Just as she was about to turn around and grab a chair, she felt Zeke lean over her and pull them down. His body was so close to hers that she could feel the heat coming off it. She swallowed hard. God help her, this was the last thing she needed, but it was one hundred percent what she wanted in that moment. It was a long time since she had been with a man, and she was feeling it. Her heart raced in her chest and there was an ache growing deep in her belly.

"Here ya go," he said, handing her the two wineglasses.

She took them from him and set them on the kitchen table as he sat down.

"White or red?" she asked, opening a slim cabinet. She had found it the day of the dinner at the farm, and thank God she had because she was in need of a drink to calm her nerves.

"Whatever you like is fine with me," he told her in a way that made her want him even more. She needed to calm herself down. It was as if his magic was calling out to hers, seducing her in ways she'd never experienced before.

She took a long moment looking at the wines, willing her magic to calm the hell down. It was like dealing with teenage hormones, and they would not listen to reason.

She finally decided on a red cabernet, and uncorked it, sending a popping echo through the house. She noticed him looking at her strangely as she poured the wine, and she wondered whether he could see how wild her magic felt.

"Do you plan to stay in Wales?" he asked, breaking the silence.

"I can't stay," she told him even though she was still undecided.

"Are you going to keep this place? It's a great little house," he said. He took a long sip of wine and pulled his lips in to lick off the trace amounts.

"Yeah, I think so. It doesn't feel right to sell it, ya know," she said, also taking a long, drawn-out sip of wine. The tension in the room was so thick she could have sliced it like bread. *Why in God's name did I ask him to come in?*

"You said Betty's house was on your way home. Do you live close?" she asked.

He lifted his hand up and ran it through his thick golden hair. "Yeah, my workshop is just a few miles down the road," he said raising his arm and pointing in the opposite direction of Dwyer farm. "I have an apartment above—" It was then that she noticed something. There was a leather cord peeking out from the edge of his shirt. A necklace of some kind, with something tucked against his chest.

"What's that you have around your neck?" she asked, cutting him off mid-sentence.

He stopped and looked at her, confused, then pulled the leather cord out of his shirt. There, hanging from it was a small black sack, one that looked just like hers. One of Karena's protection charms.

Chapter Forty-Nine

STRANGE CONNECTION

The air in the room was heavy with secrets as the necklace dangled between Zeke's fingers. Ionna couldn't hide the look of shock that she was sure washed over her face upon seeing it. There was a long, drawn-out silence between them until Ionna pulled an identical-looking necklace out from her own shirt.

Zeke's eyes grew wide with curiosity. "How do you know Karena?" he asked, staring down at the tiny black bag attached to the leather cord around her neck.

"I don't really know her that well; she's kinda helping me with a problem," Ionna answered as vaguely as possible.

He paused for a beat before he spoke again.

"I take it this problem needs … a special kind of help?" he asked, picking up his wineglass again and taking a rather large sip.

"Yeah, I guess you could say that. What about you?" She paused. *What am I doing? We are running out of time.* Malachi's powers were getting stronger by the day—even by the moment. This was her chance to stop the charade and get to the bottom of things, figure out where he fit into the puzzle. Maybe she just had to rip this off like a Band-Aid. She sighed. "I think we both know what these charms are, so what's yours for?"

His chestnut eyes widened, but then his expression softened.

"You're right. No need to play around this. It's for nightmares. I started having them about a month ago. They got so bad that even during the day if I closed my eyes, I would have visions, like waking dreams," he said, finishing off the last of his wine. "This past week they got so bad that I decided to go see Karena. I figured that maybe she would have something that could help. Last resort kinda thing."

Ionna sat there, deep in thought for a moment. His nightmares had started around the same time as Betty's death. She had a hunch it wasn't a coincidence. There had to be a connection there, something that linked all of this together.

Just another mystery to add to the mounting pile in her mind.

"What about you? Why do you have a charm?" he asked, pulling her back into the moment.

She considered her words. "It's a very long story. But the short version is that I also seem to have a darkness following me around," she said, trying to ease into it. She was relieved that he believed in the supernatural enough to seek Karena's help. It gave her hope that he was open-minded about this kind of thing. Maybe confiding in him wouldn't be as hard as she had originally thought. "Has the charm worked for you?" she asked him, pouring him another glass of wine and then topping hers off.

"It seems to be. I haven't had any dreams since I put it on.

But I still have this uneasy feeling," he said.

"I know what you mean. That feeling has been following me around too. Can I ask you a question?"

"Shoot."

"When we were down by the river and you took my hand, what did you see?" she asked him, the wine finally taking hold, giving her the courage to be more forthright.

He tilted his head. "A glow," he said. "Like the luster you get when gold is polished." He looked at her. "You noticed it too. I saw it on your face."

She knew he had seen it; the look on his face had been undeniable. But she wasn't convinced he knew what it was. "Yeah, I saw it too. Is that the first time you've seen that kind of glow?" she asked.

"No," he said with a small, awkward laugh, as though he was embarrassed about what he was going to say next. "I started seeing that kind of thing around the time the nightmares started. To be honest, I thought I was having a stroke and went to the hospital. They did all the tests and scans and stuff, but they couldn't find anything wrong. I thought I was going crazy. Then when the nightmares got worse, I went to Karena," he said, swirling the wine around in his glass.

"You're not crazy," Ionna said. "I think that—we can see another plane of reality. Like, people and objects that hold a special kind of energy, like magic."

She waited for his response. This was the moment he would either up and go or tell her what was really going on. She watched his face, trying to determine how he was taking it in. After a few moments, he broke the silence.

"I think you're right. It seems to only be around objects that already seem kinda mystical, like Karena and her fortune-teller stuff. What I don't understand is why you and I have it?" His eyes were on her, but she could tell it wasn't her he was looking at, it was her glow. "But your light is different—it's white like mine, not blue like the others I've seen."

"I don't fully understand it either. All this is new to me too. I just started seeing the glow a few days ago. But whatever it is, it seems that you and I share something."

She stopped talking and took another sip of wine, trying to summon all the power inside her to tell him the whole truth. But something was stopping her.

"I'm sorry, I didn't mean to take you hostage. I'm sure you have things you need to be doing," she told him, getting to her feet and walking over to put her empty wineglass in the sink.

"You're not taking me hostage. I had a great time today, and the wine was much needed."

He got up and walked his half-empty wineglass over to where she stood. She reached out for it, and as she did, her fingers grazed his, sending tiny flecks of golden energy into the air around them. They hovered between them for a second, like firefly trails, and then dissipated.

He stared down at her, his eyes rimmed in the same shade of gold that had come from their touch, and she felt the magic in her awaken again. It took everything in her to keep from leaning in to kiss him. It was as if her magic was being pulled to his like a moth to a flame. She could feel it racing around inside her, looking for an escape, and, boy, did she want to let it out.

He ran his fingers down her forearm and watched as the sparks rose up and floated away. She had to suppress a shiver. His touch was like nothing she had ever experienced before. It left her tingling from her head to her toes. She wondered if he was experiencing the same thing when he leaned in closer to her, their faces only inches apart, and gazed into her eyes as if he, too, was intoxicated by the magic.

Just as their lips were about to meet, there came a knock at the door, breaking the enchantment and jolting them back to reality.

Damn!

Flustered, she turned from him, placing the wineglass in the sink and then going toward the door, leaving Zeke standing in the kitchen alone to cool down.

"One second!" she called out, partly annoyed and partly thankful to whoever it was for giving her a much-needed distraction.

She peeked out the window to see Owen and Kate standing on the doorstep, whispering to each other. She opened the door to greet them, and the dewy air blew in past her ankles as if an invisible creature had just scooted into the house. The sensation caused the hairs on the back of her neck to rise, and a shiver chased down her spine.

"Hey, we're not interrupting anything, are we?" Owen asked with a raise of his eyebrows and a tilt of his head, gesturing toward Zeke's van in the driveway. Kate elbowed him in the side. "What? I'm just asking. We didn't expect him to be here," he said to Kate with a mischievous grin.

"Oh, course not, come in," she told them, swinging the door wide and exposing Zeke, who had made his way into the tiny entryway. "You guys know Zeke, right?" Ionna asked, trying to be casual.

"Hey, mate," Owen said, giving him a nod as Kate just smiled sheepishly.

"What's up?" Ionna asked, noticing that Kate was holding a book in her hands.

Kate looked at Ionna apprehensively, not knowing if she

should say anything in front of Zeke or not. Ionna gave her a slight nod of her head, indicating that it was okay.

"I wanted to show you something I found in my grandfather's genealogy book," Kate told her, holding the book out.

"Well, I better head out and let you guys catch up," Zeke said, skirting around the kids to the door.

Ionna stepped up as he opened it. "Thanks again, Zeke. Maybe you can show me that trail one of these days," she said before she could stop herself.

"Yeah, weather looks good the day after tomorrow. You free then?" he asked, seeming as eager as she was to get back to where they'd left off.

"Sounds good. Just give me a call, and we can set up a time."

She watched him walk to his car, his glow shining like silvery white moonlight all around him. He waved goodbye to her as he drove off into the dusky evening.

When she turned around and shut the door, Owen and Kate were looking at her with wide, knowing smiles.

"What?"

"Oh, nothing, just nice to see you made a new friend," Kate teased.

Ionna figured she had that coming after poking her about Owen earlier. "Ha ha. Now show me what you found," she said, walking into the sitting room and turning on the two side lamps.

Owen sat in one of the large navy armchairs, and Ionna and Kate sat together on the sofa. Kate rested the large book in her lap and began flipping through the pages, sending the smell of old paper drifting into the air.

"My abilities were passed down to me through my ancestry from Lady of the Lake," she said. "You see, she had three sons, and this one." She pointed to the name "Einion" on a family tree.

"He's my ancestor. Every two hundred years, a descendant from his line was born during a lunar eclipse with powers of the old gods, me being the most recent. It got me thinking about the other sons. Did they also have descendants with special abilities?" she said, flipping the pages of the book again. "My grandfather didn't do much research on their families' lines, but I had the first three names to go on. So Owen and I spent the day online researching where their family lines ended up." Kate pulled a stack of papers from the back of the book, fanning through them until she found the one she wanted. "Lady of the Lake's other two sons—Cadwgan and Gruffudd—their families ended up in different places in Europe. One of those places was Ukraine. Gruffudd's family settled there. You're not going to believe who we traced back to him. Artemas was one of his direct descendants." Kate paused to let this information sink in. "It must be why my magic took me to him when I flipped. It was drawn to its own source in a way."

"It makes sense. The magic in their bloodline pulled them together. Like metal to a magnet," Owen said, leaning forward with his elbows on his knees.

"I can see why Karena said he had magic like none she had seen before. It was powerful because it was the magic of the old gods," Kate said.

"Everything seems to lead back to Nyneve. Zeke told me today that she was the one who gave King Arthur the sword Excalibur," Ionna told them.

"Well, I could have told you that," Owen joked. "Everyone from these parts knows that story."

"Yeah, I actually knew the story as well. It was one my father used to tell me at bedtime. It just took hearing it from someone else before I put two and two together," Ionna said. The thought of calling Adam her dad felt strange to her now, knowing he wasn't her true father.

Ionna looked down at the printout of a family tree dating back hundreds of years, and at the very bottom was the name Neala, her birth name. The puzzle pieces were all beginning to fit together, but she still felt lost.

"Remember in Karena's story about Lady of the Lake, how her mother cast a spell on the realms so that the only way for Malachi to escape was through Nyneve's bloodline? Once you went through the veil, you literally became his key," Owen said.

"Well, that's a terrifying thought."

"It is, but knowing helps us. The more knowledge we have, the better we can prepare," Kate said sagely.

"You're right, Kate. You both did a great job digging this up. I couldn't have done it better myself. Now, we need to figure out how to stop Malachi," Ionna said.

Kate smiled and closed the book, tucking the papers back inside.

"Well, I think we better figure it out sooner rather than later. Something happened to me today when I was out with Zeke." She paused for a moment. The palms of her hands were slick with sweat. "It was right after Zeke told me that Excalibur was given to Arthur by Nyneve. All of a sudden I felt Malachi all around me. It was as if he squeezed the air right out of my lungs, and then I heard his voice in my mind. He told me to give up, that there was no defeating him," she told them, a sick feeling coming over her at the memory. "I couldn't move. I couldn't speak. I couldn't do anything. He was in my mind and had control of my body—"

"Oh my God, Ionna, are you alright?" Kate asked.

"I'm okay." Ionna nodded, but she knew she was trying to convince herself as much as the others. "I'm just... concerned that he was able to do that. Even with the protection charm on.

You know? He's getting stronger."

"Sounds like you struck a chord that caused him to lash out. That means we're getting closer to answers," Owen said.

"I think you're right," Ionna said. A shiver went up her spine, and she glanced over her shoulder, into the shadows.

"Did you try calling the Fern library place again?" Kate asked.

"No, not yet. Zeke and I were gone most of the day. We only just got back a bit before you got here."

"Maybe you should try again. Most people are home for dinner around now," Owen suggested.

Ionna walked out of the room and into the kitchen where she grabbed her cell phone off the table. She turned it on and searched for the saved the number, then walked over to the phone and dialed. As the phone rang, she felt as if the temperature in the room had dropped ten degrees. Thick, sickly dread crept over her. It was the same feeling she'd had when she was under Malachi's grip, and in that moment, she knew he was there lurking, watching.

"Hello?" A woman's voice answered on the third ring. The voice sounded younger than Ionna had expected, and she was American, which threw her off a bit.

"Oh, hi, is this the owner of Fernbeg Cottage?" she asked, her stomach turning in knots.

"Yes, but I'm not looking for a roof replacement or a lawn service or even an extended warranty for my car. Thank you, but no thank you," the woman said abruptly as if she was about to hang up.

"No, no, I'm not a salesperson. I think you might have known my father, Artemas," Ionna blurted, trying to get the words out before the woman hung up.

There was a long silence.

"You sound too young to be Artemas's daughter," the woman finally said.

"And you sound too young to have known him," Ionna answered.

Another long silence followed, and the only indication that anyone was still present was the barking of a dog in the background.

"What did you say your name was?"

"I didn't. It's Ionna Bellmore."

"My name's Helen. Yes, I knew your father a long time ago. He was a dear friend of mine," she said with a sadness in her voice that was palpable.

"I believe you may have helped him when I was younger," Ionna told her, then waited before going on. "He came to Fernbeg to find a cure for me when I was a baby. I'm hoping that you might be able to help me with something similar."

"What is it that you're looking for?" Helen asked.

"I need a spell. When I was a child, I almost died. My father brought me back through the veil, and when he did … a demon came with me. We're tethered to one another. He was able to put a spell on the demon to contain it for many years, but it's gotten free. I need a spell to break the tether between us and send it back."

There was a long pause. It sounded as if Helen was walking around.

"I think I might have what you need, but it's going to take me some time to find it. Give me a day and I'll get back to you. What's your email?" Helen asked.

Ionna told her and thanked her for her help. Just as she was getting ready to hang up, she heard Helen say, "You're more than welcome. This is the least I can do to repay your father for the gift he gave me."

Ionna placed the old corded phone back in its cradle, then headed back into the living room where Kate and Owen had been eavesdropping.

"So, what did she say?" Kate asked.

"She's going to try and find what we need and email it to me in a day or two," Ionna told them. She should have felt relieved, but she didn't. She couldn't help but think Malachi was listening to their every move, and if he was, he was already one step ahead of them.

"What's wrong?" Owen asked, seeing the look on her face.

"Nothing, I'm just a bit tired out from the day," she told them. *Not a complete lie, but close enough.* "You guys did a great job finding the link between Kate and me. Did you ever figure out where the descendants of Cadwgan went?" Ionna asked.

"We didn't get that far. Once we found Artemas in Gruffudd's bloodline, we came right over," Owen said.

"We can look into it though. We bought a subscription to one of those genealogy sites today," Kate told her.

Owen glanced at his phone. "Kate, we better go. I promised your nana I would have you back for supper tonight,"

"Yeah, okay," Kate said and turned toward the door. "We'll come by tomorrow if we figure anything else out. If you get that email, let us know," she told Ionna as she and Owen stepped out into the cool evening air.

"Sounds good. Be careful, you two," Ionna said, a deep-seated worry filling her every cell as she watched them walk out into the darkening night.

Chapter Fifty

THE FIRST

Kate and Owen drove up the long driveway and back onto the dirt road toward Kate's house just as the sun fell beyond the horizon. The sky burned with orange hues as night began to descend.

"I'm a little worried about Ionna. Did she seem off tonight?" Owen asked, following the beam of his headlights down the drive.

"Yeah, but after everything that happened with Malachi today, I don't blame her for acting a little weird," Kate said.

"Yeah, that's some scary shit."

"How well do you think these charms really work?" Kate asked, pulling hers out from inside her shirt and looking at it.

"Well, he was able to talk to her, but he didn't *hurt* her," Owen replied, trying to sound reassuring.

"He managed to stop her from breathing though. I'd say that's pretty serious. We have to figure out how to stop him before he gets any stronger. I don't wanna end up like those sheep, driven to their own deaths," Kate said, her mind racing with all the things that could go wrong. Then, more quietly, she said, "I don't want anything to happen to my nana."

"I know," Owen said gently. "We're going to figure this out, just not tonight. Nothing's going to happen to your nana. I promise. And you're not going to end up like those sheep. You'll be off at uni before you know it."

"Ha, well, deciding what uni I want to go to doesn't seem like such a big deal now. Here I thought I was going to spend a relaxing summer in the country trying to sort myself out," Kate half-joked.

"Yeah, I know what you mean. Puts things in perspective," Owen said.

Too soon, Kate found him pulling into the tiny parking spot outside her grandmother's house.

"Hey, good job today with connecting the dots. I couldn't have done it without you," Kate said.

"I would have never even thought to look if it wasn't for your suggestion," he said as he put the car into park and turned to look at her.

He had gotten a sunburn across his cheeks and the bridge of his nose, bringing out the light freckles that were almost invisible otherwise. Kate smiled looking at them.

"What?" he asked, wondering what was amusing her so much.

"I haven't seen those freckles since you were twelve," she said with a wide smile.

"Oh, these things?" he said, running a finger over the bridge of his nose and then down over his cheek. "They only come out around pretty redheads."

Kate blushed, making her own freckles stand out. She glanced down in embarrassment. That's when she felt his hand softly tilt her chin up so that she was looking into his eyes once again.

"I like that we have matching freckles," he said as he leaned forward and kissed her.

His lips tasted like licorice, and a tiny bit of stubble he had grown throughout the day tickled her upper lip. His kiss was soft and gentle, and she wanted to melt into it, but something held her back. Reluctantly, she pulled away, wondering if he thought she was a bad kisser. She'd only kissed a few guys before, and it wasn't like this. Her insecurities had broken free and spoiled the moment. But as their lips parted, Owen seemed oblivious to her apprehension, flashing a broad grin.

"I've been waiting to do that since we were twelve," he said.

"Shut up," she said, pushing him backward in his seat.

"No, I'm serious. You've always been the one that got away. Even if you got away in pigtails," he joked.

Kate was speechless. In no way had she ever thought he liked her like that. He was way out of her league.

"But you've always been too cool for me," she said, her cheeks fading to a light pink hue.

"Are you kidding me? You have superpowers. Doesn't get much cooler than that." He laughed softly in the darkness of the car. "Plus you're probably one of the nicest people I know and a hell of a speed reader." He leaned in again, this time to brush a strand of hair from her face.

She hadn't thought of it like that before. She did have something that made her special, something that made her unlike the other girls he had been with before. She had the magic of the old gods running through her veins. *But is that the only reason he likes me?* she wondered, doubt threatening to spoil the moment once more.

She dared herself to look at him. At his easy smile. The look of anticipation on his face, waiting for her to say something, waiting for her to do something.

Inching forward, she kissed him, fully embracing the moment. She ran her fingers through his hair as the kiss deepened. Pulling him close, as if she couldn't get enough of him. His kisses in turn became more hungry. They kissed with the passion only teenagers possess, becoming lost in each other.

Neither of them noticed the world outside the car had changed. The seasons spun, from summer to autumn, then winter to spring.

Her grandmother's house, which had sat snuggly in the field, faded away and was replaced with a thick forest of giant trees.

They flipped through the centuries, flickering past them like the pages of a book, and when their lips finally parted, they had returned to her grandmother's driveway, both oblivious to the fact that Kate had spun them through time.

Chapter Fifty-One

THE SONG OF COPPER

Ionna woke the next morning to the sound of thunder rumbling off in the distance. She climbed out of bed and went to the window, looking out toward the field between Betty's house and the Dwyer farm. The rain was coming down so hard that she could barely see the edge of the driveway. The sky was covered in a blanket of dark clouds, and the fierce wind blew small branches and other debris into the yard. There was a staleness to the air, and it was humid in the house, so Ionna pulled off the sweatshirt she had worn to bed, tossing it into a small pile of dirty clothes that had been growing on the bedroom floor. She wondered if there was a washer and dryer tucked away somewhere she hadn't noticed yet.

A large crack of thunder rang out. Jasper came running into

the bedroom from the hallway and jumped onto the bed, clearly deciding it was the coziest place in the house on a day like this. Ionna had half a mind to climb into bed next to him and doze off for a few more hours as she hadn't gotten much sleep these past few nights.

The night before she had stayed up till the wee hours looking through Artemas's journal again, searching for anything she might have missed. She had discovered a spell that offered the possibility of protecting them from Malachi's prying eyes, and she knew she had to try it. Even now, she sensed his shadowy presence close by, concealed in the space between, just waiting to strike.

If Karena's dream about Nyneve was true, Malachi would be hell-bent on destroying all of the bloodlines, putting not just her life in jeopardy but also Kate's. Not to mention his threat to wreak havoc on humanity as a whole. Even without his full strength, Beddgelert had already received a taste of what Malachi was capable of.

She pulled her protection charm out of her shirt and looked it over, making sure everything was still closed up and knotted properly. She had a hard time believing this tiny charm was the only thing keeping Malachi from possessing her, but she wasn't taking any chances. She tucked it back into her shirt, then grabbed Artemas's journal off the nightstand and went into the kitchen.

As she made herself a coffee, she flipped back to the page she had marked with an old wine bottle label. The cloaking spell was written in deep onyx ink and looked to be one of the simpler spells in the book. She had come across some requiring upward of twenty ingredients, most of which she'd never even heard of—agrimony, datura, henbane, and galangal, just to name a few. Then there were others with incantations written in Ukrainian, which she was unable to read.

She poured herself a cup of coffee and brought the book into the study. She'd felt more drawn to the room over the past two days, so she decided to give in to what her magic was trying to tell her and follow her intuition. She found herself sitting at the old hand-carved desk once again. As she began to read the spell, she became aware of a low hum coming from something in the room. It sounded like an electric heater, but there was nothing of the sort in there; in fact, the temperature in the room was typically ten degrees cooler than the rest of the house.

She stood and walked toward the window, but the hum grew faint, so she turned and walked back past the desk and over to the wall with all the bookshelves. The hum quickly evolved into a ringing sound. It grew so loud that she stuck her fingers in her ears, fearing it would damage her hearing. She couldn't figure out where it was coming from. Instinctively, she closed her eyes and removed her fingers from her ears. As she did, the sound changed, dying back down to a light, lulling hum.

When she opened her eyes, she saw it. Sitting there on the top shelf of the bookcase was a small copper bowl that held a line of books upright, like a bookend. And it glowed; it glowed with the brightest blue light she had ever seen. She knew just what it was; she had seen it in her vision of Artemas's death. It was his cauldron.

She dragged the old captain's chair over and stood on it, reaching up and removing the bowl from its resting place. The books toppled over like dominoes, releasing a plume of dust into the air that rained down on her, causing her to sneeze.

Ionna climbed down off the chair with the copper bowl in her hands. It hummed with the magic of a thousand spells mixed within it, each one leaving a residue of its power. Setting it down on the desk next to the book, she ran her fingers around its rim and felt the magic break from its binds and enter the tips of her fingers. She picked it up, flipping it over to expose the bottom of its base. There, carved into the copper, were the initials ACR. She traced them with her finger. Her father's initials. She stood there staring down at them, wondering if Artemas had planned to pass the bowl down to her when she was older.

The thoughts of everything she'd missed, the fact she'd never even had a chance to know her real parents sent a soul-deep sadness through her. An ache of longing she knew she would never be able to satisfy. A tear broke free and slid down her cheek, softly landing on the journal. It soaked into the old, weathered paper, and then something happened: the darkened spot where her tear had landed started to shift and turn, and right before her eyes, it formed into the shape of a heart. She spun around quickly, feeling another presence in the room.

"Betty, is that you?" she asked the air.

She remained there, still, for a long time, attempting to communicate with Betty in some way. But the room felt empty, and she couldn't sense the presence she had only moments before. She looked down at the book, to where the heart had been—now nothing but a darkened circle on the page.

She knew that Betty's spirit was still lingering in the house. There had been so many strange occurrences, and she could swear she'd caught sight of her out of the corner of her eye on more than one occasion. She didn't understand why Betty was staying hidden from her. She hoped that with her magic and the right kind of training, they would be able to communicate with each other.

A crack of thunder came suddenly and Ionna screamed. Thinking about ghosts and spirits was obviously getting to her. She opened the desk drawer and pulled out a pen and paper, then transcribed the list of things she would need for the spell.

The first two items were a white candle and sea salt, which were the easiest to find. Then came amaranth, chamomile, mugwort, and mullein, which she was hoping would be out in Betty's herb stash in the barn.

After finishing the list, she folded the paper up and stuck it in her pocket, then walked to the kitchen. She only made it a few steps past the phone when it rang. She hesitated for a second, wanting to continue her hunt for the things she needed, but decided she'd better pick up in case it was Kate or Owen.

"Hello?"

"Ionna?" a broken-up voice asked from the other end.

"Yes, who is this?" she asked, straining to hear past all the static on the line.

"It's Helen. I think I found what you…" Her voice was cut with static so badly that Ionna couldn't make out anything she said after that.

"Helen, I'm having trouble hearing you. Can you say that again?" she asked.

"You're going to need to…" Helen said, then nothing. The buzz of static grew so loud that Ionna had to pull the phone away from her ear.

"The storm must be messing with the lines. Let me call you back when it calms down here," Ionna said, unsure if Helen could even hear her. She waited a moment for a response and when none came, she hung up and went back toward the kitchen when the phone rang again.

"Hey, can you hear me?" Ionna asked loudly into the phone as she answered the call.

"Yeah, loud and clear, no need to yell," Owen's voice said on the other end as clear as day.

Ionna paused, surprised that it was Owen and not Helen. "Owen, what's up?" she asked.

"Just wanted to let you know we'll be over soon. Help you do some more digging around. You gonna be home?" he asked.

"Yes, come on over. I'll be here all day."

"Okay, we'll see you in a bit then."

"Sounds good, bye," Ionna said, hanging up.

There must be an issue with the line on Helen's end in Scotland. Maybe bad wires or something, she thought. She hurried back into the kitchen and grabbed her cell off the table where she had saved Helen's number, then returned to the phone and called her back. However, as soon as it began to ring, the static started again. It got so bad so quickly that it drowned out the ringing.

Then, in the midst of the scrambled static, she heard something else.

A voice.

Malachi's voice.

"Oh, poor little Ionna. You have no idea what you are doing. You think you have the power to stop me, but in reality, you are nothing more than a glove to be worn. Your efforts to send me back are laughable."

His thunderous inhuman voice shook her to her very core. Fear held her captive as she stood there, holding the old powder-blue phone to her ear. She opened her mouth to speak, but before she was able to say a word, his voice stopped her.

"You have no idea the chaos I am capable of. I could wipe out this entire town with the flick of my wrist if I wanted to, but instead, I think I will take my anger out on something a little closer to home. How's Kate doing today? And Owen? How about I make them suffer long, painful deaths, just like Betty?"

The words cut through her like a cold blade, but the fear

woke up her magic fully.

"If you think you're going to scare me into being complacent, then you don't know who you're dealing with," she said, the words flowing from her like a river.

Another strike of lightning flashed so brightly it lit up the entire yard, blinding her temporarily. There was a huge *thwack*, the sound of splitting wood, and beneath her the ground trembled. When her vision came back, she saw one of the oak trees that stood guard at the entrance to the driveway had been struck. Half of it lay across the driveway in broken, smoldering pieces.

She slammed the phone down on its base, grabbed her jacket off the hook by the door and walked out into the storm.

"You don't scare me, asshole," she yelled into the wind, then headed into the barn as the storm raged on around her.

Chapter Fifty-Two

WATER'S END

The next morning, Kate awoke with the sweet memory of Owen's kisses still lingering in her mind. Despite longing for a repeat of their tender moment, she was unsure about taking things any further with him. They came from two different worlds, and she would be headed back to hers at the end of the summer. The situation was already complicated enough and adding these newfound feelings into the mix seemed like an unwise move. The uncertainty of their survival also hung over everything they did, souring the thought, as Malachi's powers seemed to grow stronger by the hour.

She climbed out of bed and went down to the kitchen, greeting her grandmother with a mindless "Good morning" as she sat down and poured herself a cup of tea. The far-off look in her eyes didn't escape her grandmother's notice.

"Well, well, someone's head's in the clouds this morning. Wouldn't have to do with a nice farm boy we both know, would it?" she teased Kate as she buttered two slices of toast and set them on a plate for her.

Kate managed a smile, then continued mulling over whether or not she should let things move forward with Owen. She wished it was as simple as her grandmother thought but her and Owen's story wasn't a typical teenage romance. *We have demons to slay,* she thought as she picked away at her toast. *Actual demons.*

"Okay, now I know you must be in love. You haven't even asked for bacon or flapjacks."

That caught Kate's attention. No way was she in love with Owen—it was just a little crush.

"Nana, I'm not in love with Owen," she retorted, stuffing toast in her mouth.

"Could have fooled me. I remember that very look in your mother's eyes when she met your father. Head over heels." She patted Kate on the shoulder and walked over to put more water in the kettle.

She couldn't help but feel that "her parents" and "love" were two words that didn't go together. Her parents *had* to have been in love at some point, yet the bitter outcome of their relationship served as a harsh reminder of how love could go wrong. *No, there is no way I'm falling in love with him;* but it did seem like more than a crush. She'd had crushes on boys before, but she hadn't really gotten to know them as she had Owen. Those boys had brought out the dancing butterflies in her stomach, but Owen made her heart race as if it might leap out of her chest just to be closer to him. The thought she might like him more than she cared to admit scared her.

When it came to relationships, she lacked good role models in her life. Her parents couldn't manage to stay in stable relationships even after their divorce. And even her grandparents' seemingly perfect marriage turned out to have its secrets.

"You sure you don't want me to whip you up some eggs?" her grandmother asked.

"No, I think I'm going to go take a bath before Owen picks me up. We're going to head over to see Ionna this afternoon," she told her, standing up and putting her mug in the sink.

"Okay, just make sure you're back by six. Your mother is calling tonight to talk to you, and she won't be happy if you're not around."

"Yeah, of course," she said, swallowing down the bitterness she carried around for her mother. Most likely she was calling out of obligation rather than love. Kate had no delusions when it came to her mother; she knew she had been counting down the days until Kate was out on her own. Which was fine with her—eighteen years with that woman was long enough.

She walked down the hallway and entered the bathroom, flipping on an old sconce light to the right of the mirror above the porcelain sink. Another storm had moved in, making it abnormally dark outside and leaving the bathroom dim even with the light on. Only the area around the sink was illuminated by the sconce's warm golden glow, leaving the remainder in shadows.

She went over to the old cast iron tub and turned on the water, adjusting the shiny brass knobs until the temperature was just right. Once the stopper was secured, she stripped down and got in. She sat there as the water rose up around her, bobbing her toes in and out of its surface. Despite her efforts to push them away, thoughts of Owen and their kisses kept creeping back into her mind. She surrendered to the memories, lying back and closing her eyes, remembering how his kisses felt. She smiled, thinking about the tiny bit of stubble that had tickled her lip. She let herself sink deeper into the tub, the water now covering her chest and rising up over her collarbone.

When she opened her eyes, she saw that the water had risen almost to the edge of the tub. She sat up and quickly turned off the faucet.

As she settled back against the tub, her gaze fell to something dark floating near her feet. It was small and black, roughly the size of her thumb. She couldn't recall it being there just a moment ago when she shut off the water.

She sat up, her eyes fixed on the object, when suddenly she was forced under the water. Panic surged through her as she struggled to break free of the surface, her limbs kicking and thrashing against the unseen force that held her down. With every passing second, her lungs screamed for air, and she clutched the sides of the tub with all her strength, desperately attempting to lift herself those mere two inches to reach the surface. The water seemed to resist her as fear held her firmly in its grip.

The harder she fought, the stronger the force seemed to get, pushing her head down until it almost touched the bottom of the tub. Her lungs burned. Her mind begged for her to take a breath. Without oxygen, her body weakened. She could feel her mind slipping, going foggy at the edges. She knew her only chance was to flip herself out of the situation. She reached for the charm around her neck—her hands closed around nothing but water.

It wasn't there.

Her vision was darkening now; her throat was on fire.

It was then that she realized what she had seen floating in the water. Her protection charm.

She closed her eyes and pulled on every ounce of energy she

still had. She felt the shift happen, like a ripple through the water.

She opened her eyes; she was lying on the floor—cold, wet, and completely naked, taking in giant gulps of air and choking out the water that had snuck into her lungs. She looked around, terrified of where she might have sent herself.

It was the shoes lying next to her on the floor that she recognized first: an old, worn pair of Adidas trainers with a blue drip of paint on the toe. When she looked up, Owen was standing there staring down at her, his eyes wide with surprise and confusion.

Kate immediately covered herself with her arms and crossed her legs, folding herself into the fetal position on the floor.

"Oh my God, Kate! What the hell just happened?" he asked, concern filling each word.

She was sopping wet and still gasping for air as his words broke through the fear permeating every cell in her body.

"Can you get me some clothes?" she choked out, not looking him in the eyes, the fear quickly fading to humiliation. Her cheeks might as well have been the color of Christmas with embarrassment. She wished he hadn't been in his room so she could have stolen some clothes and just snuck out.

"Well, this is definitely not how I pictured the first time I'd see you naked," he joked as he threw her an old T-shirt and sweatpants, then turned around to give her some privacy as she put them on.

"Ha ha. Very funny."

"Seriously, how did this happen?" he asked, peeking over his shoulder to see if she was dressed.

"You can turn around now," she told him, getting to her feet and going over to his bed. She was still out of breath, and her muscles ached from the struggle. She sat down. "I was taking a bath when I noticed something floating in the water. It was my protection charm, but before I realized it, something pushed me under the water and held me there. Just before I passed out, I flipped," she told him, the fear coming back into her eyes as she looked up at him. "I thought I was going to die."

"Holy shit, Kate. Are you okay?" He sat next to her on the bed and wiped a tear from her cheek. He brushed her hair away from her face and over her shoulders, looking at her with concern.

"What is it?" she asked.

"Go look in the mirror," he told her.

She got up, walked over to his dresser mirror, and looked at her reflection. There, as if Malachi's grip was still around her throat, were the marks. Bruises that were becoming more prominent by the second, forming two perfect handprints wrapping themselves around her neck.

"We need to get you home right away and get that charm back on you," Owen said, pulling his own out from his shirt and inspecting it. "This thing is going to do everything in its power to get to Ionna and you are directly in its path." He came over and stood behind her, putting his hands on her shoulders and gently turning her from her reflection. "I can't let anything happen to you," he told her, leaning in and kissing her softly on the lips. She kissed him back, soaking in every feeling until their lips parted.

"Now, let's get you back to your nana's," he said, walking over to his bedroom door and opening it.

She followed him out and down the hallway. They had almost made it to the front door when Ben caught sight of them. He raised his eyebrows as Owen said, "Morning, Dad," and pulled Kate out the door dressed in his clothes.

"Oh my God, Owen, your dad is going to totally think I slept here last night," she said as they ran to the car in the pouring rain.

"Yup, probably. I'm sure I'll be in for a safe sex talk when I get home."

"Oh God, cringe," she said, mortified.

Owen pulled out of the driveway and started down the road to her grandmother's house. Thunder rumbled overhead in warning. By the time they pulled up outside the cottage and parked the car, the rain was coming down in sheets, and the sky was so dark it looked like evening.

"Okay, I'll go knock on the door and say I'm here to pick you up. You sneak in while I have her occupied, okay?" Owen told her, pulling his sweatshirt hood up.

"Okay. I'll go around the back and in through the bathroom window," she told him as she got out of the car, shutting the door as quietly as possible and skirting her way around the edge of the house in the downpour.

When she got to the window, she hesitated, looking in for a brief moment as if she might see the demon in there waiting for her return. But the only thing she saw was the soft glow of the light coming from over the sink. She pried the window open and climbed in, falling to the floor as she entered and bringing the rain in with her. She closed the window quietly and rushed over to the tub that was still full to the brim with water, retrieving the necklace and fastening it around her neck with a double knot. She reached in and pulled the plug and watched the water swirl into a mini vortex as it drained, thinking how that very same water had almost been her demise. The remnants of the struggle still lay in puddles on the bathroom floor.

There was a knock at the door, startling her and making her jump.

"Kate, dear, Owen is here," her grandmother called to her.

"Okay, Nana. Tell him I'll be right out," she said, stripping off his clothes and pulling her own back on. She looked in the mirror and grabbed some concealer from her bag. As she looked at the ghostly imprints that Malachi had left on her neck, her stomach turned. *He almost killed me*, she thought as she traced her fingers over the lingering marks. She dabbed concealer over the bruises until they were at least muted, then swept her hair over them.

Gathering Owen's clothes into a ball, she tucked them under her arm and opened the door. Looking back at the tub, a sudden knot formed in her stomach. She could still sense an unsettling presence in the air, like an invisible weight pressing down on her. She took a deep breath and willed the feeling of dread to go away, then slammed the door shut behind her.

Chapter Fifty-Three

THE RAGING STORM

When they got to Betty's house, they were greeted by a distressing sight—one of the guardian oak trees was split down the middle, its broken half lying across the driveway, blocking the entrance. Owen had no option but to park the car at the top near the road. Kate tucked her bag under her sweatshirt, and together, they braved the downpour and ran down to the house.

The windows were lit with a warm, inviting light, but the window to the right of the front door glowed white with something else. Owen rapped on the door with a quiet knock. Kate stood next to him, staring at the glow as an unexplainable sensation tingled through her, as if the very air crackled with an abundance of magic seeping out through the window. As they waited, Kate saw

Ionna peek her head out from behind the curtain, her face softly lit with the glow. Ionna vanished behind the curtains and opened the door a moment later.

"Hey, I wasn't expecting you so soon," Ionna said, swinging the door wide.

Stepping inside, Kate pulled her bag out from under her shirt and set it down on the side table. They hung their wet things on a small pegboard by the door before answering her.

"Kate almost drowned this morning," Owen blurted out.

Kate shot him a look like he could have broken the news a little better.

"What? How?" Ionna asked, a look of fear washing over her face.

"You might want to sit down for this," Owen told her.

Ionna walked them into the living room and sat on the sofa, while Kate and Owen took the two armchairs. Kate told her what had happened and that it was because her protection charm had come off.

"Oh my God, Kate. Are you okay?"

"I'm okay, just a little sore," she said, pulling her hair around to the front, trying to cover the marks that Malachi had left. Ionna was noticeably upset, and she didn't want to make it any worse by showing off the bruises.

"I was worried something like this was going to happen. Malachi warned me of it today," Ionna told them.

"Wait, what? He spoke to you?" Kate asked.

"Yes. Helen called to give me the spell but Malachi messed with the phone lines and he spoke to me instead. I think Helen must have found something because he made sure I couldn't talk to her."

"What did he say?" Kate asked.

"Oh ya know, the evil villain opening speech. I'm going to hurt you and everyone you love," Ionna joked, trying to lighten the dark situation.

"Okay, his powers are definitely getting stronger. That's scary as hell," Owen said.

"You need to get a hold of Helen," Kate said, nervously picking at her fingernail.

"Maybe she emailed you," Owen suggested. "We could head over to my place and check. Can't go to the rock for service in this kind of weather."

At that moment a large crack of thunder rumbled, then a flash and a flicker, and the lights went out.

"Well, I guess that's not going to happen now. It's always hours before they get the lights back on during storms like this," Owen said.

"Seems like Malachi is doing his best to keep us from finding out what Helen has," Kate suggested as another loud crack of thunder shook the house.

They all got up and grabbed the oil lamps from each of the side tables, lighting them one at a time. It was then that Kate noticed a funny smell coming from the hallway. She looked out the door and toward the study. The white glow was straining through the cracks in the door as if it were desperately trying to get out.

"What's that smell?" Kate asked, her eyes still transfixed on the glow.

"I was just about to try and cast a cloaking spell before you got here," Ionna told them, looking toward the room as well. "I figured we needed a place where there were no prying eyes and ears."

"I was just thinking about that on the ride over. If Malachi can be anywhere he wants, then what's stopping him from spying on us and knowing everything we plan to do," Kate asked, turning back toward Ionna.

"My thoughts exactly. I just prepared everything. All I need to do is the spell itself now," Ionna said, her voice giving away her apprehensions.

"It's a good idea. If he can't see or hear what we're doing, we just might have the element of surprise," Owen said, picking up Jasper, who had come in to greet them.

"Don't let us hold you up. Go ahead and do it," Kate said.

Ionna grabbed one of the lanterns and walked toward the study. Owen rose to his feet as she passed him.

"I think I have to do this on my own," she told him with a smile that looked half forced.

Owen nodded, then sat back down and began petting Jasper. Kate looked at Ionna and gave her a soft smile, quietly wishing her luck. She leaned back in her chair and opened up her bag, pulling out her grandfather's book and resting it in her lap as Ionna exited the room.

Even without electricity, the study was aglow with magic. Every inch of the room looked as if it was dusted with glitter, as if the magic was anticipating what she was about to do. Ionna walked over to the desk, which she had cleared off and made into her altar. In the center was the brass bowl, along with the herbs, salt, candle, and book, open to the page that housed the spell. She looked down at the words and read them to herself for what must have been the hundredth time.

What happened to my life? she thought as she set the candle in a small pewter stand she'd found in the bathroom. Only a few short weeks ago she was going to work, coming home to a glass of wine and a cozy book. Her life was simple. Now, she was about to perform a spell and fight off a demon. Things were so much easier when her life was on a normal plane of reality and not this supernatural rollercoaster.

Maybe she had fallen and hit her head that day she left the office in a huff, and this was all just a bad dream she was having in some sort of coma state.

She almost wished that was true, but then there was a part of her—an ever-growing part—that felt more alive than she'd felt before in her life. The magic that ran through her veins was intoxicating. When it came out, she felt in control of herself. Powerful. Maybe she wasn't meant to be Ionna anymore. Maybe it was time to return to being Neala.

With that thought, she gathered the salt and formed a circle around the copper bowl. Then she lit the candle and added the amaranth, chamomile, mugwort, and mullein into its center. As she lifted the candle and lit the herbs, she closed her eyes and let the words flow from her. They came like an ancient song, something she knew deep within her core, and with them came the magic. It filled her every cell, pulsing and pouring out of her.

> "Cloak this dwelling from evil's eye,
> Hide all within, like the darkest sky.
> Let no prying eye or ears break through,
> Seal every crack with magic's glue.
> From now until I wish it be,
> Keep all within safe and free.
> By the power of three,
> So mote it be."

She chanted the incantation three times, working the smoke up and around the room and guiding it to its four corners. She watched as the candle burned down to a small cinder, and as the final tendrils of smoke rose from it, blue beams of magic shot into the corners of the room, then bounced off the walls and came back to its center, creating a perfect pentagram. As quick as it had come, it disappeared into the air, and she felt a lightness fall over the house. *It worked.*

As soon as she felt the magic surge out of her, her body grew weak, and her head began to throb. She stood there for a moment, hoping it would pass. The spell had taken a toll on her, and she needed to regain her composure. She flipped Artemas's journal shut and was about to turn and leave when the hair on the back of her neck rose.

Out of nowhere, a hand touched her shoulder.

She spun around in shock to find nothing there but the air, crackling with sparks of leftover magic.

"Show yourself," she demanded, looking feverishly around the room but seeing nothing. Had she cast the spell wrong and Malachi had broken through it? *No, the energy feels light, not threatening.*

A flicker by the window caught her attention. At first, she thought it was just a flash of lightning from the storm still raging outside. Then she saw it again. This time, the flicker took on the shape of a man. She stepped closer, but it faded out and disappeared.

"Artemas? Is that you?" she asked, looking around the barren room for another sign he was still there.

She wished he would show himself, to help guide her and let her know she was doing everything right. She waited another minute. When nothing happened, she finished cleaning up the remnants of the spell and walked back out to where the kids were.

"How did it go?" Owen asked as soon as she reappeared.

"She did it," Kate said. "I felt a shift, a kind of lightness come over the house."

"Yeah, I think it worked. I could feel it too," Ionna said, looking back over her shoulder at the study.

Chapter Fifty-Four

READ BETWEN THE LINES

Kate sat in one of the overstuffed armchairs, flipping through her grandfather's book, looking for anything else that might help them piece together what they needed to do. She had read through the book more times than she could count at this point, finding nothing more that stood out, but every time she set it down, something called her back to it. The book didn't hold magic like Artemas's journal but there was a kind of supernatural pull to the tales within. As she reread the story of her ancestor who was hanged for being a witch, a thought came to her: maybe there was magic in the book, but it took a special set of eyes to see it.

"Ionna, have a look at this," Kate said, standing up and walking over to where she sat on the sofa. "Do you see anything special in its pages?" she asked, handing the book over.

Ionna took the book and began slowly turning the pages. "Not sure what you mean by special, but I don't see a glow."

"Look harder. I swear there's something there. I can feel it, I just can't see it," Kate said, looking over Ionna's shoulder.

Ionna flipped through the pages again. This time she pulled at her magic to assist her, but there was still nothing there other than handwritten stories.

She was just about to hand the book back to Kate when something caught her eye. A word on one of the pages was glowing. She looked down at the singular word "In" illuminated in a soft blue glow.

"What is it?" Kate asked.

"It's just the word 'In.' It has the blue glow around it," Ionna said, staring down at the aged paper of the book where the word sat.

She began to turn the pages slowly, looking for any other words that might stand out. It wasn't until she hit page twenty that she found another word lit with magic.

"Owen, please go in the kitchen and grab me the notepad and pen on the table," Ionna told him.

Owen grabbed a lantern and left the room, coming back seconds later with the items in his hands. Ionna took them and began to write the random words down. She flipped page after page, transcribing the glowing words until she came to the end of the book. There, on the pad of paper, was a single sentence.

"'In order to defeat evil all bloodlines must be bound together and made whole once more,'" Ionna read aloud from the paper.

"Okay, what does that mean?" Owen asked.

"Not sure," Ionna said, closing the book and looking down at the notepad.

"Would be nice if everything wasn't a freakin' cryptic

message," Owen retorted.

Kate sat there silent for a moment, the gears in her head spinning. "It must be talking about the Lady's three sons. Bringing them back together as one."

"I think you might be right. It makes sense, but we still don't know where the third bloodline went," Ionna said, getting up and walking over to the table where Artemas's journal sat.

"Maybe it wasn't a spell we needed from the Fern library; maybe it's Helen. She could be the third bloodline," Owen suggested.

"You might be onto something, Owen. That could be why my father was so drawn to her. It's that same pull of magic that Kate described," Ionna said, flipping to a page in the journal where Artemas talked about the bond he shared with the woman who owned it.

"Have you tried calling her again?" Kate asked.

"The phone line is still nothing but static," Ionna told her.

"I don't think we have time to sit around and wait for the power to come back on," Owen said. "Malachi might just keep messing with the phone lines and electricity and keep us from reaching her. I think we should just go there."

"Owen, that would take hours to get there and it's storming out. Remember what happened last time we drove in this kind of weather?" Kate said, running her fingers nervously through her hair.

"Kate's right. It's too dangerous to go today."

"Listen, I'm not going to sit around here just waiting for that thing to come after you again. You guys stay here. I'll go and get her," Owen said, walking out of the living room.

Kate and Ionna followed him into the small entryway.

"Seriously, Owen, just stay," Kate said walking up to him.

The concern in his eyes made Kate's heart drop. He stepped up to her and bent down, kissing her in a way that made her heart skip a beat, but also made the worry sink in deeper.

Owen gave her hand a gentle squeeze before letting go and grabbing his damp sweatshirt off the hook.

"I'll be fine. I should be back here with her first thing tomorrow morning," he said as he opened the door and stepped out into the storm.

He'd only gone a couple of feet up the drive when Kate noticed him turn and look out toward the field. She followed his gaze; something was odd. The storm clouds seemed to only be over the small valley where the house sat; on all other sides, the sky was blue to the horizon. Malachi had them trapped, using the storm as a cage.

Ionna stepped up next to Kate in the doorway and they watched Owen make his way up the drive toward his car. He was only feet away from it when a bolt of lightning came down, striking the other half of the old oak, sending its massive trunk down onto Owen's car, crushing it. The force of the strike was so powerful that it sent Owen flying back, landing in the yard just feet away from where the tree had fallen.

"No!" Kate yelled and rushed out the door, running as fast as her legs would take her over to where Owen lay motionless.

She fell to the ground, resting her head on his chest, hoping beyond hope that she would hear the beating of his heart. There was nothing for a moment, and then she heard one light, slow beat. She scooped his head up, resting it in her lap, and waited for him to come to, tears streaming down her face. The air around them smelt singed with electricity and she looked to the sky in anticipation of another strike.

Ionna made it to her side a second later.

"Is he okay?" she asked, winded.

"He's breathing," Kate said, looking down at him as he lay motionless.

The rain poured down, and the sky rumbled with the aftermath of its lightning.

"We need to get him back inside."

Ionna bent down and lifted his shoulder. Kate stood up, lowering his head softly, and grabbed his other shoulder. They dragged him half upright all the way back to the house as the storm raged on around them.

Once inside, they rested him in one of the armchairs. His breathing was shaky, and his eyes flickered back and forth under their lids.

"Is he going to be okay?" Kate asked, her voice cracking as she held back tears.

Just then, his eyelids lifted slightly and then opened.

"Oh my God, are you okay?" Kate asked, the tears breaking free now and sliding down her cheeks as she looked down into his blue eyes that lacked their normal spark.

"I think so," he said, slowly sitting forward. "What happened?"

"A bolt of lightning hit the other half of the oak, and it landed only a few feet from you," Ionna told him.

Owen slowly got to his feet, still weak, and looked out the window to see his car completely totaled under the weight of the tree.

"Shit," he said as he got his balance.

"Are you sure you're okay?" Ionna asked, still worried about his state.

"I'm fine. I think the force of the strike just knocked me out. I didn't get hit," he reassured her.

"I knew he wasn't going to let you get her," Kate said. "He's desperate now that the house has wards up and he can't know what our next move is."

"Kate's right. We need to get that spell and end this before he kills one of us," Owen said.

"Owen, you should go home. This is getting too dangerous."

"I'm not going home, Kate. Why are you trying to push me out?"

"Owen, you aren't safe as long as you're around us," she told him, tears filling her eyes again as she thought about the fact she might lose him.

"Listen, we're in this together. Don't worry, I'm going to be okay. We just need to get this spell and finish this."

"Let me go and try to call Helen again," Ionna suggested, walking over to the phone and dialing the number she had taped to the wall next to it.

At first, the line was clear and she was able to hear the ringing on the other end; then as soon as Helen answered, the line went to static again. Even if Malachi had no idea what they were planning, he was well aware that there were only a few paths to the information they needed, and he had successfully closed them all.

"Nope, still nothing but static," she told them as she walked back into the living room.

"We need to figure out a way around this," Owen said. The color was beginning to return to his cheeks and the brightness back into his eyes.

"If Malachi is tethered to your soul, he must have to stay where you are unless he's feeding off another host. If Owen and I can try and get away from here, maybe we'll have better luck getting hold of Helen," Kate suggested.

"That's not a bad thought, but I don't want you guys going

anywhere in this storm. I mean, look what just happened," Ionna said, taking on a sort of motherly tone.

"The storm is only over this valley. If we can make it to town, I guarantee there'll be power and internet," Owen said.

"Okay, but how do you propose to get out of this area without getting killed?" Ionna asked.

"What about another spell? There must be something that could help us," Kate said, picking up Artemas's journal and handing it over to Ionna.

She took it and flipped it open to the back where the spells were held, reading the title of each one. There were spells for a variety of things, but nothing stood out. Then she went back to the cloaking charm she had just used on the house. The magic inside her began to churn, and she felt it move down to her fingertips, begging to break free.

"Hand me that pen and pad," she said to Kate.

Kate obliged, and Ionna began to write. Her hands glowed, and her eyes turned a pale shade of gray as the words poured from her and onto the page.

> "Cloak this body, flesh and bone,
> Cloak my spirit from the unknown.
> Mask me from this evil eye,
> Shield me from the forces that pry.
> Wrap me in a cloak of power,
> Keep me safe, hour by hour.
> By the power of three,
> So mote it be."

The words flowed through her as if she had always known them. She walked into the study, grabbed the bowl and leftover herbs, then headed into the kitchen. She cleared the table off and ground the herbs with a small mortar and pestle. Once the herbs had been broken down, she added them to the bowl and grabbed the rest of the box of salt. This time she laid a circle of salt on the floor, just large enough for Owen and Kate to stand in.

Owen and Kate had followed her in and were looking on in amazement as she went about creating the spell. It was as if she had done it a thousand times before—her movements were methodical and precise, and she glowed with the white-hot light of the spirit realm. It was astonishing and terrifying at the same time.

"Come here. Make sure you step over the circle of salt and don't disturb it," she instructed them.

Carefully, they entered the circle. It was small and they had to stand face to face, only inches apart. Kate wanted so badly to kiss him. After that scare she realized just how much he meant to her, and she couldn't ignore it or push it away. Maybe her nana was right; maybe she was falling in love with him. She knew this wasn't the time, but she longed to tell him how she truly felt. He grabbed her hands and held them in his, squeezing them tightly, as Ionna began walking around them.

"You both need to be completely still and silent while I do this, understand?" she said. She pulled a white candle out of a drawer.

They nodded and stood there staring into each other's eyes as she began the spell.

Ionna set the candle down and carved a symbol into its soft wax, then muttered something under her breath as she lit it. She moved the lit candle around the bowl three times and then tipped the candle in and lit the herbs on fire. Before the flames got too much, she blew them out, leaving a rich, aromatic smoke billowing from the bowl's center. She took the bowl over to the circle where Owen and Kate stood. Speaking the words of the spell, she walked around them, weaving the smoke like a rope into the shape of a wreath. It hung in the air above them. By the third time around, the smoke began to glow with the white-hot light of Ionna's magic. As she spoke the final words, the light broke free and enveloped Owen and Kate.

"I think it worked. Look at Owen," she said.

Kate looked at the outline of his body. A faint shimmery blue glow hovered just above the surface of his skin. Kate smiled.

"I think you're right. He has a glow around him."

"I don't see anything," Owen said, looking down at his hands.

"Trust me, it's there."

"I have no idea how long this will last," Ionna said, "so don't waste too much time."

Chapter Fifty-Five

OBSIDIAN SKY

It was shortly after twelve o'clock when Owen and Kate left Betty's house and headed toward the Dwyer farm on foot. Ionna watched with clenched teeth, praying that the spell would hold and keep them safe. They passed Owen's wrecked car, and her shoulders tightened in anticipation of something happening. Even once they'd made it to the road, she watched them until they were out of sight.

Now all she could do was wait. She had to remain in the house to keep Malachi close to her and away from them. She rubbed her temples, trying to release the tension headache that was coming on, and walked into the kitchen to make some tea.

After drinking a steaming mug and trying to calm her nerves, she decided to use the time to continue to do some digging around. It was possible there was something in the house that she had overlooked that might aid them in ridding her of this curse.

She headed back into the study with Jasper at her heels. The light in the room was dim due to the darkening sky, so she lit one of the oil lamps that sat on a small pedestal table by the window. She set it on the desk, then walked over to the wall of books. Closing her eyes, she listened for the hum of magic. But the room stayed silent, all but Jasper's soft purring as he curled up on the old Turkish rug.

She hadn't felt quite right since she had performed the cloaking spells. Not only did her head still ache, but she had also begun to feel a bit feverish. A bead of sweat broke free from her hairline and slipped down the side of her face as she scanned the titles of the books. There were two that stood out to her, the first being *A History of the Welsh Highlands* and the second a small book of King Arthur's tales. Taking them from their shelf, she sat down in the old captain's chair. At this point, her head was beginning to feel swimmy, and she rested herself against the chair's back.

She wasn't sure if it was the toll of doing real magic for the first time or if she was coming down with a cold. Whatever it was, it had her feeling completely out of sorts. She decided it might be a better idea to take the books into the living room and lie on the sofa. She stood up, feeling off balance, and gripped the edge of the desk to steady herself. The room was spinning, and her vision was coming in and out of focus. She grabbed the books off the desk and exited the room, Jasper, up from his nap, following behind her.

As she entered the living room, her vision dimmed, and weakness overcame her. Her grip loosened and the books tumbled to the ground. With her next step, her legs gave way, and she collapsed onto the floor.

Kate and Owen had made it back to the farm without any incident and walked into the house looking like a pair of drowned rats, completely soaked to the bone. The truck was gone out of the driveway, which meant that Ben had left for his produce deliveries already, leaving them stranded without a vehicle.

When they entered the house, the electricity was still out, painting the inside in a murky light. Owen walked over and picked up the phone attached to the living room wall and put it to his ear.

"Nothing, not even a dial tone," he told Kate.

Kate went over to the windows that faced the field between the farm and Betty's house and pulled open the curtains, trying to let in what little light there was outside. Her throat tightened as she stared out at the unnatural weather. Her stomach dropped as she noticed that the clouds had grown darker over the small valley in Ionna's direction.

"Let me go and get us some dry clothes. You still into sweatpants?" Owen joked.

She cracked a smile. He went upstairs and came back down a few minutes later with a pile of dry clothes. He handed them to Kate, and she went into the bathroom that sat to the right of the living room.

She stripped off her wet clothes and threw them in a heap on the floor. Pulling on the shirt and then the sweatpants, she cinched them as tight as they would go, then looked at herself in the mirror. The rain had washed the concealer off her neck. The bruises stood out as a dark reminder of the grip this creature still had on them.

As she stared at Malachi's ghostly grip around her throat, she began to burn with anger, and as it built she could feel her body begin to shift, like she was about to flip time.

Panicked, she reached for her charm, finding it still snug against her chest. She breathed a sigh of relief and went back out to the living room.

"You okay?" Owen asked, looking at her worriedly.

"Yeah, fine," she said. They both knew it was a complete lie.

He grabbed her hand and pulled her along with him into the kitchen.

"Well, I guess we better take the time we have and refuel," he told her, letting go of her hand and reaching for a loaf of bread on the counter. He stopped mid-reach and picked up a piece of paper resting on the counter next to the coffee pot.

Headed to Gensin Market to drop off the week's produce, be back at 2

"Looks like we just missed him," Owen said.

"Shit, I didn't think he would be gone so long. What are we going to do now? We have no way to get into town," Kate said, pulling out one of the old kitchen chairs and slumping down into it. She looked up at the clock, which read quarter to one. Time was not on their side.

"Maybe while he's gone the power will come back on," Owen suggested as he pulled down two plates from the cupboard and began making ham sandwiches.

"Maybe. I don't know. I have a bad feeling. I don't want to leave her there too long by herself," Kate told him.

Owen walked over to the table with the two plates in hand and set one down in front of Kate.

"I know. I'm worried about her too, but I'm more worried about you right now. You look pale. Eat something," he said, pushing the plate closer to her.

She picked up the sandwich and took a tiny bite. But she had no appetite; she was already too full of worry.

"Do you really think we should drive all the way to Scotland to get that woman?" she asked, picking at her food.

"I think we need to if we can't get a hold of her. But let's try getting into Ionna's email when we get to town," he told her, taking a large bite of his sandwich.

They sat in shared silence while they ate, both lost in thought. Kate kept looking over her shoulder out of the window toward Betty's house, hoping that the storm had begun to let up. But every time she looked, the clouds seemed darker. At this point, it was as if the sky over Ionna was made of pure obsidian, a reminder of what was to come.

The silence was broken by the sound of tires on the gravel outside. Owen walked to the window and glanced out.

A gray van pulled up next to the barn. Zeke stepped out, his jacket pulled up over his head, and ran to the front door.

He was knocking feverishly by the time Owen let him in.

"Zeke, what's up, mate?" he asked.

Zeke pulled his head out from his jacket and wiped the rain from his face before he spoke.

"Owen, glad you're okay. I just drove by Betty's place and saw your car. I walked down to see if you were there but no one answered the door. The storm is so bad over there I nearly got blown away in the wind trying to make it back to my van," he said.

Kate came out into the entryway. "Wait, you knocked and no one answered?" she asked, her face molded in worry.

"Yeah, I knocked for a while but no one answered, so I came here to make sure Owen was okay."

Kate looked at Owen, her eyes growing wide now with fear.

"Ionna's there, we just left her. She should have answered."

"Maybe she was in the shower or something," Zeke suggested.

"I don't think she would have dared to do that after this morning's events," Kate said to Owen, who now also looked concerned.

"What events?" Zeke asked.

"I'll tell you on the way. We need to go back there and check on her. I don't have a good feeling," Kate said, grabbing one of Owen's old jackets on the hook by the door and throwing it on.

"She's right, we should go check on her," Owen said, taking an old baseball cap off the hook and pulling his hood up over it.

They ran out to Zeke's van and got in, the rain battering down on its roof like gunfire. Zeke pulled out of the farm and headed toward Betty's house, squinting through the windshield even with the wipers on full power. There was an unnatural thickness to the air, making it hard to breathe. Almost as if Malachi was pulling the moisture out of the air itself to create the storm. The sky over Betty's house had become so distorted in the darkness that it looked as if the devil himself was looming over it.

Before the van even came to a stop, Kate's heart sank deep into her chest. Something was very wrong. She could feel the magic in the air around her, dark and menacing. As soon as the van stopped, she jumped out and ran as fast as she could down to the house.

Chapter Fifty-Six

THE TOLL OF MAGIC

Kate burst through the door and into the house. She had only taken two steps into the small entryway when she caught sight of Ionna, sprawled out on the living room floor. She ran in and fell to her knees beside her.

"Ionna!" she cried out, pressing her ear to her chest to listen for a heartbeat.

Her breathing was weak, and her heart was beating so slowly that it was barely detectable. Her body was drenched in sweat, her hair hanging wet with perspiration in clumps around her pale gray face.

"In here!" Kate yelled when she heard Owen and Zeke enter the house. They ran in to find Kate leaning over Ionna's body.

"Let's get her onto the sofa," Zeke said, bending down and

grabbing Ionna's shoulders while Owen lifted her feet. He rested her head gently on a cushion. "She's burning up."

Owen looked at Kate. "What do you think happened to her?"

"I don't know, she was just lying there when I came in," she said, her eyes wide with panic.

"Kate, go get a cold wet cloth," Zeke told her, sitting down next to Ionna and taking her wrist in his hands, looking at his watch. "Her pulse is very weak, we need to get some water in her. With a fever this high, she probably passed out from dehydration."

Kate came back in with a wet washcloth and set it on top of Ionna's forehead. She winced from the cold, the first sign that she was in any way responsive.

"Ionna, can you hear me?" Kate said softly to her.

Ionna's eyes began to flick back and forth under her eyelids and then they slowly eased open. She looked around, dazed. There was a fogginess to the green of her eyes that made her look as if she were blind.

"Are you okay? You scared the hell out of us," Owen said.

"What happened?" Ionna asked. She tried to lift her head but it felt like a lead weight.

"We were hoping you might be able to tell us that," Zeke said, taking her hand in his.

Kate looked at their hands. Zeke's was glowing white with magic in harsh comparison to Ionna's glow, which was barely visible. The only way she knew it was still there was by the tiny sparks of gold that floated in the air between them at Zeke's touch. Kate looked on with amazement, while Owen sat there, seemingly oblivious to the light show taking place right in front of him.

Then Ionna spoke, breaking Kate's bewilderment.

"I'm not sure. I was going to read but then I started to feel sick, so I came in here. I must have passed out," she told them, pulling herself up to a sitting position on the sofa.

"You're sick alright, you feel like you're on fire," Owen said.

"Is there any paracetamol somewhere?" Kate asked.

"If there is, it will be in the bathroom cupboard," Ionna replied.

As Kate walked out of the room, Zeke sent Owen to get some water. When he left the room, Zeke spun himself around and sat next to Ionna.

"Are you sure you're okay? You must have taken a pretty hard hit falling on the floor like that."

"I'll probably feel it tomorrow," she tried to joke but began to feel dizzy again and rested her head against the back of the sofa.

Just then Owen returned with the water, icy cold from the faucet. Ionna drank the whole glass in one long gulp.

"Thank you," she said breathlessly, handing him back the empty glass.

"I couldn't find any," Kate told them as she came back into the room.

"Someone's going to need to drive into town and get some. We can't let her fever get any higher or she'll be headed to the hospital," Zeke told them. "But for now, let's get her into bed."

"Take my phone so you guys can check my email. My screen code is oh-nine-one-nine," Ionna told him as they got her to her feet.

Owen nodded then grabbed Ionna's cell phone off the side table and slid it into his pocket. They each took Ionna's arms and guided her into the room and into bed. Kate sat down next to her and grabbed her hand.

"We didn't get into town. Ben was gone with the truck and the power is still out."

"It's okay, we'll figure it out. I take it you didn't have any trouble on the way back?" Ionna asked, trying to find out if the spell had held without coming out and asking in front of Zeke.

"Yup, no trouble at all," Kate told her with a sly smile, knowing just what she meant.

"Zeke, can you do me a favor and grab the books I dropped on the floor so I have something to read?" She needed to get him out of the room for a minute so that she could talk freely with Kate and Owen.

"Sure, I'll grab you some more water too," he said, slipping out of the room.

"Kate, give me your hand quickly," Ionna insisted.

Kate stuck her right hand out and rested it on her lap. Ionna picked it up, her eyes turning a pale shade of gray as soon as their hands met. With the little strength she had left, she pulled on her magic once more.

"North, south, east, and west.

Let this hand guide the rest.

Earth, wind, fire, sea,

Let it find the missing of the three.

So mote it be."

As she spoke, Ionna ran her pointer finger from the base of Kate's middle finger to her wrist and then from the right side of her palm to the left, creating a cross. As soon as the final stroke of her finger touched the edge of Kate's palm, the lines lit up with a bright blue glow that faded back into her skin.

"What was that?" Kate said, looking on as Ionna's eyes returned to their normal shade of green.

"It came to me when I was passed out. It's a charm meant just for you," she said with a cough. Her face was paler than it had been just moments ago. Ionna turned her head to cough again when Kate noticed something on her neck. She leaned forward and brushed her hair away, revealing four small red patches on her skin.

Kate's heart sank. She had seen patches like this before when Ionna was a baby. Her sickness was coming back. All at once, she remembered the helplessness she'd felt the first time she had seen her so little and weak. It was crushing. And this time there was no Artemas to help.

Just as she was about to say something, Zeke came in with the books and water.

"Here ya go," he said, setting the books down next to Ionna and handing her the glass of water.

She was only able to get a few sips down when the coughing began again, and once it started, she couldn't stop. The fit went on for minutes before she was able to catch her breath.

"I think we better get her to a doctor," Zeke said.

"No, I'm fine. I just need to sleep," Ionna said hoarsely, lying back and closing her eyes.

Soon, she was sleeping. They all quietly left the room and gathered in the kitchen.

"Why don't you guys take my van and go get some medicine for her in town? I'll stay with her," Zeke said, putting the kettle on the stove and lighting it with a match.

Owen glanced at Kate, who looked apprehensive about leaving Ionna. After a moment, she gave him a reluctant nod of the head.

"Okay, be back as quick as we can," Owen said as Zeke threw him his keys.

The rain hadn't let up, still coming down relentlessly as the sky hung dark as night with clouds.

"Owen, I don't think Ionna is just sick. I think she might be dying," Kate said, her eyes filling with tears.

"What do you mean? She's just sick. Probably caught something at the market. There were loads of people there that day," he said, brushing her off as if she was overreacting.

"I'm serious. Did you see the red patches on her neck? She has measles again. It's all the same symptoms as when she was a baby."

Owen was quiet as they got into the van and pulled out onto the road.

"That can't be," he said eventually, his brow furrowed. "Why would it all of a sudden come back?"

"I don't know, but I think we need to call Karena."

"That's not a bad idea. After we get her some medicine let's use the Wi-Fi at the supermarket to call."

The town, as Owen suspected, had not been hit by the storm. It was a bright, sunny day there and if they hadn't just come from Betty's house they would have never known a storm was raging just a couple of miles away. They went into the market and picked up everything they thought she might need, then headed to the checkout. As Kate paid, Owen pulled out Ionna's phone and checked her email to see if Helen had got in contact, but there was nothing other than a few spam emails.

"Nothing," he told Kate.

"Okay, then let's give her a call," she said, walking over with the groceries and standing next to Owen.

Owen dialed the number, waiting to hear static on the other line. Surprisingly, it rang.

"Come on, come on," he urged under his breath, willing Helen to answer the call.

He let it ring ten times, and then waited another five.

Kate raised her brows at him in anticipation.

"Nothing," he said, hanging up. "She must not be home, and there's no voicemail."

Kate took a deep breath and let it out in one long, controlled exhale. It was always one step forward, two steps back, but she needed to stay calm and rational. If this was a Steven King novel, what would his next move be for the characters? Maybe they needed to look at this in a different way. Maybe they weren't meant to find the missing descendant of the Lady's bloodline yet, maybe that was meant to happen later when they needed someone to swoop in and save the day.

But this was real life, she reminded herself, not some fictional novel. They had no time to sit and wait for the right moment.

"I think it's time to call Karena," Kate said, hitting the speaker button on the phone so they could both hear.

The phone only rang once before Karena picked up.

"Kate, Owen, hello," she said, in no way sounding surprised to hear from them.

They shared a smile with one another, still surprised at her abilities.

"Yes, it's us. We have a question for you," Owen said.

"Go ahead."

"Ionna is sick. I think it's the same sickness she almost died of when she was little. Do you know what might be going on?" Kate asked in a hushed voice, glancing around. A couple of shoppers laden with bags gave them funny looks as they passed, and Kate gave them an awkward smile.

"I was afraid this might happen," Karena's voice blared out of the phone. "I told her to be careful, that casting spells requiring large amounts of magic could leave an opening for Malachi to feed from. He has found a way to siphon off her magic when she uses it. The power of the other realm was what brought her back from death's grip when she was a baby. It is the magic that keeps her alive. Any time her powers emerge now, he knows how to feed off of them, removing that same magic that's sustaining her. What kind of spells has she performed?"

"Well, that's the thing, she hasn't done much—she put a cloaking charm on the house, and then Owen and me," Kate told her.

"Why didn't the protection charm work? How can he be feeding off her magic?" Owen asked.

"Those were not small spells. Cloaking charms take a large amount of magic. Enough magic to crack open the door to the soul. That is why the protection charm did not work. As soon as she opened that door, Malachi was able to slip in and grasp hold of her magic. Now he's attached to her soul's magic, his powers will grow." She paused for a moment as if she was deep in thought. "It seems the more she uses magic, the more he can pull from her life force to strengthen his own powers. He has found a way to use her magic against her. You must keep her from using any more magic until you break their bond," she warned them.

"I don't understand. He needs her alive. Why would he risk killing her?" Kate asked, looking over her shoulder again to see if anyone was listening in on their conversation.

"Remember, it's not her physical body he needs to stay in this realm, it's her soul's magic. If she is weak and can't fight against him, he will be able to consume all of it. If he succeeds in that, then he will be able to take physical form. He will no longer need her as a host. And he will have her power. This is what he wants. You must find a way to sever the link before it's too late," she said, with audible concern in her voice.

After a few more funny looks from passing shoppers, they

headed out of the supermarket and toward the van.

"We're working on that but we can't get through to the woman who has what we need," Owen said.

"She will get it to you, be patient. Your job right now is to keep Ionna from doing any more magic, which will be difficult now she has opened that door. It will want to come out even if she doesn't want it to."

"How will we do that?" Kate asked, as she opened the door and got into the passenger seat of the van.

"Make her a strong cup of chamomile tea and add some valerian root to it along with a pinch of sage. It should make her sleep and keep her magic at bay until you have what you need."

"Thank you, Karena," they said at the same time.

"Good luck, you two. I'm always here if you need me," she told them before she hung up.

Kate sat back in her seat and looked out the window in thought. It all made sense now. Ionna had only started getting sick after she used her magic on the cloaking charms.

Then it dawned on her—she had spelled her hand before they left, and fear shot through her. If Karena was right, then she had unknowingly fed Malachi again and would be growing sicker.

"Owen. We need to get back right now."

Chapter Fifty-Seven
UP IN SMOKE

Kate and Owen had almost made it back to Betty's house when they hit a wall of rain, entering back into the demon's domain. The faint glow of the sun was barely visible over the mountains as it moved into the darkness of evening.

As they made their way down to the house, the air grew heavy. Kate couldn't shake the feeling that the dark magic was intensifying with each passing minute.

The inside of the house was dimly lit, the only light coming from the windows in the living room and a small oil lamp Zeke had left on in the kitchen. Kate's heart quickened, and anxiety rose up in her throat as they got to Ionna's room. She knew without even seeing her that she had gotten worse.

Zeke was sitting in one of the kitchen chairs, pulled up next to the bed with a washcloth in his hands. When he saw them come in, he stood and ushered them into a corner.

"Thank God you're back," he said in a low voice. "We need to take her to the hospital. She's got worse. I tried to call an ambulance but the phones are out from the storm."

"Let's just get the medicine in her first and see if it helps bring down the fever," Kate told him, knowing no hospital would be able to do anything for her condition. Plus she didn't even want to think of the havoc Malachi might wreak there. The only thing that would help Ionna now was ridding her of this demon, and fast.

"Okay, but if the medicine doesn't bring her temperature down, we have to take her," Zeke said.

Kate didn't respond; she walked over and sat on the bed next to Ionna, pulling the medicine out of the bag. "Ionna, can you hear me? I need you to sit up and take this."

Ionna slowly opened her eyes. Too weak to even speak, she gave a small nod of the head. Zeke helped her sit up and lifted the glass of water to her lips so she could swallow the medicine Kate gave her. She lay back on the pillow with a blank kind of look in her eyes, and then they began to change. Their once mossy-green tone gradually faded into a ghostly gray, like the eyes of a corpse.

Kate knew what was coming. Ionna's eyes only changed color like that when her magic was about to be let free, so she quickly grabbed both of her hands.

"Ionna, listen to me, do not let your magic out. It's what's making you sick. Hold it back as best you can until I can make you something that will help."

Kate squeezed her hands as tight as she could until Ionna's eyes returned to green again. She closed them and fell back to sleep.

Zeke looked on in disbelief. "Does either of you care to explain what just happened here?" he asked.

Kate took a deep breath, realizing what she had just said. She had been so caught up in the moment trying to keep Ionna's magic from coming out that she'd forgotten Zeke was still in the dark about everything.

"This is going to be hard to explain," she said.

"Well, give it your best shot," he replied, crossing his arms and looking at her the way her father did when he found out she was lying to him.

Kate took a breath. "Okay. This is going to sound crazy but I just need you to listen and trust us. Ionna is … special. She holds a kind of … magic inside her. This isn't just a normal fever. She has a darkness attached to her, and it's feeding off her each time she does anything that calls upon her magic."

"Is that why she has the protection necklace on?" Zeke inquired, exhibiting a level of calmness she hadn't expected.

"How do you know about that?" Kate asked.

Zeke slid his fingers around the back of his neck and pulled an identical protection charm from his own shirt. "Because I have one too. Ionna saw it the other day and she gave me some vague answer about hers," he said as he looked down at Ionna, who was still sound asleep.

"I don't understand. Did she tell you about her magic?" Kate asked.

"She didn't need to tell me, I could see it. She has the glow, just like you."

Kate looked at him, opening her eyes to the magic in the room. Then she saw it; there was a white glow around the edges of his body, just like Ionna's. She'd thought she'd seen it earlier but he was so close to Ionna that she assumed it was her magic surrounding him. But it wasn't. This glow was his own.

"But how?" she asked, not able to take her eyes off him.

"I'm not sure. I couldn't see it until about a month ago, but Karena told me I've had the glow since I was a baby. She said it was because I almost died at birth. I was born with the umbilical cord wrapped around my neck, and they had to revive me."

"Oh, that's awful," Kate said.

"Wait, how do you know Karena?" Owen asked.

"She's my aunt," Zeke said, leaning forward and wiping Ionna's forehead with the wet cloth.

Well, that makes sense as to why he seems so open to all this supernatural stuff. His aunt is a freakin' fortune teller, she thought.

"Karena saw something about a sword in a vision. She told us that it belonged to the person who would be able to help Ionna. It wasn't until Uncle John gave us your card that we realized it was you," Owen said. "Karena must have known. I don't understand why she wouldn't just tell us."

"Okay, now I'm lost. How is it that I'm going to help her?" Zeke asked.

"We don't know yet," Kate said, standing up. "Karena told us how to keep her magic under control for now. I have to go and make her this tea before she wakes up again. Owen, fill Zeke in on everything else." She walked out of the room and down the hall into the kitchen.

As she rooted around in the cupboards, she could hear Owen explaining the whole thing to Zeke. It was a good thing he had been exposed to this stuff since he was a child or he might have thought they were all insane.

She finally found the cupboard where Betty kept her tea. She thought her nana had a big collection, but Betty's beat hers by about double. She searched through the huge selection and eventually came up with a tea that was one hundred percent pure chamomile. However, there was no valerian or sage.

"Crap," she said, shutting the cupboard door. She took the chamomile tea bag and placed it in a mug, hoping it would be strong enough to help without the other herbs Karena told her to use.

Kate was about to light the old gas stove when she almost tripped over Jasper, who must have slinked into the room.

"Jasper, what are you doing there? Crazy cat," she scolded.

Then she remembered something Ionna had told them. She had found Jasper in the barn the day she fell and hurt herself in Betty's herb room. Maybe that was where she could find the sage and valerian. With that, she raced to the door, slipped on her shoes, and ran out into the rain toward the barn.

She pushed open the sliding door just enough to squeeze in. As soon as she entered, she had a flashback of holding baby Ionna in that very barn years ago. She quickly turned around to check her surroundings as the memory flooded her with fear. It was dark in the barn, and everything lay eerily still. The only sounds Kate could hear were the raindrops hitting the tin roof and the beating of her own heart.

It was the sweet sound of barn swallows that dispelled her anxiety and brought her back to the present. She took several slow, deep breaths, trying to calm herself before searching for the room that housed the herbs.

After a few moments, her eyes adjusted to the dimly lit space and she was able to make out a small door off to her left; she approached it apprehensively. She turned the old glass knob and pulled the door open with a loud creak. It was completely pitch black inside, and she ran her fingers along the wall looking for a light switch, then remembered the electricity was still out.

Now I wish I'd kept my phone on me; at least I'd have had a torch. She took a step inside. The floor was gritty, and with each step, it sounded like glass crunching under the soles of her shoes. When her eyes finally adjusted to the dim light, she could make out an oil lamp on the long counter. She ran her hands along the counter's dusty surface, feeling for matches. After finding a tincture jar, dried herbs and what she thought might have been a dead mouse, she finally came across a small matchbox tucked up next to the wall.

She struck the first match, sending the darkness back and briefly lighting the space before it quickly went out. The second match burned out quicker than she could get it over to the wick of the lamp. It wasn't until the fourth try that she successfully got it lit.

The flame flickered, and shadows danced on the walls around her. Bundles of plants hung from the ceiling, dangling just above her head. It was then that she realized she wouldn't know which herbs were which. She was no botanist. The only plant she was certain she could identify was marijuana, and that was because of the patch Stevie had on her backpack.

Squinting down at the counter in the twisting light, she noticed near the back were rows of glass jars with labels on them. Most looked to be oil tinctures but there were some on a shelf above that she couldn't quite see. She stepped closer and stood on her tippy toes, pulling each one down and holding the label to the light.

The first was a large jar full of buckthorn, then a jar with echinacea root. She pulled down Moonwort and Belladonna next. Then she saw it; toward the back was a small glass jar labeled "Valerian Root." She reached up and grabbed it, pulling a plume of dust along with it that caused her to sneeze. After the sneezing fit ended, she tucked the jar into the pocket of Owen's jacket.

Next, she searched for sage but found nothing. It was weird. Sage was such a common herb she figured Betty must have grown it.

As she moved her way down the length of the little room looking for the sage, she wondered why Betty had collected so many herbs. Had she wanted to continue Artemas's herb garden in remembrance of him, or had she figured out the magic that they held?

She heard a creak in the open part of the barn. A shiver ran down her spine, and she drew her arms close to her sides.

Two out of three isn't bad, she thought, deciding to get the hell out of there. The place was creeping her out, and she was ready to be back in the house with everyone else.

She turned to leave when the door to the room slammed shut. Startled, her arm knocked over the oil lamp and caused it to shatter on the floor. The oil spread across the old porous wood and the fire along with it.

"Shit, shit, shit," she muttered, trying to stamp it out. But the more she did, the more fuel she gave the fire.

She ran to the door and yanked the handle with both hands, but it was jammed.

"Come on!" she yelled, gritting her teeth as she pulled with all her might. She tried to twist the doorknob one way and then the other, but it remained inflexible. Behind her, the fire popped and licked heat up the back of her legs.

Looking over her shoulder, she saw that the fire had spread to the back wall and caught one of the herb bundles. Her stomach sank. She was in a room full of kindling. One by one, the bundles went up in flame, quick fuel for the fire as it ate its way to the ceiling.

She began to cough. Her throat felt like it was burning. The smoke was so thick now that she had to crouch. Panic surged through her, igniting her primal instinct to survive. *I need to use my powers and try to flip out of here.*

She grabbed the protection charm out of her shirt and tried to pull it up over her head, but the triple knot she'd tied after almost drowning in the bathtub made it too small.

Crouching down against the door, she tried frantically to untie the knot. Her heart thumped against her chest, its rapid beats reverberating through her entire being. The sound echoed in her ears, drowning out the noise of the fire, but her fingers were blunt against the knot.

"Argh!"

She gave up on the notion of flipping herself out of there. She brushed aside the debris and laid down on the floor, kicking at the door with as much force as she could, her fear fueling her effort.

As the first blow landed, a searing jolt of pain shot up her right leg, causing her to cry out. The pain rushed through her body, momentarily paralyzing her. The fiery heat was at her back, and above her all she could see was black smoke speckled with sparks, like fiery stars in the night sky. She gathered her strength and prepared for a second attempt. Adjusting her stance, she angled her legs to the side, positioning them for maximum impact. Summoning every ounce of strength left in her, she thrust her legs forward, striking the door with double the force. It remained shut.

The smoke scorched her throat, and now her lungs felt like they were on fire with each shallow breath she managed. She steeled herself for another attempt, but the thickening smoke had already swallowed the room entirely. Before she could even muster another kick, darkness overcame her and cinders rained down on her like fireflies.

Chapter Fifty-Eight
SHADOW IN THE MIST

The faint sound of a man's voice was the first thing Kate heard as the world around her tuned back in. Her head ached, and she fought to open her eyes as her vision waxed and waned. When her sight finally came back into focus, she saw Owen leaning over her, framed by the dark sky. Rain fell lightly on her face, and there was the smell of smoke in the air. All at once everything came rushing back. She sat bolt upright and looked around. The movement sent her into a coughing fit, and she leaned forward and threw up.

"Careful there. Take it slow," Owen said, resting his hand on her back for support as she teetered back and forth.

Kate turned herself around toward the barn. Smoke seeped from the cracks in the walls, thick black wisps snaking their way out of the barn and disappearing into the black sky. Zeke emerged from the barn with a piece of cloth wrapped around his face and a large fire extinguisher in his hands.

"It's out. Most of the back room is destroyed, but the structure didn't take a hit," he called out to them.

It was the first time the rain had let up all day, and Kate now longed for its cooling touch. Malachi obviously hadn't wanted to assist in putting the fire out, slowing the rain down to nothing more than a sprinkle. He probably was hoping the fire would rip through the barn and then onto the house.

"How did you know about the fire?" Kate asked in a hoarse voice.

"Ionna. She woke up and told us you were in danger," Owen told her. "I couldn't find you in the house, and when I looked out the window, I saw your footsteps in the mud heading out to the barn."

Through the haze and shock of all that had happened, Kate felt a foreboding in the pit of her stomach. Ionna had accessed her magic even in a dead sleep.

"You're lucky," Zeke said. "By the time we got out, the room was more or less engulfed. Thank God Betty had one of these in the barn," Zeke said, setting the empty extinguisher on the ground. "Another minute or two and things could have been much worse."

"Let's get you inside for some water," Owen suggested as Kate got to her feet, letting out a long string of coughs.

The three of them walked into the house, bringing with them the stench of smoke that clung to their clothes and hair. Kate felt like it was coming out of her very pores. They were surprised to see Ionna up and standing in the living room, looking out the window toward the barn.

"Ionna, what are you doing out of bed?" Zeke asked, walking over and putting his hand on her shoulder.

She turned to look at him, her eyes a pale gray.

"Ionna. Hey. Come back to me," he said, grabbing her.

Nothing happened. Her eyes remained in their ghostly state.

"Ionna, it's Zeke. Don't let the magic take you over. Fight it," he told her, taking her hands in his.

Kate looked on as Zeke unknowingly created a channel for his magic to flow into Ionna's. As he gripped her hands in his, her magic seemed to settle. As the pallor of her eyes faded and the green shone through once more, she slumped forward onto him.

"Owen, help me get her to the sofa," Zeke said, holding her body up.

Owen helped Zeke bring her over and lay her down. Kate saw that she was now covered in the red welts that had first shown up on her neck.

Kate stuck her hand in the pocket of Owen's jacket and found that by some miracle the glass jar of valerian root hadn't broken when she fell. She rushed into the kitchen and lit a match, igniting the old gas stove and setting the tea kettle on top. She shook a few bits of the root into a cup with the chamomile tea bag in it.

It seemed ages before the water boiled. She paced the kitchen, anxiety filling her stomach and making her feel as if she was going to retch again.

How had things worsened so quickly? Just yesterday Ionna was fine. Now it seemed like she was slowly dying. Kate assumed it was her body's natural reaction—to let the magic out when she was in danger. But her magic didn't understand that it was feeding Malachi, and in turn, making her gravely sick. *It's a losing battle*, Kate thought.

The kettle finally announced its boiling point, and she

finished making the tea, adding a touch of milk to cool it down so that Ionna could consume it as soon as possible.

When Kate entered the living room, Zeke was pacing near the windows, and Owen sat next to Ionna on the sofa, looking at her with concern. She lay there, still as stone, her eyes shut and her face a milky white beneath the red blotches. She looked just as she had the night Artemas pulled her back from the veil. Kate feared they were quickly running out of time.

Owen stood, giving Kate his spot on the sofa. She sat down next to Ionna and ran her hand over her forehead. It was still hot to the touch, the fever medication not doing much to slow its progress. She'd known it probably wouldn't.

"Ionna, I need you to sit up and drink this," Kate said softly to her.

Ionna didn't respond, her eyelids still resting heavily.

Setting the tea down on the side table, Kate took her hands. "Ionna, you need to gather every ounce of strength inside you and drink this tea. It will help," she said in an assertive tone.

Ionna lay there, no movement to her other than her weak and ragged breathing. Zeke knelt beside her and grabbed her hands, his glow pouring into her, where hers sat dormant. This time, no sparks of magic came from their touch, and he looked up at Kate with worry in his eyes.

"Something's wrong," Zeke said. He squeezed Ionna's hands tighter, as if willing her to get better. "Come on, Ionna."

At that, her eyes began moving under the lids, and she slowly opened them. She tried to say something from her dried and cracked lips but nothing came out.

"Don't try to speak, just drink this," Kate said, putting the cup up to her mouth as Zeke propped her body upright.

Ionna took a few small sips and then began coughing, her

breath shallow between each rasping inhale.

"Just a few more sips," Owen said, standing over Kate's shoulder.

She took three more sips, and then her eyes started to roll back in her head, turning the pale color of magic once again. She turned toward the windows that faced the driveway, lifting her arm weakly and pointing, then her eyes fell shut, and she was out again.

"Let's hope that keeps her out until we can figure out how to stop this," Kate said, setting the half-empty cup on the side table.

"What was she pointing at?" Owen asked, walking over to the window.

"Maybe it was about the fire in the barn?" Zeke suggested, standing up and walking over to the window beside where Owen stood.

It was then that they caught sight of a figure walking down the driveway. The mist in the air hung around the figure like ghostly rain, casting it in shadow.

"Were you guys expecting someone?" Zeke asked, pulling the curtains aside to get a better look.

"No," Kate said, standing up and walking over to the window.

Nearing the house down the long, winding driveway was the figure of a woman with long hair, carrying a duffle bag over one shoulder. Striding alongside her was a dog, unusually large, almost resembling a wolf. If Kate hadn't known better, she might have mistaken it for one. The woman appeared to be in her early thirties, and she bore a striking resemblance to Ionna with her long dark hair.

When she finally arrived at the doorstep and knocked, Kate was the one to open the door.

"Hello, is this Ionna Bellmore's house?" the woman asked as

she stood there, shoulders back, holding Kate's gaze. She snapped her finger, and the wolf-dog obediently sat.

"Yes, who are you?" Kate asked. They didn't have time for realtors or bible pushers, and she wanted to get right down to the business of telling the woman to get lost.

"I'm Helen Kent. I spoke with Ionna on the phone the other day."

Kate's eyes grew big and began filling with tears. She had to hold herself back from throwing her arms around the woman. "Oh my gosh…"

"Helen! Thank God you're here," Owen blurted out from behind, obviously as relieved as Kate was.

"Come in out of that nasty weather," Zeke said, stepping forward and holding the door wide for her to come in.

"This is my companion, Storm. Is it okay if he comes in as well?" Helen asked, giving the dog a scruff on his head.

"Of course," Kate said, moving aside for them to enter. "I'm Kate, and this is Owen and Zeke."

"Is Ionna not home?" Helen asked, looking around the dimly lit house.

"She is," Kate said, walking her into the living room where Ionna lay motionless on the sofa. "But she's very sick. Every time she uses her magic, she gets weaker. I gave her some tea to try and sedate her, but…" Kate trailed off.

"I was worried this might have happened," Helen said. "When I wasn't able to reach her in any way—phone, email, nothing—I knew something supernatural was keeping me from her. That's why I decided to come."

"I'm surprised you made it here," Owen said.

"Well, it certainly wasn't easy, and it took a strong protection spell to aid me," Helen said.

"I don't know how much she told you but we need to cut the tie between her and the demon before it's too late," Kate said, her voice cracking as she held back the tears.

"She told me that Artemas pulled her back from death when she was an infant. Demons only have a few ways of entering the human world. One, by summoning them, and the other, by attaching to a soul in between worlds. The second way makes them much more difficult to shake," Helen said, unzipping her duffle bag and pulling out an old leather book.

"It's draining her life force," Owen confirmed.

"I think I have something in here that might help," Helen said, opening the book.

A quiet descended on the room while Helen looked for the spell. It was a quiet that unnerved Kate. A waiting kind of quiet. She had been so wrapped up in Ionna and making her the tea that she hadn't thought about how quiet Malachi had been. Ionna was so weak now, so near to death. Why was he being so silent? The thought sent a wave of panic through her. Suddenly, she felt as if she was walking into a minefield, just waiting for an explosion that was certain to come.

Chapter Fifty-Nine
MALACHITE

Helen laid the book down on the table next to Betty's ashes, fanning through its pages until she came to a page marked with a single black feather.

"I think I know how to rid her of this demon," she said. From her bag, she pulled out glass ball jars with herbs inside and set them on the table alongside the book. "I have everything we need here except for a piece of malachite. It's a mineral and a key component of the spell. My friend Connor is searching for some — once he finds it he'll bring it to us."

"Did you say malachite?" Owen asked. "Don't you think that's a bit odd how close the names are? Malachi, Malachite?"

"Well, there was a reason the goddess guided me to that spell. I think we can safely say it's the right one," Helen said.

"What if your friend can't find it? I don't think she has much time left," Kate said, looking over at Ionna, whose face was now almost entirely covered by red welts.

"She's still in this realm; her glow is weak but not gone," Helen reassured her.

"I know where we can get the malachite," Zeke interjected, looking deep in thought. "There's an old copper mine not far from here. Malachite tends to be found alongside copper ore."

"Go if you know where to find some," Helen said with some force.

Zeke nodded once, like he'd already decided he was going, then walked over to Ionna and bent down, giving her hand a gentle squeeze. "Hold on," he whispered to her. "We still need to go on that hike, remember?" He stood and looked at Owen. "I'm going to need your help."

"Yeah, of course," Owen said, following him out of the living room.

Kate quickly followed behind them. "Owen, are you sure?" she asked in a hushed voice, not wanting him to leave.

"Kate, we have to do this. She isn't going to make it much longer, and who knows if Helen's friend will even find the malachite in time. If Zeke is sure we can get some in the mine, then I have to go and help him."

They looked at each other for a moment, Kate trying not to show the emotion she was feeling. Owen pulled her into him and kissed her deeply. It was an agonizing kiss, as if he thought he might not see her again.

She pushed against him. "Don't kiss me like that until you get back," she said, then pulled him to her in a fierce hug. His arms were tight around her, and she could feel his heartbeat through her own chest.

Then he let her go, grabbed his sweatshirt, and followed Zeke out the door.

"Kate, come here," Helen yelled out from the other room, and Kate rushed back in to see Ionna sitting up.

"Go with them," she told her in a barely audible voice.

"What? No. I can't leave you," Kate said, kneeling down beside her.

"Kate, you have to go with them. They're going to need you," Ionna said, her eyes closing again as she fell back into the tea's coma-like state.

Kate looked wordlessly at Helen, who nodded and gave a reassuring smile.

"Go. I'll keep her safe until you get back."

Kate leaned forward and kissed Ionna's forehead, then sprinted to the door and out into the mist.

On the way they swung by Zeke's place, and he grabbed a few things before heading for the old mine. Sygun Copper Mine hadn't been functional since the early nineteen hundreds. Now it was a tourist attraction, offering guided tours during the day. At night, the entrance was closed off by a gate, so Zeke drove further down the road and pulled the van off in an inconspicuous spot.

"We'll have to go from here on foot," he said, shutting off the engine.

They got out, and Zeke opened the van's back door, pulling a duffle bag to the edge and unzipping it. Inside were three headlamps, two pickaxes, a set of bolt cutters, and a small dagger. Zeke handed Kate one of the headlamps and the bolt cutter, then handed the second headlamp and one of the axes to Owen.

"These only have a battery life of two hours, so we need to

make this quick," Zeke said as he strapped the last headlamp on himself and grabbed the other pickaxe and the dagger.

Owen raised his eyebrows at Zeke when he stuck the dagger in a sheath on his side.

"Just in case," Zeke said.

He closed up and locked the van, then headed up the road toward the mine, Owen and Kate trailing behind him.

"I don't have a good feeling about this," Kate said as they fell behind Zeke.

"Yeah, I never really liked this place. My mates used to sneak in once the tour guides left for the day and do a bit of drinking. It always creeped me out knowing that miners had died in there. Plus the bats, I hate bats," Owen said, moving his shoulders side to side as if to shake off a chill.

They walked the rest of the way in silence until they came to the gate. The chain was padlocked from the outside, but there was just enough space for them to squeeze through between the gates without having to cut the bolt. Once they were inside, they walked up a long gravel driveway to the mine's main entrance, which was a large industrial-looking metal building, aged with rust.

The doors were locked, but Zeke scooted down the side of the building to a door with a chain through its handles.

"Kate, hand me the bolt cutters."

Kate took a step forward, glanced around to check if anyone was there, and then passed the cutters over to Zeke. A loud snapping sound echoed off the steel building as he cut the bolt. He opened the door just enough for them to get through and turned on his headlamp. Kate and Owen did the same and followed him into the pitch-black space. Once the door shut, their headlamps illuminated a landing above a wide, open room the size of a gymnasium.

"Loading docks," Zeke said as he began descending the long set of metal stairs.

Kate and Owen followed carefully behind him, looking down at each metal-grated step as they went.

When they arrived on the loading dock floor, Zeke led the way down a long hallway that brought them to another staircase. This one descended into one of the mine shafts.

"How do you know your way around here so well?" Owen whispered to Zeke, which didn't matter as his voice echoed off the walls and down the shaft anyway.

"I may or may not come down here every once in a while to mine a bit of copper to play with. I like to add a little bling to my hilts sometimes," he said, cracking a sly grin.

Owen smiled back. Zeke had a bit of a bad-boy side to him.

"How much further?" Kate asked, not liking the idea of going so far underground.

"We need to make it down into one of the older sections—that's where the malachite will be."

They made it off the stairs and headed down a long carved-out area where another staircase sat, leading down into an older section of the mine.

Kate peered down over the edge of the stairs before they began their descent; it seemed to be a never-ending drop, a bottomless pit to hell. The beam of light from their headlamps seemed to barely penetrate the darkness spreading out below. She didn't want to think what might happen if one of them tripped or a stair gave loose. The thought made her stomach churn and bile rise in her throat.

The deeper they went, the colder it got, and a damp, earthy smell permeated the air, making it almost hard to breathe. The walls were like that of a cave, dark and damp as if they had walked into the belly of a dragon.

They made it down only a few steps when Zeke heard something. He stopped abruptly, causing Kate to collide with Owen's back. He looked up, his headlamp lighting the chamber ceiling—and a large population of bats.

"Get down!" he yelled as the bats swooped from the ceiling.

Kate let out a scream. Dropping to their knees, they covered their heads with their arms, cutting off the light from their headlamps and plunging themselves into complete darkness.

The eerie screeches and clicking of the bats echoed off the walls. Their wings beat frantically, churning the air as they flew past and faded into the distance.

They waited a few seconds in the dark. Zeke was the first to remove his hands from his head, lighting the space up and sending their fears back. They clambered up from the ground, dusting themselves off.

"Okay, I should have warned you about that. Happens every damn time I come down here," Zeke said as he began moving forward down the next flight of stairs.

"Yeah, a heads-up would have been great. Like I said, I hate bats!" Owen said, clearly annoyed.

These stairs were considerably older than the ones they had previously been on. Zeke explained how they were part of the original mine and hadn't been upgraded like the ones used for tours. The metal grates were rusty, and the bolts were loose from corrosion.

"We should take these slow and space ourselves out. We don't want to put too much weight in one spot," Zeke said. As if to underline his point, his foot scuffed off a flake of rust from one of the steps. It bounced off the step below it, sending the sharp ringing sound of metal on metal bouncing off the mine's walls.

Kate waited for a beat before continuing, giving care to each step she took as the haunting sound of the metal groaned under her weight. With each movement, she half expected the stairs to give way and send her plummeting into the open mouth of darkness below. Owen was only a few steps behind her, but his movements sent vibrations on the rickety stairs, setting her nerves on end.

By the time they neared the bottom, the staircase was beginning to sway. Owen was last off, and when his feet touched solid ground, they all let out the breaths they had been holding.

"Over this way," Zeke announced, pointing his headlamp off to the right where there was a wall that glistened with moisture.

As they got closer, Kate could see the drips of water leaking out of the ceiling and down the wall.

"If it's anywhere, it's going to be here."

Zeke went to the wall of rock and ran his hand over it. There was a long vein of copper running through it. He pulled the pickaxe back and struck the wall, breaking a small hunk of rock off. He picked it up and held it out to them; he shone his headlamp at it, and the copper glimmered under its light.

"See this," he said, "that's unrefined copper ore. The malachite should be here where the water runs. Now it's just a matter of finding it."

Owen approached the wall and took a swing at it with his axe. Nothing broke off, but the force sent him backwards few steps. He swore under his breath and rolled his shoulder.

"Woah there, you're going to hurt yourself doing it that way," Zeke said. "You need to find the weak spot in the rock first and aim for that. See this line here, where the water has worn the rock down? That's the spot you want to hit." He took a swing and broke out a large chunk of rock.

"What does this malachite look like anyways?" Kate asked, picking up the piece he had just chipped off and looking at it.

"Malachite looks sort of like jade. A rich green color," Zeke told her as he struck the rock again.

The mine shaft was damp, and the cold was working its way into their muscles as they worked, slowing them down as their bodies grew tired. They picked the wall for over an hour with no luck when their headlamps began to flash and gutter.

"I think we better start back up," Zeke said, wiping his brow of sweat. "We only have about twenty minutes of battery life left, and that'll be just enough to get us back up. I'm sorry, guys, but I just don't see any of it here. We gave it our best shot. Let's hope Helen's friend had better luck than us."

Kate looked down in defeat, willing away the tears that began to form. The idea of letting Ionna down and not being able to save her gnawed at her insides. Owen took her hand and gave it a gentle squeeze.

"It's okay, we'll figure something out," he whispered.

They gathered their tools and headed back up the long, creaking staircase to the second chamber. They made it about two-thirds of the way up when Kate caught sight of a small section of wall with water running down it.

"Look," she said, pointing her light over at the wall.

There, on a small overhang, was a rock that jetted out in which a thin vein of malachite flowed until it widened into a pool of green at the rock's point. Kate's heart fluttered with hope.

"Good eye, Kate," Zeke said.

"Do you think you can reach it?" she asked.

Zeke leaned over the rusty railing with his pick out and measured the distance for his swing.

"Yeah, I think I can get it. Owen, I need you to go back down a few steps and try and catch it when it loosens," Zeke told him. "Kate, you go up a few steps. I need a good amount of space to swing, plus we can't put too much weight in one spot. We've only got one chance at this."

Kate nodded and quickly moved up and out of his way.

Zeke pulled his arm back as far as he could and then used the weight of his body to swing the axe over the rail. The staircase groaned and swayed, sending chunks of rust raining down into the shaft. His axe struck the stone, missing the malachite by an inch, and broke off a fist-sized piece of rock instead.

"Heads up, Owen, move out of the way!" he yelled down as the stone fell.

It was a long time before they heard it hit the ground. The staircase must have been suspended over another shaft.

"Okay, one more go," Zeke said, swinging the axe again, this time coming in full contact with the malachite. It broke loose in the size of a golf ball, and he yelled to Owen, "Nailed it!"

Owen reached out over the railing and caught it just before it tumbled down into the shaft below. There was a loud groan from the metal rail as he leaned over, sending shivers up the stairs to where Kate stood. Everyone froze, waiting for the stairs to steady themselves and stop moving. Once the danger of the moment passed, they all smiled, celebrating their small victory.

"Nice catch," Zeke said, shooting Owen a thumbs-up before he scooted up past Kate to take the lead once again.

Owen walked up to Kate, beaming with pride, and handed the stone to her.

"See, things are going to be okay. We've got this," he said, giving her a reassuring smile.

Kate took the stone and tucked it into her pocket, the tension finally leaving her shoulders.

The batteries in their headlamps continued to drain as they made their way toward the surface again. At one point, Kate's light cut out altogether until she hit it a few times with the heel of her hand, coaxing a pale glow from it. They quickened their pace. It was time to get out of there. They had found what they'd come for, and now it was only a matter of time before they would rid Ionna of Malachi.

They had almost made it to the second shaft when they heard a high-pitched metallic creak followed by a deafening crack that resonated off the wet stone walls. Kate froze, midstride between two stairs, fear causing her heart to jump into her throat.

"Everyone okay?" Zeke yelled from up ahead as the staircase trembled.

"We need to get out of here," Kate blurted in panic, her voice thin and high and not her own. She felt the weight of the malachite in her pocket. She couldn't lose it.

"You're okay, Kate," Owen said, a few steps behind her. "Just take it slow."

They were positioned far between each other on the stairs so even the beacons of their lights didn't touch one another. Kate told herself to keep calm, to just breathe.

"Just wait a second for the stairs to settle, okay?" Zeke called out.

Kate's headlight began to cut out once more. She didn't dare hit it again in case the movement caused the staircase to move more. "Okay," she said back, gritting her teeth.

"I'm right with you, Kate," Owen said.

She turned her head to look back at him when something gave way.

The stair below shifted beneath her foot, and she grasped onto the rusty railing as her heart broke into sprints. Before she could even say his name, the staircase broke free.

The last thing she saw of Owen was a glimpse of surprise and fear in his eyes as he plummeted into the darkness.

Chapter Sixty

THE DARKNESS

Kate's screams echoed down into the dark as she watched Owen fall into the nothingness below her. In an instant, Zeke was behind her, holding her back from diving after him.

"Owen! Owen!" Her screams rang through the caverns, but no response came. The only sound that could be heard was her own voice bouncing back up at her.

She sat there, three steps from the jagged end of the broken staircase, and cried. Hot tears streamed down her face as Zeke held her shoulders from behind.

"Kate, he's gone," Zeke whispered gently in her ear. "We'll send someone for him, okay?"

But she wouldn't move; she just sat there staring down into the darkness.

"Kate, we have to go. We need to get back to Ionna," Zeke said. "It's not safe here. We have to leave."

"I can't leave him." She sobbed, turning back and looking at Zeke, tears streaming down her face.

"If we don't go, and Ionna dies, then Owen's death will be in vain," he reminded her.

"No!" she cried out. She could feel her heart ripping in two. She needed to flip back before it all happened; she needed to save Owen. She had done it before. This was why Ionna had sent her. She must have known Kate was the only one who could save him.

Slowly, she stood up, looking down into the seemingly endless drop, and pulled her protection charm out from her shirt. She fumbled around with the knot, trying to untie it, but it wouldn't loosen. "Zeke, I need you to cut this off me," she said, lifting the necklace out and away from her neck.

"Why? I don't think it's a good idea," he said, hesitating to break the one thing that was keeping her safe.

"There's no time to explain. Do it, now!" she demanded, a look of utter desperation in her eyes.

Zeke slid the dagger from the sheath at his side and grabbed hold of the leather cord, cutting through it with ease.

As soon as she was free of the necklace, she tucked it into her pocket and closed her eyes. With everything in her, she called upon her magic to shift time, searching for that feeling inside her to grab onto, but there was nothing. Nothing was happening.

"Are you okay?" Zeke asked, looking at her with concern.

Tears flowed down her cheeks and speckled the gray jacket she wore, Owen's jacket. She tried again, but still nothing. She couldn't feel even a spark of magic inside her. It was as if that part of her had died with Owen. She pulled the charm out of her pocket and handed it over to Zeke.

"Hold this," she told him in between sobs.

He took it from her, and she sat back down, putting her hands to her temples, and looked down. But as hard as she tried, she just couldn't seem to push herself through time. It was as if her magic was completely gone.

"No!" she cried out, slamming her hands onto the metal grated steps, making the staircase shake side to side.

"Woah there, easy," Zeke said, resting his hand on the railing as the stairs shifted back and forth. "Kate, we have to go."

She didn't move. She didn't say anything. She just sat there in complete shock. Owen was gone, and so was the one thing that could save him — her magic. All she could think of was the biscuits, the stupid ginger biscuits. If she'd never said yes when Owen asked her to flip back for them, maybe none of this would ever have happened. She wouldn't have gotten stuck in 1951 and met Artemas, she wouldn't have saved baby Neala, and maybe the great rift between her mother and grandparents wouldn't have come to pass. She could have continued in blissful ignorance, spending summers with her grandparents, spending summers with Owen. Maybe she and Owen would have drifted apart as they grew older, but she didn't care about that — all she cared about was saving him. She would undo all of it; she would give up her powers, her love for him. The way he looked at her and made her feel ... if she could just bring him back.

Zeke tugged her up onto her feet. She pulled back, resisting him.

"No." She sobbed.

As another deafening creak reverberated through the stairwell, Zeke's grip tightened, yanking her upward with urgency.

"Kate. Please."

They surged forward, narrowly avoiding the collapse of yet

another section of stairs, just where Kate had been sitting moments before. Desperately, she reached back into the darkness, mustering every ounce of strength to call out to Owen one final time, but her voice was drowned out by the sound of the crumbling structure. Zeke pressed on, pushing them both to crest the top of the stairs and onto the safety of the floor above.

Kate walked mindlessly, her tear-stained face and eyes cast in the shadow of the closing day. By the time they got to the van, it was twilight. There was an eeriness to the darkening of day, and everything felt wrong. Zeke opened the door for her. On the passenger seat was Owen's baseball cap; he'd tossed it there before they left. She lifted it to her nose and took in the smell of him, causing her to cry even harder than before. Zeke looked at her with pity, obviously not knowing what to do or say to comfort her.

Here she was, a time flipper, and she wasn't even able to save the one person she cared most about, the person she loved. Owen had told her it was her superpower, but it felt more like a curse than ever now. Knowing that she might have been able to save him but couldn't was more than she could bear. Her heart felt as if it had been ripped out of her chest and tossed down the old mine shaft along with him.

The drive back seemed endless, and neither of them said a word. Kate held the stone inside her pocket, squeezing it so tightly that the jagged edges cut into her hand. When they arrived back at Betty's house, it was almost completely dark outside. Zeke parked the van next to Owen's smashed-up car.

He turned off the ignition and sat there for a long moment, still gripping the steering wheel. Kate could see the guilt and sadness in his eyes. He was obviously in shock, like she was. He loosened his grip on the wheel and turned to her, placing his hand on her shoulder, trying to help steady not only her but himself as well. He let out a long breath before he spoke.

"Kate, we can't say anything to Ionna about Owen just yet. We need her to be strong right now, which means I need you to be strong too." His voice cracked with emotion.

Kate just looked at him wordlessly and wiped the tears from her eyes. She knew he was right, even if it did sound callous. Owen wanted to help save Ionna, and if she could help make that happen, she was going to put everything she had into it. *His loss will not be for nothing*, she thought, as she took in a deep breath and opened the door, then followed Zeke.

The windows were dark. Not even a glow from one of the oil lamps could be seen as they made their way down the long driveway to the house.

Kate's stomach dropped. The front door was wide open. *Something isn't right.*

"Zeke, do you still have my charm?" she asked.

He pulled the charm necklace out of his pocket and wrapped it around her neck, giving it a surgeon's knot where he had cut it. The necklace now sat up close to her throat, like a choker. She moved it side to side as if it was too tight, trying to stretch it out a bit more.

"Something feels off," Kate said as they entered the dark house.

"I feel it too," he said as he stepped in behind her.

The house was pitch-black inside, and there was a staleness to the air, the same as the storm had brought.

"Helen?" Zeke called out.

He stepped in front of Kate, turning on the headlamp that still sat on his forehead. The batteries were almost dead, causing the light to flicker and dim, sending back the darkness in spurts and revealing Helen's body lying on the living room floor.

"Oh God," Zeke murmured.

They rushed over to her and checked for a pulse when they heard a voice break the silence.

"She's not dead, just knocked out and probably won't be quite the same again."

It was a deep, dark voice, like a shadow.

Zeke looked up, shining his sputtering light over toward where the voice had come from. The beam fell upon Ionna sitting in one of the overstuffed armchairs with her legs crossed and her hands resting in her lap. The red patches were gone from her skin, and the color had come back into her cheeks, but there was something wrong with her eyes. They were no longer the beautiful green of spring grass but pools of infinite darkness. Looking into them was like looking into the underworld itself, and it was with that they knew it was no longer Ionna but Malachi speaking through her.

"I see you came back missing one," she said, a sick smile lifting the sides of her face in a devilish grin. "Zeke, you should have known better than to take them down there into that old rusty place. Such a shame the stairs gave way," Malachi said, snapping his finger. The light turned back on, and the house began to hum with electricity once again.

"Fuck you, asshole. I'm going to dance on your ashes when we send you back to hell!" Kate yelled. The rage within her churned like a vortex, drawing her deeper into its currents.

Ionna's obsidian gaze slid to her. "Oh, poor Kate, you finally find a guy who doesn't think you're a total loser and poof, just like that, he's gone," she said, cocking her head to the side and pretending to wipe a tear from her cheek.

Kate lunged at her but Zeke grabbed her before she could get too close.

"What do you want?" he asked, holding Kate as tight as he could and pulling her back next to him.

"What do I want? I want you ants to get out of my way and let me get on with this. It was fun playing with you at first, but I've grown tired of it, and I'm ready to be rid of you pests," Malachi said, standing up.

She was no taller than five feet four inches, but when she rose from the chair she seemed to tower over them with the power that was emanating from her. Kate and Zeke took a step back, not knowing what to expect.

Kate looked over to where Betty's urn rested and saw the spell book and ingredients laid out next to it. If Zeke could distract Malachi just long enough for her to try and perform the spell, then they still might have a fighting chance. She glanced at Zeke, and then over at the table quickly. With a nod of his head, he took out his dagger.

"I will kill her if it means stopping you," Zeke warned.

Ionna just stood there, an evil grin playing across her lips as she waited for Zeke to make his move.

Kate saw her chance and grabbed the book while Zeke tried to distract the demon.

"She would rather die than have you use her soul to destroy humanity!" he yelled out.

"Oh please, you humans only care about yourselves. Plus, there isn't much of her soul left to care," Malachi said.

Kate pulled the piece of malachite from her pocket and set it next to a bowl Helen had filled with the herbs from the jars. She read the spell as quickly as she could, trying to understand what it said. She grabbed a box of matches from inside Helen's bag and struck one, tossing it into the bowl filled with the herbs, catching them on fire. Then she picked up the malachite and dropped it into the burning mix. As soon as the stone hit the bottom of the copper bowl, it threw a plume of aromatic sparks up into the air.

"By words of power, this spell I cast,
To rid a soul of demon's grasp.
The Light and darkness that entwined,
Must now be parted—"

Before she was able to finish the last of the spell, Ionna thrust her hand into the air, and the book went flying across the room, landing near the window.

But the demon had no idea what a voracious reader she was.

"Must now be parted, fate unbind," she continued, yelling now.

"Banished forever, the demon's plight,
The soul restored, in radiant light.
Darkness sent, through veil's divide,
Banished back, where shadows hide.
By the power of three, so mote it be."

Ionna raised her hand once again and swung it forward, knocking Kate to the ground and sending her back against the wall. She turned and did the same to Zeke, sending him smashing up against the fireplace.

"By words of power, this spell I cast,
To rid a soul of demon's grasp.
The Light and darkness that entwined,
Must now be parted, fate unbind.
Banished forever, the demon's plight,
The soul restored, in radiant light.
Darkness sent, through veil's divide,
Banished back, where shadows hide.
By the power of three, so mote it be," she yelled out once more.

She got to her feet and ran to the table, grabbing the stone out of the burning ashes in the bowl and repeating the spell for the third and final time. The flesh of her palm burned as she walked toward Ionna, the stone held out in her fist. Ionna stepped back, and Kate lunged forward, pushing the burning stone onto Ionna's chest just above her heart.

Ionna dropped to her knees, her head hanging low.

Zeke got to his feet and looked on as Kate bent forward.

"Ionna, is that you?" she asked, sticking her hand out to help her to her feet.

Ionna raised her head, the darkness still pooling in her eyes, and began to laugh.

"You didn't think some stupid little spell was going to send me back, did you? I'm much too powerful for that kind of child's play now." Malachi laughed once again, standing up.

With a flick of Ionna's wrist, Malachi sent Kate flying across the room. She landed in a crumpled heap on the floor. The sound of breaking bones was the only noise that filled the space as defeat set in.

Chapter Sixty-One

OBSIDIAN POOLS

Kate lay in a heap on the floor, clutching her arm as tears of agony slipped down her cheeks. Malachi, wearing Ionna's skin, walked over and kicked her hard in the ribs, causing the air to burst from her lungs.

"Oh, Kate, you had such potential. At first, I thought possessing you for your skills would be most enjoyable. Just a quick trip into your body to wreak a little havoc throughout time. But sadly your powers are too weak to hold a god such as myself," Malachi said as he prowled around her like a predator around its prey.

Kate lay there, clutching her ribs with her good arm, trying to find the breath that had been kicked out of her.

"I can sense how much Ionna cares for you, which makes it all that much sweeter that I get to kill you with her hands," Malachi said, taking another step forward.

Zeke sprang up and knocked Ionna's body to the ground in one swoop with his foot. Ionna's body landed hard on the ground, giving Kate just enough time to scramble to her feet and make it over to where Zeke stood. From within Ionna, Malachi snarled.

"Zeke, we need to combine all three bloodlines. We need some of Ionna's and Helen's blood. Helen might be the last remaining descendant. It's our only chance at this point," Kate told him.

Zeke didn't hesitate. He bent down and sliced into Helen's palm, laying open a thin line. Blood ran from the cut, and Helen stirred, the pain reaching her in her concussed sleep. Then he spun around and slashed Ionna's calf as she tried to get to her feet. She fell to the ground, a long vertical cut running scarlet down her leg.

Ionna screamed out in pain as the demon that lived inside her attempted to pull her back up onto her feet. Zeke's blade had made something happen. It was as if it jolted Ionna awake on the inside. Her eyes flashed green, giving them hope that she was still in there and fighting.

Kate looked up, catching something move out of the corner of her eye. A tall, shadowy figure stood next to the small side table. It flashed and flickered, then came into focus. Artemas's spirit stood there, looking down below where his feet hovered, and with all his strength, he slid the piece of malachite that had fallen under the small side table during the commotion over to Kate. She smiled at him just before he faded back into the in-between. Taking the malachite in her fist she squeezed it, the broken edge of the rock breaking through the burned flesh of her hand. The pain was intense but she didn't cry out; instead, it fueled her determination.

"Zeke," she called out, catching his attention and tossing the stone over to him with her good arm.

He looked up and caught it just before Ionna made it back to her feet.

He looked down at it, stained with Kate's blood, and knew what he needed to do. He wiped his blade off on the stone. A mix of Helen's and Ionna's blood slid off the blade and onto the rock. He stepped forward, pressing the stone to Ionna's chest as she turned around to face him.

He had expected something explosive to happen, but Malachi just stood there in Ionna's form looking annoyed.

"You mortals never learn," Malachi said as he ripped the rock from Zeke's hand and threw it across the room.

Ionna's face began to grow pale once again and the red blotches returned, blooming like poppies on her skin. The darkness in her eyes faded, and the green broke back to its surface. Her body hung limp, as if the only thing holding her up was the air itself.

She lifted her eyes to Zeke.

"You have to kill me. It's the only way now," she pleaded, using what little strength she had left.

She teetered, and Zeke stepped up to catch her. As he did, Ionna's eyes changed once more and he felt the blade of his own dagger plunge into his stomach.

Kate looked on in horror as he took two steps back and ran his hand down to the hilt of the blade. His eyes gave away his fears, knowing where it had landed was a mortal wound.

As he looked down at the dagger lodged in him, a bright white light emanated from the edges of the wound, so brilliant that he had to avert his eyes. Where his blood should have been, light streamed forth.

Kate ran to his side as he dropped to his knees, his hand still resting on the dagger.

"Ionna, if you're in there, you need to stop this. You need to fight!" Kate screamed at her.

Zeke slowly pulled the dagger from his stomach, and as he did, the light became so intense that he had to shield his eyes with one hand. No blood flowed from the wound. His skin appeared as if it had never even been touched. The blade, however, had changed; its once silver luster now shone with the white glow of the old gods.

As he held the dagger, his eyes changed as well, emulating the light coming from the blade.

"It's you. You're the blood of the third son," Kate said, looking at Zeke, her eyes wide with astonishment.

The light seemed to drive Malachi back, like some creature unaccustomed to it, something that had grown twisted and dark without light, and Ionna's eyes morphed into their soft shade of forest green again.

She smiled at Zeke weakly. "You know what to do," she said, with a slight nod.

The soft green of her eyes lasted just a moment before they faded back into the obsidian pools of evil. She spun toward Zeke, her arm outstretched as if to cast a spell, but before she could even take her next breath, Zeke plunged the dagger straight into her heart.

"Zeke, No!" Kate called out—too late—as she watched Ionna's body fall to the floor.

Zeke bent down and pulled the dagger from her chest. A long stream of dark smoke seeped from the wound and snaked its way into the air.

"But how? My power is stronger than any human, even halflings such as yourselves?" Malachi's disembodied voice said.

Kate stepped forward, her shoulders back, and looked at the demon who had just taken everything from her. Nothing more than a bit of smoke in the air now.

"You're right, I wouldn't have been able to defeat you on my own. It took all three bloodlines combined. It was the weapon Nyneve left for us to fight against evil like you," Kate said, looking over at Zeke, who still held a defensive position.

Malachi hovered over Ionna's body, swirling about, desperately trying to reenter his host. With every failed attempt he became weaker, his dark tendrils disintegrating into small wisps. His blackened soul faded to a smoky gray as he tried to claw his way back. He tried to speak but his voice was no more than a crackle of energy in the air around them. Then, as though the veil between realms had parted, a thin white light entered the room, wrapped itself around what was left of Malachi, and carried him back through the opening, vanishing.

The blade faded back to its natural color of hammered steel, and Zeke's eyes followed suit, changing back to their chestnut hue.

He tossed the blade to the floor and looked down at Ionna's lifeless body. Her eyes, with their forest-green color, stared blankly up at the ceiling. Her chest was still, no ebb or flow of breath visible. Yet no blood flowed from the deadly wound in her chest.

Zeke knelt down and felt for a pulse, but there was no heartbeat. Kate collapsed onto the floor beside them and began to cry, her hot tears falling onto Ionna's cool skin.

There was complete silence until a low sigh pierced the tense atmosphere. When they glanced around, Helen tried to get up but was to weak, so she scooted closer to them.

"What happened?" she asked, looking to Kate for answers.

"We managed to send Malachi back, but…" Kate's voice trailed off as she turned her gaze to Ionna.

Helen's face fell. "I'm so sorry. I wish I could have done more," she said, her words filled with regret and sorrow.

Zeke picked up the dagger from the floor and sliced into the flesh of his arm, bringing forth a trickle of blood that ran down his arm and onto his hand. He leaned forward and let the blood drip onto Ionna's chest.

"Zeke, what are you…?" Kate asked.

"The power of the bloodlines," was all he said, handing her the blade.

She looked at him, a newfound hope arising in her eyes, and without hesitation, she cut into her hand. She placed her bleeding palm down on Ionna's chest where Zeke's blood had pooled. If their blood combined had the power to send a demon back, then maybe it held the power to bring Ionna back as well.

Once her hand connected with Ionna's body and Zeke's blood, a bright white beam of light shot out from around it, then sank into Ionna's chest. Slowly, Kate took her hand away and looked down, hoping beyond hope that the magic of their blood would bring her back to them.

Ionna's body remained motionless, and at first, it appeared that nothing was going to happen. But then the red spots on her skin began to fade, and a slight pinkness returned to her cheeks.

"Look!" Kate whispered, pointing.

Ionna's chest started to rise and fall in slow, steady breaths. Her eyes twitched, and then she looked over to where Kate and Zeke were sitting alongside her. She gave a faint smile and murmured, "You did it.".

Kate fell forward onto her and hugged her so tightly with her good arm that Ionna could barely breathe. "Thank God! Ionna, we thought we lost you," she cried, a mix of happiness and sadness pouring out of her.

"It's okay. I'm here. We're all okay," Ionna said.

Through her tears, Kate looked over at Zeke.

Ionna sat up and looked around. "Where's Owen?" she asked.

Tears broke free from Kate's eyes and flowed like a river down her white cheeks. Ionna knew he was gone without having to ask. Her eyes welled up as Zeke and Helen helped her to her feet and over to a chair.

"How?" she asked, looking at Zeke.

"The mine. He fell," he said, sorrow thickening his voice.

"Kate, you have to flip back and save him," Ionna said desperately.

"You don't think I've tried?" Kate said, exasperated. "My magic won't work. It's gone."

"It's not gone, Kate, but it's fading," Helen told her, looking at the magical aura that surrounded Kate.

"What do you mean 'fading'? How?" Ionna asked, her essence now returning to its normal state.

"When she cut her hand and brought you back, it was the essence of her magic she used to do so," Helen explained. "Without her full magic, she won't be able to flip."

Ionna looked at Kate and ached for her. "There must be something we can do?"

"There is. But it will mean losing your powers forever. Both you and Zeke. Zeke also only holds half the power he once had, and in order for Kate's magic to be whole, she will need all she can get from both of you," Helen told them, a serious look in her eyes.

"If there is even the slightest chance we can save Owen, then I would give up a hundred lifetimes of magic," Ionna said, looking at Kate and giving her a sad smile.

Helen turned to Zeke, who was now sitting next to Ionna on the sofa, holding her hand. He looked down at the sparks of magic floating between them and hesitated for a split second before he said, "I lived without it my whole life, so what's the difference?"

Ionna squeezed his hand. "We'll find those sparks in other ways," she reassured him, seeing a sadness in his stare. He smiled and nodded.

"Okay, I'm going to need you all to link hands in a circle," Helen instructed.

Kate stood in front of them, and they all joined hands.

"Now, Ionna, I need you and Zeke to repeat this incantation. It will only work if you are one hundred percent willing to give up your magic. Even the slightest hesitation will cause this to fail."

"We understand," Ionna said, nodding.

"Then let's begin.

I strip my magic from my soul.

I gift it forth to make one whole.

With my power, I willingly part.

And gift it with the purest heart.

By the power of three,

So mote it be."

Ionna looked at Kate, who still had tears streaming down her freckled cheeks, and repeated the words. Zeke did the same, and after the third and final time, Zeke's and Ionna's chests lit with the glow of their magic. The glow moved down their arms and into Kate's, lighting her up like a star.

Kate's back arched, and her head tilted to the sky, the magic running the length of her body in one long electric pulse.

"It worked. I can feel it inside me," she said, looking down at her hands as she broke apart from Ionna and Zeke.

"It did," Helen said, smiling.

"Okay, Kate, now use that power and go get him," Ionna said.

Zeke stood and picked up his blade, walking over to Kate with it in his hands. He reached out and broke the leather roping of the protection charm that hung down around her neck and gave her a smile.

"You got this," he said, placing his hand on her shoulder and giving it a gentle squeeze.

Chapter Sixty-Two
THE PULL OF LOVE

Kate sat herself down in one of the armchairs and closed her eyes, letting the magic flow through her. She felt it move and shift inside of her. She took in a deep breath and pictured the moment that Owen fell, the look of fear in his eyes as he plummeted into the darkness. Her heart began to race, fear building up in her throat. She could feel the shift start, then stop, then start again. Her body vibrated and pulsed, and her lungs grew tight. But just when she thought she was about to flip, it stopped again.

She opened her eyes.

"I can't do it. I'm trying but nothing's happening," Kate said, frustration filling her voice.

"Think back to the moment in time you want to go and focus on that," Helen suggested.

"That's what I've been trying to do," Kate told her, anxiety beginning to take over. What if she couldn't do it? Or worse, what if she flipped and ended up somewhere she didn't want to be and got lost in time trying to find her way back? After all, all of this had started because she flipped herself too far back. The worries and fears raced around in her head, and she sat there tapping her foot incessantly on the floor.

"No," Ionna said, "don't think about the moment. Just think about Owen. Let your love for him guide you."

Kate looked out of the window and thought back to what Artemas had tried to teach her all those years ago—that love was a stronger emotion than fear. Back then, it hadn't worked for her, but she hadn't loved anyone the way she loved Owen.

When she glanced back at Ionna, she could see the faint outline of Artemas standing behind her, his hand on her shoulder. He smiled and nodded, as if to say *Go ahead and give it a try*.

She closed her eyes again. This time she concentrated on pushing the fear, the pain, the grief away and just focused on Owen's face. His smile, his laugh, and the way he made her feel. She thought about everything they had done together, horseback rides in the fields, picnics at the cabin, reading in the hayloft. And everything she still wanted to do, like snuggling on the sofa watching Netflix, going to their first concert together, and making love for the first time. As she let the memories of him fill her, she began to feel the shift. Every cell vibrated and pulsed in a rhythm she had not experienced before. There was no tightening of her chest, no sensation of spinning. She felt in control. Without fear, without anger, without pain. She allowed her love for him to guide her to the precise moment she was meant to be.

The sound of birds could be heard off in the distance and a warm summer breeze blew around her. When she opened her eyes, her heart sank at the scene before her. She was standing near a crystal blue lake in the Welsh highlands, far from where she intended to be with Owen. Panic set in, but just as it threatened to consume her, Nyneve materialized from the depths of the water.

Her long flowing hair, intertwined with lake weeds, cascaded over her shoulders. Bathed in the ethereal glow of the old gods, she exuded an aura of serenity, and Kate's fears faded as she looked into Nyneve's watery blue eyes. She walked up to Kate, rested her hand on her shoulder, and smiled.

"You did good, my daughter. Now go and finish your quest so that you may begin your own story," she said to her in a voice as pure as the sun, giving her shoulder a gentle squeeze.

Kate smiled and then closed her eyes once again, letting love guide her to where she needed to be. This time it was as if she was the wind itself blowing through the wrinkles of time, flowing like the current of a river.

She opened her eyes to darkness and the damp, earthy smell of the mine. When her eyes adjusted to the dim light, Owen was standing there on the staircase in front of her, handing her the piece of malachite he had caught. A look of pride played across his face as she took the rock from his hands.

"You okay?" he asked.

She realized she was staring at him.

His voice. She'd thought she would never hear his voice again. It was the most wonderful sound.

She grabbed him, pulling him into the fiercest hug she had ever given anyone. He looked at her with bemusement.

"You're welcome. Wish I knew you liked rocks so much," he joked.

She looked up into his big blue eyes and smiled. She didn't say anything; she just tucked her head back into his chest and let the shift carry them out of the mine.

When she felt the shift spiral down and the cells in her body calm, she opened her eyes. Owen was still there, and her arms were still wrapped around him. She pulled him in and kissed him as though it was the first time all over again.

When they eventually separated, Owen looked around, puzzled. They were in Betty's living room. Zeke, Ionna, and Helen stood around them with broad smiles on their faces.

"Can someone explain to me what's going on?" Owen asked.

"I figured out how to flip us to when it was all over," Kate told him, smiling from ear to ear. He gave her a questioning look, and she said, "I'll explain later," as she tilted her head and kissed him again.

When they broke apart, Ionna pulled Owen into a hug, and Zeke patted him on the back.

Owen was full of questions, and Ionna and Zeke attempted to answer as many as they could. However, Kate was the one who would have to break the news of his death to him when the time was right.

In the commotion, Helen drew Kate aside. They stood by the windows that looked out over the long, winding driveway.

"You did a very brave thing saving Owen like that," she said. "I'm sure you know that for every action in the magical realm, there is always a reaction. You have Owen back, but I believe your magic is gone forever, and I don't think you will be able to flip through time again."

Kate looked at her hands, no longer glowing with magic as they once had. Then she looked at Helen and smiled. "It's the smallest price I could have paid to have him back," she said.

Bright light swept through the cottage, and Kate glanced back out the window to see a car parking at the top of the driveway. A shadowy figure of a man and a large breed of dog exited the car and descended down the drive.

Helen went to the door and opened it, and Storm came bounding in alongside a tall, handsome man.

"I checked all four shops, and it wasn't until the last one that I finally found it," he said in a thick Scottish accent, holding out a polished green stone.

Helen just smiled and looked into the living room where everyone was talking animatedly and laughing.

"I'm too late, aren't I?" he asked.

"Maybe just a little," Helen joked as she led him into the living room.

"Oh, by the way, I found Storm up the road chasing a cat," he said as Storm tromped around everyone looking for attention.

"I guess it's not just chickens he likes to chase," Helen joked as she turned toward the others. "Guys, this is Connor. He brought us some more malachite." She laughed, holding the stone up for everyone to see. "Connor, this is Owen, Kate, Zeke—and Ionna, Artemas's daughter," she said. There was fondness in her voice and a look of remembrance in her eyes.

"Hey, mate," Owen said, lifting his arm from Kate's shoulder to wave.

"Nice to meet you," Kate said.

While the others greeted Connor, Helen took the opportunity to pull Ionna aside.

"You know you look like him?" she said. "Artemas."

Ionna's heart ached a little. She smiled sadly. "Really?"

"He was my mentor for many years. He taught me so much about magic, and about myself. I'm only here now because of him. But more than that, he was a cherished friend. He had a heart of gold and a spirit freer than the birds. I wish you could have known him," Helen said.

Ionna smiled again, a tear breaking free and rolling down her cheek. "I wish that too," she said, a longing in her voice.

Helen squeezed Ionna's arm and gathered her things, placing them back in her duffle bag. Before zipping it up, she reached in and removed three leather-bound books, bringing them to Ionna.

"These are some of your father's journals. I know it's not the same but maybe this will help you to know his story a little better," Helen said as she set the books into Ionna's hands.

Ionna bit her lip as emotion shook through her. "Thank you, for everything. I'm not sure we would have been able to do this without you." She pulled Helen in for a hug. "You guys are more than welcome to stay the night. It's been quite a long day, after all," she joked.

"Thanks, but I rented us an Airbnb for the night," Connor broke in from the other side of the room. A devilish grin played across his face.

Helen walked over and elbowed Connor in the ribs, shooting him a smile. "Thanks, Ionna. Another time, for sure."

They followed Helen and Connor out into the cool evening air to say their goodbyes. The storm had lifted, and the sky was peppered with stars. The moon hung low above the horizon, giving a calmness to the night around it.

They watched as Helen and Connor made their way up the long driveway, Storm bounding in circles around them. Then out of the shadows, Jasper came running up the pathway and into the house.

Owen placed his arm around Kate when she shivered, pulling her into the warmth of his chest. Her heart skipped. She could feel energy pour off him into her. However, it wasn't magic she felt, it was love. She buried her nose into the crook of his arm and breathed in his scent, never wanting to let go.

Chapter Sixty-Three

A NEW STORY

Soon after Helen's departure, Kate and Owen left as well. Kate was running late for a phone call with her mother, and Owen had told her he didn't want to get on Flora's bad side. They said their goodbyes and hugged Ionna before heading home, leaving behind a quiet house wrapped in newfound serenity.

Ionna and Zeke found themselves alone together. The house seemed transformed, exuding an air of calm that hadn't been present before. It was no longer a mere structure but held the feeling of home — a far cry from the stranger's house it had been when Ionna first set foot there. Feeling the weight of the day, she settled down on the sofa, her body relaxing as she let go of the fear and tension she'd been harboring for days.

"Are you sure you're okay?" Zeke asked, sitting down beside her.

"Yeah, I feel fine, considering."

"Considering you were taken over by an evil god, died and came back to life?" he half-joked.

She gave a sleepy laugh. "It's a lot to take in, that's for sure. I think I'll be processing this for a while."

"I know what you mean. It's all so surreal. It was as if the world was coming to an end just hours ago and now everything is fine." He paused and looked at her, the levity in his eyes becoming something more somber. "How do we just go back to normal now?"

Ionna thought for a moment. "I suppose we don't. We just … adjust. To a new kind of normal, I guess," she said, resting her head back and looking up at the ceiling.

He did the same. "I think you're right," he said.

She felt his hand brush against hers, though he was still looking at the ceiling. She let her fingers intertwine with his.

There were still sparks between them, but of a different kind, she mused. It felt right. After all she had gone through in the previous week, if not the previous five years, she felt it was time for things to fall into place for her, and Zeke was the first piece.

"You must be starving. How about I go and cook us something to eat?" Zeke suggested, looking down at her.

Ionna smiled back. "I could eat."

"Okay, you rest here, and I'll go figure out something to make."

"Zeke," she said as he was about to walk into the kitchen.

He stopped and turned to look back at her.

"Thank you for stepping up and doing what you needed to do." She swallowed. "I mean, plunging that dagger into me couldn't have been easy."

He waited a moment before he spoke.

"It wasn't. But ... in that brief moment when you broke through, I knew it was what I needed to do. I don't know how I knew, but I did. Like something was guiding me."

"It was your blood," Ionna said. "Deep down you knew what to do because you had the knowledge of the old gods running in your veins."

"I'm just glad it kicked in when I needed it."

"Me too," she said.

"Well, being a demi-god was short-lived and not all it was cracked up to be. Now it's back to just ordinary old me," he joked.

"I think ordinary you is pretty great."

He smiled and glanced down, like he was suddenly bashful. When he looked back up at her, his gaze was warm and steady. "You're not bad yourself," he said, then turned toward the kitchen.

Smiling to herself, Ionna stood and went to the table where Betty's urn sat alongside Artemas's journals.

"It's over," she murmured, looking down at the urn as if she was reassuring Betty herself. She reached down and picked up the picture of Adam. He may not have been her blood, but he was her father. Now she understood the reasons behind his actions, the decision to keep Betty and the truth about Wales from her. It wasn't driven by selfishness; quite the opposite—he had given up everything in order to protect her. She would never know if he or Betty knew the whole story, but they had understood she wasn't safe in Wales and had sacrificed their own relationship to keep her out of harm's way.

Tears welled up in her eyes as she gently set the picture back down beside Artemas's journals. Her biological father, Artemas, had also gone to great lengths for her, laying down his own life to save hers. When she had first come to Wales, she might not have understood that level of devotion. Things were different now. She had experienced that profound connection—the kind that ran so deep that you were prepared to lay down your life. She would have made that kind of sacrifice if it had ensured Kate's and Owen's protection. Just a few weeks ago she'd had no one, really, besides Meg. But Kate and Owen had become her family—her chosen family. She would have done anything to keep them safe.

From the other room, she heard the popping of a wine cork and then Zeke's voice saying, "You up for some wine? Or maybe something harder after the day we've had?"

Laughing, she turned from the table that housed the last remnants of her old family and walked toward the doorway. Just before she walked through, she glanced over her shoulder, catching a glimpse of a shimmery figure standing next to the window. She knew that Artemas's spirit still lingered in the house, standing guard over it. She smiled as she walked out of the room toward Zeke in the kitchen.

Meg was right. It was time she stopped focusing on other people's stories and started writing her own. And that was just what she intended to do.

EPILOGUE

"I'll be back to pick you up at three," Zeke said, grabbing his jacket and keys from the table.

"Perfect. That'll give me just enough time to do a few things around here," Ionna replied. She rose onto her tiptoes and planted a kiss on Zeke's lips. She wrapped her arms around him, pulling him close and deepening their kiss before reluctantly letting go.

"Don't kiss me like that or I'll never want to leave," he said.

"Well, that's kind of the point," she teased, pulling him back in for one last kiss. He smiled at her as he stepped toward the door.

"If I don't go get those pie tins Ben ordered before three, he's going to kill me. Then what will you do?" he joked. "See you in a few hours."

"Bye, Z."

Ionna watched him walk to his van and pull up the long driveway. She couldn't get enough of him. Not only had they reignited the sparks they'd lost, but these sparks felt even more magical than the first. It had been four months since she decided to return to Wales, and their relationship had blossomed. Hardly a day went by when they didn't see each other. She was genuinely happy—for the first time in a long time—not just because of Zeke but also because of the sense of belonging that had returned to her life.

In early July, she flew back to Maine and spent a week packing her belongings to be shipped over and put her house up for sale. Even after such a short trip, she was glad to get back to Wales. Maine no longer felt like home; it had become an empty shell, especially now that her parents were gone, and Meg had moved south to be with her boyfriend. It was time for Ionna to start living life anew, and she knew that Wales was where she wanted to make that fresh start, surrounded by the people she loved.

In the past month, she had found a job with a local paper. It was a rather quiet gig, with the most exciting story so far being the sighting of a black panther on the mountain trail behind the Dwyer farm. But Ionna was content with the slow pace of the job; it gave her plenty of time to work on a book she was writing. She had decided to write the story of her fathers. To the world, it would be a fictional tale of a wizard battling a malevolent god, a girl moved through time, and the man who raised her as his own. In reality, it was her way of paying homage to her two fathers, who had saved her life in different ways. It was a means of sharing their story, revealing the true heroes they were. She had chosen to write it under the pen name Neala Rogowski, which felt fitting.

As she walked toward the living room, the phone rang, pulling her from her thoughts.

"Hello?"

"Hey. Owen wanted me to call and see if you would bring

over Betty's old apple peeler," Kate said on the other end. "Ben just broke his, and if we're going to process these apples in time for the autumn market, we need to borrow it. My hands are killing me from peeling with a knife. Can you bring it over when you guys come later?"

"Sure, does he know where it is?" Ionna asked.

Kate's voice was muffled as she yelled to Owen and then relayed his response. "He thinks it's in the pantry on one of the top shelves."

"Got it. I'll have a look," Ionna said, making her way to the kitchen. With the phone cord stretched to its limit, she rummaged around the old pantry until she found the apple peeler. "Found it. Is there anything else you guys need?"

"No, I think that's good. Maybe you can come a bit early, though. We'll be baking pies until midnight at this rate."

"Sure, I'll message Zeke and tell him to come straight back here after he gets the tins."

"Okay, great. Hey, before I let you go, I wanted to tell you that my mum is coming for a visit next weekend. It's the first time she's been here in years, and I was kinda hoping that maybe you would come over for dinner," Kate said.

"Really? That's a big deal. Yeah, of course, I'll come," Ionna replied, appreciating the significance of the invitation. "Thank you for asking me."

This dinner marked a significant step for Kate and her grandmother. Kate's mother had initially distanced herself when Kate decided to stay in Wales and take a year off to figure things out. After a month of no communication, her mother called one night, and they had a heart-to-heart conversation. During the conversation, Kate's mother explained the reasons for her estrangement from her parents. She had blamed them for Kate's disappearance the summer she was twelve, saying they neglected their responsibility in looking after Kate properly. Kate was her only child, and the fact that her father had made up some song and dance about her disappearance had caused the rift between them. But it seemed to be mending now.

"Oh, good. Alright, I'll fill you in a bit more on everything later today. See you in a bit."

"Sounds good. See you," Ionna said, hanging up the phone.

She walked into the living room, where a small fire crackled in the old hearth, filling the room with a cozy ambiance. She glanced over at Jasper, who was curled up sleeping next to Betty's urn on the table. She had told herself she was waiting for the right moment to lay Betty to rest, but deep down, she knew it was an excuse. She hadn't been ready to let go just yet.

Looking out at the leaves turning to gold on the trees through the old glass panes in the living room, Ionna realized she had waited long enough. She picked up the urn and headed out into the brisk afternoon.

Late autumn had arrived, and its low-slung sun cast golden hues over the land. The air was crisp and calm. She walked over to the flower beds near the base of the old oak tree in the backyard and uncapped the urn. Slowly, she reached in and began to sprinkle Betty's ashes over the bed of wilting flowers. They drifted down gently, settling like dust on the withered petals and the soil littered with fallen leaves.

Jasper watched as Ionna made her way around the entire house, ensuring no flower bed went untouched. As she reached the bottom of the urn, a sense of closure and peace washed over her. It was the conclusion of Betty's story, one that she believed Betty would have appreciated. The end of one story always marked the beginning of another, and Ionna's story was just starting.

She reached into the urn one final time, scooping up a small bit of ash.

"Bloom with the spring, my dear sister," she whispered to the wind as she let go of the last of Betty's ashes. A gentle breeze swept them up just before they touched the ground and carried them away into the dusty blue sky.

Made in United States
Cleveland, OH
01 May 2025

16542981R00322